OTHER WORLDS, BETTER LIVES

A HOWARD WALDROP READER

Selected Long Fiction
1989-2003

OTHER WORLDS, BETTER LIVES

A HOWARD WALDROP READER

Selected Long Fiction
1989-2003

OEB
Baltimore • 2008

Published by Old Earth Books
Post Office Box 19951
Baltimore, Maryland 21211
www.oldearthbooks.com

Book Design by Robert T. Garcia / Garcia Publishing Services
919 Tappan Street, Woodstock, Illinois 60098
www.gpsdesign.net

First Edition
10   9   8   7   6   5   4   3   2   1

Hardcover ISBN: 978-1-882968-37-4
            (1-882968-37-9)
Trade Paperback ISBN: 978-1-882968-38-1
            (1-882968-38-7)

CONTENTS

ACKNOWLEDGEMENTS

"Size Matters" by Howard Waldrop, Copyright © 2008 by Howard Waldrop.

A Dozen Tough Jobs by Howard Waldrop, Copyright © 1989 by Howard Waldrop. First published by Mark Zeising, 1989.

"Fin de Cyclé" by Howard Waldrop, Copyright © 1991 by Howard Waldrop, From *Isaac Asimov's SF Magazine*, Mid-December 1991.

"You *Could* Go Home Again" by Howard Waldrop, Copyright © 1993 by Howard Waldrop. First published by Cheap Street Press, 1993.

"Flatfeet!" by Howard Waldrop, Copyright © 1996 by Howard Waldrop, From *Isaac Asimov's SF Magazine,* February 1996.

"Major Spacer in the 21st Century!" by Howard Waldrop. Copyright © 2001 by Howard Waldrop, First published in *Dream-Factories and Radio-Pictures* as an e-book by Electricstory.com, 2001 and as a book by Wheatland Press, 2003.

"The Other Real World" by Howard Waldrop. Copyright © 2001 by Howard Waldrop. From *Sci-fiction.com*, posted July 18, 2001.

A Better World's in Birth! by Howard Waldrop, Copyright © 2003 by Howard Waldrop. First published by Golden Gryphon Press, 2003.

All afterwords by Howard Waldrop, Copyright © 2008 by Howard Waldrop.

To Oso, Washington, bastard-child of
the North Fork of the Stillaguamish River.

SIZE MATTERS

"Hi-ho, everybody!" as the late Rudy Vallee used to say.

Welcome to the second volume of my *Selected Fiction*, culled (if that's the word) from my shattered and fragmented attempt at a career.

These are the longer pieces, including two published as books, what they used to call "separate publication" in the bibliographic biz.

There's a simple reason for the length of these stories—they came to me in a longer form. The standard rule is, if a piece of fiction is straight-forward, it's a short story; if *other* things are going on besides the main narrative, it's a novelette or novella.

Boy, is there *lots* going on in these stories. (I'll get to them in the brand-new afterwords to each story.)

People used to argue that the ideal form for SF and fantasy was the novella and novelette—the story has room to grow; you can fill in the background at more length, bring in plot complications, etc. etc.

That's not the way *I* do it, of course. (*Booklist* just referred to me as a "beloved genre wildman"—I don't know *what* that means, but I *like* it.) Anyway, I'll tell you why I wrote most of these.

As I said, the ideas came to me in longer forms—I can usually tell within 500 words or so *how long* something *has to be* when the idea comes to me. (I'm sometimes, but rarely, surprised.) Since I was so busy with short stories (including those in *Things Will Never Be The Same*— vol. 1 of this set.), I made up file folders for the longer stories, with whatever notes I could make *without* doing lots of research (which is what I do right before I'm ready to write a story).

Along about 1988 I looked through my story log (yes, Mr. Genre Wildman has 4 books of those—when the story idea came, when the first and final drafts were written, who it went to, where and when it sold [*if ever*] what I was supposed to be paid and when; when it was supposed to be published, etc. You know, some of the donkey-work you have to do as a freelance writer.) Anyway, I was looking at my story logs, and I noted for some reason the *last four stories* I'd written had come out at almost *exactly* 5600 words, typical short story length.

"I was in a rut without noticing it." I said to myself, "Time for some *longer* stuff."

If you read the first volume of this *Selected Fiction*, you know that one of my goals is to never write the same story twice (which is why I'll *never* be rich.) I've stuck to that goal since I started in this pretty thankless business in the late 1960s. If you do it *right*, it's much harder to repeat yourself at longer lengths than if you're doing short stuff all the time.

In the next few months, after cranking myself in a new direction, I did three of these, including the 35,000 worder. I was mighty pleased with myself. I'd broken out of my same-length rut (to my way of thinking) and was stretching the old writing muscles.

Best of all, the more I wrote at longer length, the more ideas for longer stories came to me (two ideas, for "You *Could* Go Home Again" and the forthcoming *The Moone World* [Wheatland Press] came to me within five minutes of each other one hot sweaty day in 1989, when I was trying to nap on a couch in an unairconditioned South Austin house). You tell kids that stuff nowadays, they don't believe you.

And between shorter stuff, I'd dip into the long-story notes I'd made for years, seeing if I could crank up some fresh enthusiasm for *any* of them. And of course the new ideas kept scratching at my brain.

Part of my enthusiasm for longer stuff was because of the rise of small-press publishers who were looking for a) short story collections and b) novellas to be published as separate editions. (In other words, the stuff big publishers didn't want to go *near* with a 3.183-meter pole.) The pay usually wasn't great (but if I were totally in it for the *money*, I *wouldn't* be writing short science fiction, would I?) but it was pay of some kind, and what you usually ended up with was some great-looking, beautifully illustrated (and in some cases) handcrafted book in a slipcase that'll still be around a hundred years from now.

To quote a famous moron: Bring it on.

My career at that point, and the startups (and continuations) of some swell small-press publishers coincided. They usually *only* wanted edition rights, or some month's exclusivity, and I could sometimes sell them to the magazines later.

Also, as you'll see in the story afterwords, Ellen Datlow bought some for *Omni Online.com* and its adjuncts, successors and bastard children (*Event Horizon.com*, *Sci-fi.com*)—earlier when *Omni* had been a magazine, she could only publish one, or at most two, pieces of fiction a month, usually short stories. If you're just burning photons, there's *no limit* on length (except reader fatigue).

Anyway, you'll get more than you *want to know* in the story after-words—here they are, all the longer stuff (that fits). There are more that aren't here for various reasons—they've just been reprinted in fairly permanent form by someone else somewhere else; none of the longer collaborations are here—those are in *Custer's Last Jump and Other Collaborations* from Golden Gryphon Press, which I see by my latest royalty statement sold a big 28 copies in the last 6 months. (I'll be laughing my ass off in five years when people are paying $150 for third-hand ex-libris copies off e-Bay, though neither me, my buddies, nor Golden Gryphon will get *any* of *that*. Golden Gryphon has vowed to keep the book in print as long as they're able, but *eventually* they'll all be gone, and people who want one will be in the tender care of sharks and wolves . . .)

I'm proud to have done each and every one of these. For some reason, 2007 is turning out to be the Year of Long Waldrop, with the printing of these, and *The Search for Tom Purdue* (Subterranean Press, forthcoming) and *The Moone World* (Wheatland Press, ditto).

Next year, maybe, back to the good old *short* stuff.

Howard Waldrop
Friday, July 15, 2007

A DOZEN TOUGH JOBS

I

It was so early in the morning that the birds wasn't even up yet, to my way of thinking,and here I was down to the gate of the Old Egypt Cemetery tryin' to decide whether to tell a white woman a lie or not.

Miz Eustis had sent me down to see whether the old church cemetery needed the fall cleaning yet—she was of course a Baptist but some of the earliest town settlers was buried out here and the hoity-toity white folks always turned up two Saturdays a year, whenever Miz Luvsey told them to, and worked themselves up almost to a sweat and then had a stand-up ice cream social afterwards.

I was standing in front of Old Man Chop's tomb. It was big and pointy-looking, about twenty feet on every side. His brothers Myron and Keiffer's tombs was about the same (though Mr. Myron's looked taller because it was on a little rise). They was this big stone lion out front of the three tombs that they'd brought all the way down from Cairo, Illinois, to put in front of the vaults long before the war. Somebody was gonna have to decide what to do about Mr. Keiffer's tomb—it looked terrible. It had once been covered with imported limestone, but in the middle of the Civil War they came out and found somebody had busted chunks off it to make whitewash with, and what with rain and all there was only about a third of it left now, since they'd started at the bottom it looked all jaggeldy up at the top.

Miz Eustis thought it should stay like it was to remind people of the sacrifices of the war. So had her mother-in-law and *her* mother, so it had just gone to hell for sixty-some years.

1

Well, the cemetery didn't look too bad to me, but I'm not an expert, and I don't like being around them even in daylight. But now that the cotton's all picked and white kids is back in school, and nobody pays attention to anything because football's already started at Ole Miss and MSC, it'd probably do the white people some good to work this Saturday.

So I went back east, crossed over Niles Creek, and went back to the big house to tell Miss Luvsey Eustis that the Old Egypt Cemetery was in sorry shape, but when I got back, Uncle Romulus told me I'd dawdled so long that Miz Eustis had gone into town already to see to the shopping and that I was supposed to go find where she was and wait outside the store for her, and tell her the condition of, as Romulus said she put it, "the former necropolis." And that should be P.D.Q.

Mr. Eustis—Boss Eustis—had left earlier that morning to go over to Anatolia County to see Boss Primagenus about some Democrat Party business, so Uncle Romulus was on a tear, being absolute monarch in the absence of both owners of the house.

"Get moving, I.O.," he said, "or I'll be telling Miz Eustis you're being obstreperous again."

"I ain't. I'm tired."

"Don't be thinking you'll get the use of a horse, either." He looked at the big Regulator clock in the kitchen. "It's seven thirty-two. I want to hear from Miz Eustis that you found her before 8 A.M. by the courthouse clock, else I'll be serving you up a extra big helping of that Whipme-Whopme pudding I keep behind the smokehouse."

I took off at a trot, cutting through the low pasture, taking the short-cut over the two ditches and headed fast as I could down the old bridle-path toward downtown Anomie, Mississippi, U.S.A.

* * *

I got to the eastern edge of town—Darky Town they of course call it, and turned up King Bull Street, which was the widest thing in that part of town. Old Man Asher, who'd tried making a go with a line of cattle called King Bulls, had put up lamp posts on every corner decorated with cement cows, and being a thinking man had made them so they had an easy time making them over for electric lights. 'Course, when he'd done that, white folks lived on this side of town; first thing you know there was some Cajuns from Louisiana, then some Mexicans—the ones with money the white folks called 'Spaniards'—and the next thing you know, ain't nobody here but us dark people. 'Course, moving the Interurban line back before the Great War had more to do with it than anything. Then King Bull Street was on the wrong side of the tracks. It's still the only street over here with lights on the corners at all, and the bulbs slowly burn out during the year, or kids slingshot 'em, and every year, just before Christmas, Prometheus Gundlefinger brings his power company truck and a ladder, and puts new bulbs up. It's about all the Christmas some folks get around here. But the cows all look nice and bright while the bulbs are still new.

There wasn't too many people on the streets. I could see all the way to town, the hub of commerce, and there wasn't much there either.

Then I saw someone standing on the front gallery of his house, not moving. He had a guitar under his arm. He was an old, old man and he wore a pair of dark round glasses. I slowed down, trying to walk real quiet. I was on the other side of the street. The old man's head turned toward me. I took a few steps and his head turned with me. I stopped.

"What you stoppin' for, I.O.?"

"Damn if I know, Blind Bill," I said.

"Mister Blind Bill to you, young pissant," he said. "You see that no-good white paperboy?"

Just as he said that a kid came zooming around the corner of Delphi Street leaning over on the sidewalls of his bike tires. His paperbag buckles was sending up sparks and he had one foot out like a motorcycle state trooper, and his taps were sparking, too. He had a mean look and his cap was down at a chilling angle.

"He don't much like being in this part of town,"said Blind Bill.

The paperboy only had four subscribers in Darky Town, and didn't care either way about the dime a month he made or not, they were so far apart. For some reason Blind Bill Orff was one of them—folks said it was something that happened between him and the newspaper editor years ago.

"On the sidewalk!" yelled Blind Bill. The paperboy was oblivious—it didn't even look like he would throw a paper. He came by a blur, and a paper was flying through the air, twenty feet up, bounced off the tin roof on Bill's house and end-walked back down the rock path to a stop a couple of inches from Blind Bill's feet.

The kid was already out of sight before the paper stopped moving.

"Hee-hee-hee," said Blind Bill. "Can't wait to hear my Thursday paper. Come on and set down and read it to me, I.O."

"I can't Bi—Mr. Blind Bill. I got to go find Miz Eustis down to the mercantile and do some bowin' and scrapin'."

"What you mean? How the hell am I gonna be well informed somebody don't read the weekly paper to me?"

"Well, where's your nephew?"

"That no-good sumbitch was out tom-cattin' around and ain't come back yet. I hope he gets the goddam clap and that's the truth." He picked up the paper. "Come on in and read to me."

"I ain't got the time, Mr. Blind Bill, I really ain't."

"Damn, does everybody in your generation got no respect for they elders?"

"We're a lost generation, Mr. Blind Bill."

"What the fuck you talkin' bout? You ain't lost, you right here!"

"Something in a book I read, Mr. Bill."

"*You* read a book?"

"I sneaked it off Miz Eustis's bookshelf the other night, read it real quick, she never noticed it gone."

"What's it about?"

"A bunch of crazy mixed-up white folks in Paris, France. One of 'em had his hammer shot off in the war."

"What's it called?"

"*The Sun Also Rises*, Mr. Blind Bill."

"That so? That's from *Ecclesiastes*. See? While you was yammering to me you coulda been reading. Get busy."

"I ain't got time. Miz Eustis gonna get Uncle Romulus all over my ass already."

"Well, dammit! Read me the column."

I sighed, "Alright, Mr. Blind Bill. I'll read the column to you, but that's all I can do. Really."

"Set. Read," he said. He walked back to the porch like he had eyes, sat down in his rocker and put down his guitar. He folded his hands on his lap and waited while I put on the glasses Miz Eustis had me fitted with last year. I unfolded the paper.

"*Spunt County Shouter*. Week of September 26, 1926," I said.

"Hell, I know that!" said Blind Bill. "Read 'The Pea-Patch Poet' column."

The Pea-Patch Poet Column, by Virgil Homer

Well, the crops are in, and I guess if you hunker down on your nail keg there, we can get back to whatever it was we were talking about, and what all's gone on in the county while you were out following the mules or the combine machine, or fiddling with the cantankerous engine on your John Deere Model 21s, like I heard you were last week.

Where was I? Lessee . . . I could tell you about some more adventures of hometown boys in the Great War—I already told you about Paul Minius—he went over and joined the Canadian Army before the United States got into the war, and he got to see the famous boxing match in '17 between Man-Mountain Mannon of Syracuse and Kid Troy from over in Anatolia County. People who saw it are still talking about it.

Or I could continue the story of U.S. Gant who left France in 1918 and hasn't made it home yet. Not that he ain't trying—his wife keeps hearing bad things, but his Aunt Hera keeps getting postcards from people all over the world who've seen him—they say he looks determined, grim and a lot thinner than he used to. He's on some Caribbean island, supposedly. He's taken more ships that have sunk or wrecked or run aground than any man alive.

"I heard enough about that asshole," said Blind Bill. "I hope he don't get off yammering about him again."

"Let me read, Blind Bill."

But you've probably heard enough. Maybe he should sign up with one of those people who are always trying to fly across the Atlantic Ocean in an aeroplane. He couldn't do any worse than he has already, except maybe be killed outright.

So I'll devote this column to the greatest event ever in this county —for those of you who have been dead or on the Planet Mars for the last two weeks.

I'm talking about The Game.

As everybody knows, Ap Low is the best checky-player in Spunt County. A Napoleon of the draughts, a General Pershing of the harlequined gaming board. Well, he's probably even better than that. When he visited Corinth last year to see his brother Jupe, he played everybody there, too. Most of the games was over faster than you can say Jack Robinson.

Anyway, Ap was as usual over at the picnic table in front of the Spunt County Courthouse, taking on all comers.

As they tell it, down at the depot the noon train pulls in and a guy dressed in his Sunday best (this was Tuesday) steps off and he's got no luggage, just a big flat box under his arm. Merk Jones, the Western Union boy, said he didn't ask anything, just looked around till he saw the courthouse clock and started walking that way. (I myself was witness to most of what happened but I'm relying on eyewitnesses as to events which happened before my hurried arrival on the scene.) Anyway, old

Eb Short was as usual warming his spot on the green park bench when he saw the stranger approaching. He said what attracted his attention, besides the flashy suit, was that the man walked with sort of a stopped walk, like his feet was on the wrong legs, and that he had a long thin face with a big nose and he was wearing a goatee beard, first one seen in Spunt County, I'm told, since Professor Panteen closed the Lyceum back in '88. So Eb watched and listened real close.

The stranger came right up to the picnic table. Ap was just clearing off four of Jimmy Theyer's kings in one jump, as he usually does. The stranger said:

"Are you Mr. Ap Low?"

"Yep," said Ap.

"I hear you play some checkers."

Ap leaned back and looked the stranger over.

"I been known to. What can I do for you?"

"My name's Bill Marshius. I come all the way from Crossett, Arkansas, and I aim to beat you in a game of checkers."

The crowd gasped. Last time somebody said that was back in 1911, and you all know what happened to him.

Ap's eyes narrowed.

"You play hafta-taka-jump?"

"Either way's fine with me. I done beat everybody in Arkansas both ways."

"Best two-outta-three, don't hafta-taka-jump?" asked Ap.

"Fine with me," said Marshius. "Do you want to make it interesting?"

Ap Low sat there like a rock for about fifteen seconds, then he reaches in his overalls and takes out a fifty dollar gold piece. They said you could see the eagle blink as it came out of his pocket. He put it in the middle of the checkerboard. (Jimmy had cleared off the board while all the talk was going on.)

"Boy," said Blind Bill. "That Virgil Homer sure can write!"

"Bill, let me finish this thing! I'm late already. Miz Eustis's probably having a hissy fit already!"

"Go on, go on," said Blind Bill.

Marshius started to reach for his billfold.

"I don't want your money," said Ap. "That money's what you get if you beat me two out of three games."

"What do you want, then?" asked Marshius.

Ap looked him up and down. "I assume you got a way of getting home?"

"I certainly got money for a ticket home."

"Well," said Ap, "if I win, I want everything you're wearing except your wallet. All the way down to your birthday suit. Right here on the square. And you got to walk from here to the depot."

"You asking me to get arrested for indecency?"

"Oh," said Ap, looking around and winking at Deputy Marshal Marshall who had stopped to listen. "I think we can get the law and some of the ladies to look the other way."

Marshius looked at him real hard. "That what you want? Me jay-bird naked if I lose? You're betting $50 against that? That what you want?

Ap looked him over again, real hard and slow like. "Mr. Marshius, I think you're the kind of man who would take that bet even if I didn't have a dime."

"Let's get this straight. Two out of three. Don't have to take a jump. Your fifty dollars against me stripping off naked and walking to the depot. That it so far?"

"Yep."

"And we play on my board?"

"Fine with me," said Ap.

"Then mister," said Marshius, holding out his hand. "You got a deal." The man took the box out from under his arm. He laid it on the table, opened it. He took out a hinged checkerboard. It was made of white marble and onyx. The crowd gasped again and people went running off to get everybody, including me.

Then, according to Eb, Marshius brought out his men. They were made of round and polished ebony and ivory. Jimmy Thayer picked two up, then held them behind his back. Then he held his clenched fists out.

"Call it, Mr. Marshius," he said.

"Left hand."

Jimmy opened it. "White," he said. "That means you move first."

"I know what the hell it means, kid."

They set the counters up. By now there must have been a crowd of 200 people around, me included, and more every minute.

Then Ap Low looked across the table and he said, "Mr. Marshius, let's play some checkers."

CONTINUED NEXT WEEK

* * *

"I'll be goddamned," yelled Blind Bill. "That ain't right!" You're just saying that cause you're in a hurry. Read me the rest o' it."

"That's all, Mr. Blind Bill. I didn't know it was coming!"

"He always says continued next week, but he always tells a whole story, goddam him!"

"Hell, Bill, everybody knows how that checker game came out! Why—"

Blind Bill clamped his hands over his ears. "Don't you tell me! Don't you dare tell me!" he yelled. "I don't know. I don't want to know. Goddam you, just for that you be here with the paper first thing next Thursday morning and you read me what happened, you hear me? What a nasty-ass trick to play on a poor blind man!"

He took his hands away from his ears. He was right, Virgil Homer had never done a column that way before.

Everybody but Blind Bill Orff knew how that checker match turned out anyway.

"You just be dammed sure you be here next week, you young turd!" He picked up his guitar and put a sawed-off sanded-down end of a Coca-Cola bottle on the little finger of his left hand. "Damn Virgil Homer!" he said. He pulled a screaming slide note with a quick jerk of both his hands. It sounded like a rusty two-handed file pulled across a loose nail on a wet day. It hurt my ears.

I took off running for town. I didn't want to be real close when Blind Bill started playing. He pulled a long wailing note, then another. I turned onto Delphi street to put some houses between me and him. Then he started singing, growling loud and nasty:

> Go tell Aunt Rhody—ahhhr!
> Go tell Aunt Rhody—oowah!
> Go tell Aunt Rhody,
> That ol' grey goose is dead.
> Yahhhhh!
> One she been savin',
> One she been savin' lordy lordy,
> One she savin',
> Make a feather bed!

They said Blind Bill lost his wife a long, long time ago, and he never got over it, which is what made him such a mean old man. But that was way before my time.

II

I ran in toward the square, crossing the old interurban tracks and leaving Darky Town.

There was a clatter of hooves on the side street and I stopped. The sounds got louder and then came out onto the main stem.

Everybody referred to them as the Horsey Set, or the Riding Club, only there wasn't one in this burg, not officially anyway. In the front was Mr. Ness—he was the guiding light, and his father'd made all the money he lived on. He was only about thirty, but him and his bunch had been riding their horses—Kentucky thoroughbreds all—all over the county since I was a baby. They were always on picnics or hunting or fishing trips. That must be where they were going today because Mr. Ness had on that big ol' fishing vest with all those reel-and-rod plugs stuck all over it, some of them must have had fifteen hooks each on them. Ness was about the only man in the county to use a reel-and-rod. I've seen him fishing from the saddle with the horse standing in shallow water. In fact, I ain't ever seen Mr. Ness or none of the others off their horses that I remember. I probably wouldn't recognize them standing on their own two legs.

It was early in the day so they weren't drunk yet. You only had to watch out for them in the evenings and at night when they sometimes rode hell for leather through town on their way to Ness's house, where, rumor has it, the revels continue late into the night. Where they find all the liquor I don't know; all I know is it drives them crazy when they've had some.

A couple of them had saddlebags on their mounts. I nodded to Miz Dianne Rio whose mother my older sister had worked for before she ran off to Memphis. Miz Dianne looked like she hadn't got much sleep—she wasn't as old as Mr. Ness and the others—she'd only been running with them for four or five years. I waited till they turned off toward the Creek Road Bridge and ran on down to the courthouse square.

It was already 8:10. Uncle Romulus was gonna whop me sure when Miz Eustis told him I was late.

I passed some people coming out of the Prokrus Mattress and Furniture Store wrestling a big ol' chair out onto the sidewalk. (I'd of built the doors of a furniture store wider.) Then as I was hurrying by the Apex Theater I saw they had some new handbills up where the announcement of the next movies should be.

I already had seen the movies playing this week—Charlie Chaplin's *The Gold Rush* and *The Wizard of Oz* with an actor named Larry Semon, and a comic Negro actor named G. Howe Black who didn't even notice when lightning struck him in the head. (The film wasn't much like the book—Oz is where Czecho-Slovakia is on a map, and Semon and some fat man dress up like the Scarecrow and Tin Woodman for about two minutes—it was a real bad print, too, and from way up in the balcony where us folks have to sit, you couldn't see much.)

But these notices weren't for a movie. Mister Ashneel's Traveling Players was coming to town for three days next month. They were doing a play a night for three nights—*The Little Killt Babies, Who's Been At Mother?* and *Murders in the King's Palace* plus an 11 P.M. performance "for gentlemen only" called *Girls With Big Jugs (of oil)*. Admission to the other plays was 50¢, the late show was a whole dollar!

The courthouse clock chimed the quarter hour.

I ran into Coretta, Miz Eustis's help, standing outside the Jitney Jungle.

"There you is, you no good whelp!" she said. "You done dawdled so long Miz Luvsey done all her shopping already 'cept for some stuff in there, and she's ready to go. Now she got somethin' else for you to do. You supposed to go down to the courthouse and wait all day, if necessary, for a man to show up who's gonna be working for Mr. Eldridge."

"But Coretta, I ain't even . . ."

"I do not want to hear it. Mr. Eldridge had to call all around town by long distance from Acedia all the way over in Anatolia County till he found Miz Luvsey—he'd forgotten all about the man till Boss Primagenus reminded him."

"How'll I know him? All white folks . . ."

"Don't the hell give me that, I.O. You's supposed to meet him at the sheriff's office. You just look at every white man comes in there and listen to their business until you find the right one. You oughta like this, I.O. They got lots of stuff you can set on your ass and read at the sheriff's office."

"Coretta, I'm afraid of the sherriffs!"

"Well, you should be, rightly so, and someday you might have to deal with them, but I guarantee one thing—you don't bring that man back out to the place you gonna be dealing with Uncle Romulus in ways you ain't *never* seen!"

"Aww . . ."

"Get your black butt down to the courthouse and don't come back till you got the man or till they lock the place up tonight. Don't you make me put these packages down!"

I started away. "Tell Miz Eustis that cemetery looks like an afterbirth!" I said. I ran toward the courthouse, past the usual bunch was sitting on their chairs and benches, but the closer I got the slower I went.

The sheriffs' truck with the wire cage on the back wasn't in its spot, so I knew they were gone, there being three sheriffs and no deputy, the place would be locked up while they were out on a run.

I was heading toward the south door when I saw the strangest thing I ever saw coming from the west side of the square, and heads was turning all over the place.

It was a man about five feet tall, but about half that wide at the shoulders so he looked like a walking icebox. He had a big thick square beard that looked like the business end of a coal scoop, and on his head was a black and yellow cap. He didn't have on a shirt and wore a pair of bib overalls, only they were made with just one strap over the right shoulder, and from here they looked like they were made of brown leather. It made my butt tighten just to think what it must feel like in there on a hot day. He had on some boots made out of another kind of hide, lighter in color than the overalls. He went up the west steps and out of sight.

I went in and down the cool corridor and turned left, and there was the man coming down the hall at me, looking up and down at the signs over the doors. I stopped and he went by, and I saw there was a big square folded piece of yellow and blue paper sticking out of the back pocket of his leather coveralls. Right away I knew he'd been brought out of prison to finish his time working somewheres.

I went to the sheriffs' office, which was of course closed, with a sign saying, "Be back whenever justice is meted out." Then there was a shadow on the door beside me. I turned. It was the man in the leather outfit. He was looking at me with the most piercing grey eyes I'd ever seen. I sort of jumped.

"They sure know how to hide a sheriff's office in this county," he said.

I swallowed. "Well, sir, it ain't in the usual place."

"Hey!" said a voice down the hall. "Y'all got business there?"

It was Deputy Marshal Marshall standing with his hands on his belt. Just like we got three county sheriffs and no deputy, we got one town deputy and no marshal.

"I have to report to the county sheriff," said the man.

"I reckon I'll do while they're gone. Come on down to my office. What about you?"

"I'm supposed to meet a man here coming to work for Boss Eustis."

The deputy laughed. "I see a pattern developing here. Ain't but one reason a man coming to work for Boss Eustis would have to be met at the sheriffs' office. I think that there's your man. Come on along."

This is the kind of stuff Boss Eustis gets me into. What now? We went out the steps and around to the marshal's office in the basement. Marshall took off his hat. "Where's them damn forms?" he said, searching through his desk. "Here they are. Lemme see your papers."

He looked at the yellow form. "This here's Boss Eustis's charge alright," he said to me. "Things has come to a might lax pass when The Boss sends a little nigger boy down here for a man what did five years hard time."

"I didn't know anything about it, Mr. Marshall. I thought it was just somebody coming here to work for Mr. Eustis."

"I guarantee he'll work, all right. Let's get this stuff down here on the paper. Name?"

"1213—" the man started, then said, "Lee, comma Houlka, no middle name."

"Age?"

"Thirty-two."

"And you're a Caucasian male by the looks of that there beard. Which prison?"

"Parchman Farm."

Marshall whistled. "That's where them muscles come from. I think there's only been one white man come from Parchman in the last ten years. Occupation?"

"Convict."

"Before then, dammit."

"You might say I was a wildlife management specialist."

"Home?"

"Route 1, Box 2, Mt. Oatie, Mississippi."

"Next of kin?" Then Marshall looked at the yellow form. "Well, you pretty much took care of that, didn't you? Next next of kin?"

"Al Lee, Route 1, Box 4, Mt. Oatie."

"Relationship?"

"Twin brother."

"Read and write?"

"Some."

"Alright. I'm gonna read this to you then. You gotta tell me you understand, cause you mess up, or don't please the Boss, we get your ass back to Parchman P.D.Q."

He pulled out the county form.

"You are hereby remanded to the custody of the below-named person to work for him for the rest of your term, being a period of," he looked down on the other form, "—one year from today's date.

"The following terms apply:

"You will work for two dollars a month and keep. This rate is set by the state. You cannot work for any other wages, tips or salary, and you cannot be lent out for money hire by your employer. Employer is to provide one hot meal a day and two others. Employer is to provide one change of clothes and shoes or boots and one extra shirt, pair of socks and a light jacket during each year or portion of a year.

"You are not to associate with known criminals, parolees or persons of low morals. You are not to have in your possession firearms, concealed weapons, or knives with blades longer than three inches. You are not to have in your possession proscribed articles, drugs, or alcohol. Prohibition is the law of these United States, the State of Mississippi and every county therein. You are not to leave the county under any circumstances unless your employer requires it and gives three days advance notice in writing to the county sheriffs. You are not to use profanity or blasphemy. You are to perform your work in a courteous and expedient manner. Your work-release depends on the good will of your employer and you can be remanded to custody for transportation back to the prison you came from at any time during the period, with no option for further buying-out of your time. Escape or attempts to escape will result in the return to prison with an additional two years added to your original sentence. Do you understand all this?"

"Yes, sir."

"Sign here."

Mr. Houlka Lee picked up the fountain pen and carefully and slowly wrote out his name.

"I'm gonna let you take this man out to the Boss's place, but you tell Mr. Eustis next time send a man in to do this job. And he runs away before you get him home, I'm gonna put your ass in Parchman."

"Yessir."

Marshall wrote out "for Eldridge Eustis, employer" on the bottom of the form and pushed it over to me. "Make your mark, then tell me your name," he said.

I took up the fountain pen and signed "Invictus Ovidius Lace."

Marshall looked up at me. "I'll remember that next time, Invictus."

"They call me I.O., Mr. Marshall."

"I'll put these under the sheriffs' door," he said. "Git."

* * *

I took Mr. Lee out to the Boss's place. Things was in an uproar there—some circuit court judge had died four counties away, and you'd think the

Moon had fallen into the Pacific Ocean the way people was yelling on phones and roaring up and jumping in and out of cars, and with Boss Eustis still over in Anatolia County.

I found JimBob, the Boss's overseer. "Take him out to Roskus's old shack, the one next to yours. Clean it up and scrub it down. He'll eat with the second shift of white folks in the kitchen. The Boss'll see him tomorrow."

He turned to Mr. Lee. "We gonna have any trouble with you?"

"Not that you can tell."

"If we are, tell me now; we'll get you back up to Parchman tonight. Mr. Eustis is doing this as a favor to some friends up in Corinth, same's they do for him. We'd as soon have one person as another."

Houlka didn't say anything, and we went out and made a start cleaning up the shack.

III

Boss Eustis sat back in his big half-barrel chair on the front porch.

"Well, hee-heee-hee!" he said. He was a dried-up prune of a little man, looked about four hundred years old, although I looked in the Big Bible once, on the family tree pages, and he wasn't even born when the War for Southern Independence ended, though he looked like he'd been around when George Washington was a surveyor.

He hasn't changed a speck since I saw him the first time leaning over the old dresser drawer they said they used for my crib. That was the first bad scare I ever had in my life.

I was scared pissless of him till I was around ten years old. Usually white folks when they get old they fall apart all at once—one week they're middle-aged, the next they're toothless old noddies being pushed around by their grandkids in a wheelbarrow. Black folks just get older and a little grayer and a little shorter and then they die.

The Boss was the only white person who got old that way.

"I done brought you out of Parchman on the advice of my cronies. You understand the terms of your employment?"

"Yes."

Boss Eustis was a little taken aback. He waggled his finger in his ear like he was clearing it out. "What wuz zat?"

"Yes, sir," said Houlka Lee.

"That's better. Well. You gonna get to start early. I'm sorta responsible for everything in this county that don't come under the heading of the judge's or the sheriffs' business. We got us a re-port this morning that they's a cougar tearing up hell in the northeast section just above the Lake. Your job's gonna be to get rid of it. Run it out of the county, trap it, I don't care, just so long's I don't have to hear people squawk about it. Take that pissant there with you," he said, pointing at me. "Can't let you have a gun, of course, but you'll have to figure something out."

"Yessir."

"JimBob," said the Boss, "get someone to drive 'em out to Skeeno's place. Make sure this man gets whatever he needs, short of firepower."

"Sure thing, Boss."

Houlka and me went out back. He looked around. "Get me the sharp-est axe on the place," he said. I went out to the tool shed and came back with the Michigan double-bit. Houlka took it and walked out to the woods over the back fence

"What's this?"

"That? Oh, that's one of them damn olive trees the Frenchman who owned the place before the Boss's folks bought it tried to plant. He had some notion Mississippi would become the olive-oil capital of the world. Only two or three of them lived."

Houlka put his foot on it and started chopping. The trunk was nine inches in diameter and about eight feet up to the first branches. He chopped it down, started working it on one end with the edge of the blade held close to his hand. Then he whacked it off about four feet up and smoothed that end.

"Let's go," he said.

We went back out front where the truck was waiting. Some of the men on the porch started sputtering and laughing.

Then I saw something I hadn't seen in three years. Boss Eustis stood up.

"You mean you're going after a mountain lion with a stick? You ain't taking any traps or nets or stuff to make a deadfall? No dogs?"

He even walked to the edge of the porch. "You go on. You just go on. I find out you're just out there settin' somewhere, I'll send you back to the farm."

We got in the truck and they drove us out to above Lake Yuksino.

* * *

"I think you should cut up from the stomach and around the ribcage," I said.

"There's more than one way to skin a cat," Houlka said. He cut a little nick in the heel of one of the cougar's legs he'd nailed to the fence rail. He grabbed with both hands and started pulling and walking.

The skin started turning inside out, and I'll be damned if it didn't pull off, over the butt, around the other leg, off the chest, up the neck and down the chin. When he finished, there was nothing but the white carcass and the whole skin joined by two little-bitty pieces to the lips and one leg. He came back and made three quick cuts with his Ka-Bar knife.

"Know anybody who needs two hundred pounds of meat?"

"I can't believe Mr. Eustis didn't want the skin," I said.

"I told him I needed a new coat this winter. He saw it as a way not to have to spend any money." He took off his yellow and black Lion Feed cap and held it up next to the cougar's head skin. "Should just fit," he said. We carried the carcass to the butcher's, who ran it through a bone saw four or five times, then on to the orphan asylum.

"Venison," he said to the lady in the orphanage kitchen.

"It ain't deer season yet."

"It had an accident," said Houlka.

*   *   *

I was in my shack when JimBob knocked on the door. "Get ya butt out to the porch. Him too," he said, nodding toward Houlka's cabin.

Houlka and I went out front where Boss Eustis and the others were holding forth. It was the first time Mr. Eustis had seen Houlka's outfit—the leather coveralls he always wore, the boots, and now the coat made out of the cougar hide with the head still attached that he wore pulled back like a cowl on his neck. He was carrying his big club.

"Halloween ain't for two more weeks yet. Damn if you ain't dressed to win every contest in this town," said the Boss. "Then again, I ain't ever paid a man for the way he looks, either. Never let that be said, or Goober over there would be broke all the time." They all laughed.

"You did so well with that panther you're wearin' that we done thought of another call along the same lines. We want you and the boy there to go over and clean up all the snakes from Mr. Hyder's pools."

"Ooh, they's moccasins in there eight feet long, I hear," said Goober. "That set right with you?"

"Fine," said Houlka. "I been killing snakes since I was a baby."

"Dr. Sclape's been warned to look out, you might be being brought in to his clinic," said JimBob.

"Well, if they's bit, they sure as hell ain't gonna make it back to town, JimBob," said Boss Eustis. "Who you better call's the undertaker."

I was shaking in my shoes.

"You got a frog-gig for the boy?" asked Houlka.

"Fix 'em up, JimBob."

* * *

We was in the thick of it, down in the muddy bottomland, and there was already a snake every twenty feet just gettin' to the ponds. I saw one on the path and raised up the gig to get it.

"That's a rat snake," said Houlka.

"A snake's a snake!" I said.

"You want rats eating the butts off every baby in Spunt County, go ahead."

I let it slide away.

"I hope your eyes is quick and good," I said. "Can't nobody fish here anymore it's so full of snakes. Used to be the best fishing in the county."

The ponds covered five acres or so in all. As we came over a little rise I saw a bass that must have weighed five pounds come out after a snake doctor. You could almost see the bottom of the pond it knocked so much water up when it arced.

"We need to make some torches," said Houlka. "Use it when they strike, hit back when they recoil. You'll get the rhythm soon enough."

* * *

Snakes flew around like they had wings. Loops flopped around on the ground. You could smell their flesh burning. I was scared and the air was full of their venom smell. One struck at me, I lowered the torch. Its fangs knocked sparks off. As it pulled back, I stuck it with the gig, twisted to break its back, and shook it off the tines.

Houlka used the torch and club. He flipped the bashed snakes behind him. There were two in front of him, seven, eight feet long. I tried to watch, then another one came at me. I missed with the gig and it started winding around the haft up toward my hand. I caught its head between the torch and the handle. Its flopping and coiling twisted the gig from my hands.

I heard Houlka yell and thought sure one of the snakes had got in.

I looked over. Both snakes were mashed in three or four places. Houlka jumped around. I'll be damned if there wasn't a crawdad pinching his leg with both claws. It must have been flipped up in the melee and landed on his coveralls.

Houlka pulled it off and laughed.

* * *

We got our breath back finally. We'd piled the snakes up on the sides of three of the ponds. It looked like stacks of tires at a service station. One of the Hyder family came over the rise, stopped stock still.

We walked up to him.

"That's all the mocassins and copperheads, except the little ones that swam out to the middles of the ponds. Weren't any rattlers. If somebody comes back tomorrow with a .22 they can take care of all the little ones. Anything big that's left is just a mud snake," said Houlka.

The man's jaw hung open.

"You satisfied?" asked Houlka.

The man nodded his head, still staring at the nearest pile of bloody snakes.

"Then if you could tell Boss Eustis our work's done when he calls, we'll be on our way."

The man looked at the other two piles.

"I'll be godddamned," he said.

IV

People had come to give Houlka a wide berth whenever he had to go into town. Deputy Marshal Marshall had been talking, as had the Hyders and Skeenos, and all the cream of Spunt County who spent all their time on the Boss's front porch. Wearing those coveralls and the lionskin didn't help much, but it did let them see him coming a long way off.

Miz Eustis had him doing odd jobs around the place. The big house had never looked better—she had us planting and cleaning and painting. Houlka just did his work and didn't say much of anything till he was through. I don't think Miz Eustis gave him much thought at all except just as another handyman around the place.

Boss Eustis though—he fumed and he pondered on what to do, and him and his buddies was always thinking of ways to humiliate Houlka with menial stuff. Me, I came in for my share of it, but after awhile they tired of that stuff, like it wasn't fun any more to make us wash their cars, like it was them being belittled, not us.

After the cougar and the pond cleaning, and having to go run down that old razorback that had come all the way over from Arkansas just before Thanksgiving—we had hog along with turkey and put up two hundred pounds of pork besides—there wasn't as much hoorawing on the front porch as there once had been.

It was on a cool day, December 1st, and we was all lined up because it was payday on the place. If you didn't go see Boss Eustis sittin' in his cut-down half-barrel chair, you didn't get paid. Some of the farmers who were on pay-and-cost instead of shares had to come seven or eight miles, but by eight in the morning there was ten or twelve wagons and a couple of trucks parked outside on the road. They were full of kids and wives and there were always dogfights.

"Well, Elmer," said Boss Eustis to the farmer who stood in front of him, "I done heard you been drinkin' again. That right?"

"Boss," said Elmer, "I don't rightly see how a man with eight kids, a wife, a mother, four mules, two horses and twelve dogs to keep up would have the time or money to drink, do you?"

"Besides," he added, "I been spending all my time finding a covey of quail for you. I know just where they keep in the south field."

"Hee-hee-hee," said the Boss. "Give him his pay, JimBob."

"Sure thing, Boss." Mr. Eustis always paid in solid dollars and change.

"Who's this?" asked the Boss, squinting up. "Why, Leroy. How many fines Leroy got last month?"

"Only three, Boss."

"Only three! Why, that's like a miracle. Not going to church Sunday before last on there? I know he didn't go; I asked."

"It's down here, Boss," said JimBob.

"I'll be damned. Give him his pay minus the dollar-fifty then, JimBob. When's the last time he collected his full earnings?"

"April, 1925, Boss."

"Keep getting better, Leroy, and you're gonna break me at full pay. Hee-hee-hee."

I was next.

"I suppose just because your mother worked for me for twenty-seven years you'll be wanting another dollar-fifty this month to spend on ice cream, huh, Invictus Ovidius?"

"Yes, sir, Boss Eustis," I said.

"Any fines on this one?"

"Romulus says he slammed the screen door twice last month."

"Oh, Mr. Eustis. I been telling Romulus that door needs fixin' for the longest time."

"Well, why didn't you fix it, then?"

"Nobody *told* me to, Mr. Eustis."

"That's the kinda help I got here. Let's say the door slammed itself once, and you did the other. Give him his money minus a dime. And fix that damn screen door."

"Yes, Mr. Boss Eustis."

Houlka was behind me. He just stood there. Boss Eustis looked at him.

"Give the man his two dollars," he said.

"Sure thing, Boss," said JimBob.

* * *

That same afternoon the Boss sent us off up northwest in the hills. He wanted us to find out where that Horned Doe was. People had been seeing her for four years now. She had only one set of antlers—on the left side. Must have been damned uncomfortable, her head to one side all the time.

The Boss had said, "I want to know exactly where she is. Time somebody shot it. People must have expended more ammunition than was used in the Great War on that thing last year and nobody even hit close. I'm thinking of taking a little hunting trip. You show me exactly where she is, hear?"

We was given a ride out to the edge of the flat Woods. We got off the truck and it turned around and left.

Houlka sniffed the wind. "It's going to snow," he said.

"What?" I looked at him like he'd grown a turkey beak. "This is the 1st of December. The earliest Spunt County's ever had snow is December 26th. We never had a white Christmas, or a white anything before then."

"I hope your coat and shoes is plenty warm," said Houlka, "because it's going to snow."

"Hah. 'Scuse my laughing. Y'all may get snow up around Corinth and Mt. Oatie in July for all I know, but we don't here. Besides, it's at least sixty degrees out here. I'm takin' off my jacket already. Gets any hotter I'll take off my shoes, too."

We walked deeper into the wood. I unbuttoned the top button on my shirt.

* * *

An hour later, after the wind shifted and the clouds rolled up, and it thundered, and the temperature dropped like an anvil, the snow started falling. It was covering the bushes and trees and some of it wasn't melting off the leaves on the woods' floor.

"Godawmighty I'm cold!" I yelled. I stooped down and filled up my jacket with handfuls of leaves from way down under the snow. "Geez!"

Houlka was looking at some pine needles.

It started snowing so hard I had to take my glasses off. That meant I couldn't see anything more than twenty feet away, if there'd been anything but snow twenty feet away.

Houlka was gone. "Hey! Mr. Lee? Where are you? Where are you?"

I started wandering around crashing into stuff. Finally I gave up and just sat down under a tree and watched the snow pile up two inches deep on the leaves, and the wind picked up more and the snow was like a big white flag in front of my face.

Through the wind, I heard a sound to the left.

"Mr. Houlka, is that you?"

* * *

We stood beside the truck that had given us a ride back into town. The driver was gunning the motor. We'd slipped and slided all the way back from the Flat Woods.

I'd seen Uncle Romulus at the window when we'd pulled up. As we'd gotten out, Mr. Eustis and his cronies filed out onto the snow-laden front porch.

"I figured you'd be back. You better know where that doe is, or was. I find out you two been drinkin' coffee in a diner somewhere for six hours, I just don't know what I'll do."

"I know exactly where she is," said Houlka.

"Do you now?"

"I could take you there this very minute."

"A man would have to go crazy and back to hunt in weather like this. I wouldn't open the back window in the kitchen to shoot her if she was standing in the back yard eating Luvsey's poinsiettas today." All his friends laughed.

"You don't want to hunt her today?"

"Hell, no," said the Boss, lost for a second in a swirl of snow from the roof. "Damn! And you know you gonna have to go back and look again before I can hunt her, 'cause this damn freak weather's gone make every deer in the county leave their usual lies. Just be ready to leave first thing in the morning. Write today off as experience."

"Alright, Mr. Eustis. You don't want to shoot her today, that's fine with me." Houlka went to the back of the truck with all the boxes and tarps there. He reached in, jerked off a rope from some canvas near the tailgate.

She stood up then, in the falling snow. She was a tawny gold color like old money and she had an antler with twelve points on the left side of her head. She was five feet high at the shoulder and built like a ten year old buck. I was close enough to her to see the reflection of the snow falling in her big brown eyes. Steamy breath came out of her nostrils. She looked directly at Boss Eustis for what seemed like a full twenty seconds. Then she was gone.

It must have looked like magic from the porch. One second she was standing stock still in the back of the truck, the next the spot was empty.

From my side of the truck I saw her clear the bed, take the distance between the truck and the nearest tree in three jumps, change direction, clear the fence and sail past the road, and turn into the woods.

Boss Eustis and his pals all stood there slack-jawed and with eyes wide as Miz Luvsey's blue-willow china saucers.

"I'll be goddamned," said somebody.

* * *

For Christmas I got a Ralston-Purina checkerboard giveaway knife and a pair of socks and a shirt and a new pair of pants, some apples, tangerines, filberts and almonds. I thought I was king of the world.

There was a New Year's shindig at the place. I was hoping 1927 would be a better year than 1926 had been. While the white folks was whooping it up in the big house, we was having a barn dance in the barn and shooting off skyrockets and Roman candles. I had been dancing with Emzee Dacy and she was dressed in her new Christmas stuff, and we were cutting a rug, if there'd of been a rug. Then her mother took her away early, and the fun sort of went out of everything for me.

I went back to my cabin while they were still dancing and blowing themselves up with fireworks. Up at the big house, I could see the thoroughbred horses of Mr. Ness's bunch tied up at the front, but all the people were inside. There was lots of yelling and lights and whooping, and occasionally someone would come out of the house onto the drive to pee or shoot off a pistol or throw up; old Southern white customs. They scared the horses.

It must have been after about the fifteenth chorus of "Auld Lang Syne" from the big house that I heard footsteps and a knock on the door.

"Who is it?"

"It's Houlka."

I opened the door.

"I just wanted to wish you a happy new year 1927," he said.

"Thank you, Mr. Houlka. The same to you."

He went on over to his place.

I went to bed feeling better about myself.

* * *

We spent most of January getting rid of the crows at Mr. Staempfel's farms. Old people said they were as thick as passenger pigeons had been forty years ago. All that month you could hear limbs breaking like thunder when they roosted at night. What they were eating, or why they were just roosting on Staempfel's land I don't know.

But we finally got rid of them after a solid week of hard work, and they didn't come back. Even the game warden and the county agent came out to see how Houlka did it.

We all wondered why Boss Eustis had taken such a special interest in Staempfel's problems, until I heard Mr. JimBob and the others talking, and it came out that Mr. Eustis was buying an undivided Half-interest in the place for what was considered a very low sum in these parts.

Figures involving more than two dollars give me a headache, so I don't worry about what white folks do with their money.

V

It was February and still cold. It had been the wettest winter in my fourteen years; not freezing stuff, just rainy and cold after that first snow back in December.

Boss Eustis had called for Houlka in the morning. Mr. Eustis was in a bad mood. He'd gotten a phone call from Senator Bilbo or somebody like that that had caused him not to be able to finish his breakfast. Him and the boys must have thought a long time on things these past weeks, because the Boss told Houlka to go over to Mr. Augie's place and see about a little job he had for him.

It was about six miles and we didn't get there till close to eleven in the morning. I was getting really hungry by then.

Mr. Augie lived in a falling-down old place that had once been a big plantation house like the Boss's, only three of the rooms had caved in and half the roof on that side was leaning on the ground.

The closer to the house we got the more horses you could hear neighing and whinnying from the back of the place. It sounded like there was fixing to be a cavalry charge back there or something.

A bunch of no-neck kids played in their coats on a busted-down divan on the front porch. The house looked like it had once been painted purple.

A kid ran in the door hollering daddydaddy.

A one-eyed fat man came out, hands on his hips. He had on a gray workshirt, gray workpants and a gray hat he looked like he'd been born in.

"I'm Houlka Lee. Mr. Eustis sent me."

"He tell you what it's about?"

"No," said Houlka.

"That one o' Boss Eustis's nigger boys or one o' yourn?" asked one of the kids.

Without looking, Mr. Augie slapped him sideways.

"This is business talk; you shut up," he said to the boy. Then to Houlka, "You might call it in the nature of a sporting proposition between me and Eldridge." I had to keep telling myself that was Boss Eustis's name. "See, he was bragging on how you could do any kind of work, real P.D.Q., so we got to debating that. I wagered as how I had a job you couldn't do, and he philosophized as to how you could, and it got to be a matter of five hundred dollars."

Houlka just leaned on his big club and listened.

Mr. Augie turned to his kids. "Y'all get back there and put them animals in the back pasture."

"Aw, gee, dad," said one. Mr. Augie turned and looked at him. As one, the kids all filed inside the house where they made a lot of thumping noises.

"You ain't a gimp, are you?" asked Mr. Augie, nodding toward Houlka's stick. "This job'll kill a strong man—but it would be just like Eldridge to send a spung to try to do it."

"No, I'm not," said Houlka.

The kids came back out dressed like they were going for a long trip to the planet Mars—heavy coats, Boss Mule work gloves up to their elbows, rubber boots to their butts. Two carried ropes and one a whip.

They went around the fallen-down part of the house. Directly we heard yelling and yipping and screams, fenceposts getting torn up, whinnying and the wet sounds of hooves in mud.

"Sarey," yelled Mr. Augie. "Bring out three cups of mocha joe."

He went to the door. three steaming cups were handed out. He gave two to Houlka, who handed one to me.

"Thank you, sir," I said. Mr. Augie didn't say anything. We drank the bitter coffee. One by one the kids staggered back around the house. The sound of horses was further away now. Mr. Augie threw the grounds from his cup out into the yard.

Two of the larger boys carried a third between them. All the kids were covered with mud and horse manure.

"What happened to that 'un?" asked Mr. Augie.

"One of them stepped on him, Daddy."

"Well, put him on the couch there and have your mama give him some coffee." He turned to us. "Let's go look this proposition over."

We went out back of the house. What was left of the barn—no roof, two walls, some timbers where the other ones had been—stood like a wet gray owl with broken wings in the middle of what had been a feed lot 2 acres in size.

Everything, everywhere you looked was covered with horse shit three feet deep. It was piled in drifts like black snow, grey and green snow, against the fenceline and the barn. It was broken only by hoofprints, a metal water trough, the signs of recent struggle with the kids. The place stank to the heavens, and that was on a cold wet day in February. How they stood it in the summer I don't know.

That there's what were talking about," said Mr. Augie. "See, I bet Eldridge you couldn't move all that out past the fenceline in twenty-four hours. Being as how it's already noon, I'll give you a break and let you start seven A.M. tomorrow morning."

* * *

"I'll need to look around," said Houlka.

Mr. Augie lost his demeanor. "You mean," he said, looking at Houlka with his one good eye, "that you're damnfool enough to try? Why, man, they's been horses in there for nigh onto five years. We put 'em in one day, sorta forgot about them but to feed and water 'em. Whole generations been born and died in there. And you gonna try? I thought this was gonna be the easiest five hundred dollars I ever made.

"Shit," he said then. "Look all you want. You can stare at it till seven in the morning for all I care. It ain't gonna get any smaller."

"I have to move it all past the fenceline?" asked Houlka.

"Every bit of it."

"Well, I'll look around then, and be back tomorrow morning at seven, if that's when you want me to start."

"Just you. One man. One job. The nigger boy can't help, not that even that would give you a Chinaman's chance."

"Very good, Mr. Augie."

* * *

"Mr. Houlka," I said. "He's right. You might's well give up. I know you're big and strong, but you couldn't get the top six inches off that stuff in a solid week. They ain't no use you killing yourself for the Boss's five hundred dollars. It's as good as Mr. Augie's right now.

Houlka was studying the farm, if you could call it that. We couldn't see a single horse, though it sounded like there was a thousand just beyond the trees. We walked by the back side of the lot. We passed a pond like one of Mr. Hyder's we'd cleaned of snakes back in October.

We stepped through a gully, still trying to get a look at the horses, and came out on a little rise. It sounded like horses were going crazy, or playing football or something off to both sides of the farm. Hooves were thundering just like Zane Grey says.

"How much taller are you than me?" asked Houlka.

"Half a head, Mr. Houlka. What the hell kind of question is that?"

He took the old rolled up Lion Feed cap out of his pocket and put it on my head. "Okay, I.O., we're going to play a little game." He looked back to where Augie's kids were watching us; they'd followed us since we left the front yard. "I want you to walk all over this place where I tell you to. Every time I tell you to stop, I want you to jump in the air, turn around three times clockwise and put your hand on top of the cap with your little finger straight up in the air."

I looked at him like he had lizards up his nose.

"Just do it," he said.

We walked *all* over that place, and Mr. Houlka would send me off and yell and I'd jump up and turn and put my hand up, and then he'd send me somewhere else, and I'd do it again. Well you could imagine what all those kids were thinking, and one of them ran off and got the gray woman, and she left and came back with Mr. Augie, and he watched us till he got tired, and he left, then the woman left, and two or three of the kids drifted away, and the rest just sat down in what little grass there was at the back of the house, and would only look at us occasionally.

Because we was still doing exactly the same damn thing. We went up through the woods and by the ponds and through the woods and under the outer fence and over the rise and across the gully and across the rise and beside the house and over to the other side and across the road and in the pasture and back to the horse lot and back to the ponds where we started. Every damn time Houlka would send me off and holler and I'd stop and jump and turn and hold up my hand.

Then we went back by the house.

Mr. Augie was outside, hands in his butt pockets. "If you're crazy enough to think you can shovel that stuff out, you're probably crazy enough to think you can hoodoo this place. But I don't get the heebie-jeebies, no sir, and Eldridge is barking up the wrong tree if he told you that."

"See you at seven in the morning, Mr. Augie," said Houlka.

It was late afternoon.

"I.O., I need the name of a man who'll do something improper for a dollar. He can't be in trouble with the law, and he has to be a white man."

I named the few I knew. Tomorrow was not going to be easy to watch.

* * *

Boss Eustis had a man drive us out before the sun came up. We sat bouncing around in the back of the bobtail truck. I was worried. Houlka had a big toe sack with him that had the handle of a shovel sticking out of it. He'd gone to town and come back after I'd gone to sleep last night, worn out from all the foolishness.

We got out of the truck. What little sun there was was just coming up behind a flat deck of high clouds.

Mr. Augie's whole family, except the woman, was waiting for us.

"One thing I can say you're punctual. In two minutes, you'll have twenty-four hours, and they ain't no lights out here at night, and I don't advise shoveling horse manure in the dark. You sure you won't just give up right now? Save your back?"

"I'm ready," said Houlka.

"Well, start—right—NOW."

Houlka reached in the bag and took out a two pound claw hammer and five pounds of #16 nails and handed them to me.

"Wait right here," he said. He took the sack with the shovel handle sticking out and walked down toward the lot.

"Moving mighty slow," said Mr. Augie, "for a man who's gotta shovel nine hundred cubic yards of shit today."

Houlka went around the lot.

"What the hell?" said Augie.

"That man's crazy, Daddy," said one of the girls.

"I knowed that yesterday, honey," said Augie.

Houlka went over the gulley and into the far stand of trees.

"Now I seen it all," said Mr. Augie. Then Houlka was lost to sight for a while.

"Do you have any *idea* what he's doing?"

"I'm as lost as you are, Mr. Augie. I been lost since about noon yesterday."

After a few minutes Houlka came walking at a brisk pace back up the rise, like he had some purpose in mind. Then he leaned down and was doing something we couldn't see.

There was a huge explosion from back in the woods that jarred our teeth.

"Holy Christ!" yelled Augie. A plume of debris rose in the air from the woods—mud, grass, small tree limbs. Then there was a low roar from that direction.

"That sonofabitch blew the seal on my minnow pond!" yelled Augie. We could see a brown ribbon snaking its way through the woods toward us, knocking down bushes, coming toward the small gully. I looked at Houlka. He was watching the rushing water. Then he turned, leaned down, then stepped back real quick about fifty feet.

The water got to the gulley and began to fill it.

There was another, closer explosion—I thought Houlka had blown himself up. There was a huge roaring torrent shooting straight out into the air above the rise.

The heavy mud-laden water came down the rise, met up with the water that had just reached the gulley (and seemed to me to leap uphill) and came across and slammed into the feed lot, making a hollow clanging sound like a bell as it beat against the metal water trough. The water turned instantly black, seemed to lift up in its tracks, and flowed what looked to me like uphill again to the gulley in a big churning whirlpool. Then it rushed like a big flat black snake into the woods where it had started from.

The flow from the first pool had stopped and the second was slowing down. There were two streams, the whirling mass, the outflow from the lot. The barn was shaking. The fence on the far side was under water for a minute or two before it re-emerged.

Mr. Augie had his mouth open. "Why . . . why . . . he blew up my catfish pool. My minnow pond. My catfish!"

The kids were yelling and clapping their hands until Mr. Augie looked at them. The water from the second pool over the rise slowed to a trickle, and we could see Houlka shoveling at its levee. Then he walked back into the woods where the minnow pond was. After a few minutes he came back by the second pond and shovelled some more.

The water had moved out of the barn lot and was moving away and getting back into the woods. I could see black water among the roots of the trees there. Houlka finished shoveling and came down toward us.

I didn't know whether Mr. Augie was going to get a gun and kill him or just explode where he stood. Houlka held out his hand. I gave him the hammer and the nails. He walked down to the lot, miring up to his ankles in the muddy ground. He paused to throw a couple of shovelfuls of manure over the fence. Then he came back up the hill and handed the bag to me.

"You'll be wanting to go pay Mr. Eustis now," said Houlka.

He walked away. Mr. Augie was hissing like an old stove, shaking in his clothes.

* * *

Houlka was asleep after a bath. I was at the front of the house.

Boss Eustis was rolling on the front porch, crying, he was laughing so hard. The Spunt County chorus was falling all over itself.

"And then . . . and then . . ." tears squirted out of the Boss's eyes, "then Augie says, but he blew up my minnow pond and my catfish! I says, but that lot's clean as a whistle, I hear, and it ain't even a quarter to nine . . . anything . . . anything . . . else you want him to do in the other twenty-two hours and fifteen minutes, like . . . like . . . blow up your house, or kill all your horses or anything? Hee-hee-hee."

Ed Bender couldn't get his breath and Mr. Jones fell off his nail keg.

"'Sides," said Mr. Eustis, "I hear he only blew the top two feet off each levee and closed them up before he came back, even fixed that . . . damn ol' rickety fence for you. Hee-hee-hee."

"Didja . . . didja take his money, Eldridge?"

"Hell yes. He lost the bet. You shoulda seed the expression on his face. Then I handed it back to him and gave him another thousand dollars besides, and I said, Augie, you done give me fifteen hundred dollars worth of entertainment this morning, you sure have. Buy yourself some new catfish—besides, you get off your lazy butt and get someone . . . someone to plow that bottom where all that stuff went and soaked in, you'll get forty bales to the acre off'n it. Hee-hee-hee."

"And," Mr. Eustis caught his breath, "I says, Augie, you just better be mighty careful how you bet from now on out! Hee-hee-hee."

I went back into the kitchen. Every time anybody new would pull up out front, he'd start in again, and tell the whole thing, and you could hear people falling off their chairs all afternoon.

VI

The next time we got our pay, Houlka went down to the Western Auto store and bought a bow and arrow set. It had a forty pound pull, he said. He bought a bunch of target arrows, and me and him spent some days in the old tumbledown blacksmith shop pounding out hunting arrowheads out of the old bladestock iron in there.

Then Boss Eustis had us go over to the edge of Lake Yuksino and catch this big damn old bull that had gotten loose and was tearing up the countryside. That thing ran us up one side of the county and halfway across it before Houlka managed to bull-dog and hogtie it.

That's also when the rains really started. There was talk the River was higher than it had ever been, and this was only March, so the ice wasn't even off it in Yankee-land yet. We got fourteen straight days of rain, then it cleared off for a day or so, and Miz Eustis sent us off to go take some medicine and stuff to a bunch of people who farmed one of the Boss's places about seven miles northwest of town. Then, she said, you go check on the Old Egypt Cemetery for me again on the way back in, in case we have clear weather and get to work on it.

So we set off, me carrying the bundle, and Houlka with his big club and bow and arrows.

* * *

We moved over so a wagon could pass us. I'd heard it coming up behind us for five minutes or more. A big chestnut mare came by about half asleep, pulling a shay that had been cut down so that only one seat was left.

I looked up, then looked back real quick. The man driving was the Reverend Mr. East. He had on his preaching suit, out here on this road. On the back rail of the wagon was his two boys, dressed up, too.

Mr. East nodded, then put his eyes back on the road.

"Somebody out here must have died," I said. "Nobody wears clothes like that on a Tuesday. Can't figure what his sons are doing with him. He's a preacher, a real hell-fire and brimstone boiled-in-the-word-of-God book thumper," I said. Houlka didn't say anything. He knew by now I'd keep on talking anyway.

"He raised his boys to be just like him. When they turned sixteen and seventeen, they ran off to Atlanta and Memphis, one after another. They showed back up four years later, and it nearly killed the old man. They'd become preachers, too, only one is a Baptist and the other's a Methodist. He prayed three weeks, then got so sick he almost died, and Dr. Sclape gave him some medicine that kept him in the outhouse for three solid days—the neighbors said you could hear him holler, 'Oh Lordy, Lordy, take me now, take me now, end this misery!'"

Houlka smiled a little, hummed, then sort of sang:

> *David the King, he wept and wept.*
> *Saying, Oh my Son, Oh my Son!*
> *I would have died, had not it been*
> *for my chamber, chamber!*

"That's one of Mr. Blind Bill's songs. Where'd you hear that?"

"People around Mt. Oatie been singing that for a hundred years," said Houlka.

I looked on up the road. There were a couple of wagons and a Model T parked off of the mud on the side of the road to the right, and the preacher's wagon was turning in at the fence row.

"They ain't no house here," I said. "If somebody's dead they would have taken them to a house before they called a preacher. Wonder what's up?"

We came even with the thicket on the right where the fenceline started, and there were eleven or twelve people there, and the preacher and his two boys was getting out and walking into the field. A man in bib overalls stood there. He had on a big pair of work gloves and a straw hat. He held the handles of a little-bitty one-wheeled single-spade garden cultivator, the kind town wives use to put in tomato patches, and it was hooked up with twelve-strand rope to the biggest ox I'd ever seen in my life.

"It's a field-blessing," said Houlka. "I haven't seen one since I was your age."

"I ain't ever seen one! What's it like?"

"Hush, and you'll see."

We stopped at some respectful distance back, but where we could see and hear. Nobody noticed us. They were attending to what went on out in the field.

Well, it wasn't a field, not yet anyway; more of an open place about four, maybe four and a half acres, to where some trees curved around on both sides. There were some old dead weeds about a foot high, and some new grass just coming up, even after all the rain. That was about all you could say for it.

"*This* is the place you want me to ask God to make stuff grow on?" asked Reverend Mr. East. He had a big loud voice and the ox's eyes rolled when he started yelling. It headed for the woods. Mr. East's two sons grabbed an ear each and held on. It tried to kick out of its rope and pulled the cultivator over. The farmer grabbed the handle and stuck it back into the ground.

"I can't believe *anybody* would be idjit enough to try to grow something on this sorry piece of land," yelled the preacher. "Did you get your brains out of a feed sack?"

The farmer scuffed his boot back and forth in the weeds, not looking at the preacher.

"*This!*" Mr. East spread his arms all around the extent of the field. "Haven't nothing but thistles and briers grown on this place since the flood. And you expect me to ask favors for you?"

The ox jumped again. Mr. East's sons were talking into its ears, soothing and gentling it down, though we couldn't hear what they were saying.

"You must be as dumb as that plow-rig you got," said the preacher, loosening his tie. "I'm getting mad just thinking about what am I doing here in this wilderness when there's the sick to visit; I could be evangelicizing down at the jailhouse, but no, I have to get all dressed up, and drag my two boys out away from their good works, and come out to this sorry-ass place and try to get God to bless it?

"Another thing. You probably can't plow any better than this place can grow things. You and this piece of desert deserve each other! You'll kill yourself and that there ox, and this place'll grow weeds and brush and little oak trees, and you'll make half a bale of cotton off the whole damn thing! Who ever told you you were a farmer? I guess it was easier than getting a real job, huh? Trying to grow things with everything against you is bad enough—the sun, the weather, cyclones, hail—when you're a mental giant. But somebody like you; well, it's a wonder this whole country, sea to shining sea, could raise enough food to get Spunt County past peach-picking time if all the farmers out there are like you trying to provide the nation's breadbasket!

"And that ox! Not only is he hooked up wrong, but it looks as dumb as you are. Couldn't be dumber. You didn't see *it* buying this piece of trash land, did you? Whoever sold you this place is probably laughing his ass off and getting liquored up with your money right now.

"Go ahead. Don't let me stop you. Just go ahead and try to plow a straight furrow with this contraption. It'd be just right—they could let a crazy man out of the Europa Clinic and he could hook a soup ladle up to a cat and plow a straighter line than that—look at that. Straight between here and that dead tree yonder, not all over the place!"

When the preacher had told him to, the farmer'd dug the plow into the ground and slapped the ox with the tail end of the rope that was doubled over three or four times to the single-yoke and the ox had begun to pull. The ground rolled up and over in front of the plow, like there was a big gopher running just in front of the wheel. The two preacher boys held the ox's head and every time it would try to pull straight, they sort of guided it the other way. They were still talking into its ears as they handled it from each side.

The farmer went out from the edge of the field in a short half-circle, twisting the ropes and trying to keep the ox going straight, then got him going fairly well in a long line, then what with one thing and another the ox turned around and was heading back almost at a trot in another long line paralleling the first. The farmer hung on for all he was worth, trying to keep the plow in the ground; his feet only touched the ground every ten feet or so. The two young preachers ran beside the plow animal now, still holding onto its ears, still talking.

"Look at that idjit!" the preacher turned to the crowd. "I been on some stupid errands in my life in the Name of the Lord, but never anything like this. Stop that thing before it plows under my wagon!" He yelled to the farmer. "Stop it, you agricultural maladroit!"

The farmer let the ox drag him another few feet by the ropes, then got to his feet and stuck the plow into the ground and wrapped the free ends of the ropes around the cultivator handles. He was panting and covered with mud, grass and sweat. He was twenty-five feet from where he'd started.

"You consarned idjit. I'm gonna have to come back in a few weeks and say your obsequies. You'll let that ox plow you and the fence and the road and Spunt County under. Damn! Damn! Damn!"

His two sons joined the preacher.

"Since I've come all the way out here I might as well get this over," said the Reverend Mr. East. "I guess we better bow our heads." There wasn't any sound for a minute but the ox cropping dead grass.

"Dear Lord, help this moron in his time of need. If anyone ever needed it, it's him. And his family, for having a fool at the head of it. If he has to kill himself trying to make a go of this piece of wasteland, we ask that you make his death a quick and speedy one. Try not to be too hard on his ox; it was fashioned as one of your creatures and cannot help it if someone was venal enough to sell him to the first idjit with a loose nickel in his pocket, not knowing he'd work it to death on a worthless piece of rocks and stumps like this. We ask all this in your name. Amen."

"Amen," said the crowd. The preacher looked around at the farmer, his ox, the plow, the field with the long single rounded-and-straight continuous cut line in it, and the people in the crowd, and shook his head sadly. Then he and his sons climbed up into the shay.

The farmer handed him a dollar in quarters.

"It'll never grow a single goddam boll," said Mr. East. Then he turned his mare around and headed back toward town.

The crowd broke up and went back to its wagon and the car. The farmer, alone in his field next to the harnessed ox, scanned the sky for coming weather.

We went on down the road and left him to his worries.

* * *

We had delivered the medicine and come back to town and gone to Old Egypt Cemetery.

First thing I noticed was that the recent rains had played hell with everything. Some more of Mr. Keiffer's tomb had cracked off and was laying in piles around the base. Two or three tombstones were leaning over.

I heard a crash of glass out in the far edge of the graveyard just as we got to the gate, which was mighty rusty.

"Miz Eustis is really gonna throw a hissy fit," I said. "She'll have white folks all over this place this weekend, hell or high water."

There was a moan from the back of the place. It stopped, then came again. "Oh, Mama, Mama," it said, deep, a man's voice.

I looked around Mr. Myron's tomb. There was a man at the back by the fence looking down at the ground where a tombstone had fallen completely over. "Who did this to you, Mama?" he asked. Then I recognized who it was.

"That's Mr. Anse," I said to Houlka. "He's mean, he's drunk. He loved his mother and something's happened to her tombstone. Her grave was the only one that was always clean. Let's leave *now*," I said.

"Who's there? Who the goddam hell kicked over my mother's stone?"

"Wasn't us, Mr. Anse," I said.

"Since when's niggers allowed in here?" he yelled.

"Come on, I.O.," said Houlka, going toward the gate.

"Where you think you're going, Mr. Cougar Man?"

"We came to check on the cemetery for Mrs. Eustis. We're going now."

"The hell you did!" Mr. Anse came around the three tombs and walked between them and the big stone lion. He was drinking from a Mason jar. "Come to kick over some more old ladies' tombstones, Mr. High 'n' Mighty?"

"You're intoxicated and we're leaving."

"First you defile the grave of the greatest woman who ever lived, then you think you can just walk away?"

Houlka sighed. "If it'll help things, I'll aid you in putting your mother's tombstone aright."

Anse turned and smashed the liquor jar against the nose of the stone lion. "You set one foot on her grave and I'll cut off your neck and shit down your throat."

He made a sneer that showed his teeth and beckoned with his fingers.

"Don't force me to fight. I have no quarrel with you," said Houlka. "I've never been here before in my life."

"Not so brave, huh? Big man with a bow and arrows. Like a wild Indian. Big man with a club. All talk."

Houlka turned to walk away. Anse charged him with the jaggeldy jar.

Houlka turned, tapped the jar so it cracked to pieces with his club. Blood appeared on both their faces from flying glass. Then he threw the club down and jerked his bow and arrows to the ground, and they smashed together like tigers.

They rolled over and over in the glass splinters, then they were up and bleeding, smashing into Mr. Keiffer's tomb and falling behind it.

By the time I got around they were already over at the back by Mrs. Anse's grave, snarling and roaring. Mr. Anse was bigger and had reach on Houlka and was trying to get at his eyes with thumbs. Houlka rolled them over and came out on top.

They were up and down and up. Then down. Houlka threw Anse fifteen feet, but when he hit he came right back up. Blood flew off both of them in a mist every time they collided with each other. Houlka threw him down and he came up again. He got one hand in one of Houlka's eyes.

Then Houlka lifted Mr. Anse; all six foot six and three hundred pounds of him, up in the air in a bear hug from the back, and he started squeezing, and pushing the back of Anse's neck with his chin; Anse's face was purple and this sound came out of him like when you step on a toad-frog, and sinews popped and Anse went limp two feet up in the air.

There was a squeal of brakes behind me, and I jumped and kept jumping because the squeal turned into the long loud wail of a siren. I came down crawling backwards.

The black Model T truck with the iron cage on the back had come to a stop six inches behind where I'd been standing. The wail was still coming out of the siren. There were three faces filling the windshield of the truck. Their eyes were looking everywhere—at me, the cemetery, Mr. Anse, Houlka, the tombstone, the broken jar, the smear of wet on the lion.

Sheriff Mr. Manfred's hand was still on the siren handle. Mr. Maurice was watching everything from the middle, Mr. Jack leaned his head out the driver's side, took two quick looks at me and Houlka, then all three of them were back inside the truck.

Then Sheriffs Manfred, Maurice and Jack Eumenides jumped out of the truck, ran over to Mr. Anse where Houlka had dropped him to the ground, felt his chest, picked him up, ran to the back, threw him in, shut the cage door, jumped back into the front seat. The truck spun around, turned and was gone through the cemetery gate. The siren's wail started, and through the brush I saw the black truck shoot by, Mr. Manfred's arm working the siren crank.

The sound faded away toward town.

I turned back to Houlka. He was bleeding all over. He sank slowly toward the ground. I grabbed him.

* * *

"Ain't no use goin' to Dr. Sclape's," said one of the old men who had a warped place shaped exactly like his butt on the bench in front of the drug store. "He just lit out in his wagon to go birth some babies out to the Mannon place."

Houlka was still bleeding pretty badly from the head. "Where's Nurse Ramis?" I asked.

"I reckon she's over to the Ladies Church Aid Society with them others," he said, nodding his head to the northwest part of town. He stopped and put a squirt of tobacco juice about fifteen feet out in the street. "They's decoratin' for the young folks' Jesus social tonight."

"Thank you," I said, and led Houlka over to the edge of the square. I was holding him up, and carrying his club, and it was killing me. I never realized how heavy it was. He had his bow and quiver on his shoulder where I'd put them.

We cut past the Mercantile and went up Second Street till we came to the railroad tracks about two blocks west of the depot. There were two signalman up working on the thru-light panel. One of them was holding up one of the big green lights. We cut across the track right under them.

"Damn if that ain't the sorriest sight I ever seen," said one. "That guy looks like a gorilla, and that nigger boy with him looks like a monkey."

Houlka straightened a little, tried to clear his head. He only made it bleed faster.

"Hey. Get your dumb asses off the tracks. You want to be run over?" yelled the other guy up there. "Don't you know better? I seen brighter turnips than you two."

"What you wanna go that way for?" asked the first. "Way to the insane asylum's out the other side of town." They laughed and yelled, and one of them threw a greasy rag down at us. "Hey! Gorilla! Climb up here and beat us up. I'll give your monkey a banana, too!"

They were still hooting when we crossed Apple Street and turned down Peach. The First Baptist Church was at Third and Peach, but the social hall was out with the Sunday School wing where Third crossed Pomegranate. There weren't any lights on there even though it was getting dark outside.

"Hello the hall!" I said, banging on the side doors. There was noise inside then the door opened. "Oh, my," said a woman's voice.

"They told us Miz Ramis was here," I said. "Mr. Lee's got a bad head cut."

"Oh, my. No. Bring him in. Miss Ramis just got sent for by that old hypochondriac Methodist lady on the other side of town. Here," she said. She had pulled one of the chairs out from along the wall, one of the big old chaperone chairs, and we eased Houlka into it.

"Wait," I said. I pulled the bow, quiver and the lionskin coat off him and unbuttoned his overall strap. I put the cloak in the chair so it wouldn't get blood on it, then we eased him back down.

"Goodness. I'll get Mrs. Dimmitt," said the woman. I was holding Houlka's head up when I heard a voice I knew.

"Why, I.O.! What in the world are you doing here?" I turned my head in the tiny bit of light still coming in the windows. Sure enough it was Emzee Dacy.

"I'm trying to keep Mr. Houlka here from bleedin' to death. The doctor's gone and some fool told us Miz Ramis was over to here."

Emzee was just my age. Her people now worked for Miz Snooks who owned the Mercantile—her mother was the cook and her father was the car-drive and handyman.

Everybody calls her Emzee, though that was from her initials, M.Z. Emzee'd been born just as this crazy two-hundred-year-old great great aunt was about to die—Emzee's folks had told her she could name the baby if she could live long enough to see her born, and an hour after the child was birthed, they'd taken her in to the old biddy, who hadn't opened her eyes for three weeks and whose breathing was so shallow they'd taken to putting a mirror up to her nose a hundred times a day, and they brought this squalling baby in, and the old lady opened her eyes and said: "Mercurochrome. Zipper." And then was dead as a hammer, so what could Emzee's folks do?

"Miz Ramis was here. But she had to go over to Ol' Miz Haigis's because the old lady had the vapors." She leaned down real close. "Uh-oh! He's really hurt."

"Yeah, and if someone would turn on the damn lights, I could see where to sop."

"Can't," said Emzee. "That crotchety old Mr. Moper came in while ago and was fixing some outlet plug or something and blew out all the damn fuses. He's gone over to the hardware store to pick up some more. I swear he gets more scatter-brained every day!"

"Emzee!" said a sharp white woman's voice. "What have I told you?"

Emzee scrunched all up. "I'm sorry, Miz Dimmitt."

The woman came up beside me. "I can't see anything. Get in there and get me a candle. There's some in the second right hand cabinet. Cory? Cory? Where *is* that girl?"

Emzee's voice came from far back in the kitchen part of the social hall. "Don't know, Miz Dimmitt. We was playing this afternoon but I ain't seen her in a long while."

"Co-ry! I never can find that girl when I need her. Hurry up with that light."

"All I can find's this little old stub here," said Emzee's voice.

"Well, light it and get in here."

"I can't find no matches, Ma'am."

"Hold his head up more," she said to me. "You're one of Mr. Eustis's help, aren't you?"

"Yes'm. This here's Mr. Lee. He's been brought out of Parchman. We was at the cemetery. Mr. Anse—"

"I don't care about anything unless someone was killed out there."

"No'm. The sheriffs was there and they took Mr. Anse . . ."

"Co-ry!" she hollered. "Cory! If she was here at least she'd be able to find me the matches."

"I'm tryin'!" yelled Emzee from the other room. I heard a match strike.

"Bring the dishtowels with you when you come, if you can do two things at once," said Miz Dimmitt.

Emzee came in with about an inch of lit candle and a bunch of rags.

"Goodness gracious!" said Miz Dimmitt when she saw Houlka's head. The skin had been sliced back above the left eye. His whole face and shoulder were covered in blood.

"Damn!" I said. I grabbed at the towels, put one behind his shoulders. Miz Dimmitt wiped his head.

"Get some water in here, Emzee. Some to wash him with and some to drink."

"I think there's about one more piece of candle in there," said Emzee. She left. It was really dark in the place now, except for the little candle. Emzee came back with a basin and a glass of water. I put it to Houlka's lips and he spilled it all over his beard. Miz Dimmitt got most of the old blood off his face and got a wet rag up against the cut to slow the bleeding down. The water in the basin was already dark.

Houlka's stomach gave a big rumble.

"Have y'all eaten lately, or is he going to upchuck?" asked Miz Dimmitt.

"We ain't eaten, ma'am."

"Emzee. Find some food for these people."

"Ain't none here yet, Miz Dimmitt. Miz Leda was supposed to be here by now, but she probably done looked over from her house and didn't see any light on and didn't think we were here yet."

"How'm I supposed to see what this place needs for a social if nobody's done anything yet? And where is Cory?"

"I told you, I don't *know*, Miz Dimmitt."

Houlka stirred again and his stomach rumbled.

"Well. Go see what's left from the prayer breakfast and fix that. The stove should be hot enough by now."

"Yes'm." She went off and made noises with pots and pans.

"Hold this rag up here," said Miz Dimmitt. "I've got to find that daughter of mine. I'm worried about her now."

She went to the dark doorway. "Cory!" she called. "Co-reee!" She walked outside. I heard her calling all around the building and up toward the church.

I washed Houlka's head some more. He might be okay for a while, until we could get him over to Dr. Sclapes, whenever he came back tonight.

My eyes were getting used to the candlelight. There was some streamers hung overhead that I hadn't noticed till now, and there was crêpe paper all over the walls.

Emzee brought in two steaming hot bowls of something. "All I could find was some old oatmeal, no telling how long it's been in there, probably since the McKinley Administration. I can't find any sugar and they ain't no milk I could find in the ice box so I crumbled up some julep that's growing in a pot in there. I hope you like it."

"Hold this bowl while I get some of this into him," I said. I blew on the spoon and put some in Mr. Lee's mouth. He swallowed it even though his lips were cut and swelled all up. I tried not to get it all over his beard.

I eased his head back. He must of been having bad dreams, 'cause his lips were moving and he was real restless.

"You better bandage that up else he's gonna start bleeding again."

I tore up one of the dishcloths and wet another rag and put it on the cut, then tied it on with a dry rag around the back of his head. He seemed to be turning his head away from the candlelight.

I took his cougar-skin cloak and put it over his head to keep the light off him.

Miz Dimmitt was still out calling when Miz Leda came in with a whole plate of roasting ears and Emzee jumped up and took the candle in the kitchen with her.

"We gonna go out and look for Cory," said Emzee as she and Miz Leda went out through the door.

It was dark and close in the building. Now both the candles was in the kitchen. I could tell Houlka was still hurt because he was moving under that skin.

The screen door opened and Miz Dimmitt came in. She was so upset she was crying.

"I just don't know about that girl," she said, sitting down in one of the folding chairs against the wall. She listened as the calls of the women moved further away. "She's a bright girl, but she just wanders away sometimes and can't be found." Then she really started crying.

"I'm sure it'll be fine, Ma'am. She's a lucky girl. Some people's folks don't even care if they're around or not."

She quit crying; I could see her rubbing her eyes.

"How's he doing?" she asked.

"Some better," I said. "He still ain't easy. He feels like he might have a fever."

She got up to come over, watched him turning and tossing, reached under the cougar skin and felt his head. "He *is* burning up." Then she looked back out the darkened windows. "I wish they'd find that girl!"

"Yes'm."

"What in the world did Emzee fix you?" she asked, noticing the bowl on the floor beside the basin. I'd forgotten about mine, picked it up and ate some. It was minty, and the oats was like wet paper now, but it was good.

"Whatever it is it's just fine," I said. "Sometimes you can be happy with just anything."

The screen door slammed open. We both jumped a foot.

At the same time the lights came blazing on, blinding me completely. "Here she is!" said Emzee.

My eyes came back to normal. Emzee stood in the door, holding Cory Dimmitt's hand. Cory was a couple years younger than me. She was covered with streaks and on her clothes.

"Where have you *been?*" asked her mother, going to her.

"She was asleep down in the coal bin when I found her," said Emzee. "Me an' her used to go down there during hide-and-go-seek."

Her mother shook her shoulders till I thought her teeth would all fly out; then she stopped and hugged her and kissed her. Cory still wasn't wide awake.

"Don't you ever run away like that again," said Miz Dimmitt. "Promise me!"

"I won't, Mama," said Cory.

Over in the big chair, with the skin over his head, Houlka began to snore like a freight train.

VII

The white folks cleaned off the old cemetery again, then the weather set back in. The Mississippi River busted through the levees all the way from Missouri down to the Gulf of Mexico, and President Coolidge came down to look at Louisiana from a train. People in Greenville was living in tents on the levee, and looking at a sheet of water forty miles wide broken only by the tents on the Arkansas side of the River. It was still raining and the River hadn't crested yet.

Mississippi had just gotten over the War For Southern Independence when the depression of 1893 hit; they were coming out of that when the bottom dropped out of the cotton price; they all got out of the cotton business just when we got into the Great War; everybody rushed to grow cotton while the price was sky-high and along came the boll weevil; they were just over that and Boom! Ol' Man River came to live on their farm. Now they were staying on a levee, and if they looked real hard, they could see their grandmother, dead and buried twenty years ago, come floating by in her coffin full of wet rats.

The papers were full of stories like that everyday. In Spunt County we were fairly warm and dry, as long as you could stay inside, which wasn't often. Miz Eustis sent me and him out to the Diamond Horse Farm to help round up a couple of dozen equines who'd run away when their stalls flooded and the fences washed away. Those horses of Mr. Augie's had sounded mean, though we never saw a one of them. These things was mean. They'd try to eat your arms and legs off if you got within a hundred yards of them. I thought we was gonna be killed half a dozen times an hour. Houlka gentled a few of them down; those he couldn't he just dragged them back to the rebuilt stables.

That was at the end of April. By May the river was beginning to crest, if you call it that, and was starting to drop, if you could call it that. Every river in America was backed up and flowing uphill. The rain went from the Noe's Fludde it had been to just plain rain. There were even a few days where there was no rain at all. It was May, but it was cool.

* * *

"I heard you done your work right fine," said Boss Eustis. "Well, boys," he said, looking around the verandah at the Colonels and toadies, "What we gonna do to keep Mr. Lee occupied in this nice weather?"

There was some hurried consultation among the great minds of Anomie and Spunt County, then they all looked back up at Houlka, some of them smirking.

"They's this house of ill-repute in town." Someone snickered, Boss Eustis looked at him, went on. "Anyway, it's run by this Mrs. Hippola, a European Lady. I'd like you to go ask her if you could borrow her corset. The red one."

Then everybody on the porch guffawed and kicked their heels up and down.

"Is that all?" asked Houlka.

"For right now," said the Boss. "You be careful now, you hear, 'cause if you don't hit her in just the right mood, she can be meaner than Uncle Cato Hacker."

We left the front yard, walking toward town. Houlka shouldered his club on the left shoulder. His right had been giving him trouble since the fight in the graveyard. He waited till we got far down the dirt road.

"Why they think this will be harder than any of the other things?"

I didn't know where to begin. "I'm not up on all that stuff, Mr. Lee. But I hear Mrs. Hippola's mighty proud of that corset. It used to be people was always trying to get their hands on it—college boys from Corinth and Arcola always being sent down by their fraternities. She's seen and heard about every kind of ploy there is. She's ready for any shenanigans. And . . ."

"What?"

"Well, she runs the house but . . . she ain't one of the kind of women who likes men. Know what I'm sayin'?"

"I think so," he said. We walked on for another few yards.

"Who's Uncle Cato Hacker?"

"Who *was* he, thank God. He was the meanest man that ever walked this county, maybe the whole U. S. of A. Thank the Lord I was too young and little and nobody ever took me near him; he died four years ago before I could run into him on my own. They still gonna be talking about him a thousand years from now," I said.

"I'll just tell you one thing—Virgil Homer wrote about it in his column, so everybody in the county knows it by heart—ain't a house around here don't have that one column clipped out and put up somewhere—and you can figure out the rest. Anyway, it was six-seven years ago, 1920, and Uncle Cato Hacker was about eighty-four then and he was going to the 54th Muster of Nathan Bedford Forrest's regiment which was to be held at the King Cotton Hotel in Memphis.

"He stepped off the train. (He was with Mr. Doakes and Mr. Jenkins, who were younger than he was but in worse shape.) Uncle Cato was in his full dress uniform. (He'd been a sergeant. It still fit him like a glove, and he'd walked all the way home from Athens, Georgia, in it when the war had ended.) He was ramrod straight (I was trying to remember it like Virgil Homer wrote it) and picked up his bag and started walking toward the King Cotton Hotel. It was a cool night and they came out of the station and there, sitting on the curb beside the baggage handling area was this wreck of a man. He had one right leg and one left arm, and that arm was so twisted around all it could do was hold a cup in the lap. The whole right side of his face was gone. There wasn't an ear on the left side. The one eye he had was pretty clouded over and the man was shivering in the cold and his homemade crutch was lying in the gutter.

"He was wearing what was left of a blue coat, and the cap he had on had a G.A.R. badge on it.

"Uncle Cato Hacker walked over to him, reached in his pocket (he wasn't a rich man) and put a twenty-dollar gold piece in the man's cup.

"The cripple looked up at Uncle Cato Hacker and leans up so he can focus on him, and sees his uniform and all, and he asks, 'You're a Johnny Reb, ain't you?' and Uncle Cato says, 'That I am,' and drew himself up to his full height and the man says, "Then why would you do something like that for me? A Yankee?'

"And Uncle Cato says, 'You're the first one I've ever seen trimmed up just like I like 'em.'"

* * *

We had been in town watching Mrs. Hippola's place in the afternoon. Houlka watched the comings and goings before they opened for business, and got the layout of the place. It's not very easy watching a brothel without making someone suspicious.

The moon was in the west early in the evening and we stayed around till close to midnight, listening to the music and laughter coming out of the place. Houlka was very still, and I thought I saw him brush his eyes with the back of his hand like he'd been remembering something and was ready to cry.

Even though the Delta was still under water, we'd had a break for some days. We were walking home when Houlka said, "Any place we can take a swim around here?"

"Well, yeah, but it'll be cold as a well-digger's ass and it'll feel like a mudbath."

"Maybe that's what I need."

I got my bearings and set off to what used to be the county's favorite swimmin' hole. It had a long rock ledge above it, and was deep enough to dive off in. Houlka took off his lionskin and coveralls and boots and jumped in. He swam around a few minutes, spitting water into the air like a whale.

"You're right; it's gritty."

I stood up and stripped off my stuff and went down to the water and put a toe in. Damn, it was cold!

Houlka quit splashing and looked at me. The moon was just fixing to set, and you could see the reflections of it all broken in the water. The air smelled fresh and green like there was a hall full of hay somewhere around.

I jumped in and damn near died of a heart attack. "Wooie!" I yelled. "This is just what I need!" I felt my heart hammering in my chest and all of a sudden Houlka was right there beside me in the water and his hands were on me.

I thought he was just goosing me, so I moved away, but he came back and put one of his arms on my shoulders. His beard sparkled with water and I could see his eyes shine in the moonlight.

"What are you doing, Mr. Houlka!" I said.

"Give me some sugar, I.O.," he said.

I jerked myself around. "What you mean? I like girls too much, Mr. Houlka."

"So do I. That's why I have to remind myself they're not all there is," and he opened his lips to kiss at me.

I swung my arm and hit him and brought my knee up where it would do the most good. He never expected it or it would have been useless. He bent and his mouth went underwater and he came up coughing and reaching for me.

I knew where the ledge was behind me and he didn't. I got up on it. "Let me be, Mr. Houlka," I said.

He roared then like a bull and started out of the water. "Jesus!" I said. I kicked him in the chest and he slipped back down on his knees on the ledge and his head slid against the rocks. "Arrr!" he yelled.

I backed up, grabbed my shirt and pants and scrambled up the rise. He came out wet and dripping from the water, holding the side of his face and there looked like there was blood on it. He picked up his club and looked around. I saw that his dong was nearly as big and stiff as the club, and I took off with him right behind me.

* * *

I was running through the woods and falling down and I stuck a stob in the side of my foot and was limping and crying. My shoes and glasses were back at the creek but I wasn't going back for them ever. I thought I heard Mr. Lee crashing around in the trees. I couldn't see anything. I couldn't breathe good anymore. I didn't know if I wanted to.

After a while I just fell down in some brush, somewhere on the south side of town. I could have tried to go back home, but I didn't want to run into Houlka again tonight, or be anywhere near him. I figured he might cool down if I could keep away from him long enough.

Then I started crying. I was mad at him, but I felt sorry for him too. I didn't know what to do, or what I wanted, or anything. I couldn't even keep two thoughts in my head at the same time.

I must have gone to sleep for a second because I woke up with a start. I couldn't stay there and have him find me. So I started walking.

I could see a little now, like just before the moon comes up, but it had already set, so I guess I was just getting some night vision. I found the old Indian Trail that cut over to the main highway just below the cabinet shop and walked along that. Nobody used it much anymore except the Riding Club. Once so many Chickasaws used it it was worn down lower than the ground around it by two feet or more. It went on out of town and joined up with the Natchez Trace over by the Mangum Mounds forty miles away. Some man from Alexandria, Virginia, came through two years ago walking it—the *Spunt County Shouter* had done an article on him. He was making maps of all the aboriginal trails in the South.

It was slow going tonight. There were bushes growing out of it, and roots, and the sides were falling in in some places. It was like walking through a new-plowed field. I was sure if Mr. Lee was anywhere around he could hear me huffing and puffing a mile away.

Then I was up on the highway cut and I climbed and started walking along the cinders. There was a ditch on either side and I could see along the road in case Houlka was waiting for me. But I got out at the first cross street at the back of town and cut through it.

I was parched as a mule and my feet hurt. The night was still and calm. There must of been a warm front coming in. There was no noise except my feet in the dirt. I knew it was going to be a long time before I could find some water to drink.

Then I saw a coal-oil lamp lit over off the road, and heard a door open.

I wasn't exactly sure where I was, but thought I must be somewhere near the old Interurban tracks, and could use them to cut off half a mile of walking, so I turned off through the field.

A voice, a soft woman's voice, carried to the road.

"You, out on the road? You thirsty?"

"Yes, ma'am," I said.

"Come up and get some well water then."

"Can't rightly do that ma'am, but thanks anyway."

"What's the matter? Are you injured?"

"Some, ma'am. But I'll be alright."

She was quiet a moment. "Are you a Negro man?"

"Negro, Ma'am. Man, no."

"Well, hell then," she said, "Come on up in the yard and don't stand in the road hurt and thirsty."

The door opened and shut again and the coal-oil lamp lifted up inside and the door opened, and a woman came out dressed in a nightshirt like old white men wear. I couldn't see too well in the glare but she had her hair pulled back—all I could see was the side of her face and the nightshirt and her right hand as she held the lamp up.

"You're a mess, son," she said, looking up and down. "Get some well water from that bucket over yonder and cool down. Did you know your foot was leaking like a bad pump suckerwasher?"

I looked down at the hurt foot, but she took the lamp back inside and set it down again and moved around inside the shack, tearing up cloth, it sounded like.

I hobbled over to the bucket and looked around for the dipper. There wasn't one, and there was a big watering trough under the pump. So I dipped out a couple of handfuls of water. It sure was good and cool. I broke out in a sweat as soon as I drank some.

Then the woman was back. "Sit down on the trough there," she said. "Let me clean that foot off. You'll get dew poison or lockjaw walking around barefoot with a cut like that.

"It wasn't by choice," I said. I tried to take my foot away.

"Hold still, dammit," she said. "I don't bite."

She bent down and poured water on my foot, which was bad enough, then put something on a piece of cloth and put it on my cut.

"JESUS CHRISTAWMIGHTY LADY?" I yelled. Tears jumped out of my eyes it hurt so much. It was like jumping into a patch of bull nettles. I bit my lips. "I'm sorry, ow-ow-ow . . .," I said

"They say if it doesn't burn it doesn't do any good. Hold your foot still while I wrap it to keep the dirt out." She wound a long strip of cloth from what looked like an old sheet around the instep of my foot then fastened it across the top with a safety pin.

"That too tight?"

"Some. Not too much." The stinging was going away. "Thank you, ma'am. Thanks for the water and for wrapping my foot. I have to be getting home now."

She stood up. "You look like a hurt little puppy," she said, holding the lamp up high. "I think you'll be alright." Her eyes got a funny look, showed a little white under the bottom of the pupil. I'd never seen that before.

"Rest awhile," she said. "Are you hungry? I've got some cornbread and milk left from supper."

I didn't want to stay, but suddenly I got really hungry. I realized I hadn't eaten since yesterday evening.

"Well, ma'am . . ."

"Stay here." She got up and went back inside leaving me and the kerosene lamp outside. She lit a candle in the house and moved back and forth across the place three or four times. I watched the shadows on the floursack curtains. She might have been dancing for all I know.

I heard a sound then and looked around and I'll be damned if there wasn't the biggest buck deer standing ten feet away looking at me with his big old eyes. Then I'll swear he lowered his head and shook it back and forth just like a man shaking his head no.

I turned real slow so as not to scare him, and there was a big boar shoat with his snout right next to my hand. His eyes were big and black and he was looking at me and not moving anything but his nose that was twitching and wet like there was a real slow fountain inside.

The door opened and the white woman came back out with a glass. In it was crumbled up cornbread and milk with a big blue-speckled spoon stuck in it. The buck and boar looked at her. She lifted one of her hands and put two knuckles against her forehead like she had a headache. When I looked back around the hog and deer had turned and were walking away.

"That's the damnest thing I've ever seen," I said.

She handed me the cornbread and milk. I took it. She sat down on a little chair on the little front porch.

"Go ahead and eat," she said. "I'm not hungry." She looked over at the place the deer had been. "They're real tame. They come around to drink out of that old horse trough."

I ate the wet cornbread with the spoon. It was the best I'd ever had. It had a taste like she'd used onions and garlic in the grease she'd cooked it in.

She leaned over and blew out the lamp without lifting the chimney. "I'm low on coal-oil," she said. "It's getting so a body can't hardly afford it anymore. They want 11¢ a gallon down at the big station for it."

I finished eating the chunks of cornbread and turned up the glass and drank the corn mush in the bottom. It had the consistency of wet sand. I could have eaten another whole glassful, but I didn't dare ask. "You *were* hungry," she said. I started feeling uncomfortable. I could tell she was watching me in the dark.

"Well, thank you ma'am," I said. "Can I wash these out for you here in the trough?"

"I'll take care of it," she said. "Aren't you sleepy?"

As soon as she said it I felt tireder than I ever had in my life. I couldn't keep my eyes open. But I knew I needed to go home soon.

"I . . . I . . . gotta . . ." I couldn't even talk.

"It's alright," she said. "You can sleep right here on the porch steps."

"But . . . ma'am . . .," I said, nodding.

"It's alright," she said. "You'll see. Just go to sleep."

"But . . .," I said. "But . . ."

* * *

I was lying on the porch, everything was sideways. I was fighting going to sleep. I didn't know how I got there. There was someone standing over me. I could see bare legs. Beyond them was a yard and a pump. The yard was full of animals. A horse and a bull. A buck deer. A dog or two. Rabbits. A hog. A big wading bird. A snake. A cougar. A bear. They were all looking at me, not moving.

A hand was on my head, rubbing it. I tried to look up, couldn't.

"Don't fight it," the woman said. The voice had been crying. "Don't fight it. Just let go."

I just let go. It all went away.

* * *

There was a puppy in the yard with me. I loved to play with that puppy. I was happy. We would run around and around the yard. We would chase the ball and chase the ball and we would yell and laugh and fight and run and yell and fight and play with rags and the woman would laugh and laugh then she would cry and then she would make me and the others sit still and watch close and she would say things and point with the long stick at the big flat thing with the pretty circles and then she would talk and talk and cry then she would laugh again and we would all be happy and after it was day and night and day again and the air was full of different smells some more men came and the woman made us all go to the shed out back and then we came out and she would point with the long stick at the pretty circles on the big flat thing again.

Then it was day again and me and the puppy played in the yard then there was a man standing outside the yard looking and the woman came out and the man said something and the woman was upset and ran to me but the man got there first and I was watching and I knew I liked the man but just before he reached me my ear started to itch so I scratched it with my right foot and then he picked me up and I knew I liked him so I licked him on the face.

VIII

When I woke up my head was a log and the sky was a wedge and the light was a sledgehammer. I was on the front porch of Houlka's shack. It was afternoon and the sun was out.

There was a rasping sound nearby. I got my eyes to sort of focus.

"You better watch drinking that moonshine," said Houlka. "You never know what that stuff's got in it."

He was sitting out under the tree sharpening his arrows with a bastard file. The sound was worse than the sunlight.

"Please. Don't. Mr. Houlka."

"Sorry." He put down the file.

A bird whistled somewhere. Its song was a fishhook through both my ears. I winced all over.

"This must be your first big drunk."

"Please, Mr. Houlka. Don't make me talk."

"All right," he said. He came over to me. I was trying to remember all that had happened since we left.

"What is today?"

"It's three days since we left," he said.

Some of what happened came back to me.

He was watching my eyes. For the first time since that day in the courthouse he looked away from me. He slowly put his hand on my shoulder. "I'm sorry about what made you run off. It won't happen with you again. There are plenty of people who don't mind at all. But I won't bother you again. I never should have gotten so close to Mrs. Hippola's without going in. I have a temper. It gets the best of me sometimes. That was one of those. Did anybody ever tell you what I done time for?"

"I didn't ask. I didn't want to know. Did it have anything to do with what you tried with me?"

"No. It was for my temper. I had a fit and killed my wife and kids."

I started shaking, from hearing that and from whatever it was I'd drunk. "Shouldn't they have put you in Starkville?" I asked.

"The judge didn't see it that way. But it made a lot of people mad, including some of Boss Eustis's friends, who don't think prison was rough enough on me."

I tried to sit up.

"Better not do that. You understand, though, that what happened won't happen again? Shake on it?"

I held out my hand, shook his. "I'm shaking enough already," I said.

"Houlka, I . . . there was all these animals . . . I . . . think . . ."

"Don't try that either. You better try to get some more sleep now. I'm gonna put a bucket of water beside your head, cause next time you wake up that's all you're gonna be thinking about. Your glasses and shoes is in your shack. After you feel better, I got a little errand for you."

I went back to sleep.

*   *   *

Houlka was right. I woke up, turned over and drank half a bucket of water. Then I had to pee for fifteen minutes. Then I drank the rest of the bucket. Houlka was snoring inside his cabin.

I went into the kitchen of the big house. Romulus didn't lecture me. He said God was punishing me enough and to remember the way I felt. I ate some milk and cornbread and tried to remember things but it was no use. Houlka must have told them only that he found me drunk in a ditch somewhere, and that I had been poisoned by bad liquor, which is what I got from the context. Then Miz Luvsey came in and said, "You poor boy," and, "I suppose you have learned a great lesson," and so on.

I left the kitchen. It was just getting dark. Houlka was awake.

"Feeling any better?"

"Meep. Nerx. Some," I finally managed.

He reached under his cot and brought out a package neatly wrapped with some leftover Christmas stuff from the storage house. He handed it to me and then brought a long-stemmed rose.

"Don't worry. I asked Mrs. Eustis for it. First one of the year, it's been so wet. Take these to Mrs. Hippola's house. Don't take any guff off anybody. You're to give this package and the rose to her personally, and you're to say 'The message is thank you for the loan.' Got that?"

"Thank you for the loan."

"No. 'The message is thank you for the loan.'"

"*The message* is thank you for the loan."

*   *   *

I was walking into town with the stuff and I'll be damned if I didn't hear shooting or fireworks coming from it, and car horns and bicycle bells and Halloween and New Year's noisemakers. What would people be celebrating in May? Maybe the state of Mississippi was seceding from the Union again.

I took the back streets. Even they were noisy, people walking back and forth across them, neighbors talking. The main streets sounded like the Barnum and Bailey Circus was out there. None of this was really helping my head.

I went to the back door of Miz Hippola's. It sounded like they was throwing a *charivari* in the parlors and upstairs.

I knocked. I had to knock about ten times before the door was opened. A man that could have been Uncle Romulus's twin brother smiled, then turned it into a frown.

"I'm sorry, young gentleman," he said. "Mrs. Hippola's caters only to a white clientele. If you'll go five blocks back down, and two blocks right, you'll find Miss Reba's establishment."

"I have a package for Miz Hippola," I said.

"I'll see she gets it," he said, holding out his hand.

"I have to deliver it personal."

"I'm sure a quarter would obviate that necessity," he said, reaching in his vest pocket.

"No, sir." I said. "I have to deliver it personal."

"That will take some doing. As you can see, we're busy with one thing and another."

I held on to the package.

"Very well. Wait here in the kitchen." He showed me in then left through the hanging beads.

There was a Negro woman cooking and washing up dishes. There was a table that seated twenty. The place was smoky. There was yelling and laughter from the parlor, even more from the street outside. I could hear a piano, banjo and kazoo playing some jazz song, but it sounded like it was a million miles away it was so noisy in town.

Then the beads parted and a white lady in her early forties came in. She had on a blue dress that pushed her titties up so far it looked like they were going to run away. She had black makeup around her eyes, her lipstick was bright green and her hair was coiled up like a big snake on top of her head—it must have been six feet long.

"What is it? This is the busiest night since election day three years ago."

I held out the package. Then I took the rose from behind my back and handed it to her.

She looked at the flower, like she already knew what was in the wrappings.

"The message is thank you for the loan."

"The answer is once ain't enough," she said.

"Once ain't enough?"

"*The answer* is once ain't enough," she said.

"The answer is once ain't enough," I said. She took the things. "Now git. I'm busy."

"One thing, ma'am," I said. "What's everybody so excited about?"

The Negro woman dropped her peeling knife. Miz Hippola laughed.

"They musta kept you *way* down in the well this week," said the Negro woman.

"I been—out of touch, ma'am."

"That calls for a drink, Beulah. Get him some needle-beer."

"If it's all the same to you ma'am, that's what made me miss most of this week."

"Well, well. More for the customers then. You really ain't heard?"

"No, Ma'am!"

"Lindy made it!" she said.

IX

It's only after you spend three day trying to drive cattle from one side of a county to the other do you know what tired really is. Overland through muddy fields and around people's pastures, across what few bridges that ain't been washed out this spring and across the creeks where they have. Wasn't no William S. Hart heroics involved. Boss Eustis was supposed to have called around and told everyone we was coming and not to give us no lip, but the Boss probably got to telling stories on the porch one day, and didn't call Mr. Jerry Younts, so there we was in a yelling match, with fifty head of cattle, and all I wanted to do was go bury my head in the ground like an ostrich while Houlka straightened it out. Mr. Younts sure has *some* vocabulary.

We was taking the cattle of course to the land where Mr. Boss Eustis had the undivided half-interest.

We staggered-ass back home, and I wanted to sleep for a week. But of course that wasn't to be. It all started, like so many things do in Spunt County, with a casual visitor's remark.

* * *

Miz Eustis had me weeding the walk-border that leads up to the front porch. It was a sunny day and all the Boss's friends was there, and someone had brought this new guy to meet the Boss while he was doing some business in the (what used to be) sunny Southland.

He was dressed like a Yankee—dark suit, hat, vest, white tie, pointy little shoes. The guy had introduced him as T. Harris Stottle, who was an adviser to "Big Al Up North."

He had a very peculiar way of talking, even for a Yankee. After the usual amenities, and many stories swapped, he was explaining about some exploit that had just happened.

"So I says, Al, you are being taken for the chump. The guy's house is all mutted up. His nightclub *habitues* drip mink and use Jacksons to fire their ropes. Enough ice goes in and out the place as'll put the Frigidaire people to shame. Then he gives you this balloon juice as how his patrons want more malt and less hootch, and just because you go back together since before they built Syracuse, you buy it. Use your peepers, I says.

"So Big Al says that sombitch he puts one over on me I feed his dick to his youngest daughter; I trust him that much or I never say such a thing.

"Well three days later, Big Al's in his friend's own club when guys come in and it clouds up with Cicero lightning and Chicago thunder, and they fog the place up pretty bad only Big Al never got his hair mussed. What with a little nudging around, Big Al finds out the man with the rhino for the pop was his good friend, Mr. Poor Mouth.

"So Big Al says, Stottle, Stottle, you spent time in the knowledge box, what would you do with a friend like that so it hurts for a long time?

"I said Al, it ain't so much the hurt as the surprise you want.

"Al, you got to make with the wide eyes, like you could never in eight hundred and two thousand seven hundred and one years figure out why someone would do such a insane thing as shoot you. Then you invite him and twenty of your best friends to a party, only one person of whom will not be in on the joke. Meanwhile you have rented the vacancy and fixed things up nice, and you go find yourself a powder monkey from a good soup factory and he makes some alterations to the building code. Night of the big senior prom comes; you got lights on and a phonograph in the house making with the party noises, and here comes Mr. Long Face and up he walks and toots the dingdong, and the last thing he is thinking as his beezer goes through his goozle is, I wonder who coulda done this, 'cause Big Al was just absolutely fakelooed by my act!"

Most of the men on the porch laughed a little nervously.

"Then I tod him, Al, you're a great guy, but you gotta start looking around you with your own gleepers. It's surprising, Al, what you can tell by giving things a glim."

"Like what things, Mr. Stottle?" asked JimBob.

T. Harris Stottle looked out at the road from where the sound of horses' hooves came. It was Mr. Ness and the others. Some of them nodded toward the Boss.

"Well, for instance," said Stottle, watching a minute. "Two of them's drunk. One has a hangover. One of them just didn't get any sleep last night; he's dragging his piles. One has Cupid's itch and is upholstered, but he ain't gettin' any because too many people know. That woman at the back ain't drunk; she's either blizzarded out or all gowed up."

"What you mean?"

"Gold dusted? Joy powdered? Happy timed? Mudded? On a sleigh ride? Sucking Bamboo? White crossed? Kicking the gong around? Whatever you people call it down here."

"You mean *dope*?" asked JimBob incredulously.

"Cocaine or opium, one or the other," said Stottle.

"White people? In *our* town?" asked another.

"I'm a total stranger here," said Stottle. "You hand me five hundred dollars and give me thirty minutes in this burg, and I shall come back to this very porch and build you a snowman."

"I'll just be goddamned," said someone.

I watched the Horsey Set ride away with some new respect.

* * *

Then it began to rain again, and it was the rain that brought on the next thing.

Houlka and I had been coming back toward town on the old Indian Path from some damnfool errand Miz Eustis sent us on, and a storm caught us, and we crawled under some blowed-over cane in a brake and was fairly dry. It slowed after a while, then stopped. While everything was dripping dry, we heard horses going by on the path, a bunch of them.

The wind came up and started drying everything off, and we got back on the trail and was heading for the railroad tracks when we saw the horse standing in the middle of the trail and heard the crying.

It was Miz Rio. She was sitting in a muddy place and was soaked, and she still held the reins of her horse. She was sobbing into the sleeve of her coat.

"You thrown?" asked Houlka.

She looked up at us. Her eyes were like skull sockets there were such big black circles under them. She'd lost maybe twenty pounds since the last good look I'd gotten at her.

"I can't take it anymore. I can't go on," she said.

"We'll take you home then," said Houlka.

"I . . . don't have one anymore, except Ness's place. I don't want to go back there. I'll die if I go back there. They'll find me wherever I am," she said, crying again. "I want to quit. I can't go on anymore."

Houlka looked at her. "Are you sure?"

"Yes. Yes. I'll die if I go on this way."

Houlka turned to me. "I been doing stuff just for the Boss long enough. Time I did something for someone else that don't make the Boss richer. Take Miss Rio's horse over to Mr. Ness's stables. Tell him she told you to. Tell him you met her on the trail, she asked you to take her horse home and tell them she doesn't want to ride with them any more. Then go home. I'll be back there before you do."

He handed me the horse's reins and picked up Miz Rio and started for the town.

I took the horse over to Mr. Ness's place. The horse wouldn't let me ride it. I tried to get on it seventy-eleven times. I pulled and pushed it till I got him walking down the road to Mr. Ness's house.

The place was already lit up and there was music and racket coming from it by the time I finally got the horse there.

Mr. Ness, sitting on his horse, was waiting at the gate to the place.

I walked up to him, held out the reins, wiped sweat off my head. "I met Miz Rio on the old Indian Trail," I said. "She asked me to bring this here horse back to you and to tell you she don't want to ride any more, Mr. Ness."

He looked at me with them deep green eyes, then looked back past me up the road, searching. then he looked back at me, took the reins, turned and took the horses toward the stables.

Damned if I wasn't tired of walking all over Spunt County.

* * *

They called me around to the front porch next morning and there wasn't any laughing going on.

Mr. Ness and all the others in the Riding Club were sitting on their horses in the yard.

Boss Eustis started right in on me. "I.O. Lace. They's a thing that don't happen nowhere I know of. That's that a white woman disappears and a nigger boy shows up where she lives and tells somebody that she don't want to live there any more and gives those people the woman's horse. You know of anywhere that happens, I.O.?"

I looked at the men on the porch. they were looking at me like I'd never seen before.

"You want me to shoot your ass right here, or give you to Mr. Ness so he can drag you downtown and they can cut your balls off and put an Alabama necklace on you and light it 'n' haul you up the schoolhouse flag-pole, or what?"

I never saw this coming. I started feeling all cold in my gut.

"Mr. Eustis. All I know's is what I told Mr. Ness. I ran into Miz Rio on the Indian Trail comin' back from taking them preserves out to Hankin's place for Miz Eustis. Miz Rio was all upset about something, but it wasn't my place to ask. She told me to take her horse over to Mr. Ness's stables and to tell them she didn't want to ride any more. That's what she said. That's what I done, honest to God, Mr. Eustis. What you think I done?"

"She ain't come back, I.O. People's upset. They liable to think all kinds of things, even though you're only a boy, you're a Negro boy and that's rea-son enough sometimes."

"Boss, if I'da done something bad you think I'd take her horse back where she lives after I done it? I ain't smart, but I'm smarter than that."

"Dammit, I.O., I ain't never had one of my ni-groes lynched, and I don't aim to start now. I'll take care of you myself if you're lyin'."

"I ain't lyin' Mr. Eustis."

"Why the hell would you take a white woman's horse back with a story like that in the first place, I.O.?"

"'Cause she told me to, Boss Eustis. That was what she told me to do! Have you ever known me to do anything without somebody *telling* me to?"

The Boss looked at me a minute. "Normally, that would make me believe you, 'cause it's true. That would be the clincher. But I got this feel-in', I.O., that you're holding something back. You skatin' on thin ice."

I sighed. "She gave me a dollar to do it," I said.

I fished around in my pocket and pulled out a big greenback dollar. "You know I ain't never had more than a dime on me by this time o' the month, Boss."

"Now we have come to the crux of the matter, ain't we, I.O. If you'da said that and showed me that dollar first off, you'd still have it. Give it to JimBob—I'm finin' you for causing all this grief 'cause you ain't forthcom-ing with the Pure-D truth. You can think about all the ice cream cones you could be buying with it right this minute."

He turned to Ness. "There you have it," he said. "She told him to do it and gave him a dollar, and that's what he did."

Ness nodded his head toward the back of the house.

"Where was your big friend Mr. Houlka while all this palaver was going on?"

"He'd done done cut off toward town by then," I said. "He said he had to go pick up that crowbar at the hardware store that we need if you want us to move that second outhouse like you said you wanted."

"They's a new crowbar in the tool shed," said JimBob.

The Boss turned his head sharply toward JimBob. "Since when does a ex-con get to sign for my tools at the store?"

"Well, hell, Boss," said JimBob. "Him and I.O. does three-quarters of the work gets done around here, I put him on the list."

"Well be damn sure about everything on the account, you hear?" said Mr. Eustis.

"Sure thing, Boss."

Mr. Eustis turned to me. "I.O., I want you to tell me one more time, and Mr. Ness here, too, exactly what happened from the time you two left here yesterday. Don't add nothing, and don't leave nothing out."

I told them again.

"You heard him, Mr. Ness. I got no choice but to believe him. I'm sorry one of my boys was involved in this in any fashion, but he won't do anything like that again, not for no amount of greenback dollars, he'll do some thinking first. You can go to the sheriffs if you want to from here, but I'm satisfied. You can send the law out, or you can look somewhere else."

Ness looked at me, then cut his eyes toward the back, where Houlka was piling brushwood. Then he turned, and he and the others rode out the driveway.

* * *

I was shaking so hard all over I had to sit down on my porch. I'd never thought when I took that horse back it wouldn't be the end of it. Me and Houlka'd gone over the story last night, and he'd given me the folding dollar. While I had been standing there this morning I remembered what had happened that night last month with Houlka, and what if it had happened to Miz Rio? Oh god, if something had happened to her.

Houlka walked over to me.

"Soon's you quit shaking, we got us an outhouse to move," he said.

* * *

I don't know how he did it, but he did all his work, kept Miz Rio hidden out somewhere, and didn't let anyone find her. Some nights he must not have slept more than an hour—he'd get away after dark and not come back till just before sunup.

One night I thought I heard hooves outside. The next morning I got up early and went outside. There was a torn envelope stuck to Houlka's porch post with a banana knife. I took it down.

It was a letter postmarked Starkville, with no return address but the envelope addressed to Mr. Ness. It was short. It told him she was drying out and that she was okay, not to bother her, and that she was sending another letter to the sheriffs so no one would worry about her.

Houlka came out while I was reading it. I handed it to him, indicating the banana knife in the post. I pointed to the hoofprints outside.

Houlka was looking down. There was a package beside the post.

It was full of little cellophane envelopes full of white powder.

Houlka looked at them a minute. He sighed. Then he picked them up, went inside and threw them into his cook stove fire.

* * *

A week later, Miz Rio went back to the Ness place and picked up her stuff and moved to a boarding house. A couple of days after that, I was out front at just dark. The Riding Club came by, on the way back from a fishing trip. The others went on, but Mr. Ness turned into the drive. He rode up to where Houlka was leaning on the pruning bill he'd been using on the willow tree. He stopped in front of him. He just looked at him for a minute, then nodded, turned his horse around and rode off to catch back up with the others.

* * *

Two nights after that, around midnight, I hear Miz Rio sneaking into Houlka's shack. After awhile there was such a rattling and shaking as you ever heard. I was sure it was gonna wake up everyone in the big house, but it didn't.

Just great. I thought. I'm gonna have to lay here all night and listen to them porking. My glands was already raging anyway.

Then I heard steps outside my porch. My first thought was that it was Mr. Ness or some of them, or the Boss or Mr. JimBob, and Houlka's on his way back to Parchman two months before his time's up, on the charge of fornication.

I went toward my door. It was a pitch-black night.

There was a little knock.

"Who's there?"

"I.O. It's me. Emzee."

"Emzee?" My head was swimming.

She came in the door. I could smell vanilla. "I been dying to tell you but I couldn't till now. Mr. Houlka done had Miz Rio hid out at our place. That's where she was all the time, before she moved to the boarding house. I don't never want to see a body go through that again."

"Emzee," I said. A moan came from next door.

"I knew Miz Rio was coming out here tonight," she said. "I thought you'd be lonely having to listen to all that."

Then she was on me like a snake and put her tongue in my mouth.

X

The Spunt County Glee Chorus sat on the front porch. It was ten in the morning and finally already hot.

Boss Eustis leaned forward in his chair, holding his fan still. "I got a piece of paper here signed by the sheriffs," he said, taking it out of JimBob's pocket and holding it out to Houlka. "It says here you can be out of the county for me on business for three days, starting tomorrow morning. I want you to go see a man about a dog." He laughed at his own joke. "It's down in the Delta way back in what little woods they is there. This here other piece of paper," he said, giving him another one, "got his name and address on it. I want you and the boy," he sniggered and the others joined in, nudging each other in the ribs, "to go down there and bring the dog back for me. I'm interested in a little sporting action this fall."

We left the front yard.

I looked at the papers, the sheriffs' forms. Then I looked at the address.

"Oh, Mr. Houlka," I said. "Boss Eustis done signed our death warrants!"

"What you mean?"

I read the address. "Mr. Pluto Dees. Rural Route 3, Box 293, Avernus, Mississippi."

"Who's that?"

"Mr. Dees. Pluto Dees. Royal Kleagle of the Knights of the Ku Klux Klan."

"What you know about him?"

"He's the kleagle, that's all any black person has to know."

"Who knows something about him?"

"Mr. Blind Bill. He's the one had so much trouble with him so long ago. He's one of the few black men that ever laid eyes on him. But he won't talk about it, I can tell you that."

"How does he know it was him, if he's Mr. Blind Bill?"

"He wasn't blind before he met him," I said.

* * *

Blind Bill was playing a quiet little tune to himself with his guitar when we came up his walk. He stopped.

"I ain't studying you, I.O. Lace! I been mad at you ever since you didn't come back to read me that column. I had a hell of a time finding out how that game came out. Get the hell outta my yard!"

"I'm sorry Mr. Blind Bill, I really couldn't and I knew you'd pester somebody and get them to read to you."

"I still ain't studying you or your friend there."

"Mr. Blind Bill, this is Mr. Houlka Lee."

"You the one I heard about. Let me feel that cougarskin."

Houlka stepped close. Bill reached up and felt the headskin and the shoulders. "I used to know a tame one," said Blind Bill. "I used to play and he'd come up and lay down beside me. That was a long time ago. Thanks."

"Mr. Blind Bill. We're in trouble," I said. "We gonna have to go down to the Delta. Boss Eustis sending us to see Mr. Pluto."

Bill stiffened. He put down his guitar, reached up to his eyes.

"I'm sorry," I said. "We just gonna need all the help we can get. We supposed to go pick up a fighting dog from him."

"Oh, God," said Blind Bill Orff. "I hoped never to hear that name again as long as I lived. I swore I'd kill the first person ever brought his name up."

"It ain't us. Boss Eustis must think it's some kind of joke."

"You don't joke using Mr. Dees," he said. "Oh, lordy lordy. Boss knows he'll probably just shoot you on sight, I.O. He'll take his time with your white friend here for bringing a Negro to him. He don't let black people live within thirty miles in any direction."

"They must not get much cotton picked down around there," said Houlka.

Blind Bill laughed. "You bet your ass on that, Mr. Lee. I never thought about it quite that way. Hee-hee-hee!"

Then Bill sobered up. "Ain't no laughing matter. Mr. Dees don't care whether cotton get picked or not. People always dying. He owns just about every tombstone company in this state, and everybody buys from him, too." Bill leaned back in his rocker, making short little jerky rocking motions.

"There's one person in the world got Mr. Dee's respect. It's the only way you gonna be alive after you get there. Mr. Dees had a cruel upbringing, not that I care, but one person treated him fair. That was his fourth grade teacher. She was as rough on him as everybody else, but she was fair, and she the one who set him on his way being a mortuary tycoon. He never forgot her, and when she was ready to retire, he sent her a golden rule, a real golden ruler, twenty-four carat, and a lot of money, but it was the ruler that meant the most to her. It paid her back for all those years teaching peckerwoods and rednecks, told her she'd touched someone's life.

"Trouble was, she was in a car wreck the next year and went sort of crazy in the head. Claimed she could tell things that was gonna happen."

"You mean she could see the future?" asked Houlka.

"Naw. Naw. She had been a history teacher. Claimed she could see into the past, see what was gonna happen in the past."

Houlka didn't laugh. I did. "You talking about that crazy old bat, Miz Commer?" I asked.

"That's it. That's her new name."

"New? Bill, she done been retired and married twenty years. I been hearing about her since I was a baby."

"You go out where she is. You ask about that ruler. All she can say is no, then you're dead men soon as you get down to the Delta."

"What about the dog?" asked Houlka.

"Won't be the same ones. Be their great-great-grandpups. Mean, real mean. I seen one tear a bobcat to pieces. Big old heads and jaws, almost no hind legs at all. Mr. Dees breeds 'em for dogfights and for sickin' on black people for fun about twice a year. White people that cross him, too."

"Boss Eustis wants me to bring it back."

"Then you're dead. You might kill it, but you ain't gonna catch hold of it. Sorry I told you about Miz Coomer. I thought you just had to kill the dog."

"I got to try," said Houlka.

"Well, I suppose so. Go out to Two Gates Farm. I wish you luck. It'd be worth my eyes again see somebody get something over on that sombitch Mr. Dees."

"Thank you, Blind Bill," I said.

"How many times I got to tell you it's Mister Blind Bill to you?"

"Sorry."

As we left, he started singing, soft and slow, "Swing Low, Sweet Chariot."

* * *

There *were* two gates, about fifty yards apart.

One of them was covered with steer horns of all kinds, longhorn, shorthorn, goat horns, rams's horns and deer antlers. The other one was made out of elephant tusks.

"Mr. Coomer was a safari guide in Africa," I said. What he did coming back to Mississippi and marrying a schoolteacher from Spunt County's more than I can figure."

You could see the drive curve in from both gates, all overgrown, and beyond, the corner of a big house. Tall trees arced over the place.

We opened the righthand fence gate with the elephant tusks all over it, stepped in and closed it behind us. I looked around. I musta been wrong, I couldn't see the house from here. Houlka took a few steps, then he stopped. He looked behind us. We couldn't have taken more than a few steps, but the road curved back behind us out of sight, and we couldn't see the gate.

"Wait," said Houlka, looking back up the road. "Back up. Don't turn around." I backed up into the gate hard. The loose ivory rattled like elephants was fighting behind me.

I reached around and opened the gate chain and backed out with Houlka. That's when we saw the sign that had fallen down, saying, "USE OTHER GATE." Houlka pounded it back onto its bent nail.

We didn't say anything, went to the antlered gate on the left, went in and got to the house in about a minute. I didn't look the other way up the drive, I didn't want to. Things was spooky enough already.

* * *

There was a man sitting on the wide verandah, drinking. He had on a white jacket and was wearing a pith helmet. He wore a walrus mustache. "Hello," he said, standing. "I'm Jock Coomer. And you?"

"Houlka Lee." They shook hands.

"Admirable bow," he said to Houlka. "Might I see it?" Houlka handed his bow over to him. He flexed it. "Forty-to-forty-five pound pull. Quite sufficient. I've seen pygmies drop a Kudo on the run with one that only pulls twenty."

"This is I.O."

"Oh, I know this chap." He came down and shook hands with me. "One of Mr. Eustis's boy-of-all-work, isn't it? How are you?"

"Not so good," I said.

"Oh, beastly. Can I do anything?"

"We actually came to talk to Mrs. Coomer," said Houlka.

"That will be quite hard. This isn't one of her good days. I believe she's finally gotten to sleep." There was a noise in the back of the house.

"I could be wrong, of course. Cybil?" he called. "Cybil? We have company."

The screen door opened. I wasn't ready for what I saw. She was maybe sixty years old, had on an old wrap. Her hair looked like a brush heap a crazy man piled. Her eyes were wild and round—the bottoms showed like that white woman's at the house I got drunk at that night. She was holding her arms over her head, looking off into the porch ceiling.

"These men wish to talk to you, darling. I'll just find some little chore to do."

"You might nail your gate sign back up," said Houlka.

"Which?"

"The elephant one."

"Oh? Hope you weren't too inconvenienced. I'll just pop out there and repair it." He picked up a claw hammer and some nails and set off up the right-side driveway.

The woman had a long thin object wrapped in paper in her hand.

"This is what you came for," she said, handing it to Houlka.

The hair stood up on the back of my neck.

"Please return it," she said. "It has great sentimental value."

"I'll do my best, Mrs. Coomer."

"Mrs. Coomer," I said, gulping. "I thought you could only see into the past."

"All times, all places in the past," she said.

"Then how could you have seen this, know what we was coming for?"

"I saw all this tomorrow morning," she said, and went back into the house.

We went back up the left-hand drive, passed Mr. Coomer coming back down.

"Going to be a pleasant day," he said. "Probably very hot. I hope you'll come again soon."

Mr. Coomer went back toward the house, whistling. We went out the gate. I closed it. It rattled. I looked up. It was covered with elephant tusks and had a sign on it saying "USE OTHER GATE." Houlka was walking on up the road. I looked back. The elephant gate was on the left and the antler one was on the right. I didn't say anything.

* * *

We rode the Interurban as far as it went, then caught a ride on a truck that took us a mile from Avernus. Water was still standing in the ditches on each side of the road.

We walked into town. People was staring at us, what few there were in town. Houlka went into the post office. He came back out. "Buck up," he said, "it ain't very far to the place."

A few people followed us, down the street, talking among themselves. We didn't look back. There were signs on the telephone posts leading out of town pointing the way we were going. Trucks passed up, people leaned out and gawked. Some of them slowed down. One actually stopped, backed up, stopped, then went on. We kept walking.

We came to a Y in the road, we took the right one, same as the arrows on the poles. The trees began to overgrow the road, making it green and gloomy. The day was hot and sticky.

More trucks and cars passed us. The road went down toward a low place. We came down and there must have been two hundred vehicles, cars, trucks, and wagons, parked there. There weren't any people there, just the sound of cooling motors as we walked through.

The pines rose higher and closed in the other side of the meadow, making it a dark green space. As we went in, people were just disappearing around the bend from us.

We got to where they'd been and there before us was the long flat black tongue of a river. Three or four kids was standing at a landing on this side, and a couple of them started crying.

There was a big island in the middle of the river, and coming back from it, guided by a rope tied off at posts on each side came a ferry being poled by one guy.

We went down to the landing. So many trees grew on the island you couldn't see anything there.

When we came down, the kids, who carried bundles in their hands, started crying and screaming again, looking back and forth from Houlka and me to the ferry boat and the island.

The ferryman was stripped to the waist and his shoulders were as big as Houlka's.

"Shut your yapping!" he yelled at the kids. "You'll get across in plenty of time. If you hadn't dawdled, you could have gone over same time as your mom and dad!" They stopped crying, and one by one they unfolded their bundles and put on their sheets, and after they got them on they turned and stared at me.

The ferry hit. Houlka put his foot on it. The kids climbed on. Then I did. I was sweating. Even if it was a hundred below zero I'd be sweating. The man went to the front, poled us out. The line sagged downstream. The man grunted and heaved, and we crossed.

The kids jumped off, getting the bottoms of their sheets wet.

"Mister," said the ferryman. "It's pretty obvious you ain't with the group rate, so that'll be two cents each."

I reached in my pocket and pulled out a nickel.

"Four cents," he said. "Not a nickel. Four cents."

"Well," said Houlka. "Hold that nickel and remember us, and we'll give you three more cents when we come back."

"I hate to make a penny that easy," said the man, and poled back into the river.

We walked into the arch of trees and turned around the first bend. We stepped into the clearing. There was people doing things like at any family reunion or picnic, talking, running, jumping, like that. Only each and every one of them was wearing a pointed white sheet. Some of them had the cowls pulled back while they did stuff.

Then a hush went across the clearing. There was some confusion, and we saw a raised platform on the other side of the field they was all looking at. They waited for a signal. They got it.

As one, they all put their sheets over their heads and turned to face us.

They all came to a sort of attention with a flutter and snap of sheets.

They stood stock still wherever they are, maybe two thousand Klansmen and -women and -children.

Houlka put his right hand on my shoulder then and started me moving toward the platform. I don't remember anything but sheets and eyes, but they moved aside and cleared a small path for us, and after two or three weeks, it seemed like, we were standing in front of the speakers' platform.

There were huge dogs tied with about eighty pounds of barge chain each to the corner posts. One of them sniffed, bared his teeth, growled.

"Well, I thought I seen everything," said one of the sheets on the platform. There must have been fifty of them there.

"It's a little early for sausage-makin', but looks like we gonna be eatin' high on the nigger tonight," said another.

"I get the brains," said a third.

"His friend there looks a little tough. Hour or two o' boiling take care of that. Let's cut off his legs, put tourniquets on them, have him eat some of his own legs before we kill him!"

"I say let's quit talkin' and do it," said another. Fifteen guns came out.

Very slowly Houlka reached in his pocket and took the golden ruler out and held it up in the air.

"EVERYBODY SIT DOWN NOW," a voice boomed from the back. You could hear the whistling of sheets and the snap of sleeves as everybody sat wherever they were.

When they were all sitting down, I saw there was a big overstuffed chair at the back with a fat Klansman in it.

"That there ruler bought you another two minutes living. Start talking."

"I'm Houlka Lee. I work for Boss Eustis up in Anomie, in Spunt County."

"Spunt County. Mighty pretty women in Spunt County. I was thinking of going up there sometime and getting me a wife," said the Klansman in the chair.

"Mr. Eustis sent me here to get your dog."

There wasn't a sound in the place except the hot wind through the pines. Then the Klansman started chuckling and the sound spread around the platform, the field, all across the island, the river. It sounded like a thousand apples falling all at once. Then the sound died away.

"Well, why didn't you say so. I got an open invitation to any of the county bosses they can send someone down here for my dog any time. Why, he'll walk right up to you. You might even say, he'll be eager to see you." He turned his hood toward me. "That still don't explain the nigger boy there, and why we shouldn't get a lot of fun out of him. This is a three-day meeting, you know?"

"I brought him to hold my bow and arrows and my club. I figure both my hands are gonna be full."

"You got that right. Only you probably won't have no head left, so it don't matter much about the hands."

"That's the only reason I brought him. Had no idea this was a holiday."

"Well, after I give you my dog, it won't matter much why you brought him 'cause that dog just sometimes don't know when to stop greeting folks."

"I came here to get a dog Mr.—mister. It's just another job to me, like mending a fence or painting a barn."

"Why . . ."

Houlka held the ruler up high.

The Klansman leaned back in his chair.

"Which one is it?" Houlka asked, looking back and forth, taking off his quiver and bow and handing me his club, at the dogs chained to the posts.

"Oh. Oh! You think it's one of them? Why, them's just puppies! Weaned last week. When you were sent after a dog, mister, you were sent after a *dog*."

The Klansman hollered over his shoulder. "Serbia! Up front, boy!"

People moved out of the way at the edge of the stand. There was a jangling of a collar and a dog the size of a bear came around, shaking off the marks the bars had made in his cage.

It came around in front of the platform and sat down on its tiny little hind-quarters. Its head was a foot wide and its front legs were the size of stovepipes.

"*That's* my dog, mister." People moved out of the way, clearing a place around me and Houlka. "You take him off this island, your boss can keep him with my blessings. You don't, I'll send your Boss Eustis a letter saying thanks for taking me up on my offer."

"See Mrs. Coomer gets her ruler back," said Houlka.

"Good as done," said the Klansman. "Any time you ready Mr. Lee."

Houlka took a deep breath. "Ready."

"Serbia," said the Klansman. The dog came up, its hair bristling, lips pulled back. It shook all over in anticipation.

"Serbia! Marcus Garvey!" said Mr. Dees.

* * *

I closed my eyes. There was a big long snarl and a smash. I opened them and Houlka was under the dog, twisting it over by the hind legs. It must have weighed a hundred-fifty pounds. It moved so fast it looked like it had three heads. It bit him on the arm and leg and the back, and then they changed ends twice and I closed my eyes again.

* * *

Dr. Sclape finished sewing up the cuts. Houlka was bruised and torn from one end to another.

The dog was back at the Boss's place, in the third cage that day. It had gnawed through two already on the way back to Spunt county. The Boss wanted him to take it right back, but the others on the porch said that wasn't Houlka's place.

Miz Rio came running in. She looked down at Houlka.

He tried to smile.

"That sonofabitch Eldridge Eustis!" she said. "I'm going to get a gun and go over there and shoot his bony old ass off."

Houlka held up his hand and mumbled something.

"What?" she asked. "What?"

I leaned down. "He said it's only seven more weeks."

"He gets you killed," said Dianne Rio, "and I'll kill him, dead, dead, dead, dead!"

Houlka shook his head.

First Miz Rio started crying, then I did.

XI

"You know what I'd like right about now?" said the Boss

"No, what's that, Eldridge?" asked one of the toadies.

"I'd like about three of them big shiny apples from Mr. Hester's orchard.

"That would be real good, Boss, but as you know, Mr. Hester ain't brought them to market yet, so you gonna have to wait."

"Well, good as they are," said the Boss, "I always thought he picked them about a week late. I think right now they would be at the peak of their perfection."

"You must have spies, Boss, cause everybody knows no one got to *sample* one of them before it came to market in thirty-five years."

"I bet if a guy was real smart, real good like Mr. Lee here, I figure he could find a way to bring me about three of them apples before tomorrow night."

"What you're advocating, Boss, is trespass and trover. At the very least, Mr. Lee would be faced with a writ of replevin. And of course you're forgetting that he might end up back at Parchman if he was doing an illegal act, *toots sweet*."

"'Course it'll never come to that, 'cause Mr. Hester would of course assume that first Mr. Lee would be coming for one of those luscious daughters of his, if it wasn't so near harvest time. He'd have three or four reasons for shooting first and asking questions later. Which means the law won't be involved at all."

"If he was caught, he would of course say you sent him which of course you would deny," said JimBob.

"Sounds like a mighty losing proposition to me. But I sure would like Mr. Lee here to bring me about three of them apples back from Mr. Hester's orchard," said the Boss.

* * *

We were on the road to the western edge of the county.

"What they said," I said.

* * *

We was on this side of the county road, and beyond was a stand of trees, then there was a field that Mr. Hester kept mowed so he could see anyone sneaking up on his place from where his big house overlooked the orchard from a rise.

There was a bridge over the creek just to our right out on the road, the one that ran through Mr. Hester's orchard, that his daughters pumped up to the orchard.

We waited in the tall August grass on this side of the bar ditch. It was noon and hot. We were going to wait till dark, I guess, but of course that's when Mr. Hester's most vigilant.

We heard trucks coming down the road and moved back into the grass. They slowed and stopped. It was the state chain gang trucks. The dog truck had pulled up about a quarter-mile back. The two trucks near the bridge were full.

"Two you boys get out them big sledges," yelled one of the guards. "A. T. Last, on the road."

There was a clanking of chains as the other men jumped down.

"Come on down here with me, A.T. You men follow us." The guard was carrying a 10-gauge pump shotgun with the barrel sawed off in front of the pump.

"A.T., you done back-sassed a captain about one time too many. That's *once*. Nobody does it twice. But we have a little ritual training exercise to drive a lesson home." The guard looked around. "Speaking of home, you was born around here weren't you?"

"Mile from here, Captain." A.T. was the biggest black man I'd ever seen in my life, built like Houlka only two feet taller. He wasn't wearing leg irons.

"Well, well. Don't think about going there today. A.T., you see that bridge piling there? You get up under that bridge piling and you put your shoulder up agin' the beam, you hear? I mean, put it up against it *good*. No, not that one out here, that one back in there about three feet. That's just about right. Now you two other boys, you knock that pile right out into the creek like it was a baseball, hear?"

There were sounds of hammering that would have killed an elephant, then a big *whoof!* from A.T. and the piling thudding into the dirt. We heard the two men with the hammers run out from under the bridge, and some timbers groan.

"Go back to the truck boys, you done good. Extra beans for the two coming up!" he yelled up to the road. Then we heard him light a cigarette. "A.T., can you hear me?"

We heard a groan.

"I'll take that for yes cap'n," said the guard. "A.T., we gonna go up the road about two mile and have our cornbread and coffee and a cigarette or two. When we get back I want to find one of two things: the taxpayers' nice county bridge here, or a pile of lumber with you under it. Ain't no third choice I can see. You understand, A.T.? You learning about back-sass under there?"

"Yes, Cap'n," he groaned.

"Well, you have a long cogitation on it, A.T. We'll see you in about an hour." The guard walked back up to the road, climbed in and the trucks drove over the bridge. "Oh lordy," we heard A.T. moan as they rolled over him.

Houlka nodded to me, pointed down the bank to the creek. We got in the shallow edge of it, walked up to the bridge. A.T. was bent, straining, eyes closed in pain.

"You from around here?" asked Houlka.

"Please don't make me talk mister," said A.T. He shifted, dirt ran down onto his head from the bridge planks. "Can't you see I got troubles?"

"You know Mr. Hester?"

"Godawmighty, mister. I worked for him for ten years, till I messed up in town and was put on the road gang."

"You reckon you could get some apples from the orchard for me?"

"You better get out from under this bridge is what you better do," said A.T.

"If you was loose, I mean?" asked Houlka.

"I could get as many as you need. But I ain't gonna be loose anytime soon. I got three more years. I can't waste my time with foolishness."

"I mean loose for a little while, today."

"I could get a whole tree worth. I killed a copperhead one time had Mr. Hester in a bad fix."

"Tell you what," said Houlka. "I fix it so you can get away for a few minutes, you get me some apples, and we'll have a little fun with the captain."

"Why you do that?"

"I need the apples. And I got no use for cap'ns."

"I'll be goddamned," said A.T.

* * *

We were in the high grass again an hour later. We'd wiped all our footprints out under the bridge and come back up through the creek to the high grass back of the bar ditch.

The trucks were coming down the road. The first one slowed to a stop in the middle of the bridge. The guard leaned over the driver and honked the horn five or six times.

"A.T.! A.T. Last? You still down there?"

"Yes, Cap'n."

"I'll be damned. Well, last part of this lesson's the hardest. You ready A.T.?"

"Ain't got much choice, Cap'n."

The guards climbed out. He waved the other trucks onto the bridge with the first. The dogs went crazy smelling the convicts.

"Jump, boys," said the guard. "Jump. Don't worry. Truck falls in, you get to spend soft time in the hospital. Jump!"

The chain gang started jumping up and down in the trucks. The dogs were barking and bouncing around in the cages. The bridge shook.

"Cap'n. Cap'n. That'd kill a weak man," yelled A.T.

"Well, well A.T. Good for you. I know your shoulder's pretty tired. Same two boys get the hammers. Three more of you come down to wrestle this piling into place. A.T., you thinking of dropping the bridge on me, you're gonna be disappointed." He waved the trucks off the bridge. "I ain't gonna get under there, you'd just be killing your grab-ass buddies."

"Never considered it, Cap'n."

"Some have, A.T. You done thought about back-sass down there?"

"Powerful lot, Cap'n."

"That was my only object."

The convicts had reached the creek bed. Two of them fell down laughing.

"I come up now, Cap'n?"

"I wouldn't advise it till they get that piling back up, A.T."

The other three convicts fell down, hands on their mouths.

A.T. stepped around the outer piling, looked up at the guard.

"You won't believe it, Cap'n, but that damn thing jumped back up about two minutes after you left, all by itself."

"What? What? What!" yelled the guard, running down the embankment. The five other convicts was rolling on the ground. The guard looked at the ground, the creek, at the piling jammed back up on its foundation, the bare ground empty except for A.T.'s footprints. "What! What!"

The men in the trucks started laughing.

"What! What!"

We crawled back through the grass with our sack of apples and headed home.

XII

Boss Eustis himself drove Houlka into town, and Miz Rio and me was waiting for them there.

We went to the sheriffs' office.

Mr. Manfred, Mr. Maurice and Mr. Jack was setting behind the big long desk at the front looking at us.

Boss Eustis pulled out the papers. "Today is Mr. Lee here's end of term. Far as I'm concerned he's a free man."

All three looked at Houlka, Boss Eustis, the papers.

Then Mr. Manfred pulled out a rubber stamp, Mr. Maurice tore off two of the four forms, Mr. Jack pulled another out of the desk. They passed the rubber stamp back and forth in a flurry of pounding and pen scratching.

When they were through, Houlka had his release, Boss Eustis had a carbon, one was in the file drawer beside the table and the other was in an envelope ready to be mailed to the Governor.

Mr. Manfred, Mr. Maurice and Mr. Jack folded their hands.

We all went back outside.

"Them Euminides Brothers ain't very talkative," said Boss Eustis, "but you gotta admit they're efficient."

Mizzus Luvsey had had Coretta load Houlka down with food and a bundle of clothes, and Miz Rio had her suitcase with her and had on a new green dress.

"Can I give you a ride down to the depot?" asked Boss Eustis.

"We're catching the bus over in Anatolia County."

"Why would you wanta do a damnfool thing like that?"

"I walked into this county under my own power, I'd like to walk out the same way."

"Miss Rio is gonna ruin her new pretty dress," said Boss Eustis.

"I want to make the walk," she said.

"Carrying that damn suitcase?"

"I.O.'s going to help carry stuff to the county line."

"Is that right? Well, well, well."

He reached in his pocket, pulled out a fifty dollar bill, started to hand it to Houlka.

"You've already paid me, Mr. Eustis, two dollars a month and keep. I've still got six dollars of that."

The boss stood there with his jaw open, closed it, put the money back up.

He held out his hand. "Mr. Lee, you're a good 'un."

They shook. "You ever want a real job making real money, you just come on back here, you hear?"

"I won't, but thanks all the same."

Then Boss Eustis climbed in his car. "I.O., you be home by dark. With Mr. Lee gone, you're gonna have to take up all the slack around the place." He roared off back toward home.

We started walking northwest on the highway that led to Acedia. Emzee was waiting where it cut past the railroad track turn, and me and her held hands and took turns carrying the suitcases and bundles.

Nobody said much. When we got to the boat camp cutoff road, we took it, since if you're walking, it's the quickest way to the county line. It crosses the Dardus River just before it enters Lake Yuksino, and the main highway's three or four miles longer.

Should have been more cars and wagons than there was on the road, coming and going. When we got a quarter mile from the river, we saw why. They was cars backed up, and two state highway trucks, and one from Spunt County.

The low water bridge was down in the middle span. The river was still up. People was turning their cars around and going back out to the highway. "We're getting the bridge crews out. This thing'll be closed for a week," said one of the guys who ran the fishing camp.

"Well," said Houlka. "Looks like we get to walk some more."

Then, from back toward the fishing camp I saw the Riding Club coming up from down the lake. I told Houlka. I sure would hate for there to be trouble for him on his first day free.

"Where?" asked Miz Rio. "I'm sure there won't be any trouble. Chuck is over all that now. And maybe we can save some time walking. There's a ford about a half mile up—it's too deep to walk with this much water in the river, but horses can walk it easy. I'll ask Chuck and the others if they can give us a ride across."

Houlka looked at her. "That's up to you," he said. "I'd just as soon walk back to the highway."

"Don't worry," she said. She ran back to the boat camp waving her arms. She stood there in the new green dress talking to Mr. Ness. He looked at her, looked up at Houlka, at the ruined bridge. He nodded.

He and another man rode up to the road while the others went back toward Anomie.

Mr. Ness had a fishing rod sticking from a saddle boot, and he was wearing that vest with all those fish plugs and lures hanging all over it. The pockets bulged with them. It musta had forty dollars worth of them on it, all shining in the sun. He wore an old felt hat.

The other man leaned his fish pole up against a tree.

"They'll take me and Houlka up there and over," said Miz Rio. "It's real muddy. We'll have to say goodbye to you here," she said. She hugged Emzee, then me. She smelled like trees. In her new dress she about the prettiest woman (white woman) I'd ever seen.

"Take care of him," said Houlka to Emzee.

Then he looked at me for a moment. He stepped forward, hugged me real hard, then knuckled my head, nearly knocking my glasses off. "Come to Mt. Oatie as soon as you can get out from under the Boss. Just come to Corinth and turn left, can't miss it. Thank you, I.O."

"I'll do that Mr. Houlka. I sure will."

Then we handed over the food and suitcase, and me and Emzee stood there and watched them walk up the edge of the old trail with the two men riding behind. Last thing I saw was the sun shining off Mr. Ness's vest, then they was all four out of sight upriver.

Emzee and me watched the Spunt County and Anatolia County crews yelling back and forth at each other for awhile, then that got old.

"I sure will miss him," I said. "Let's get on back."

We stood up. I thought I saw an old hat go floating by on the water along with the sticks and leaves, but I didn't think too much about it.

* * *

It was six years later when we got to Mt. Oatie and it wasn't a happy journey.

They'd had five kids in the six years. Miz Rio had committed suicide day before yesterday. Houlka's folks, poor country people, had laid him out on a big brush pile on the side of the mountain.

His twin brother Mr. Al Lee didn't look a thing like him. He was standing there with a torch in his hand while the kids and family was all crying. Miz Rio's new grave was about ten feet away from the brush pile.

Mr. Houlka was laid out in his boots and some new leather coveralls, but something I didn't understand, he was wearing Mr. Ness's old fishing vest with all them plugs on it over that. They'd laid his lion-head skin over his head and draped it back off the brush and crossed his bow and arrows and the big stick on his chest.

His brother handed me the torch. I walked over to the pile, stuck it in in three or four places around the bottom, then lit up the lionskin and the vest. I watched until his beard started to burn, then I turned away.

Mr. Lee's wife held out something to me. It was the old Lion Feed cap he'd had on the day he'd walked from Parchman to Anomie, and the one I'd worn when he was figuring out the lie of Mr. Augie's land. "He wanted you to have it," she said.

I put it on—it probably looked funny over my Sunday suit—and handed my hat to Emzee.

"Them poor children," she said, looking at the kids—they were too young to know what was really going on, the youngest two being carried by relatives; one of them was being wetnursed right that moment.

"We came to do what we can," I said to Mr. Lee.

"Well. We'll just have to figure things out as we go along, same as everybody's always done, I guess," he said.

"Oh!" said Mr. Lee, then breaking down. "It's too sad a story to tell." He was sobbing and his wife held him.

"Then I don't want to know it," I said. Emzee came and stood beside me.

Together, we watched the smoke rise up in a curtain, twist once, and hang high into the skies above Mt. Oatie and Corinth and north Mississippi.

AFTERWORD

I'll tell you where this one came from, one day in 1988.

I was on the toilet in a house I shared with Warren and Caroline Spector and Richard Steinberg (who's also the syndicated columnist Mr. Smarty-Pants). Richard woke up in his room in the back of the house and to lively himself up, put on Talking Heads' "Road to Nowhere."

I immediately had a vision of a guy in bib overalls with a club over his shoulder coming down a country road. I knew that this was Hercules and that this was 1920s Mississippi. The Twelve Labors of Hercules were going to happen *there*.

About this time, Mark V. Zeising (who'd been sending me literary mash-notes for a couple of years) asked me for a novella he could publish, along with the hardcover edition of my solo paperback Ace SF Special novel *Them Bones*, from 1984.

"Sure thing," I said. "It's called *A Dozen Tough Jobs*." Just like that.

I wrote it between March 5, 1988 (when I received the advance) and January 29, 1989, on and off. (The problem was *typing* it up—yes, I still write longhand and type my stuff up on the last Adler manual portable typewriter ever built, out of West Germany.) I sent it off to Andy Watson, Mark's production guy, in two batches, January 30th and 31st.

The signature plates arrived on March 16, 1989, and the book was published April 10th (the limiteds were delayed due to a slipcase error, it says here in my notes).

The history of this gets a little weird after that. First it was up for a couple of awards (the Nebula and World Fantasy Award) and came in second in the annual Locus Poll.

Then, when the paperback edition of my Ursus Books hardcover second collection (*All About Strange Monsters of the Recent Past*, 1987) came out as just *Strange Monsters of the Recent Past* from Ace Books in 1990, they put *A Dozen Tough Jobs* in *there*. Over in Britain, Legends printed the trade paperback edition of my third collection, (*Night of the Cooters*, Ursus/Zeising 1991) it put *A Dozen Tough Jobs* in *there*. So where you read it in paperback depends on *what* collection you read it in *what* country.

There was also some fol-de-rol (having to do with contracts between Zeising and Ace) whereby Zeising was paying Ace 10% of the royalties on *Them Bones*, and Ace was paying Zeising 10% of the royalties on *A Dozen Tough Jobs*. You'd think they just would, have called it a draw. . . .

Years later, a movie enters the picture . . .

* * *

I started getting letters from England (where it opened, first) about two weeks before it came out over here. The tenor of the letters was "Sue the Bastards!"

The "bastards" in this case were Joel and Ethan Coen and the movie was *O Brother, Where Art Thou?*, a version of *The Odyssey* set in 1930s Mississippi. I said I'd wait until I saw it and make up my *own* mind. I had to wait for the video release, since at the time I was living in the unincorporated village of Oso, Washington.

I watched the movie.

"No," I wrote back to my English, and now American, friends who'd joined the mob-cry. "What they did in the movie was their own version of *The Odyssey*, which has of course been lying around for the taking for 2800 years or so. By setting it in 1930s Mississippi, they *used* many of the same things I did—the prison-release stuff; if the hero visits the Underworld, it of course has to be a Ku Klux Klan meeting, etc. It comes out of the materials and the setting. Trust me. And if," I said, "You're ripping off a writer named Howard Waldrop, you *don't* name one of your characters Vernon T. Waldrip, do you?"

The Coens did a fine job on the movie. So have other people. Martin Scorsese, for instance. In his 1985 movie *After Hours*, which is about a guy trying to get across Manhattan one night. There's an Aeolus episode (his *only* money, a $20 bill, blows out a cab window): *anytime* he does *anything* that keeps him from getting home *immediately*, he ends up in deep *kimchee*, wanted for rape, etc. An ice-cream truck driven by Katherine O'Hara is a symbol of the Furies, etc.

As I said, the classics are there for the grabbing, from James Joyce to a 1930s Robert Armstrong movie about a crippled railroad engineer and his beautiful wife, called *Danger Lights* (1932, I think). At one point—if I'm lyin' I'm dyin'—Armstrong passes by a Vulcan stove in the kitchen.

Neither me nor the Coens could have made that up if we tried.

FIN DE CYCLÉ

A. Gentlemen, Start Your Stilts!

There was clanking and singing as the company came back from maneuvers.

Pa-chinka Pa-chinka, a familiar and comforting sound. The first of the two scouts came into view five meters in the air atop the new steam stilts. He storked his way into the battalion area, then paused.

Behind him came the second scout, then the cyclists in columns of three. They rode high-wheeled ordinaries, dusty now from the day's ride. Their officer rode before them on one of the new safety bicycles, dwarfed by those who followed behind.

At the headquarters he stopped, jumped off his cycle.

"Company! . . ." he yelled, and the order was passed back along by NCOs, ". . . company . . . company . . . company! . . ."

"Halt!" Again the order ran back. The cyclists put on their spoon-brakes, reached out and grabbed the handlebars of the man to the side. The high-wheelers stood immobile in place, 210 of them, with the two scouts standing to the fore, steam slowly escaping from the legs of their stilts.

"Company . . ." again the call and echoes, "Dis—" at the command, the leftward soldier placed his left foot on the step halfway down the spine of the bicycle above its small back wheel. The others shifted their weight backwards, still holding to the other man's handlebars.

"—mount!" The left-hand soldier dropped back to the ground,

79

reached through to grab the spine of the ordinary next to him; the rider of that repeated the first man's motions, until all three men were on the ground beside their high-wheels.

At the same time the two scouts pulled the levers beside the knees of their metal stilts. The columns began to telescope down into themselves with a hiss of steam until the men were close enough to the ground to step off and back.

"Company C, 3rd Battalion, 11th Bicycle Infantry, Attention!" said the lieutenant. As he did so, the major appeared on the headquarters' porch. Like the others, he was dressed in the red baggy pants, blue coat and black cap with a white kepi on the back. Unlike them, he wore white gloves, sword, and pistol.

"Another mission well done," he said. "Tomorrow—a training half-holiday, for day after tomorrow, Bastille Day, the ninety-ninth of the Republic—we ride to Paris and then we roll smartly down the Champs-Élysées, to the general appreciation of the civilians and the wonder of the children."

A low groan went through the bicycle infantrymen.

"Ah, I see you are filled with enthusiasm! Remember—you are the finest Army in France—the Bicycle Infantry! A short ride of seventy kilometers holds no terrors for you! A mere ten kilometers within the city. An invigorating seventy kilometers back! Where else can a man get such exercise? And such meals! And be paid besides? Ah, were I a younger man, I should never have become an officer, but joined as a private and spent a life of earnest bodybuilding upon two fine wheels!"

Most of the 11th were conscripts doing their one year of service, so the finer points of his speech were lost on them.

A bugle sounded somewhere off in the fort. "Gentlemen: Retreat."

Two clerks came out of headquarters and went to the flagpole.

From left and right bands struck up the Retreat. All came to attention facing the flagpole, as the few sparse notes echoed through the quadrangles of the garrison.

From the corner of his eye the major saw Private Jarry, already placed on Permanent Latrine Orderly, come from out of the far row of toilets set halfway out toward the drill course. The major could tell Private Jarry was disheveled from this far away—even with such a job one should be neat. His coat was buttoned sideways by the wrong buttons, one pants leg in his boots, one out. His hat was on front-to-back with the kepi tied up above his forehead.

He had his toilet brush in his hand.

The back of the major's neck reddened.

Then the bands struck up "To the Colors"—the company area was filled with the sound of salutes snapping against cap brims.

The clerks brought the tricolor down its lanyard.

Private Jarry saluted the flag with his toilet brush.

The major almost exploded; stood shaking, hand frozen in salute.

The notes went on; the major calmed himself. This man is a loser. He does not belong in the Army; he doesn't deserve the Army! Conscription is a privilege. Nothing I can do to this man will *ever* be enough; you cannot kill a man for being a bad soldier; you can only inconvenience him; make him miserable in his resolve; the result will be the same. You will both go through one year of hell; at the end you will still be a major, and he will become a civilian again, though with a bad discharge. His kind never amount to anything. Calm yourself—he is not worth a stroke—he is not insulting France, he is insulting *you*. And he is beneath your notice.

At the last note the major turned on his heel with a nod to the lieutenant and went back inside, followed by the clerks with the folded tri-colors.

The lieutenant called off odd numbers for cycle-washing detail; evens were put to work cleaning personal equipment and rifles.

Private Jarry turned with military smartness and went back in to his world of strong disinfectant soap and *merde*.

After chow that evening, Private Jarry retired behind the bicycle shop and injected more picric acid beneath the skin of his arms and legs.

In three more months, only five after being drafted, he would be released, with a medical discharge, for "chronic jaundice."

B. Cannons in the Rain

Cadet Marcel Proust walked into the company orderly room. He had been putting together his belongings; today was his last full day in the Artillery. Tomorrow he would leave active duty after a year at Orleans.

"Attention," shouted the corporal clerk as he came in. "At ease," said Marcel, nodding to the enlisted men who copied orders by hand at their desks. He went to the commanding officer's door, knocked. "*Entre*," said a voice and he went in.

"Cadet Proust reporting, *mon capitaine*," said Marcel, saluting.

"Oh, there's really no need to salute in here, Proust," said Captain Dreyfus.

"Perhaps, sir, it will be my last."

"Yes, yes," said Captain Dreyfus. "Tea? Sugar?" The captain indicated the kettle. "Serve yourself." He looked through some papers absent-mindedly. "Sorry to bring you in on your last day—sure we cannot talk you into joining the officers corps? France has need of bright young men like you!—No, I thought not. Cookies? Over there; Madame Dreyfus baked them this morning." Marcel retrieved a couple, while stirring the hot tea in his cup.

"Sit, sit. Please!" Dreyfus indicated the chair. Marcel slouched into it. "You were saying?" he asked.

"Ah! Yes. Inspections coming up, records, all that," said the captain. "You remember, some three months ago, August 19th to be exact, we were moving files from the old headquarters across the two quadrangles to this building? You were staff duty officer that day?"

"I remember the move, *mon capitaine*. That was the day we received the Maxim gun tricycles, also. It was—yes—a day of unseasonable rain."

"Oh? Yes?" said Dreyfus. "That *is* correct. Do you remember, perhaps, the clerks having to take an alternate route here, until we procured canvas to protect the records?"

"They took several. Or am I confusing that with the day we exchanged barracks with the 91st Artillery? That also was rainy. What is the matter?"

"Some records evidently did not make it here. Nothing important, but they must be in the files for the inspection, else we shall get a very black mark indeed."

Marcel thought. Some of the men used the corridors of the instruction rooms carrying files, some went through the repair shops. There were four groups of three clerks to each set of cabinets. . . .

"Which files?"

"Gunnery practice, instruction records. The boxes which used to be—"

"—on top of the second set of wooden files," said Marcel. "I remember them there. I do not remember seeing them *here*. . . . I am at a total loss as to how they could not have made it to the orderly room, *mon capitaine*."

"They were checked off as leaving, in your hand, but evidently, we have never seen them again."

Proust racked his brain. The stables? The instruction corridor; surely they would have been found by now. . . .

"Oh, we'll just have to search and search, get the 91st involved. They're probably in *their* files. This army runs on paperwork—soon clerks will outnumber the generals, eh, Proust?"

Marcel laughed. He drank at his tea—it was lemon tea, pleasant but slightly weak. He dipped one of the cookies—the kind called a madeline—in it and took a bite.

Instantly a chill and an aching familiarity came over him—he saw his Grandmother's house in Balbec, an identical cookie, the same kind of tea, the room cluttered with furniture, the sound of his brother coughing upstairs, the feel of the wrought iron dinner table chair against the back of his bare leg, his father looking out the far kitchen window into the rain, the man putting down the burden, heard his mother hum a tune, a raincoat falling, felt the patter of raindrops on the tool-shed roof, smelled the tea and cookie in a second overpowering rush, saw a scab on the back of his hand from eleven years before. . . .

"*Mon capitaine!*" said Marcel, rocking forward, slapping his hand against his forehead. "Now I remember where the box was left!"

II. Both Hands

Rousseau was painting a tiger.

It was not just any tiger. It was the essence of tiger, the apotheosis of *Felis horribilis*. It looked out from the canvas with yellow-green eyes through which a cold emerald light shone. Its face was beginning to curve into a snarl. Individual quills of whiskers stood out from the black and gold jaws in rippling lines. The edge of the tongue showed around lips with a faint edge of white. A single flower, its stem bent, was the only thing between the face of the tiger and the viewer.

Henri Rousseau put down his brush. He stepped back from the huge canvas. To left and right, birds flew in fright from the charging tiger. The back end of a water buffalo disappeared through the rank jungle at the rear of the canvas. Blobs of gray and tan indicated where the rhinoceros and impala would be painted in later. A huge patch of bamboo was just a swatch of green-gold; a neutral tan stood in for the unstarted blue sky.

A pearl-disk of pure white canvas, with tree limbs silhouetted before it would later be a red-ocher sun.

At the far back edge of the sky, partially eclipsed by a yellow riot of bananas, rose the newly completed Eiffel Tower.

Rousseau wiped his hand against his Rembrandt beret. His eyes above his graying spade beard and mustache moved back and forth, taking in the wet paint.

Pinned to one leg of the easel was a yellowed newspaper clipping he kept there (its duplicate lay in a thick scrapbook at the corner of the room in the clutter away from the north light). He no longer read it; he knew the words by heart. It was from a review of the showing at the *Salon des Refusés* two years before.

"The canvases of Monsieur Rousseau are something to be seen (then again, they're not!). One viewer was so bold to wonder with which hand the artist had painted this scene, and someone else was heard to reply: 'Both, sir! Both hands! And both feet!'"

Rousseau walked back to the painting, gobbed his brush three times across the palette, and made a two-centimeter dot on the face of the tiger.

Now the broken flower seemed to bend from the foul breath of the animal; it swayed in the hot mammal wind.

Rousseau moved on to another section of the painting.

The tiger was done.

III. SUPPER FOR FOUR

Three young men walked quickly through the traffic of Paris on streets aclank with the sound of pedals, sprockets, and chains. They talked excitedly. Quadricycles and tricycles passed, ridden by women, older men, couples having quiet conversations as they pedaled.

High above them all, their heads three meters in the air, came young men bent over their gigantic wheels. They sailed placidly along, each pump of their legs covering six meters of ground, their trailing wheels like afterthoughts. They were aloof and intent; the act of riding was their life.

Occasionally a horse and wagon came by the three young men, awash in a sea of cyclists. A teamster kept pace with a postman on a hens-and-chickens pentacycle for a few meters, then fell behind.

There was a ringing of bells ahead and the traffic parted to each side; pedaling furiously came a police tricycle, a man to the front on the seat ringing the bell, another to the rear standing on the back pedals. Between them an abject-looking individual was strapped to the reclining seat, handcuffed and foot-manacled to the tricycle frame.

The ringing died away behind them, and the three young men turned a corner down toward the Seine. At a certain address they turned in, climbed to the third landing-and-a-half, and knocked loudly on the door.

"Enter Our Royal Chasublerie!" came the answer.

Blinking, the three tumbled into the dark room. The walls were covered with paintings and prints, woodcuts, stuffed weasels and hawks, books, papers, fishing gear and bottles. It was an apartment built from half a landing. Their heads scraped the ceiling. A huge ordinary lay on its side, taking up the whole center of the room.

"Alfred," said one of the young men. "Great news of Pierre and Jean-Paul!"

"They arrived in the Middle Orient on their world tour!" said the second.

"They've been sighted in Gaza and bombed in Gilead!" said the third.

"More bulletins soon!" said the first. "We have brought a bottle of wine to celebrate their joyous voyage."

The meter-and-a-quarter-tall Jarry brushed his butt-length hair back from his face. When they had knocked, he had just finished a bottle of absinthe.

"Then we must furnish a royal feast—that will be four in all for supper?" he asked. "Excuse our royal pardon."

He put on his bicycling cap with an emblem from the far-off League of American Wheelmen. He walked to the mantelpiece, where he took down a glass of water in which he had earlier placed 200 drops of laudanum, and ate the remains of a hashish cookie. Then he picked up his fly rod and fish basket and left, sticking his head back in to say, "Pray give us a few moments."

Two of the students began teasing one of Jarry's chameleons, putting it through an astonishing array of clashing color schemes, and then tossing one of his stuffed owls around like a football while the living one jumped back and forth from one side of its perch to the other, hooting wildly.

The second student watched through the single window.

This is what the student saw:

Jarry went through the traffic of bicycles and wheeled conveyances on the street, disappeared down the steps to the river, rigged up and made four casts—*Bip bap bim bom*—came up with a fish on each one—a tench, a gudgeon, a pickerel, and a trout, threw them in the basket, and walked back across the street, waving as he came.

What Jarry saw:

He was carrying a coffin as he left the dungeon and went into the roadway filled with elephants, and pigs on stilts. A bicycle ridden by a skeleton rose into the sky, the bony cyclist laughing, the sound echoing off itself, getting louder the further away it got.

He took a week getting down the twenty-seven-kilometer abyss of the steps, each step a block of antediluvian marble a hundred meters wide.

Overhead, the sun was alternate bands of green and brown, moving like a newly electric-powered barbershop sign. The words "raspberry jam teapot" whispered themselves over and over somewhere just behind his right ear.

He looked into the thousand-kilometer width of the river of boiling ether. The fumes were staggering—sweet and nausea-producing at the same time. A bird with the head of a Pekingese lapdog flew by the now purple and black orb of the sun.

Jarry pulled out his whip-coach made of pure silver with its lapis-lazuli guides and its skull of a reel. The line was an anchor chain of pure gold. He had a bitch of a time getting the links of chain through the eye of his fly. It was a two-meter-long, four-winged stained glass and pewter dragonfly made by Alphonse Mucha.

Jarry false-cast into the ether, lost sight of his fly in the roiling fumes, saw a geyser of water rise slowly into the golden air. The tug pulled his arm from its socket. He set the hook.

Good! He had hooked a kraken. Arms writhing, parrot beak clacking, it fought for an hour before he regained line and pulled it to the cobbles, smashing it and its ugly eyes and arms beneath his foot. Getting it into the steamer trunk behind him, he cast again.

There were so many geysers exploding into the sky he wasn't sure which one was his. He set the hook anyway and was rewarded with a Breughel monster; human head and frog arms with flippers, it turned into a jug halfway back and ended in a horse. As he fought it he tried to remember which painting it was from; *The Temptation of St. Anthony*, most likely.

The landing accomplished, he cast again just as the planet Saturn, orange and bloated like a pumpkin, its rings whirring and making a noise like a mill-saw, fell and flattened everything from Notre Dame to the Champ de Mars. Luckily, no one was killed.

Another strike. For a second, the river became a river, the fly rod a fly rod, and he pulled in a fish, a pickerel. Only this one had hands, and every time he tried to unhook it, it grabbed the hook and stuck it back in its own jaw, pulling itself toward Jarry with plaintive mewling sounds.

"*Merde!*" he said, taking out his fishing knife and cutting away the hands. More grew back. He cut them away, too, and tossed the fish into the mausoleum behind him.

Better. The ether-river was back. His cast was long. It made no sound as it disappeared. There was the gentlest tug of something taking the dragonfly—Jarry struck like a man possessed.

Something huge, brown and smoking stood up in the ether fumes, bent down and stared at Jarry. It had shoulders and legs. It was the Colossus of Rhodes. A fire burned through vents in the top of its head, the flames shone out the eyes. It could have reached from bank to bank; its first stride would take it to Montmartre.

Alfred gave another huge tug. The chain going from his rod to the lip of the Colossus pulled taut. There was a pause and a groan, the sound of a ship on a reef. With a boom and rattle, the bronze man tottered, tried to regain its balance, then fell, shattering itself on the bridges and quays, the fires turning to steam. The tidal wave engulfed the Île de la Cité and would no doubt wipe out everything all the way to the sea.

Painfully, Jarry gathered up the tons of bronze shards and put them in the wheelless stagecoach and dragged it up the attic stairs to the roadway.

The bicyclists and wolverines seemed unconcerned. Saturn had buried itself below its equator. Its rings still ran, but much more slowly; they would stop by nightfall. Pieces of the bronze Colossus were strewn all over the cityscape.

Jarry looked toward the Walls of Troy before him as he struggled with the sarcophagus. At one portal he saw his friends Hannibal, Hamilcar, and Odoacer waiting for him. If the meal weren't to their satisfaction, they were to kill and eat *him*. He put up his hand in acknowledgement of doom.

The sky was pink and hummed a phrase from Wagner, a bad phrase. The Eiffel Tower swayed to its own music, a gavotte of some kind. Jarry got behind the broken-down asphalt wagon and pushed it toward the drawbridge of despair that was the door of his building.

He hoped he could find the matches and cook supper without burning down the whole fucking city.

IV. Artfully Arranged Scenes

Georges Méliès rose at dawn in Montreuil, bathed, breakfasted, and went out to his home-office. By messenger, last night's accounts from the Théâtre Robert-Houdin would have arrived. He would look over those, take care of correspondence, and then go back to the greenhouse glass building that was his Star Films studio.

At ten, the workmen would arrive. They and Méliès would finish the sets, painting scenery in shades of gray, black, and white, each scene of which bore, at some place, the Star Films trademark to discourage film footage piracy. The mechanics would rig the stage machinery, which was Méliès' forte.

At eleven the actors would appear, usually from the *Folies Bergère*, and Méliès would discuss with them the film to be made, block out the movements, and with them improvise the stage business. Then there would be a jolly lunch, and a free time while Méliès and his technicians prepared the huge camera.

It was fixed on a track perpendicular to the stage, and could be moved from a position, at its nearest point, which would show the actors full-length upon the screen, back into the T-shaped section of the greenhouse to give a view encompassing the entire acting area. Today, the camera was to be moved and then locked down for use twice during the filming.

At two, filming began after the actors were costumed. The film was a retelling of Little Red Riding Hood. The first scene, of the girl's house, was rolled in, accessory wings and flies dropped, and the establishing scene filmed. The actresses playing the girl and her mother were exceptionally fine. Then the next scene, of the forest path, was dropped down; the camera moved back and locked in place.

The scene opened with fairies and forest animals dancing; then the Wolf (a tumbler from the *Folies*) came on in a very hideous costume, and hid behind a painted tree.

The forest creatures try to warn the approaching girl, who walks on the path toward the camera, then leave. She and the Wolf converse. The Wolf leaves.

The second scene requires eleven takes, minor annoyances growing into larger ones as filming progresses. A trap door needed for a later scene comes open at one point while the animals romp, causing a painted stump to fall into it.

The camera is moved once more, and the scenery for the grandmother's house is put in place, the house interior with an open window at the back. The Wolf comes in, chases the grandmother away, in continuous action, goes to the wardrobe, dresses, climbs in bed. Only then is the action stopped.

When filming begins again, with the same camera location, Red Riding Hood enters. The action is filmed continuously from this point to when the Wolf jumps from the bed. Then the Wolf chases the girl around the room, a passing hunter appears at the window, watches the action a second, runs in the door, shoots the Wolf (there is a flash powder explosion and the Wolf-actor drops through the trap door).

The grandmother appears at the window, comes in; she, the hunter, and Red Riding Hood embrace. *Fin.*

Méliès thanks the actors and pays them. The last of the film is unloaded from the camera (for such a bulky object it only holds sixteen meters of film per magazine) and taken to the laboratory building to be developed, then viewed and assembled by Méliès tomorrow morning.

Now 5:00 P.M., Méliès returns to the house, has early supper with his wife and children. Then he reads to them, and at 7:00 P.M. performs for them the magic tricks he is trying out, shows new magic lantern transition-transfigurations to be incorporated into his stage act, gives them a puppet show or some other entertainment. He bids goodnight to his children, then returns to the parlor where he and his wife talk for an hour, perhaps while they talk he sketches her, or doodles scene designs for his films. He tells her amusing stories of the day's filming, perhaps jokes or anecdotes from the *Folies* the actors have told him at lunch.

He accompanies his wife upstairs, undresses her, opens the coverlet, inviting her in. She climbs into bed.

He kisses her sweetly goodnight.

Then he goes downstairs, puts on his hat, and goes to the home of his mistress.

V. WE GROW BORED

The banquet was in honor of Lugné-Poe, the manager of the *Théâtre de l'Oeuvre*.

Jarry, in his red canvas suit and paper shirt with a fish painted on it for a tie, was late. The soup was already being served.

There were three hundred people, all male, attending. Alfred went to his seat; a bowl of soup, swimming with fish eyes, was placed before him. He finished it at once, as he had forgotten to eat for the last two days.

He looked left and right; to the right was a man known vaguely to him as a pederast and a *frotteur*, but whose social station was such that he would rather have swallowed the national tricolor, base, standard, and spike, than to have spoken to Jarry. To the left was a shabby man, with large spade beard and mustache, wearing an artist's beret and workman's clothes. He slowly spooned his soup while deftly putting all the bread and condiments within reach into the pockets of his worn jacket.

Then Jarry looked across the table and found himself staring into the eyes of a journalist for one of the right-wing nationalist Catholic cycling weeklies.

"Are you not Jarry?" asked the man, with narrowed eyes.

"We are," said Alfred. "Unfortunately, our royal personage does not converse with those who have forsaken the One True Means of Transportation."

"Ha. A recidivist!" said the reporter. "It is we who are of the future, while you remain behind in the lost past."

"Our conversation is finished," said Jarry. "You and Monsieur Norpois have lost our true salvation of the Wheel."

"Bi-cycle means two wheels," said the journalist. "When you and your kind realize that true speed, true meaning, and true patriotism depend on equal size and mighty gearing, this degenerate country will become strong once more."

The man to Jarry's left was looking back and forth from one to the other; he had stopped eating, but his left hand brought another roll to his pocket.

"Does not the First Citizen of our Royal Lands and Possessions to the East, the Lord Amida Buddha himself, speak of the Greater and Lesser Wheels?" asked Jarry. "Put *that* in your ghost-benighted, superstition-ridden censer and try to smoke it. Our Royal Patience becomes stretched. We have nothing against those grown weary, old, effete who go to three, four wheels or more; they have given up. Those, however, with equal wheels, riders of crocodiles and spiders, with false mechanical aids, we deem repugnant, unworthy; one would almost say, but would never, ever, that they have given in to . . . *German* ideas."

The conversation at the long table stopped dead. The man to Jarry's left put down his spoon and eased his chair back from the table ever so slightly.

The face of the reporter across the table went through so many color changes that Jarry's chameleon, at the height of mating season, would be shamed. The journalist reached under the table, lifted his heavy-headed cane, pushed it up through the fingers of his right hand with his left, caught it by the tip.

"Prepare yourself for a caning," said the turnip-faced man. No challenge to the field of honor, no further exchange of unpleasantries. He lifted his cane back, pushing back his sleeve.

"Monsieur," said Jarry, turning to the man on his left, "do us the honor of standing us upon our throne, here." He indicated his chair.

The man scooted back, picked up the one-and-a-quarter-meter-high Jarry and stood him on the seat of his chair in a very smooth motion. Then the man grabbed his soup bowl and stood away.

"I will hammer you down much farther before I am done," said the reporter, looking Jarry up and down. People from the banquet committee rushed toward them; Lugné-Poe was yelling who was the asshole who made the seating arrangements?

"By your red suit I take you for an anarchist. Very well, no rules," said the reporter. The cane whistled.

"By our Red Suit you should take us for a man whose Magenta Suit is being cleaned," said Jarry. "This grows tedious. We grow bored." He pulled his Navy Colt Model .41 from his waistband, cocked it and fired a great roaring blank which caught the reporter's pomaded hair on fire. The man went down yelling and rolling while others helpfully poured pitchers of water on him.

The committee members had stopped at the gun's report. Jarry held up his finger to the nearest waiter. "Check, please!" he said.

He left the hall out the front door as the reporter, swearing great oaths of vengeance and destruction, was carried back into the kitchen for butter to be applied to his burns.

Jarry felt a hand on his shoulder, swung his arm up, came around with the Colt out again. It was the man who had stood him on the chair.

"You talk with the accent of Laval," said the man.

"Bred, born, raised, and bored *merdeless* there," said Jarry.

"I, too," said the man.

"We find Laval an excellent place to be *from*, if you get our royal meaning," said Jarry.

"Mr. Henri-Jules Rousseau," said the man.

"Mr. Alfred-Henri Jarry." They shook hands.

"I paint," said Rousseau.

"We set people's hair afire," said Jarry.

"You must look me up; my studio is on the Boulevard du Port-Royal."

"We will be happy if a fellow Lavalese accompanies us immediately to drink, do drugs, visit the brothels, and become fast friends for life."

"Are you kidding?" said Rousseau. "They're getting ready to serve the cabbage back in there. Do look me up, though," he said, heading back in toward the banquet hall and putting his napkin back under his chin.

"We shall," said Jarry, and mounted his high-wheeler and was gone into the darkness.

VI. News from All Over

January 14, 1895 *Le Cycliste Français*

TRAITOR ON THE GENERAL STAFF!
ARREST AND TRIAL OF THE JEW CAPTAIN DREYFUS
DEGRADATION AND STRIPPING OF RANK
DEPORTATION TO GUIANA FOR LIFE

"Secrets vital to the Nation," says a General, "from which our Enemy will profit and France never recover. It is only the new lenient Jew-inspired law which kept the Tribunal from sentencing the human rat to Death!"

VII. LIKE THE SPOKES OF A LUMINOUS WHEEL

The reporter Norpois rode a crocodile velocipede of singular aspect. Its frame was low and elongated. The seat was at the absolute center of the bicycle's length, making it appear as if its rider were disincorporated.

Though extremely modern in that respect, its wheels were anachronisms, heavily spoked and rimmed to the uncaring eye. On a close examination it was revealed the spokes were ironwork, eight to each wheel, and over them were wrought two overlapping semicircles, one of a happy, the other of a sad, aspect of the human face.

In unison, front and back, the wheels first smiled, then frowned at the world around them as they whirled their rider along the newly macadamized roads and streets.

In his sporty cap and black knickers, Norpois seemed almost to lean between the wheels of strife and fortune. Other bicyclists paused to watch him go spoking silently by, with an almost inaudible whisper of iron rim on asphalt. The crocodile frame seemed far too graceful and quiet for the heavy wheels on which it rode.

Norpois worked for *Le Cycliste Français*. His assignments took him to many *arrondissements* and the outlying parts of the city.

He was returning from interviewing a retired general before sunset one evening, when, preparatory to stopping to light his carbide handlebar-lamp, he felt a tickle of heat at his face, then a dull throbbing at his right temple. To his left, the coming sunset seemed preternaturally bright, and he turned his head to look at it.

His next conscious thought was of picking himself and his velocipede up from the side of the road where he had evidently fallen. He noticed he was several dozen meters down the road from where he had turned to look at the sunset. His heart hammered in his chest. The knees of his knickers were dusty, his left hand was scraped, with two small pieces of gravel embedded in the skin, and he had bitten his lip, which was beginning to swell. He absently dug the gravel from his hand. He had no time for small aches and pains. He had to talk to someone.

"Jules," he said to the reporter who shared the three-room apartment with him. As he spoke he filled a large glass with half a bottle of cognac and began sipping at it between his sentences. "I must tell you what life will be like in twenty years."

"You, Robida, and every other frustrated engineer," said Jules, putting down his evening paper.

"Tonight I have had an authentic vision of the next century. It came to me not at first as a visual illusion, a pattern on my eyes, some ecstatic vision. It came to me first through my nose, Jules. An overpowering, oppressive odor. Do you know what the coming years smell like, Jules? They smell of burning flesh. It was the first thing to come to me, and the last to leave. Think of the worst fire you ever covered. Remember the charred bodies, the popped bones? Multiply it by a city, a nation, a hemisphere! It was like that.

"The smell came; then I saw in the reddened clouds a line of ditches, miles, kilometers upon thousands of kilometers of ditches in churned earth, men like troglodytes killing each other as far as the eye could see, smoke everywhere, the sky raining death, the sky filled with aerial machines dropping explosives; detonations coming and going like giant brown trees which sprout, leaf, and die in an instant. Death everywhere, from the air, from guns, shells falling on all beneath them, the aerial machines pausing in their rain of death below only to shoot each other down. Patterns above the ditches, like vines, curling vines covered with thorns—over all a pattern formed on my retina—always the incessant chatter of machinery, screams, fire, death-agonies, men stomping each other in mud and earth. I could see it all, hear it all, above all else, smell it all, Jules, and . . ."

"Yes?"

"Jules, it was the most beautiful thing I have ever experienced." He stared at his roommate.

"There's some cold mutton on the table," said Jules. "And half a bottle of beer." He looked back down at his paper. After a few minutes he looked up. Norpois stood, looking out the window at the last glow of twilight, still smiling.

VIII. ONE ORDINARY DAY, WITH ANARCHISTS

Alfred Jarry sailed along the boulevard, passing people and other cyclists right and left. Two and a half meters up, he bent over his handlebars, his cap at a rakish angle, his hair a black flame behind his head. He was the very essence of speed and grace, no longer a dwarfish man of slight build. A novice rider on a safety bicycle took a spill ahead of him. Jarry used his spoon-brake to stop a few centimeters short of the wide-eyed man who feared broken ribs, death, a mangled vehicle.

Then Jarry jumped up and down on his seat, his feet on the locked pedals, jerking the ordinary in small jumps a meter to the left until his path was clear; then he was gone down the road as if nothing had happened.

Riders who drew even with him dropped back—Jarry had a carbine slung across his back, carried bandoliers of cartridges for it on his chest, had two Colt pistols sticking from the waistband of his pants, the legs of which were tucked into his socks, knicker-fashion. Jarry was fond of saying firearms, openly displayed, were signs of peaceableness and good intentions, and wholly legal. He turned down a side street and did not hear the noise from the Chamber of Deputies.

A man named Vaillant, out of work, with a wife and children, at the end of his tether, had gone to the Chamber carrying with him a huge sandwich made from a whole loaf of bread. He sat quietly watching a debate on taxes, opened the sandwich to reveal a device made of five sticks of the new dynamite, a fuse and blasting cap, covered with one and a half kilos of #4 nails. He lit it in one smooth motion, jumped to the edge of the gallery balcony and tossed it high into the air.

It arced, stopped, and fell directly toward the center of the Chamber. Some heard the commotion, some saw it; Dreyfussards sensed it and ducked.

It exploded six meters in the air.

Three people were killed, forty-seven injured badly, more than seventy less so. Desks were demolished; the speaker's rostrum was turned to wood lace.

Vaillant was grabbed by alert security guards.

The first thing that happened, while people moaned and crawled out from under their splintered desks, was that the eight elected to the Chamber of Deputies on the Anarchist ticket, some of them having to pull nails from their hands and cheeks to do so, stood and began to applaud loudly. "Bravo!" they yelled, "Bravo! Encore!"

IX. THE KID FROM SPAIN

His name was Pablo, and he was a big-nosed, big-eyed Spanish kid who had first come to Paris with his mother two years before at the age of thirteen; now he was back on his own as an art student.

On this trip, the first thing he learned to do was fuck; the second was to learn to paint.

One day a neighbor pointed out to him the figure of Jarry tearing down the street. Pablo thought the tiny man on the huge bicycle, covered with guns and bullets, was the most romantic thing he had ever seen in his life. Pablo immediately went out and bought a pistol, a .22 single-shot, and took to wearing it in his belt.

He was sketching the River one morning when the shadow of a huge wheel fell on the ground beside him. Pablo looked up. It was Jarry, studying the sketch over his shoulder.

Pablo didn't know what to do or say, so he took out his gun and showed it to Jarry.

Jarry looked embarrassed. "We are touched," he said, laying his hand on Pablo's shoulder. "Take one of ours," he said, handing him a .38 Webley. Then he was up on his ordinary and gone.

Pablo did not remember anything until it was getting dark and he was standing on a street, sketchbook in one hand, pistol still held by the barrel in the other. He must have walked the streets all day that way, a seeming madman.

He was outside a brothel. He checked his pockets for money, smiled, and went in.

X. More Beans, Please

"Georges Méliès," said Rousseau, "Alfred Jarry."

"Pleased."

"We are honored."

"Erik Satie," said Méliès, "Henri Rousseau."

"Charmed."

"At last!"

"This is Pablo," said Satie. "Marcel Proust."

"'Lo."

"Delighted."

"Gentlemen," said Rousseau, "Mme. Méliès."

"Dinner is served," she said.

"But of course," said Marcel, "*Everyone* knows evidence was introduced in secret at the first trial, evidence the defense was not allowed to see."

"Ah, but that's the military mind for you!" said Rousseau. "It was the same when I played piccolo for my country between 1864 and 1871. What matters is not the evidence, but that the charge has been brought against you in the first place. It proves you guilty."

"Out of my complete way of thinking," said Satie, taking another helping of calamari in aspic, "having been unfortunate enough to be a civilian all my life. . . ."

"Hear, hear!" they all said.

". . . but is it not true that they asked him to copy the *bordereau*, the list found in the trash at the German Embassy and introduced that at the court-martial, rather than the original outline of our defenses?"

"More beans, please," said Pablo.

"That is one theory," said Marcel. "The list, of course, leaves off halfway down, because Dreyfus realized what was going to happen as they were questioning him back in December of '94."

"That's the trouble," said Rousseau. "There are too many theories, and of course, none of this will be introduced at the Court of Cassation next month. Nothing but the original evidence, and of course, the allegations brought up by Colonel Picquart, whose own trial for insubordination is scheduled month after next."

Méliès sighed. "The problem, of course, is that we shall suffer one trial after another; the generals are all covering ass now. First they convict an innocent man on fabricated evidence. Finding the spying has not stopped with the wrongful imprisonment of Dreyfus, they listen to Colonel Picquart, no friend of anyone, who tells them it's the Alsatian Esterhazy, but Esterhazy's under the protection of someone in the War Ministry, so they send Picquart off to Fort Zinderneuf, hoping he will be killed by the Rifs; when he returns covered with scars and medals, they throw him in jail on trumped-up charges of daring to question the findings of the court-martial. Meanwhile the public outcry becomes so great that the only way things can be kept at *status quo* is to say questioning Dreyfus' guilt is to question France itself. We can all hope, but of course, there can probably be only one verdict of the court of review."

"More turkey, please," said Pablo.

"The problem, of course," said Satie, "is that France needs to be questioned if it breeds such monsters of arrogance and vanity."

"Excuse me, Mr. Satie," said Madame Méliès, speaking for the first time in an hour. "The problem, of course, is that Dreyfus is a Jew."

She had said the thing none of the others had yet said, the thing at base, root, and crown of the Affair.

"And being so," said Jarry, "we are sure, Madame, if through our actions this wronged man is freed, he will be so thankful as to allow Our Royal Person to put him upon the nearest cross, with three nails, for whatever period we deem appropriate."

"Pass the wine, please," said Pablo.

"It is a rough time for us," said Jarry, "what with our play to go into production soon, but we shall give whatever service we can to this project."

"Agreed by all, then!" said Méliès. "Star Films takes the unprecedented step of collaborating with others! I shall set aside an *entire week*, that of Tuesday next, for the production of *The Dreyfus Affair*. Bring your pens, your brushes, your ideas! Mr. Satie, our piano at Théâtre Robert-Houdin is at your disposal for practice and for the *première*; begin your plans now. And so, having decided the fate of France, let us visit the production facilities at the rear of the property, then return to the parlor for cigars and port!"

They sat in comfortable chairs. Satie played a medley of popular songs, those he knew by heart from his days as the relief piano player at the Black Cat; Méliès, who had a very good voice, joined Pablo and Rousseau (who was sorry he had not brought his violin) in a rousing rendition of "The Tired Workman's Song."

Jarry and Proust sat with unlit cigars in their mouths.

"Is it true you studied with Professor Bergson, at the Lycée Henri IV?" asked Marcel. "I was class of '91."

"We are found out," said Alfred. "We were class of all the early 1890s, and consider ourselves his devoted pupil still."

"Is it his views on time, on duration? His idea that character comes in instants of perception and memory? Is it his notion of memory as a flux of points in the mind that keeps you under his spell?" asked Proust.

"He makes us laugh," said Jarry.

They spent the rest of the evening—after meeting and bidding goodnight to the Méliès children, and after Madame Méliès rejoined them—playing charades, doing a quick round of Dreyfus Parcheesi, and viewing pornographic stereopticon cards, of which Georges had a truly wonderful collection.

They said their goodbyes at the front gate of the Montreuil house. Pablo had already gone, having a hot date with anyone at a certain street address, on his kangaroo bicycle; Rousseau walked the two blocks to catch an omnibus; Satie, as was his wont, strode off into the night at a brisk pace whistling an Aristide Bruant tune; he sometimes walked twenty kilometers to buy a piece of sheet music without a second thought.

Marcel's coachman waited. Jarry stood atop the Méliès wall, ready to step onto his ordinary. Georges and Madame had already gone back up the walkway.

Then Marcel made a Proposal to Alfred, which, if acted upon, would take much physical activity and some few hours of their time.

"We are touched by many things lately," said Jarry. "We fear we grow sentimental. Thank you for your kind attention, Our Dear Marcel, but we must visit the theater, later to meet with Pablo to paint scenery, and our Royal Drug Larder runs low. We thank you, though, from the bottom of our heart, graciously."

And he was gone, silently, a blur under each gas lamp he passed.

For some reason, during the ride back to Faubourg Ste.-Germain, Marcel was not depressed as he usually was when turned down. He too, hummed a Bruant song. The coachman joined in.

Very well, very well, thought Proust. We shall give them a Dreyfus they will *never* forget.

XI. THE ENRAGED UMBRELLA

In the park, two days later, Marcel thought he was seeing a runaway carousel.

"Stop!" he yelled to the cabriolet driver. The brake squealed. Marcel leapt out, holding his top hat in his hand. "Wait!" he called back over his shoulder.

There was a medium-sized crowd, laborers, fashionable people out for a stroll, several tricycles and velocipedes parked nearby. Attention was all directed toward an object in the center of the crowd. There was a wagon nearby, with small machines all around it.

What Marcel had at first taken for a merry-go-round was not. It was round, and it did go.

The most notable feature looked like a ten-meter-in-diameter Japanese parasol made of, Marcel guessed, fine wire struts and glued paper. Coming down from the center of this, four meters long, was a central pipe, at its bottom was a base shaped like a plumb bob. Above this base, a seat, pedals and set of levers faced the central column. Above the seat, halfway down the pipe, parallel to the umbrella mechanism, was what appeared to be a weathervane, at the front end of which, instead of an arrow was a spiral, two-bladed airscrew. At its back, where the iron fletching would be, was a half-circle structure, containing within it a round panel made of the same stuff as the parasol. Marcel saw that it was rotatable on two axes, obviously a steering mechanism of some sort.

Three men in coveralls worked at the base; two holding the machine vertical while the third tightened bolts with a wrench, occasionally giving the pedal mechanism a turn, which caused the giant umbrella above to spin slowly.

Obviously the machine was very lightweight—what appeared to be iron must be aluminum or some other alloy, the strutwork must be very fine, possibly piano wire.

The workman yelled. He ran the pedal around with his hand. The paper-wire umbrella moved very fast indeed.

At the call, a man in full morning suit, like Marcel's, came out from behind the wagon. He walked very solemnly to the machine, handed his walking stick to a bystander, and sat down on the seat. He produced two bicyclist's garters from his coat and applied them to the legs of his trousers above his spats and patent-leather shoes.

He moved a couple of levers with his hands and began to pedal, slowly at first, then faster. The moving parasol became a flat disk, then began to strobe, appearing to move backwards. The small airscrew began a lazy revolution.

There was a soft growing purr in the air. Marcel felt gentle wind on his cheek.

The man nodded to the mechanics, who had been holding the machine steady and upright. They let go. The machine stood of its own accord. The grass beneath it waved and shook in a streamered disk of wind.

The man doffed his top hat to the crowd. Then he threw another lever. The machine, with no strengthening of sound or extra effort from its rider, rose three meters into the air.

The crowds gasped and cheered. "*Vive la France!*" they yelled. Marcel, caught up in the moment, had a terrible desire to applaud.

Looking to right and left beneath him, the aeronaut moved a lever slightly. The lazy twirling propeller on the weathervane became a corkscrewing blur. With a very polite nod of his head, the man pedaled a little faster.

Men threw their hats in the air; women waved their four-meter-long scarves at him.

The machine, with a sound like the slow shaking-out of a rug, turned and moved slowly off toward the Boulevard Haussmann, the crowd, and children who had been running in from all directions, following it.

While one watched, the other two mechanics loaded gear into the wagon. Then all three mounted, turned the horses, and started off at a slow roll in the direction of the heart of the city.

Marcel's last glimpse of the flying machine was of it disappearing gracefully down the line of an avenue above the treetops, as if an especially interesting woman, twirling her parasol, had just left a pleasant garden party.

Proust and the cabriolet driver were the only persons left on the field. Marcel climbed back in, nodded. The driver applied the whip to the air.

It was, Marcel would read later, the third heavier-than-air machine to fly that week, the forty-ninth since the first of the year, the one-hundred-twelfth since man had entered what the weeklies referred to as the Age of the Air late year-before-last.

XII. THE PERSISTENCE OF VISION

The sound of hammering and sawing filled the workshop. Rousseau painted stripes on a life-sized tiger puppet. Pablo worked on the silhouette jungle foliage Henri had sketched. Jarry went back and forth between helping them and going to the desk to consult with Proust on the scenario. (Proust had brought in closely written pages, copied in a fine hand, that he had done at home the first two days; after Jarry and Méliès drew circles and arrows all over them, causing Marcel visible anguish, he had taken to bringing in only hastily worded notes. The writers were trying something new—both scenario *and* title cards were to be written by them.)

"Gentlemen," said Satie, from his piano in the corner. "The music for the degradation scene!" His left hand played heavy bass notes, spare, foreboding. His right hit every other note from *La Marseillaise*.

"Marvelous," they said. "Wonderful!"

They went back to their paintpots. The Star Films workmen threw themselves into the spirit wholeheartedly, taking directions from Rousseau or Proust as if they were Méliès himself. They also made suggestions, explaining the mechanisms which would, or could, be used in the filming.

"Fellow collaborators!" said Méliès, entering from the yard. "Gaze on our Dreyfus!" He gestured dramatically.

A thin balding man, dressed in cheap overalls entered, cap in hand. They looked at him, each other, shifted from one foot to another.

"Come, come, geniuses of France!" said Méliès. "You're not using your imaginations!"

He rolled his arm in a magician's flourish. A blue coat appeared in his hands. The man put it on. Better.

"*Avec!*" said Méliès, reaching behind his own back, producing a black army cap, placing it on the man's head. Better still.

"*Voilà!*" he said, placing a mustache on the man's lip.

To Proust, it was the man he had served under seven years before, grown a little older and more tired. A tear came to Marcel's eye; he began to applaud, the others joined in.

The man seemed nervous, did not know what to do with his hands. "Come, come, Mr. Poulvain, get used to applause," said Méliès. "You'll soon have to quit your job at the chicken farm to portray Captain Dreyfus on the international stage!" The man nodded and left the studio.

Marcel sat back down and wrote with redoubled fury.

"Monsieur Méliès?" asked Rousseau.

"Yes?"

"Something puzzles me."

"How can I help?"

"Well, I know nothing about the making of cinematographs, but, as I understand, you take the pictures, from beginning to the end of the scenario, in series, then choose the best ones to use after you have developed them?"

"*Exactement!*" said Georges.

"Well, as I understand (if only Jarry and Proust would quit diddling with the writing), we use the same prison cell both for the early arrest scenes, and for Dreyfus' cell on Devil's Island?"

"Yes?"

"Your foreman explained that we would film the early scenes, break the backdrops, shoot other scenes, and some days or hours later reassemble the prison cell again, with suitable changes. Well, it seems to me, to save time and effort, you should film the early scenes, then change the costume and the makeup on the actor, and add the properties which represent Devil's Island, and put those scenes in their proper place when the scenes are developed. That way, you would be through with both sets, and go on to another."

Méliès looked at him a moment. The old artist was covered with blobs of gray, white, and black paint. "My dear Rousseau; we have never done it that way, since it cannot be done that way in the theater. But . . ."

Rousseau was pensive. "Also, I noticed that great care must be taken in moving the camera, and that right now the camera is to be moved many times in the filming. Why not also photograph all the scenes where the camera is in one place a certain distance from the stage, then all the others at the next, and so on? It seems more efficient that way, to me."

"Well," said Méliès. "That is surely asking too much! But your first suggestion, in the interest of saving time with the scenery. Yes. Yes, we could possibly do that! Thank you . . . as it is going now, the trial may very well be over before we even *begin* filming—if someone doesn't shoot Dreyfus as he sits in court since his return from Devil's Island even *before* that. Perhaps we shall try your idea . . ."

"Just thinking aloud," said Rousseau.

"Monsieur Director?" said Marcel.

"Yes?"

"Something puzzles me."

"Yes?"

"I've seen few Lumièreoscopes—"

"That name!" said Méliès, clamping his hands over his ears.

"Sorry . . . I've seen few films, at any rate. But in each one (and it comes up here in the proposed scenario) that we have Dreyfus sitting in his cell, on one side, the cutaway set of the hut with him therein; then the guard walks up and pounds on the door. Dreyfus gets up, goes to the door, opens it, and the guard walks in and hands him the first letter he is allowed to receive from France."

"A fine scene!" said Méliès.

"Hmmm. Yes. Another thing I have seen in all Lu—in moving pictures is that the actors are always filmed as if you were watching them on stage, their whole bodies from a distance of a few meters away."

"That is the only way it is done, my dear Marcel."

"Perhaps . . . perhaps we could do it another way. We see Dreyfus in his hut, in his chair. We show only his upper body, from waist to head. We could see the ravages of the ordeal upon him, the lines in his face, the circles under his eyes, the gray in his hair."

"But . . ."

"Hear me, please. Then you show a fist, as if it were in your face, pounding on the door. From inside the hut Dreyfus gets up, turns, walks to the door. Then he is handed the letter. We see the letter itself, the words of comfort and despair . . ."

Méliès was looking at him as if there were pinwheels sticking from his eye sockets.

" . . . can you imagine the effects on the viewer?" finished Marcel.

"Oh yes!" said Méliès. "They would scream. Where are their legs? Where are their arms? What is this writing doing in my eye?!!!"

"But think of the impact! The drama?"

"Marcel, we are here to plead for justice, not frighten people away from the theater!"

"Think of it! What better way to show the impact on Dreyfus than by putting the impact on the spectator?"

"My head reels, Proust!"

"Well, just a suggestion. Sleep on it."

"I shall have nightmares," said Méliès.

Pablo continued to paint, eating a sandwich, drinking wine.

"Méliès?" said Jarry.

"(Sigh) Yes?"

"Enlighten us."

"In what manner?"

"Our knowledge of motio-kineto-photograms is small, but one thing is a royal poser to us."

"Continue."

"In our wonderful scene of the nightmares . . . we are led to understand that Monsieur Rousseau's fierce tigers are to be moved by wires, compressed air, and frantic stagehands?"

"Yes."

"Our mind works overtime. The fierce tigers are wonderful, but such movement will be seen, let us say, like fierce tigers moved by wires, air, and stage-labor."

"A necessary convention of stage and cinematograph," said Méliès. "One the spectator accepts."

"But we are not here to have the viewer accept anything but an intolerable injustice to a man."

"True, but pity . . ."

"Méliès," said Jarry. "We understand each click of the camera takes one frame of film. Many of these frames projected at a constant rate leads to the illusion of motion. But each is of itself but a single frame of film."

"The persistence of vision," said Méliès.

"We were thinking. What if we took a single click of the camera, taking one picture of our fierce tigers . . ."

"But what would that accomplish?"

"Ah . . . then, Méliès, our royal personage moves the tiger to a slightly different posture, but the next in some action, but only one frame advanced, and took another click of the camera?"

Méliès looked at him. "Then . . ."

"Then the next and the next and the next and so on! The fierce tiger moves, roars, springs, devours! But each frame part of the movement, each frame a still."

Méliès thought a second. "An actor in the scenes would not be able to move at all. Or he would have to move at the same rate as the tiger. He would have to hold perfectly still (we already do that when stopping the camera to substitute a skeleton for a lady or somesuch) but they would have to do it endlessly. It would take weeks to get any good length of film. Also, the tigers would have to be braced, strutted to support their own weight."

"This is *our* idea, Méliès; we are not technicians."

"I shall take it under advisement."

Méliès' head began to hurt. He had a workman go to the chemist's, and get some of the new Aspirin for him. He took six.

The film took three weeks to photograph. Méliès had to turn out three fairy tales in two days besides to keep his salesmen supplied with footage. Every day they worked, the Court of Cassation met to rehear the Dreyfus case, every day brought new evasions, new half-insinuations; Dreyfus' lawyer was wounded by a gunshot while leaving court. Every day the country was split further and further down the center: There was no middle ground. There was talk of a *coup d'état* by the right.

At last the footage was done.

"I hope," said Méliès to his wife that night, "I hope that after this I shall not hear the name of Dreyfus again, for the rest of my life."

XIII. The Elephant at the Foot of the Bed

Jarry was on stage, talking in a monotone as he had been for five minutes. The crowd, including women, had come to the *Theater of the Work* to see what new horrors Lugné-Poe had in store for them.

Alfred sat at a small folding table, which had been brought onstage, and a chair placed behind it, facing the audience. Jarry talked, as someone said, as a nutcracker would speak. The audience had listened but was growing restless—we have come for a play, not for someone dressed as a bicyclist to drone on about nothing in particular.

The last week had been a long agony for Jarry—working on this play, which he had started in his youth, as a puppet play satirizing a pompous teacher—it had grown to encompass all mankind's foibles, all national and human delusions. Then there had been the work on the Dreyfus film with Pablo and Rousseau and Proust and Méliès—it had been trying and demanding, but it was like pulling teeth, too collaborative, with its own limitations and ideas. Give a man the freedom of the page and boards!

Jarry ran down like a clock. He finished tiredly.

"The play takes place in Poland, which is to say, Nowhere." He picked up his papers while two stagehands took off the table and chair. Jarry left. The lights dimmed. There were three raps on the floor with Lugné-Poe's cane, the curtains opened in the darkness as the lights came up.

The walls were painted as a child might have—representing sky, clouds, stars, the sun, moon, elephants, flowers, a clock with no hands, snow falling on a cheery fireplace.

A round figure stood at one side, his face hidden by a pointed hood on which was painted the slitted eyes and mustache of a caricature bourgeoisie. His costume was a white canvas cassock with an immense stomach on which was painted three concentric circles.

The audience tensed, leaned forward. The figure stepped to the center of the stage, looked around.

"*Merde!*" he said.

The riot could be heard for a kilometer in all directions.

XIV. What He Really Thinks

"Today, France has left the past of Jew-traitors and degeneracy behind.

"Today, she has taken the final step toward greatness, a return to the True Faith, a way out of the German-Jew morass in which she has floundered for a quarter-century.

"With the second conviction of the traitor-spy Dreyfus, she sends a signal to all his rat-like kind that France will no longer tolerate impurities in its body-politic, its armies, its commerce. She has served notice that the Future is written in the French language; Europe, indeed the world, shall one day speak only one tongue, *Française*.

"The verdict of Guilty!—even with its softening of 'With extenuating circumstances'—will end this Affair, once and for all, the only way—short of public execution by the most excruciating means, which, unfortunately the law no longer allows—ah! but True Frenchmen are working to change that!—that it could be ended; with the slow passing of this Jew-traitor to rot in the jungle of Devil's Island—a man who should never have been allowed to don the uniform of this country in the first place.

"Let there be no more talk of injustice! Injustice has already been served by the spectacle of a thoroughly guilty man being given two trials; by a man not worth a sous causing great agitation—surely the work of enemies of the state.

"Let every True Frenchman hold this day sacred until the end of time. Let him turn his eyes eastward at our one Great Enemy, against that day when we shall rise up and gain just vengeance—let him not forget also to look around him, let him not rest until every Christ-murdering Jew, every German-inspired Protestant is driven from the boundaries of this country, or gotten rid of in an equally advantageous way—their property confiscated, their businesses closed, their 'rights'—usurped rights!—nullified.

"If this decision wakens Frenchmen to that threat, then Dreyfus will have, in all his evil machinations, his total acquiescence to our enemy's plans, done one good deed: He will have given us the reason not to rest until every one of his kind is gone from the face of the earth; that in the future the only place Hebrew will be spoken is in Hell."

—Robert Norpois

XV. TRUTH RISES FROM THE WELL

Emile Zola stared at the white sheet of paper with the British watermark.

He dipped his pen in the bottle of Pelikan ink in the well and began to write.

As he wrote, the words became scratchier, more hurried. All his feelings of frustration boiled over in his head and out onto the fine paper. The complete cowardice and stultification of the Army, the anti-Semitism of the rich *and* the poor, the Church; the utter stupidity of the government, the treason of the writers who refused to come to the aid of an innocent man.

It was done sooner than he thought; six pages of his contempt and utter revulsion with the people of the country he loved more than life itself.

He put on his coat and hat and hailed a pedal cabriolet, ordering it to the offices of *L'Aurore*. The streets were more empty than usual, the cafés full. The news of the second trial verdict had driven good people to drink. He was sure there were raucous celebrations in every Church, every fort, and the basement drill-halls of every right-wing organization in the city and the country. This was an artist's quarter—there was no loud talk, no call to action. There would be slow and deliberate drunkenness and oblivion for all against the atrocious verdict.

Zola sat back against the cushion, listening to the clicking pedals of the driver. He wondered if all this would end with the nation, half on one side of some field, half on the other, charging each other in final bloodbath.

He paid the driver, who swerved silently around and headed back the other way. Zola stepped into the Aurora's office, where Clemenceau waited for him behind his desk. Emile handed him the manuscript.

Clemenceau read the first sentence, wrote, "Page One, 360 point RED TYPE headline—*J'ACCUSE*,'" called "Copy boy!", said to the boy, "I shall be back for a proof in three hours," put on his coat, and arm in arm he and Zola went off to the Théâtre Robert-Houdin for the first showing of Star Films' *The Dreyfus Affair*, saying not a word to each other.

XVI. Chamber Pots Shall Light Your Way

Zola and Clemenceau, crying tears of pride and exultation, ran back arm in arm down the Place de l'Opéra, turning into a side street toward the publisher's office.

Halfway down, they began to sing *La Marseillaise*; people who looked out their windows, not knowing the reason, assumed their elation for that of the verdict of the second trial, flung *merde* pots at them from second-story windows. "Anti-Dreyfussard scum!" they yelled, shaking their fists. "Wait till I get my fowling piece!"

Emile and Georges ran into the office, astonishing the editors and reporters there.

They went to Clemenceau's desk, where the page proof of Zola's article waited, with a separate proof of the red headline.

Zola picked up the proof.

"No need of this, my dear Georges?"

"I think not, my friend Emile."

Zola shredded it, throwing the strips on the pressman who was waiting in the office for word from Clemenceau.

"Rip off the front page!" Clemenceau yelled out the door of his office. "We print a review of a moving picture there! Get Veyou out of whatever theater watching whatever piece of stage-pap he's in and hustle him over to the Robert-Houdin for the second showing!"

Emile and Georges looked at each other, remembering.

"The Awful Trip to the Island!"

"The Tigers of the Imagination!"

"First News of Home!" said Emile.

"Star Films," said Clemenceau.

"Méliès," said Zola.

"Dreyfus!" they said in unison.

* * *

Three days later, the President overturned the conviction of the second court, pardoned Dreyfus, and returned him to his full rank and privileges. The Ministry of War was reorganized, and the resignations of eleven generals received.

The President was, of course, shot down like a dog on the way home from a cabinet meeting that night. Three days of mourning were declared.

Dreyfus had been released the same night, and went to the country home of his brother Mathieu; he was now a drawn, shaken man whose hair had turned completely white.

XVII. THREE FAMOUS QUOTES WHICH LED TO DUELS:

1. "The baron writes the kind of music a priest can hum while he is raping a choirboy."

2. "I see you carry the kind of cane which allows you to hit a woman eight or ten times before it breaks."

3. "Monsieur Jarry," said Norpois, "I demand satisfaction for your insults to France during the last three years."

"Captain Dreyfus is proved innocent. We have called attention to nothing that was not the action of madmen and cowards."

"You are a spineless dwarf masturbator with the ideas of a toad!" said Norpois.

"Our posture, stature, and habits are known to every schoolboy in France, Mister Journalist," said Jarry. "We have come through five years of insult, spittle, and outrage. Nothing you say will make Dreyfus guilty or goad our royal person into a gratuitous display of our unerring marksmanship."

Jarry turned to walk away with Pablo.

"Then, Monsieur Jarry, your bicycle . . ." said Norpois.

Jarry stopped. "What of Our Royal Vehicle?"

"Your bicycle eats *merde* sandwiches."

XVIII. THE DOWNHILL BICYCLE RACE

A. Prelims

The anemometer barely moved behind his head. The vane at its top pointed to the south; the windsock swelled and emptied slowly.

Jarry slowly recovered his breath. Below and beyond lay the city of Paris and its environs. The Seine curved like a piece of gray silk below and out to two horizons. It was just after dawn; the sun was a fat red beet to the east.

It was still cool at the weather station atop the Eiffel Tower, 300 meters above the ground.

Jarry leaned against his high-wheeler. He had taken only the least minimum of fortifying substances, and that two hours ago on this, the morning of the duel.

Proust had acted as his second (Jarry would have chosen Pablo—good thing he hadn't, as the young painter had not shown up with the others this morning, perhaps out of fear of seeing Jarry maimed or killed—but Proust had defended himself many times, with a large variety of weapons, on many fields of honor). Second for Norpois was the journalist whose hair Alfred had set afire at the banquet more than a year ago. As the injured party, Jarry had had choice of place and weapons.

The conditions were thus: weapons, any. Place: the Eiffel Tower. Duelists *must* be mounted on their bicycles when using their weapons. Jarry would start at the weather station at the top, Norpois at the base. After Jarry was taken to the third platform, using all three sets of elevators on the way up, and the elevator man—since this was a day of mourning, the tower was closed, and the guards paid to look the other way—returned to the ground, the elevators could not be used, only the stairways. Jarry had still had to climb the spiral steps from the third platform to the weather station, from which he was now recovering.

With such an arrangement, Norpois would, of course, be waiting in ambush for him on the second observation platform by the time Jarry reached it. Such was the nature of duels.

Jarry looked down the long swell of the south leg of the tower—it was gray, smooth, and curved as an elephant's trunk, plunging down and out into the earth. Tiny dots waited there; Norpois, the journalist, Proust, a few others, perhaps by now Pablo. The Tower cast a long shadow out away from the River. The shadow of the Trocadéro almost reached to the base of the Tower in the morning sun. There was already talk of painting the Tower again, for the coming Exposition of 1900 in a year and a half.

Alfred took a deep breath, calmed himself. He was lightly armed, having only a five-shot .32 revolver in his holster and a poniard in a sheath on his hip. He would have felt almost naked except for the excruciatingly heavy but comforting weapon slung across his shoulders.

It was a double-barreled Greener 4-bore Rhino Express which could fire a 130-gram bullet at 1200 meters per second. Jarry had decided that if he *had* to kill Norpois, he might as well wipe him off the face of the earth.

He carried four extra rounds in a bandolier; they weighed more than a kilo in all.

He was confident in his weapons, in himself, in his high-wheeler. He had oiled it the night before, polished it until it shone. After all, it was the insulted party, not him, not Dreyfus.

He sighed, then leaned out and dropped the lead-weighted green handkerchief as the signal he was starting down. He had his ordinary over his shoulder opposite the Greener and had his foot on the first step before he heard the weighted handkerchief ricocheting on its way down off the curved leg of the Tower.

B. The Duel

He was out of breath before he passed the locked apartment which Gustave Eiffel had built for himself during the last phase of construction of the Tower, and which he sometimes used when aerodynamic experiments were being done on the drop-tube which ran down the exact center of the Tower.

Down around the steps he clanged, his bike brushing against the spiral railing. It was good he was not subject to vertigo. He could imagine Norpois' easy stroll to the west leg, where he would be casually walking up the broad stairs to the first level platform with four restaurants, arcades and booths, and its entry to the stilled second set of elevators. (Those between the ground and first level were the normal counterweighted kind; hydraulic ones to the second—American Otis had had to set up a dummy French corporation to win the contract—no one in France had the technology, and the charter forbade foreign manufacture; and tracked ones to the third—passengers had to change halfway up, as no elevator could be made to go from roughly 70° to 90° halfway up its rise.)

Panting mightily, Jarry reached the third platform, less than a third of the way down. Only 590 more steps down to sure and certain ambush. The rifle, cartridges, and high-wheeler were grinding weights on his back. Gritting his teeth, he started down the steep steps with landings every few dozen meters.

His footsteps rang like gongs on the iron treads. He could see the tops of the booths on the second level, the iron framework of the Tower extending all around him like a huge narrow cage.

Norpois would be waiting at one of the corners, ready to fire at either set of stairs. (Of course, he probably already knew which set Jarry was using, oh devious man, or it was possible he was truly evil and was waiting on the first level. It would be just like a right-wing nationalist Catholic safety-bicycle rider to do that.)

Fifteen steps up from the second level, in one smooth motion, Jarry put the ordinary down, mounted it holding immobile the pedals with his feet, swung the Rhino Express off his shoulder, and rode the last crashing steps down, holding back, then pedaling furiously as his giant wheel hit the floor.

He expected shots at any second as he swerved toward a closed souvenir booth: He swung his back wheel up and around behind him holding still, changing direction, the drainpipe barrels of the 4-bore resting on the handlebars.

Over at the corner of another booth the front wheel and handlebar of Norpois' bicycle stuck out.

With one motion Jarry brought the Greener to his cheek. We shall shoot the front end off his bicycle—without that he cannot be mounted and fire; ergo, he cannot duel; therefore, we have won; he is disgraced. *Quod Erat Demonstrandum.*

Jarry fired one barrel—the recoil sent him skidding backwards two meters. The forks of the crocodile went away—Fortune's smiling face wavered through the air like the phases of the Moon. The handlebars stuck in the side of another booth six meters away.

Jarry hung onto his fragile balance, waiting for Norpois to tumble forward or stagger bleeding with bicycle shrapnel from behind the booth.

He heard a noise behind him; at the corner of his eye he saw Norpois standing beside one of the planted trees—he had to have been there all along—with a look of grim satisfaction on his face.

Then the grenade landed directly between the great front and small back wheels of Jarry's bicycle.

C. High Above the City

He never felt the explosion, just a wave of heat and a flash that blinded him momentarily. There was a carnival ride sensation, a loopy feeling in his stomach. Something touched his hand; he grabbed it. Something tugged at his leg. He clenched his toes together.

His vision cleared.

He hung by one hand from the guardrail. He dangled over Paris. His rifle was gone. His clothes smelt of powder and burning hair. He looked down. The weight on his legs was his ordinary, looking the worse for wear. The rim of the huge front wheel had caught on the toe of his cycling shoe. He cupped the toe of the other one through the spokes.

His hand was losing its grip.

He reached down with the other for his pistol. The holster was still there, split up the middle, empty.

Norpois' head appeared above him, looking down, then his gun hand with a large automatic in it, pointing at Jarry's eyes.

"There are rules, Monsieur," said Jarry. He was trying to reach up with the other hand but something seemed to be wrong with it.

"Get with the coming century, dwarf," said Norpois, flipping the pistol into the air, catching it by the barrel. He brought the butt down hard on Jarry's fingers.

The second time the pain was almost too much. Once more and Alfred knew he would let go, fall, be dead.

"One request. Save our noble vehicle," said Jarry, looking into the journalist's eyes. There was a clang off somewhere on the second level.

Norpois' grin became sardonic. "You die. So does your crummy bike."

There was a small pop. A thin line of red, like a streak of paint slung off the end of a brush, stood out from Norpois' nose, went over Jarry's shoulder.

Norpois raised his automatic, then wavered, let go of it. It bounced off Alfred's useless arm, clanged once on the way down.

Norpois, still staring into Jarry's eyes, leaned over the railing and disappeared behind his head. There was silence for a few seconds, then:

Pif-Paf! Quel Bruit!

The sound of the body bouncing off the ironworks went on for longer than seemed possible.

Far away on the second level was the sound of footsteps running downstairs.

Painfully, Jarry got his left arm up next to his right, got the fingers closed, began pulling himself up off the side of the Eiffel Tower, bringing his mangled high-wheeler with him.

D. Code Duello

A small crowd had gathered, besides those concerned. Norpois' second was over by the body, with the police. There would of course be damages to pay for. Jarry carried his ordinary and the Greener, which he had found miraculously lying on the floor of the second level.

Proust came forward to shake Alfred's hand. Jarry gave him the rifle and ordinary, but continued to walk past him. Several others stepped forward, but Jarry continued on, nodding.

He went to Pablo. Pablo had on a long cloak and was eating an egg sandwich. His eyes would not meet Alfred's.

Jarry stepped in front of him. Pablo tried to move away without meeting his gaze. Alfred reached inside the cloak, felt around, ignoring the Webley strapped at Pablo's waist.

He found what he was looking for, pulled it out. It was the single-shot .22. Jarry sniffed the barrel as Pablo tried to turn away, working at his sandwich.

"Asshole," said Jarry, handing it back.

XIX. Fin de Cyclé

The bells were still ringing in the New Century.

Satie had given up composing and had gone back to school to learn music at the age of thirty-eight. Rousseau still exhibited at the *Salon des Refusés*, and was now married for the second time. Proust had locked himself away in a room he'd had lined with cork and was working on a never-ending novel. Méliès was still out at Montreuil, making films about trips to the Moon and the Bureau of Incoherent Geography. Pablo was painting; but so much blue; blue here, blue there, azure, cerulean, Prussian. Dreyfus was now a commandant.

Jarry lived in a shack over the Seine which stood on four supports. He called it Our Suitable Tripod.

There was noise, noise everywhere. There were few bicycles, and all those were safeties. He had not seen another ordinary in months. He looked over where his repaired one stood in the middle of the small room. His owl and one of his crows perched on the handlebars.

The noise was deafening—the sound of bells, of crowds, sharp reports of fireworks. Above all, those of motor-cycles and motor-cars.

He looked back out the window. There was a new sound, a dark flash against the bright moonlit sky. A bat-shape went over, buzzing, trailing laughter and gunshots, the pilot banking over the River. Far up the Seine, the Tower stood, bathed in floodlights, glorying in its blue, red, and white paint for the coming Exposition.

A zeppelin droned overhead, electric lights on the side spelling out the name of a hair pomade. The bat-shaped plane whizzed under it in near-collision.

Someone gunned a motor-cycle beneath his tiny window. Jarry reached back into the room, brought out his fowling piece filled with rock salt and fired a great tongue of flame into the night below. After a scream, the noise of the motor-cycle raced away.

He drank from a glass filled with brandy, ether, and red ink. He took one more look around, buffeted by the noise from all quarters and a motor launch on the River. He said a word to the night before slamming the window and returning to his work on the next Ubu play.

The word was "*merde!*"

AFTERWORD

There are wild men (and women) in literature, and then there are Wild Men.

One of the Wildest was Alfred Jarry (1875-1907). The author of the Ubu plays, precursor to Dada and Surrealism, and so on and so forth. He lived an hallucinated life (the examples I give in the story are mild compared to some real ones, but totally in character). He spoke in the royal "we," tried every drug and drink he could get his hands on, and influenced everyone around him. The books to read are Roger Shattuck's *The Banquet Years* and Bill Griffiths' (the creator of Zippy the Pinhead) *The Man With the Axe.*

Shattuck's book is about the whole Belle Epoque and was the initial inspiration for the story. All across the whole history of French art and literature in the late 1890s stretched The Dreyfus Affair, which split French society apart even more than the Vietnam War did America later. It had *everything*; militarism, injustice, anti-Semitism, and usually, Catholics vs. Prots.

Along with all that: film was just being invented (there are various inputs in the story that would take filmmakers *30 more years* to learn), aviation was just around the comer (earlier here in my story), the bicycle was changing society (the way I referred to this story years before I wrote it was as "the velocipede story"), the Eiffel Tower had just been built for the 1889 Paris Exposition.

This is the world that is, as prefigured in the story, about to blow itself up in 1914.

I wrote this finally in October of 1989—the first half anyway—which I read, with primitive visual aids, at Armadillocon. It says here that I finished it March 8 of 1990 (a really long time but I was busy with other stuff, too). I mailed it off to Arnie Fenner then at Ursus Books in Kansas City, who, with Mark Zeising, was publishing my next collection, *Night of the Cooters*, as a joint venture. (The book had a Don Punchatz cover of Slim Pickens riding an armadillo at a Martian war machine outside the Alamo.) "*Fin de Cyclé*" was the original to the collection.

Gardner Dozois (of *Asimov's*) called me, wanting second serial rights on the story. (There was a six month's exclusivity on it in the collection.) I told him he could, if he published it *after* August of 1991. He sent me a contract, and later money, and it was published Mid-December 1991 as the cover story.

The cover was by Nicholas Jainschigg, showing Jarry on his high-wheeler, leaning against a wall with his elephant gun while Saturn splashes down into the Seine.

Just after I got it, Neal Barrett Jr. called.

"I just got the *Asimov's*," I said. "I got the cover story. Not only is it beautiful," I said, "It's directly from the story."

"You're lying," said Neal, "That *never* happens."

And he hung up on me.

It really happened once. Neal, honest-to-gosh.

This one was up for the Hugo in 1992; like all of them so far, I lost handily.

YOU *COULD* GO HOME AGAIN

The Joint is Jumpin'

They had slipped their moorings at Ichinomaya, Japan, in the early evening of September 15, 1940, amid the euphoric shouts of well-wishers, fresh from the Tokyo Olympics that had just ended.

Wolfe hadn't noticed the crowds. He'd arrived late, a couple of new shirts (specially tailored—the Japanese weren't used to six-foot-six men buying off their racks, and he'd had to get the address of a British men's shop from someone at the American Embassy) in one hand, his old suitcase and bulging, torn briefcase in the other. He'd barely made it; the boarding platform was being unbolted at the bottom as he ran up to it.

He'd been shown to his stateroom; felt a lurch as they got under way. Then he'd folded down the couch that made into an upper and lower berth, and had sprawled across the lower one and had slept for a little more than an hour.

He awoke near sunset. The bell in the dining salon was ringing. He was disoriented. Then memories of the last two weeks had come back to him; the Olympics, the crowds, being a giant once more (as he used to feel in America before the operation and the weight loss) in a world of Lilliputian Japanese.

He put on his robe, found the Gentlemen's washroom for his set of cabins, showered, then shaved, something he'd forgotten to do during the last two days of *bon voyage* parties.

He went back to his stateroom, made up the couch and changed for dinner. Then he laid his things out on the desk while sitting on the folding, backless stool which fit under it. (Wolfe was glad of that: he'd usually

117

had to take the backs off chairs in the old days—his body had been so tall and thick, chairs had seemed like toys that cramped him, making him feel like a golliwog in some circus act.)

He went to the reading and writing room just after dinner (he'd had double portions of everything) and dashed off a postcard or two, which he knew he would forget about if he didn't do it then. He could have put them in the pneumatic tube that took them straight to the mailroom, but decided to take them there himself tomorrow. Instead, he read over the passenger list.

It was the usual kind for a trip going back to Europe and America from the Orient the long way, going west. Wolfe had traveled every possible way in his life: luxury liners, tramp steamers, ferries, airplanes, coal barges, buses, a thousand different trains, cars (after that National Parks thing—six thousand miles in twelve days with two guys that led up to the illness that almost killed him two years ago—he'd sworn never to ride in any automobiles but a taxi cab again), bicycles, hay wagons, once even roller-skating for two miles with some kids when he lived in Brooklyn.

There were the usual two dozen nationalities on the manifest—lots of Americans, Brits, Frenchmen, Indians, Syrians, Swedes, Germans, a Russian or two (probably White), some Brazilians and Argentines, an Italian count, and several Japanese.

In all, there were 320 passengers and a crew of 142 on the first leg of this trip. Several would be leaving in India, more no doubt getting on there, going on to Egypt, then up to Italy, and the rest of the European stops.

As he read the list, a man with sergeant's chevrons on his R.A.F. uniform came into the writing salon, nodded, sat down and began scribbling on a small pad.

Wolfe heard music in the air. They must have cleared away the last of the dishes from the evening meal, the stewards would have pulled back the tables, and the band begun to play in the main salon. He finished the postcard in his (since the operation) much smaller and more controlled loopy scrawl. He looked at his watch. It had been an hour since he'd eaten. Time had a way of getting away from him lately.

He stood, nodded to the R.A.F. man, who gave him back a strange smile. The man was heavily tanned, though blondish; his eyes stood out like bright blue marbles in a brown statue. It reminded him of the face of one of the stone angels that used to stand on the porch of his father's shop in Asheville.

Wolfe checked his own reflection in the corridor mirror—brown suit, buff vest, white shirt. Thinning on top (he turned his head far to the left, smoothed the bit of hair that always stood at right angles over the scar from the brain operation), cheeks now a little sunken in a long wide face (three teeth removed, and seventy-five pounds of lost weight), eyes too big and bright. He pulled on the knot of his black tie with its Harvard Club tie tack, grimaced to make sure there was no food on his teeth, and went back to the main salon.

He eased his way through the few couples who stood talking at the doorway of the ballroom. Art Deco metal palms arched to each side of the opening, forming a heart-shaped portal in a glassine wall.

It was smoky inside. Candles were lit on the tables; waiters went back and forth between the chairs and the dimly-lit bar on the right side. Wolfe made his way toward it, where other men traveling alone, and a few women, stood watching the band.

Bars were always something Wolfe had liked in the old days.

The band—clarinet, banjo, violin, cornet, drums, bass and piano— were on a small raised platform. The unused piano looked dull and grey from the bar area. Probably the light, thought Wolfe. The band was in evening wear. They played "Marie" but, as no one was singing, it sounded thin. A spot for dancing had been cleared; no one was taking advantage of that, either.

"Bourbon and Coca-Cola," said Wolfe to the barman. That was one thing about a trip like this. Everyone was first-class: there were no passenger divisions, no one-deck-for-you-Mr.-Average-Guy, the other for the Hoity-Toity. That was one reason Wolfe had chosen to travel this way.

He got his drink, turned, and leaned against the aluminum bar with his right elbow. He saw, with some discomfort, two women looking at him, talking back and forth. He knew, without a second glance, that they were asking each other whether that could be *him*; no, he's tall but too thin-looking, and much older than his photos. (The one on the jacket of his newest book had been taken two years ago, before the operation. Not that he didn't look bad enough then, he just looked differently, and worse, now.) Wolfe focused his attention toward the front of the salon. He'd had plenty of shipboard flings in his time. (The great love of his life, so they told him in those fuzzy first days at Johns Hopkins, had started on the *Berengaria* in 1926. To him it was only a skewed memory. When he had seen the woman, Aline, for the first time during his recovery, he had been puzzled. This woman— twenty years older than me, hard of hearing, hair going grey—was the love of my life?) But in the last two years, some memories had come back. (Wolfe sometimes viewed himself as standing on the far northern shore of

Canada, looking out to sea, and occasionally an iceberg, heavy with remembrance and emotion, would drift toward him from the North Pole of Time, crash into him, immersing him in a flood of scents, thoughts, visions, from a past usually closed off to him as if he were locked in a vault with no key.) He recalled some of the affair with Aline; the memories were fragmentary. He remembered fights as often as lovemaking, jealousy of her theater friends as well as the quiet afternoons in Paris hotels, an attempt of hers at what he first thought of as suicide, which wasn't.

Now, he was on his way to Germany to see another woman.

As he turned toward the band, Wolfe saw a huge light-skinned black man with a pencil-thin mustache sitting at a table near the front, deep in conversation with two other Negroes.

It was then that Wolfe realized how unobservant he had become. The last thing he would have thought was that the T.W. Waller on the passenger list was Fats.

Wolfe had seen him many times before. He dimly remembered trips to Harlem in the late twenties when he had still been an English instructor at Washington Square College. They'd gone to Connie's Club, where Waller was playing to packed houses. He'd had quite a following among the jazz-mad students. One night Wolfe had been surprised to hear Waller on the radio, singing some novelty tune. Then suddenly, he had been everywhere. While Wolfe had been struggling to be a playwright, Waller had three or four revues or musicals running in the late twenties—and unlike other songwriters and composers, Fats had been right there every night playing the piano for the shows.

Wolfe had seen both movies Waller had made in the thirties. He lit another cigarette, signaled for another drink. The band finished its number, "Nagasaki," a corny tribute to the land they'd just left.

The bandleader—surprisingly, the banjo player—stepped up to the star-webbed microphone (there were loudspeaker boxes at the rear of the salon so people there could hear as well as those up front) and said, "Thank you, thank you," to polite applause. "We're the Band in the Stars, and we'll be with you for the whole voyage. But enough about us—" the drummer hit his tom-tom *thunp!* "Tonight, we're honored—we really are—gee whiz! —to have a special appearance, a special guest, one of your fellow passengers—I think he'll be with us to France—" There was a yell from the audience, "England!" "—England, but he says he needs some sleep, so, tonight only, he'll be sitting in—er, ladies and gentlemen, the Band in the Stars, and the *Ticonderoga*, are proud—well, here he is, the one, the only, Mr. Fats Waller!"

Some people were taken aback—there were gasps and oohs—as the huge man stood up at his table. Waller was dressed in a black pin-striped double-breasted suit with a black vest, white shirt and a flamingo-pink tie, wide as a normal person's leg. He waved to the crowd. He would have seemed incredibly round, except that he was so tall, he seemed only plump. He walked to the grey piano—like all huge men he had a smooth grace about him, not as if he were moving in slow motion, just that thin people moved too fast; his motions reminded Wolfe of Oliver Hardy's.

"Thank you, thank you," he said, pulling out the piano bench. "I never played on an al-loomin-eum piano before. Let's see—" he ran his fingers over the keys, "my, my, that's sweet. I see it's tuned in the key of R. Well—" *Blang!* he hit the keys. "Here I am, one night only, 'cause gee I'm tired." The man at the table with him brought a full gin bottle and a glass and set them on the piano. "Oh, suddenly I ain't so tired any more!" He took a drink straight from the bottle. "Wow! That's the stuff. Now I feel like I can play till we hit an iceberg!"

The passengers laughed.

"All right. Here I am, Mrs. Waller's Harmful Little Armful, Mr. Fats himself. Let's go. One two three—" he pointed at the band, who had no idea what was coming, so waited. He broke into a medium stride measure, his left hand covering ten keys between notes, his right way down at the other end, and he began "The Joint is Jumpin'," and the Band in the Stars jumped in right behind him.

As he sang, Fats noticed a great big galoot watching him from the bar with his eyes all bugged out.

The audience roared when they finished the song. Fats drank more gin and leaned back, making tiddling noises with his fingers on the keys.

"Ain't this band sharp?" he asked the audience. "Dressed like that, you'd think the only song they knew was 'Penguins on Parade,' wouldn't you? And me as the walrus. Haha."

Then he struck up "I Can't Give You Anything But Love," and the bandleader and he did *sotto voice* repartee over it, making fun of the lyrics, themselves, the passengers. It was totally unrehearsed, so it worked.

"Like working with Charlie McCarthy," said Fats, when it was over. "'Cept he always brings that guy Bergen along. I don't know why he don't split up the act. We know who's got all the talent in that team, don't we?

"I worked with everybody," said Fats. "'Bout the only two I ain't performed with is Donald Duck and Goofy, and I hear tell Disney's trying to book me with them three weeks at the Apollo next year!"

There was laughter and more applause.

"Next thing you know, ol' Fats will be selling U.S. shares and singing on the floor of the Stock Exchange with Ferdinand the Bull! That'd be a tough act to follow, wouldn't it?"

He took a drink. "Well, we gonna hafta do it sooner or later before drunks start yelling for it, so we might as well give Hoagy his two cents now."

Then they did "Stardust" and the cornet man took a surprisingly good solo, for someone in a ship's band.

"Most beautiful music *this* side of the Monongahela!" said Waller as they ended the song. "I can say that without fear of oblooquy."

They went into a medley of five of Fats' songs, the band shifting tempo and lyrics with him as soon as they heard a few notes; these guys, they shouldn't just be playing here.

When Waller looked up again, wiping the sweat from his mustache, reaching for the bottle, he noticed that the big guy at the bar was gone.

Wolfe crossed the promenade deck and turned starboard. He went out to the observation area, with its open louvered windows and its delicate decorated aluminum railings.

They were steering west-southwest, so there was still the last vestige of a late summer sunset out the windows. A slight breeze blew in, but much less than Wolfe had expected. He barely felt it in his thinning hair. There was also a hum, like the wind, barely noticeable.

The western sky, over the South China Sea, looked like a peeled pink Crayola left forgotten to melt against a dark blue windowpane. There were stars out up from the horizon. Wolfe looked down at the sea. It was like a flat sheet of dark leaded glass full of the dot and wink of stars, merging with pale red where it met the afterglow.

He heard people passing by toward the salon behind him and the subdued music. Part of him wanted to stay here, watching full night come on, the farthest from home he'd ever traveled. The other half wanted to drink in every note from the piano. There would always be beautiful evenings somewhere in the world; there might not always be a Fats Waller.

With a last puff, he took his cigarette from between his lips, gripped it between thumb and back-curled middle finger, and with a former paperboy's sure aim, flipped it far out away from the window railings.

He watched the orange dot blinking in a long arc; leaning closer to the window he saw it part of its way down the three thousand feet where it would land in the dark, star-pinned sea.

Looking up and out, he could see one of the ten Maybach twenty-cylinder engines that pushed the U.S.I.A.S. *Ticonderoga* through the cloudless sky. He imagined, as he looked at the propellers, that the hum in the air was louder, but it wasn't.

He turned and headed back down the promenade.

Ain't Misbehavin'

He finished "Honeysuckle Rose," the fingers of his left hand splayed far across the keys between each bass note. The right hand came down in another triplet, and the salon was still. Then the roar was deafening.

"My, my, yes," he said. He smiled at the crowd. "You better stay awake, because as soon as Fats is through, he's gonna be asleep for the entire rest of this trip. Them Japanese people done partied me for a week.

"What'll we do next, boys?" he asked the band. "Maybe we could do something I played with the Little Chocolate Dandies? Or McKenzie's Mound City Blue Blowers? How 'bout the 'West India Blues' I did with the Jamaica Jazzers?"

"We don't know that!" the band yelled back.

"Well, I could do something I learned from James P. Johnson. That's how I learned piano, you know, listening to his piano rolls. I used to turn the drum one note at a time, put my hand on the keys when they went down. Seemed like the only way to learn music to me." He grinned at the passengers. "'Course I was only about nine years old then.

"I went in and auditioned for Willie 'The Lion' Smith—he needed a piano player for when he was taking a break. I was 'bout twelve years old, corner of Lexington and 114th, went down there and played for him. He pretended he wasn't even listening. I got through and says, 'What you think, Mr. Lion?' and he says, 'No pissant gonna play intermission piano for me in *shorts*' and he marched me next door and bought me my first pair of long pants.

"Well, enough of this frothy badinage, let's get busy, boys! Hang on!"

He made a run, the bandleader started snapping along with his fingers, pulled his banjo up, and the band joined in on "(You're Just a) Square from Delaware."

Fats looked up as they played. "Uh. You know that, huh?" he said over the music. "Looka that man with the horn. Blow the end off it, Lips! Oh. Here comes that hard part again. There it comes. Think I got it. Yes, yes! Let's see if we can't get the last eight bars in six!" The music got faster, lost nothing. "O-Kay!" he said, as they slammed to a finish. During the clapping, Fats reached out and shook the bandleader's hand, nodded to the others.

Then they did "Abercrombie had a Zombie," something Waller had recorded a few months before, which had become, for some obscure reason, a dance-band standard the world over.

"You boys take a little break if you want to," said Fats. "I'll doodle around on this tin box till you get back, and then we'll see if we can't blow all the rubber off this balloon."

The band rushed for the bar.

Fats straightened himself in his suit.

"You probably wonderin' what I was doing in Japan," he said to the audience. "I woke up yesterday wonderin' the same thing. No, no, don't get me wrong. I been good lately."

Then he did an instrumental version of "Ain't Misbehavin'."

He stood up when he was through. "Y'all mind if Fats takes off his coat?" They yelled approval.

Two huge wet circles plastered his shirt under the arms. "Y'all tell me the second I begin to perspire, will you?" he asked.

He leaned forward, his hands only a fraction of an inch above the keys, and he played a Bach *partita*.

Until the Real Thing Comes Along

It had been the Olympics that brought him back, in many ways.

In those strange first days in Johns Hopkins, when he was meeting his mother and sisters and friends, for the second time, snatches of his former self would come to him unbidden, but isolated, with no indication which memory came first, or how far apart they were.

Then, like Faulkner's Benjy, things had quit spinning around and settled into a smoothness. The chronology sorted itself. First, he must have done this. This before that, this memory goes somewhere between *here* and *there*.

Still, there had been no linchpin holding it together, no relation to the "me" he was.

It was in November, two months after the operation. He was still in Baltimore, in a hotel-apartment, looked after by his mother and sister.

"Well, Thomas," said his sister. "I'll be expecting you'll be wanting to see that film about the Olympic Games, especially since it's by that German woman."

"Whatever do you mean?" he'd asked from the couch.

"Well, you were *there*. It's all you talked about or wrote home about for six months."

"That's right," said his mother from the kitchen, where she was shelling butterbeans she'd somehow found for supper in November.

He had a dim memory of crowds, moving colors, events of some kind. What he remembered mostly was a pretty woman's face. Who was she?

His mother wiped her hands on her apron, stood in the doorway.

"Don't tell me you forgot that, too? You were over there for two solid months, both sides of the Games. Then you upped over to Austria and back to Holland, and who-knows-where-else you didn't tell us about."

"There are so many things, Mama. So many trips. They all run together. If you hadn't shown me the postcards, I wouldn't even have known I'd ever been in Seattle."

"Well, you went everywhere, and you was at the Olympics two years ago, and now there's a film about it," said his sister.

"I can't believe I did that and can't remember it," said Tom.

So they'd gone to the movie later that week. It was almost a mistake from the start. It was four hours long, and the first part of it was full of naked people throwing things around and running with torches with their willies out. Tom's sister covered her eyes when there were naked people up there. His mother kidded her about it.

Then the film switched to the '36 Olympics: the opening parade, the torch, events with shooting and horses, then the track and field. Lots of it was in slow motion, or from above or under the ground. Tom knew it was a great film, but he still had no sense of being there. Maybe he'd gone to Europe on a two-month bender and made up all the postcards?

Suddenly there was a Negro on the screen, getting down into starting blocks. Then a long shot of the race ready to begin. The camera lingered over the German entrant. You would think they would show more of the Negro man. Tom was irritated. The cameras panned over to the Chancellor's box. There was a shot of a fat man and a small man with a mustache. Get the camera off them, thought Tom, and back on the track. (It's a film, he reminded himself. These things are not happening right *now*.) Then the gun went off, and in slow-and-normal motion, the Negro man flew down the cinders, getting to the tape three steps ahead of the German and the rest.

There was a shot of the small man with the mustache turning his head sharply to the left, as did the others in the box, toward some commotion up and behind them.

Of course, thought Tom, that's when I yelled so loud for Jesse Owens from the American ambassador's box where I was sitting with Martha Dodd, that even Hitler was annoyed. Göring too.

"Why, Tom," asked his mother, "what's the matter?"

He was sitting still, tears running down his cheeks.

"I remember now, Mama," he said. "I *was* there."

And the pretty woman's name had been Thea Voelker.

"Mr. Wolfe?" asked a young male voice at his side.

"Yes?"

"I'm the social director on this trip," said the thin young man with black hair in a blue suit, holding out his hand. "Call me Jerry."

They shook hands.

"I'm not very sociable right now," said Wolfe. "What can I do for you?"

"Well, I have to ask you the usual questions and all. Like what do you like to do on trips like these?"

"Sleep and write. And drink."

"Hmmm. Mostly what I've got here is people who play checkers, chess, bridge, table tennis, the kinds of things young matrons—there are a few on this trip—like to do. There's skeet shooting tomorrow morning on the port side. Of course, you're welcome to come down to the activity room anytime—I see you're with us to Germany—to look over the stuff for the costume ball two nights from now. Lots of masks and things—I doubt we have any whole costumes themselves that will fit, but . . . we just might rig up something to make you very *mysterioso* . . ."

"Who's *not* going to know it's me?" asked Wolfe, quite seriously, then smiled.

The Jerry guy laughed. "I see what you mean. You're even bigger than your pictures make you look. And I saw the one of you with a German policeman under each arm."

"Really?" asked Wolfe. "Did that make the American papers?"

"I don't know. I was the games instructor on the *Bremerhaven* then. '37. When the chance came last year to sign on the *Ti*, I took it. Some way to travel, huh?"

Wolfe looked out over the dark ocean, heard the hum of the ten engines pushing them gently through the night sky at ninety miles per hour.

"It really is," he said. "My first time on an airship."

"We have tours tomorrow, eleven A.M. and three P.M. ship's time."

"I could maybe make the late one." Wolfe nodded toward the ballroom. "I'm going to watch him play till one of us drops."

"He's pretty good, isn't he? I'm not a boogie-woogie man myself," said Jerry, "but he sure beats . . ." he looked around conspiratorially, ". . . any of those guys in the ship's band."

Wolfe was looking once more at the darkened horizon aft.

"She's a great ship," he said.

"*He's* a great ship. Him," said Jerry. "That's left over from the German zeps. They called them that, for obvious reasons. Half the crew on the *Ti* and his brother ships are old U.S. Navy men. Took them a long time to get used to it; Navy still calls their airships *her*. Most of the new U.S.I. Airship Service people are trained in Germany, so it comes naturally to them. Still, there's just about a fight about it every week. President Scott, or the Congress Committee or somebody's going to have to make an official declaration, once and for all, is it *him* or *her*?"

"I didn't know that," said Wolfe.

Jerry looked around. "I didn't either, till I signed on the *Ti*. You know, Mr. Wolfe, there's one thing—"

Wolfe thought he knew what was coming. He'd heard it a thousand times since the operation, so it must have happened a million before then. There's one thing I always wanted to be—a writer, only I don't use words so good. But I've got this idea worth a million bucks. I'll tell it to you, and you write it up and we'll split the money fifty-fifty, right down the middle. Wolfe steeled himself, ready to make the usual polite denial, explain how with him, anyway, the ideas had to come from within, be driven by his experiences, his need to tell the story.

"—I bet you get tired of," said Jerry, "is people always coming up to you telling you they got an idea that'll make a million bucks, if only you'll write it up, they'll split the money with you."

Wolfe laughed nervously. Was this some new kind of preamble?

"Does that happen a lot, or am I just imagining it?" asked the social director.

"Way too much," said Wolfe, looking down at the official name tag on his blue suit coat. "Aren't you one of those people who wants to be a writer?"

"Me? Heck no!" said Jerry. "Give up a life of adventure and dames, flying all over the world, free drinks in the only official arm of the U.S. where it's legal to serve 'em? Give that up to sit in some crummy dump in the Bronx, collecting the Social, staring at a wall while the rats gnaw your feet, trying to think of something to write for *Swell Stories*? No thanks!"

Wolfe laughed again.

"Not that that's what *you* do, Mr. Wolfe," said Jerry. "I thought *O, Lost* was a really great first novel."

"Why, thank you."

"There's anything I can do for you on this trip, just let me know. Office is always open—I'm not there, just leave a message on the corkboard. It's really very nice to meet you." They shook hands again, and he was gone back toward the salon.

After watching the darkness and the stars a little longer, Wolfe went back that way too.

It's a Sin to Tell a Lie

Fats took another swallow of gin.

He saw that the big guy who'd been watching from the bar was gone again. He seemed familiar somehow. But Fats had looked at a million faces in his time.

He ran his fingers over the keys, went *plink-plonk* at the end.

"I don't know about you," he said to the band, "but I ain't making this trip for my health, no, no." He made another rude noise with the keyboard. "I'm on my way to England, Ole Blighty, right now. Gonna make some records over there for Victorola. Only they don't call it that. Over there, it's His Master's Voice. From Nipper. I knew Nipper when he was just a pup. Why, I knew Nipper when he was so little he was listenin' to two tin cans with a string tied between 'em, instead of a phonograph. That's the truth!

"Gonna record with that Frenchman Grapply. Grape-Elly. I seen him bend a fiddle inside out once, had to play the music backwards so it would come out right. He can play better with his feet than Yehudi can with his teeth. I saw them do it myself. I'm also gonna record some music in a cathedral."

He began a slow melodious tinkling on the piano that wouldn't quite become a recognizable tune.

"Then I'll be coming back to good ol' New York City, U. S. of A. Incorporated. Me and my men will be closing out the New York World's Fair this year—well, we'll be closing it down completely, 'cause when we're done, it's through with."

The drummer hit his snare.

"Thank you, thank you. Any of you people out there come to N.Y.C., come on out and give us a listen. We'll be playing at the big Bandhouse there, for your dancing pleasure. To find us, just follow the fire trucks. I might even play the Mighty Wurlitzer organ for the Aquacade. While you're there, you might want to take in the fair, too."

Another drum roll.

"You can watch me on the new tele-vision there. Hey, you hear they got a robot-man there, the Electro-Man or something like that? He can talk. He can even play little tunes and stuff. I can hear his *repertoire* now: 'Junkyard Blues,' 'Will You Love Me When I'm Oiled and Grey?,' and 'Nobody Loves You When You're Rusty and Brown.' Maybe I can get him to sit in with the band.

"We could play duets. Can't be any worse than some of the stuff me and Andreamentano Razafinkierfo—or, as he's better known to the American Society of Composers, Artists and Performers—Andy Razaf and me used to do. He used to say his playing was too mechanical, so working with Electro-Man'll be just like playing with Andy!"

Another snare drum shot, ending in a cow bell.

"Thank you. Okay, let's play something. Try to follow along, boys," he said to the Band in the Stars. "It gets too much for you, just lay down and take off your coats."

He counted off slow, then went into an easy melody with his right hand. After a couple of bars the band joined in, one and two at the time. "That's right, that's it," said Fats.

He sang "It's a Sin to Tell a Lie."

As he did so, he watched the big lunk come back in, knock back a drink, order another, pick it up and leave.

Either he don't like me, thought Fats, or the live experience of Victor's Cheerful Little Earful is too much for him.

Hold Tight (Want Some Seafood Mama)

The song, which had once had a powerful effect on Wolfe, now had another.

Intellectually, he remembered what it meant in the old days. Now, it no longer connected emotionally with anything in him, and that realization made him take his drink out of the ballroom, through the companionway, where the promenade, cabin and lower deck corridors met. His first impulse had been to go back to the reading and writing salon, but instead he went down the spiral aluminum staircase to the lower deck lounge area.

Most of the lower deck was the remainder of the cabins, two more observation areas, and farther back, crew's quarters and mess, and the freight and baggage compartments. He would see it all tomorrow; he knew this from the brochure they'd given him when he'd booked on the flight.

It was much quieter here. A few people sat about on the light but comfortably padded chairs and the settees. Most of the passengers were smoking, something impossible on the old dirigibles, before the Panhandle find of helium in Texas, and the other one in South Africa.

Two men sat at one of the only two cocktail tables—the other was occupied by a *pukka-sahib* type, and Wolfe could do without that right now.

One of the men at the table looked up—it was the R.A.F. sergeant he had seen writing earlier, the one with the sandy hair and blue eyes. Now he was in civilian clothing, khaki shirt, light wool pants—no vest, coat or tie. The other was a tall thin man with a large nose, receding hairline, dressed in a grey suit and vest, with a black tie.

The taller man said something to the other, then motioned Wolfe over. He carried his drink over to them.

"H—hello," said Wolfe, sticking out his hand.

"Join us, please?" asked the taller man. "My name's Norway. this is Sergeant Ross."

"Surely," said Wolfe. "Pleased to meet you, Mr. Norway. Sergeant. I'm an American."

"Who doesn't know that, Mr. Wolfe?" asked the sergeant. "How's the music up there?"

"It's great!" said Wolfe, loosening his tie. "Too good. I had to get away for a few minutes, get some air. I—I've seen him before, long time ago. He was great then, too." He came to a stop, aware that he was sounding like a child who'd just seen his first puppet show.

"Perhaps we'll go listen soon, eh Ross?" asked Norway. The sergeant nodded.

"I suppose I'll just have to put on a coat," he said to Norway; then to Wolfe, "Do relax."

"We were just talking about your country, about the Technocrats. Do you have *any* idea what's next?" asked Norway.

Wolfe stammered. "I'm the last person to ask about anything political. For the first four years of the Depression, all I did was write. I came up for a breather around 1935, then got back to writing and traveling around for another three years. Then I got pretty sick, I'm just now getting on my feet again. So, sorry, I can't help you very much that way."

"Well," said Norway, "I don't think your case is much different than most Americans."

Wolfe laughed. "It did seem like it happened overnight, I guess. Sort of like the Magna Carta with you people."

Sergeant Ross laughed. "I suppose so. But that wasn't in a democracy, with a constitution."

"People will do lots of screwy things when they're hungry," said Wolfe. "I try to steer clear of politics with other Americans. Saves a lot of wear and tear on my fists. Like I said, I haven't paid much attention to politics since the '32 elections."

"That was—Long and Scott?—wasn't it? I was over there while that was going on," said Norway. "Seemed like a lot of consternation after—what's his name, governor, poliomyelitus . . . Roosevelt—choked on that ham sandwich—"

"It was a chicken bone, I think," said Wolfe.

"—chicken bone just before the convention."

"Whoever was nominated was going to beat Hoover," said Wolfe. "So it was Long, and he chose Scott for veep, not because he was a Technocrat, but because he was a Yankee."

"Then Scott brought in all his Technocratic colleagues. I met most of them back in '33," said Norway. "I never thought it had a chance of working."

"Well, I don't think it would have, if Long hadn't been killed, and Scott took over. And the people hadn't voted for the Twentieth and Twenty-First Amendments."

"Well, you certainly needed the first of those. You got back your 3.2 beer."

"All of America was drunk on 3.2 beer that day," said Wolfe. "That's one thing I *do* remember. You had to ask *not* to have it if you went to a restaurant. Scott himself said, 'a little beer is good for America.'"

"He also said, 'a sober America is a working America,'" said Norway.

"Spoken like a true engineer," said Ross.

The tall man looked at him.

Wolfe saw there was an intensity about Ross that he could almost feel, like this conversation was the most important thing in the world. He'd met people like that before, but usually going along with the intensity was a heaping helping of ego. Wolfe didn't feel that from this man.

"Uh, what do you do, Mr. Norway, *are* you some kind of engineer?"

Norway laughed. "Well, yes. Aeronautical engineering."

"Why, you must feel right at home!" said Wolfe, pointing all around them.

Ross laughed very hard.

Wolfe blinked. "Did I say something wrong?"

"No," said Ross. "You said something very funny. Norway built this airship. And all its sis—" Norway looked at Ross "—brother ships. Did the designs, top to bottom."

"Really?" asked Wolfe.

"I helped," said the Engineer. "The U.S. Incorporated Airship Service called in a very *many* British and German consultants."

"Don't be quite so modest, Neville," said Sergeant Ross.

"You mustn't forget, I also helped with the *101*," said Norway, a little sourly.

There was a small pause. Wolfe remembered the disaster headlines from many years ago.

"Those were the old days. Things were different then. Hydrogen, for instance," said the sergeant.

"Hydrogen had nothing—"

Well, Mr. Ross," asked Wolfe, "what brings you halfway around the world, and on an American airship? If I'm not prying?"

"I assure you, I couldn't afford this trip on my non-commissioned officer's pay," he said, smiling. He looked away.

"Since he's too modest to tell you, I will," said Norway. "Sergeant Ross is being flown back to England to be a technical advisor on a motion picture."

"Really? What's it about? Flying? The Great War?"

Ross looked very embarrassed.

"It's about Lawrence," said Norway, looking at Wolfe, who creased his brow. "T.E.? Of Arabia?"

"Oh!" said Wolfe. "Did you serve with him?"

"I knew Lawrence in Palestine. Before the war. But the man I knew then was only slightly the one the film is being made about."

"But they still wanted you as technical advisor?"

"Yes. I told them that, but they insisted. I had studied all the man's writings, intimately. I think it was that they wanted." He struck a match against his thumbnail, watched it burn for a few seconds, put it out. "It's going to be a very strange film. Not as strange as it would be if they could find out one-tenth of the truth about him. But still, very strange indeed, if you view his life as a whole." The sergeant looked back down at his drink.

The ghost of a tune came down the stairwell. Wolfe thought at first it was one song, then it sounded like another.

Wolfe finished his bourbon and Coke.

"Well," he said, rising, "I'd better get another drink. Can I bring you something? No? This is some spectacular airship, Mr. Norway," he said, stamping his foot against the deck. "And I hope the film goes well for you, Sergeant. I'm sure we'll see each other again—I don't leave till we get to Germany. Come on up and hear the music or you'll be sorry you missed it."

Wolfe went up the circular stairs. As he rose, he looked through the aluminum trusses with the octagons cut out of them that formed the railing, saw that Ross and Norway were talking quietly again, as if he had never been there.

He was at the observation windows again. There was only a night full of stars out there. The interior lights had been dimmed to help the seeing, if there had been anything to watch. They were still running, according to the little ship they moved every hour on the world map beside the bulletin board, down the South China Sea before making the right turn that would take them to Karachi, India, the next stop on the *Ticonderoga's* around-the-world flight. It had started in New Jersey and would end there. New Jersey—Akron—Ft. Worth (for helium)—San Francisco—Honolulu—Ichinomaya—Karachi—Cairo—Trevino—Friedrichshaffen—Paris—London—New Jersey. Wolfe would be leaving in Germany. He was going to see his German publisher. Now that Germany was back on Zone Time, money, which had been locked up during the years before the Army revolted against Chancellor Hitler after the Sudetenland Debacle, was again flowing in and out of the country. Wolfe was to pick up his royalties from the last two books, and was to meet a translator, Hesse, who had done the last book there, supposedly a very good job indeed. Then he would meet Thea again, and they would have six weeks together in Germany and France, ending up at the Oktoberfest in Munich.

Wolfe lit another cigarette, and as he did so he realized with a start that it was exactly two years to the day since he'd awakened in the bed at Johns Hopkins, after the tubercule had been taken out of his brain. He reached back and rubbed the scarred place on his head.

Two women's voices drifted over from the promenade, then one of them laughed at something.

He felt a small moment of dizziness. It was him, not the airship. He still occasionally had them. He reached his hand out to the aluminum railing past the window louvers, and the world came calm again.

At times like this, Wolfe truly felt something was wrong. Not wrong with him—the doctors reassured him on that—but with everything else. The times. The world. His present life. Like there was something fundamentally wrong with the whole business of living.

He'd felt it that evening two years ago in the hospital, when he'd first come to some of his senses. He'd remembered nothing of the weeks of delirium beforehand. They told him it had been six raving weeks since he had caught the cold that led to the flu that opened the old tubercular lesion. That he had been in Seattle. They might as well have told him that he was from Mars.

He had had the same dislocated feeling many times in the past two years. He talked to the psychiatrist friend of Dr. Dandy, the man who'd operated on him. The psychiatrist told him that it was a fairly common side affect of operations on the brain that entailed any memory loss of one kind or another, and that the feeling should go away with the return of memory. But it hadn't, not yet.

It had been his books and his older manuscripts that reinforced the feeling in him. He had read them all, sometimes again and again, in the past twenty-four months. Most of them were intensely personal writings, books about a writer writing books about a writer. When his memory had begun to return, he recalled some of the true incidents which had been transmogrified into the fiction.

But they no longer connected to the person he was. Phrases, words, sentences, sometimes whole pages spoke out to him; but they did so as to a reader, not as to the man who wrote them. It was like some other guy, with the same name, had written these works, and then taken off on a long vacation while Wolfe was sick, leaving only the words behind, like some jumbled private code. It had been up to Wolfe to discover who this person was, decipher the mystery. He had failed.

He'd gone through the long manuscript he and Perkins had broken off from *Time and the River* in '34, and that he had, evidently, later divided into *The Lost Helen* and *The October Fair*, both of which he had been adding and splicing to just before his illness.

There was an aborted, limited-third-person manuscript Perkins told him was the "Doakesology"—about a guy named Joe Doakes. In other places he was named Paul Spangler. Sometimes they were Eugene Gant, in other places it was "I," in other places George Webber.

Wolfe had read the whole jumble over in two years. They were mostly full of great ringing apostrophes to night and America and food and trains. There was some good writing in them, lots of bad, too much of the mediocre. Mainly, they didn't interest him at all, because he no longer recalled the emotions that had made the Other Wolfe, as he referred to him sometimes, write them.

One chunk of manuscript from the two three-feet-by-four-feet pine packing crates full of them at the Scribner's office did interest him. It was a history, spare, told in the third person about (as Perkins and his mother told him) his North Carolina hill-country ancestors, called here the Pentlands and the Joyners. It was funny. It was exciting. It told a story. It wasn't like any of the other manuscripts that surrounded it.

It was this piece he had taken in the summer of '39, fleshed out and finished, and which Scribner's had published early this year as *The Hills Beyond Pentland*.

The reviewers, most of them, had gone crazy, taking it as a sign that a new, mature Thomas Wolfe was walking the field of letters, a writer more in control, one interested in narrative, who could write about people other than himself. (The entire narrative took place twenty years before he had been born.) That, they said, was worth the price of the book.

Others of course bemoaned the loss of the Wolfe who used to howl at the moon, the ones who wanted him to continue writing stories so that, as one of them said, "You couldn't tell if he was sitting down to a Thanksgiving dinner, or about to have sexual relations." (A line he would cherish forever.)

What neither set of critics knew was that some of the material had been written as far back as 1933. Most of it was in manuscript before the hospital stay. All he'd had to do was finish it just as he had started it; he had been capable of this book seven years before. As to the ones who wanted the Other Wolfe back, he was gone. He had disappeared into a hospital, and another writer, wearing his clothes and face, had come out. That man could no longer churn out dithyrambs at blinding speed, no longer overflowed with words like torrents of hot lava, was not a floodgate waiting to be opened by the business end of a stub pencil.

After the illness Wolfe found that sometimes the writing of a postcard could be an onerous chore. His work, his writing, now came slowly, slower than a mason with his bricks or a cabinetmaker with a piece of cedar. There were times when it did flow—a sentence, paragraphs, two, three: once a whole page. When it happened it left him feeling like he had been touched by the gods. But when it went away, there was nothing to do but go back to words, phrases, a sentence at a time. His manuscripts were now full of crossouts, big and little xxx's, six, seven, eight wrong word choices scratched through.

He asked Maxwell Perkins about it. He paused, in his Connecticut way, and then said:

"You used to write faster than any human being, Tom, but I had to have you take it out by the bucketfuls, whole chapters at a time. The stuff you're doing now is the best you've ever done. Don't worry. Just do it as it comes. You've got all the time in the world now, which you didn't used to think you had, which was what made you write too fast."

It was the longest speech he'd ever heard Perkins make.

There had been the time, just before he'd left on the western trip that made him sick, that he had almost broken with Scribner's. That terrible review by de Voto (rereading it lately, Wolfe could dispassionately see the places where it was right, the places where it was wrong) of the small book he did about the struggle to write *Time and the River*. Something about lawsuits they had settled out of court. Something that had gone on for months about a dentist's bill. (Wolfe had used Scribner's as a bank, drawing off his royalties ten and fifteen dollars at a time.) All those things meant zip now: Wolfe had found nothing as revealing as the ten-, twenty-, thirty-page letters the Other Wolfe had written in the heat of rage, sealed in envelopes, but fortunately never mailed.

The Other Wolfe had been a bitter man in 1937 and '38.

But Maxwell Perkins had stuck with him. His had been the first face he'd seen at Johns Hopkins as he came out from under the sedative; it had been the last in New York when he set out on this journey that led to this dirigible over the South China Sea.

It was very late. Wolfe was tired (he was always tired these days—how had the Other Wolfe denied that body sleep and rest for so long without wearing it completely out?), but he wanted to hear more Fats Waller. If the man were as tired as Wolfe was, he would sleep for the rest of the flight once he quit.

Your Feet's Too Big

The band kept up as best it could.

Fats slammed down on the last notes of "One O'Clock Jump." The sound was still holding in the air when he trilled his way up the scales in the opening to "Christopher Columbus." He sang, and the band joined in the vocals over the chorus. Waller went into the falsetto for the crewman's voice, and Columbus' basso, and then they went into an extended jam in the middle.

The ballroom was still two-thirds full, with other passengers coming in and going out continually. Crewmen, not allowed there except on duty, stood in the rear doorway that led to the kitchen; some danced in there, dimly seen through the cigarette smoke from the passenger tables.

The song kept growing and expanding; the bandleader took a kazoo from his breast pocket, blew it into the mike while continuing to slam-pick his banjo. He and Fats put their heads close together at the microphone, singing in good harmony.

The song rattled to its noisy close.

"Wowee!" said Fats. "Talk about a rumpus! My old heart can't take much of that. Let's see if we can't slow it down a little bit. Lessee, maybe I can think of something. Here's a thing we wrote for a Broadway revue, well, fewer years ago than it seems like. At least on the law books, this stuff don't cut it in the good old U. S. of A. any more. Believe me, this song's still true."

The bandleader was looking at him expectantly, as if, for once, he knew what Waller was going to play. He whispered to the cornet player, who stood up. Fats had just finished speaking when the horn man blew the two-bar introduction, just like on Fats' recording, in front of Waller's slow piano notes. Fats smiled for a second at the horn man, before his face went back thoughtful, and he began to sing, in the smokiest, slowest voice of the night, his song "(What Did I Do to Be So) Black and Blue?"

The noise level in the salon dropped, then stopped completely. There was only Fats' voice, a few piano notes, the quiet accompaniment of the band, the muted cornet, slow violin, occasional *tum* from the banjo.

When he finished, there was no sound at all in the place. Then there was an explosion of applause and yells.

"Thank you, thank you," he said, picking up the gin bottle. He leaned over and said something to the violin player, who put his instrument down on the edge of the aluminum piano.

Then he spun around on the piano bench, propped his immense feet up toward the audience. "You ever tried to buy a pair of Size Fifteen Torpedo Boats in Japan?" he asked. He saw, through the crowd, the big guy who'd been watching him all night from the bar suddenly break into a smile. "You saw these things coming at you on a dark night, you'd run screaming for the police." Then he looked down at himself. "Course, on me, they look positively dainty." He stood and struck a cupid pose. "But they're big, no doubt about it." He sat down and hit the opening *clump-clumps* of "Your Feet's Too Big," the song getting louder and more insistent as he played. Then, on the beginning of the chorus, he hit a note on the piano, stood up, missing two beats, picked up the violin and bow, and continued playing, pulling long vibrating sounds out of the strings, fingering rapidly. The violin looked like a toy in his huge hands, but the music from it filled the ballroom. The passengers yelled. Waller stopped, said: "It's easy, if you just know how," in a mellifluous voice, finished the chorus on the violin, sat back down, again losing two beats, and ended the song on the piano.

He had been there a long time. Waller had taken off his vest and tie, rolled up his shirtsleeves. Someone brought him a garter, and someone else found a derby hat. He put both on, and posed while the ship's photographer snapped a picture.

"Boy, does this take me back!" he said. "Whoever thought when they was playing this music in the back parlors of sportin'—'scuse my Anglo-Saxonism—houses, we'd end up playin' it in the clouds over China? That's the charm of music, the Hegemony of Harmony, the Triumph of Terpsichore, and other melodious metaphors. Right now, you listen to the Band in the Stars, while ol' Fats has to visit the Necessary Room, or whatever they call the head on this gasbag. I'll be right back."

"No, no!" yelled the passengers.

"You wanta see a big fat man explode all over a piano, or what?" he asked as he walked out the door, waving the derby.

The Band in the Stars played "Don't Get Around Much Anymore."

In three minutes, Waller was back.

Gonna Sit Right Down and Write Myself a Letter

Try as he would, Wolfe could hardly keep his eyes open, even standing against the bar. The drinks had worked on him, the smoke from the cigarettes and pipes scratched at his eyes. He could no longer drink like the Other Wolfe had. Coffee, which he'd been drinking since he was a child, now made him jumpy; it used to have a wakeful but calming effect on him. He had never really gotten his strength back after the operation.

The two men, Norway and Ross, had come into the ballroom at some point. They seemed to be enjoying Waller's antics as much as his musicianship, laughing quietly along with the rest of the crowd. At one time or another, every single person on the airship must have watched, crew included. The captain was at a corner table for a while—when he left, the second officer came back. Most of the crew Wolfe saw looked Old Navy, like the social director had said.

Fats and the band plunged ahead on "Darktown Strutters' Ball," which Wolfe knew had other lyrics than the ones usually sung in public. He was sure Waller knew them; maybe the violin player too: he had that seedy white musician look of a guy who spends his off-hours (back on the ground) at places where liquor (no matter how illegal) and other, stronger things always flow.

The passengers clapped along, faster on the climbing notes, slower on the descending ones, joining in on the chorus. Wolfe wished he felt as good as the audience sounded. He waved away the barman coming toward him, nodded goodnight to Sergeant Ross, who happened to be looking his way, stepped through the perrspex doorway with its stamped aluminum palm trees, and headed down the corridor.

He thought of looking at the stars one more time, maybe from the lower deck platform, but decided that if he were too tired for Waller, he was too tired for the most glorious night that ever was. There would be nothing to see; the little airship on the big map in the companionway was still over water.

He turned toward his cabin. Partway down the hall (outside half the doors people had set pairs of shoes to be shined by the steward) a woman in evening dress came out into the hall, Jerry behind her. She was newly made-up and looked like a million dollars. The social director was readjusting his tie.

"Ah-mmmm," said Wolfe, pointing his right index finger at them, rubbing back and forth across it with his left index finger. The woman stepped back, looking up at him, and blushed. Jerry turned his head.

"Oh, Mr. Wolfe! Still want the tour tomorrow?"

"The late one, Jerry, please," he said, holding his head, feigning drunkenness.

"Sure thing! He still playing?"

"They'll have to beat him absolutely to death with a crowbar before he'll quit," said Wolfe.

The social director laughed. "We're on our way there now," he said.

"Have a good time. You won't be able to help yourselves. Good night."

He went to his cabin, opened the door, watched Jerry and the woman turn the corner, the guy slipping his arm around her waist in the instant just before they turned the corner, disappearing toward the far sound of music.

The steward had been in and folded the back of the couch up onto its chains for the upper, and pulled the cushions out on the lower. A two-foot-long ottoman formed an extension of the bottom bunk—one of the things Wolfe had requested when he'd booked the airship. (One thing Aline had done for him was to have him a long bed built for his apartment in those days in Brooklyn—the first he'd ever had in his life that his feet didn't hang off of.)

Wolfe undressed down to his undershirt and pants, took off his shoes (not quite Waller's size fifteens, but big enough) and socks. He hung up his other clothes on the open rack opposite the window. He went to it, and something out toward the horizon caught his eye.

It was a ship. He'd been on many ships before, but none like this one. It was huge, even at this distance, this far up from the ocean. It looked like a floating city, all lights and curves; unlike most steamships it was not open-decked, but streamlined, closed in, like it was a smooth, rounded battleship. There was deck upon deck, row upon row of lighted portholes, all the way down to the waterline. It must have been ten storeys tall above the first deck, with five more below that. The funnels looked like double shark fins, silhouetted in their own pools of light.

As he watched, the ship sent a hoot of greeting to the *Ticonderoga*, a long high blast that barely carried across the miles. There was a sudden pale light somewhere beneath Wolfe's vantage point. It revolved, red white blue, red white blue, then went off. One U.S.A. Incorporated vessel greeting another. Then the ship was gone, leaving a line of swirling phosphorescence to each side of the sea to mark where it had been. The *Ticonderoga* was going ninety miles an hour; the other ship must have been making fifty knots.

It had to be the *Columbiad*, bel Geddes-designed, commissioned last year. Like the *Ticonderoga*, it went anywhere it was needed, plied all the lanes, showed the flag in every port; anything from a Caribbean cruise to an around-the-world marathon.

A thin line glowing pale green was the only thing to look at out there on the dark. Wolfe closed his window, cranked it down; the air up here was a little chilly late at night.

His tiredness had lifted for a short while—either seeing Jerry and the woman, or the liner, or both, had taken some of his bone-weariness and drink fumes away.

He sat down at the writing desk, pulled up the folding backless stool, took out a sheet of paper. Of course he could wait to write anything until the night before he got off in Germany—nothing would get to New York faster than the *Ticonderoga* itself; it would drop off its mail sacks in New Jersey nine days from now. But he had many letters to write.

There was a light above the desk but Wolfe kept it off. He reached down inside one of the pockets in his huge travelling briefcase and came up with a box nine inches by four. As he lifted it, one of the flaps on the bottom came open and two c-cell batteries fell out and rolled across the decking. "Damn!" he said, getting down and crawling after them, bringing them back. Then one of the spare bulbs fell out of the box. He caught it on the first bounce.

From inside its box he pulled a child's nightlight. It was a figure of Mickey Mouse, made out of tin, leaning against a fake red candle at the top of which was a bulb shaped like a flame. Mickey was in his usual shorts with the two big buttons, he wore the shapeless bread-dough shoes, one white-gloved hand was waving, the other cupped around the candle, supporting his weight as he leaned against it like a lamppost. On his face was a confident grin.

Wolfe turned it on, then the light above the desk.

The nightlight had been the second thing he saw in the hospital—first Max's concerned face, then the beaming face of Mickey Mouse.

He'd found that his sister had bought it in those weeks of incoherence out west, before they brought him to Baltimore for the operation. She'd gone down the street from the apartment next to the Seattle hospital and had bought the first battery-powered nightlight she had found, since they knew they would be moving him cross-country on a train soon. She had bought it because Tom had seemed, while irrational, to be afraid of the dark.

He hadn't slept a night in the two years without Mickey being on.

He smiled, took hold of Mickey's outstretched hand.

"Hello, Mickey," he said. Then he answered in a falsetto, as close to Walt Disney's as he could get, "Hello, Tom!"

He laughed in spite of himself. Then he took out his old Parker pen, unscrewed the cap, and got his reading glasses from his jacket pocket.

The stationery was official U.S.A. Incorporated Airship Service letterhead, with the embossed dirigible *Ticonderoga.*

16

September ~~15~~, 1940

Dear Max, (he wrote)

> *Somewhere way over the South China sea or the Indian Ocean as I write this. We left six p.m. Tokyo time, it must be four a.m. (that damned Fats Waller has kept everybody up all night with his piano playing!) (just kidding!) The Olympics, as I told you last letter (but this might beat it there), were great. Watched Sunpei Uto set a new 100 meter freestyle record (better than Tarzan's). Since Owens wasn't there, we lost all the dash events in track but won some distance (!) races—an American that can run more than a mile—unheard of in the 1930s! I'm sure you read all this in the papers—will tell you all about them when I get back in November.*
>
> *Saw Scott F. in L.A. before I came over—has he written you?—he looks bad, Max (don't tell him I said that). He's writing some college*

movie for Columbia (he wrote a Republic Western under a pen name a few months ago)—when are they going to stop thinking of him as a freshman?—he's in his forties. He tried to get me to stay in Hollywood and write ("just till you get your health back, Tom—lots of money to be made here"). I told him I wouldn't have any health at all if I had to write for the little tin kings out there. Scott also says, "To hell with Technocracy! I want to go into a bar in broad daylight and get drunk again."

It's not that way on this zep, Max. It flows like water. I'm glad you got me to take it, back in June when I was planning the Olympic trip. Smoother than a liner—we should already have come over 800 miles. Like riding in a fast hotel.

Did I tell you I watched the Olympics some on tele-vision? I know they have it at the World's Fair—but not like Japan. They wanted to keep the locals away from Olympic Stadium, so they broadcast it all over Japan—big department stores, town halls, etc. Saved most of the seats for the tourists. We're way behind them in the field of tele-vision. Tell Howard Scott that I said so next time you see him. Tell him to get his crackedest Technocrats on RCA's butt about it.

By the way, ask the accountant to make sure that if my U.S. Inc. shares get put in with my royalties, to turn them back in to my bank account (cashed!) please. I forgot to leave him a note before I left.

Harry and Caresse Crosby were supposed to be on the trip—but nobody's seen them. They either missed the zep, or maybe even never made it to Japan, or are in their cabin jazzing (Xcuse my French)— they saw Lindbergh land at Le Bourget, remember?—now everybody and his dog are zipping around the world in dirigibles (god, I'm beginning to sound like Fitzgerald!).

I think I saw the Columbiad *below us a while ago. You can check the shipping tables and see if I'm hallucinating, or what, Max. Had to be. Looked like Philadelphia in a canoe. Or have they turned out another one since I left? (There I go again.)*

This letter seemed important when I started it, now it just seems like a letter. Am looking forward to the rest of the trip—tomorrow (today) I get to take the tour. The Other Wolfe would have waxed poetic about it, the grandeur, the size, the mystery of all this, the zep, the people, their baggage, weighing less than this pen I'm writing with (Somebody told me the pilots like to take off with the whole thing weighing about 200 pounds—something to do with the engines.) Once I would have waxed poetic, now I'm lucky if I can wax my shoes. (Sorry.)

Hear the German guy Hesse did a great job. Did you send Rohwolt the galleys of Child By Tiger *(I'm sure you did) so they can start on that?* O, Lost *and* T.A.T. River *had great translations, everybody tells me* H.B. Pentland *(called—I forget what—*Die Alpen Forever *or something) is even better than those. In German I mean. Am looking forward to the six weeks with Miss Voelker more than anyone knows. (She said she was writing you, but is ashamed of her English, which is better than mine, Max. Did she?)*

Wolfe sat up and stretched his arms, rubbing his left shoulder. He looked toward the window. He couldn't tell if it was getting light, or what he saw was just the airglow off the ship's silver skin.

Now I'm tired Max, so will write more this afternoon. Will tell you all about the passenger list, starting with Herr Bock, Docteur Canard and Monsieur le Coq, and ascending upward to me. Also various other etceteras.

For now,
Tom

Wolfe lay naked on the bunk, orange in the glow from the nightlight. He smoked a last tired cigarette, stubbed it out in the weighted conical ashtray he'd taken off the desk and placed on the floor. There was a dull, not unpleasant throb on the deck. He put his hand up against the wall; it was there too. It must be there all the time, the tension of their passage through the air, the smooth vibrations of the engines against the structure of the ship. It was a calming thing.

He lay with his hands behind his head, staring up at the bottom of the unused bunk above him.

He was more than half a mile in the air, hurtling through the sky at nearly a hundred miles an hour, and he'd been listening to a band playing jazz as if he were in a Manhattan basement. He had never felt safer or more secure in his life.

He turned sideways, to face the dim light. All the familiar things were around him—his pen on the desk, his battered briefcase, his shoes and socks.

And the nightlight; grinning, confident, like President Scott in a pair of baggy shorts. Wolfe closed his eyes.

Into the future, then, reeking of celluloid and Bakelite though it may be, with Mickey Mouse lighting the way.

Cabin in the Sky

The passengers in the salon felt as if they had been beaten with thousand-pound feathers most of the night. Fats took another drink from his bottle, looked at it, finished it.

He'd taken off the derby hat and the garter. His shirt was transparent, wet.

The band had quit two hours before, completely worn out. They'd packed up their instruments, left the stage, now sat at tables, watching, marveling, not believing the man. Not many people noticed they'd gone.

There was a sleeping child at one of the front tables. She began to wake up.

"Here's somethin' I should have played first," said Waller. "Way back when I started tonight."

He ran a bunch of high tinkling trills with his right hand, and in a high voice began singing "Cabin in the Sky."

He finished. The forty or fifty passengers left broke into applause.

He glanced out the door where he could get an angle on a window. The sky seemed paler, the stars beginning to fade.

He looked at the child who'd awakened. Her eyes were puffy as she rubbed them with her sleeve.

"Whose baby child is that?" he asked, pointing. The woman at the next table said, "Mine." "Well, Ol' Fats is gonna sing one song, just for her, then he wants you to take her and put her in her little bitty bunk bed, and then come on back. But this one's gonna be for you, darlin'," he said, pointing to the girl. "You can help me sing it if you want to."

A man at another table looked at his Cartier wristwatch as Fats began the bass notes.

"Never mind the hour!" he said to the man, "I got the power!"

He started in, and they all—the little girl, her mother, the passengers, the band members, the crew—all joined in, shaking off their lethargy and sleepiness, as he began singing "Who's Afraid of the Big Bad Wolf?"

You **Could** *Go Home Again*
Appendix: "A Musical Interlude"

This is a list of the music on the tapes I made and listened to while I was writing "You *Could* Go Home Again." You might want to make your own version. This fits on both sides of a 90-minute cassette and half a 60-minute one. You'll notice it's not all contemporary (either the music itself, like the Dylan, or the performer, like '30s music played by '60s neo-jug and jazz bands). What I was aiming at was a mood, something either to get me butt-jumping in my chair, or to calm me down. Besides, there's lots of good music here.

1. "The Joint is Jumpin'"—Fats Waller
2. "Gonna Sit Right Down (and Write Myself a Letter)"—Fats Waller
3. "Mood Indigo"—Jim Kweskin Jug Band
4. "The Sheik of Araby"—Jim Kweskin Jug Band
5. "It's a Sin to Tell a Lie"—Fats Waller
6. "Titanic"—Snaker Dave Ray & Spider John Koerner (*they have it going the wrong way . . .*)
7. "Ukelele Lady"—Jim Kweskin Jug Band
8. "Christopher Columbus"—Jim Kweskin Jug Band
9. "Your Feets Too Big"—Fats Waller
10. "My Blue Heaven"—Fats Domino
11. "I Can't Give You Anything But Love"—Fats Waller
12. "Mississippi"—Turk Murphy Jazz Band
13. "Shipwreck Blues"—Bessie Smith
14. "Smokey Joe's Cafe"—Stampfel & Weber
15. "Corrina, Corrina"—Bob Dylan
16. "In The Mood"—Henhouse Five Plus Two (*chickens do Miller*)
17. "Aloha ka Manini"—Gabby Pahanui
18. "The Sheik of Araby"—Leon Redbone
19. "Emperor Norton's Hunch"—Queen City Jazz Band
20. "Bethena Walltzes"—Queen City Jazz Band
21. "Shine on Harvest Moon"—Leon Redbone
22. "Phonograph Blues"—Robert Johnson
23. "Willow Weep For Me"—Billy Holiday
24. "Mr. Jelly Roll Baker"—Leon Redbone
25. "Hang out The Stars in Indiana"—New Mayfair Dance Orchestra
26. "After You've Gone"—Queen City Jazz Band
27. "If We Ever Meet Again This Side of Heaven"—Leon Redbone

28. "Ain't Misbehavin'"—Fats Waller
29. "Black Diamond Bay"—Bob Dylan
30. "Yellow Submarine"—The Beatles
31. "Wear Your Love Like Heaven"—Donovan
32. "Mississippi Rag"—Turk Murphy Jazz Band
33. "Gonna Sit Right Down (and Write Myself a Letter)" Fats Waller (again)
34. "There Goes My Baby"—The Drifters
35. "Sea Cruise"—Frankie Ford
36. "Sincerely"—The Moonglows
37. "Goodnight Sweetheart Goodnight"—The Spaniels

AFTERWORD

Growing up, I knew *everything* (from what was available at the time I could get my hands on) about certain writers. I'd read their works, become fascinated by them, read biographies and critical works etc. They were, pretty much in order: Edgar Rice Burroughs; Robert E. Howard; H.P. Lovecraft; Thomas Wolfe; James Agee; Eugene O'Neill.

I'd always wanted to write a story about Wolfe (1900-1938). Norman Mailer once said, "Wolfe wrote like the greatest 17-year-old who ever lived." A few years later when the essay was reprinted, he provided a footnote: "I meant 15-year-old."

Wolfe's stuff used to speak to the young (when the young still *read*). Every writer has a Wolfe story in them, and usually wrote it (Bradbury did "Forever and the Earth.")

One of the problems of writing a Wolfe story is that they all think they have to write *like* Wolfe, which was practically impossible in the past, and must be more-so today.

Also, people who've written stories *about* Wolfe surviving his 1938 ordeal in Seattle and at Johns Hopkins always tried to make him the pre-illness Wolfe of logorrheic torrents, gargantuan appetites and world-striding gait, without taking into account the effects of tuberculosis of the brain, and the state of brain surgery in the late 1930s.

What I wanted to do was to try to imagine him as he *would* have been had he lived through *that*: I figured he'd be trying to find himself afterwards, just like he'd been trying to find the real America before.

I'd also wanted to write about Technocracy for a long time: (I think the only other story ever set in a world where Technocracy had come true was Mack Reynolds' "Speakeasy" in the early 1960s.)

It was a movement started by Howard Scott in the early 1930s, before Roosevelt's election—supposedly when things totally collapsed in the Depression (was the thinking) which looked like it would happen *any day now* under Hoover, the Technocrats (engineers and scientists, mostly) would step in, reapportion goods and services on a meaningful scientific basis—from areas of abundance to areas of scarcity—keep the railroads running etc.—I'm simplifying; but it was an all-encompassing system of social reform based on something other than straight capitalism which had gotten the world in the mess it was in. Technocracy had quite a vogue from about 1931-1933, when the New Deal mugged and kidnapped some of its best ideas. (The last vestige of it was when the Post Office adopted the ZIP code in 1964.)

Technocracy now remains as a sort of charming reminder of those long-dead Depression Thirties. If you've ever seen the *Our Gang* comedy *The Kid From Borneo*, there's a scene where Spanky (who thinks an escaped Wild Man from Borneo is his "Uncle George" and who wants to eat *him*—whereas the Wild Man only wants to eat everything *else* in the kitchen) is cornered up on the kitchen counter and tries to make conversation to get Uncle George's mind off cannibalism:

Spanky: How are things in Borneo?

"Uncle George" (busy with a ten pound ham): Yum yum eatem up, eatem up.

Spanky: Yeah, I guess things are tough all over. Have you heard about Technocracy?

Once again I have various writers doing cameo appearances (like in the movie of *Around the World in 80 Days* [1956]).

There's Wolfe front and center of course. Nevil Shute and T.E. Lawrence settle in for a nice conversation (under their real, or assumed names). And then there's Jerry.

Hard as it is to believe, the most reclusive American writer of the 20th Century was once the assistant social director on the *Bremerhaven*, or one of those luxury liners that plied the Atlantic every week between the Wars. His father, a meat importer, sent Jerome David over to Europe to check on things in 1939; he worked out his passage both ways as the assistant social director. (He was a whiz at ping-pong.)

I couldn't make this stuff up if I *tried*.

Wolfe was at the 1936 Olympics in Berlin, He *would* have been at the 1940 ones in Tokyo had not his death, and WWII intervened (in our world).

Well, I wanted a better world than that. (I also kept forgetting to put in some sports figures from John R. Tunis' *The Iron Duke* and *The Iron Duke Returns*, about the '36 Olympics, forgotten boys' sports novels. It's too late *now*. This thing is set in concrete.)

I wrote this in July of 1991. It was published in a beautiful edition of 200 or so, by Cheap St. Press in November 1993. I later sold it to *Omni Online* for the Neon Visions series (sponsored by Chrysler) for the biggest check I've *ever* gotten for less than a book-length work. The money allowed me to move (in May 1995) with everything I owned (except 8 boxes of books) and $600 cash in an '85 Toyota Tercel wagon to

Washington state, where I wrote, fished and didn't eat very well for the next eight years. I was sometimes happy as a clam. Most often, not.

(For more on Cheap St. and George and Jan O'Nale, see the afterword to "Flying Saucer Rock and Roll" in *Things Will Never Be The Same*, vol. 1 of *Selected Fiction.*)

FLATFEET!

1912

Captain Teeheezal turned his horse down toward the station house just as the Pacific Electric streetcar clanged to a stop at the intersection of Sunset and Ivar.

It was just 7:00 A.M. so only three people got off at the stop. Unless they worked at one of the new moving-picture factories a little further out in the valley, there was no reason for someone from the city to be in the town of Wilcox before the stores opened.

The motorman twisted his handle, there were sparks from the overhead wire, and the streetcar belled off down the narrow tracks. Teeheezal watched it recede, with the official sign *No Shooting Rabbits from the Rear Platform* over the back door.

"G'hup, Pear," he said to his horse. It paid no attention and walked at the same speed.

By and by he got to the police station. Patrolman Rube was out watering the zinnias that grew to each side of the porch. Teeheezal handed him the reins to his horse.

"What's up, Rube?"

"Not much, Cap'n," he said. "Shoulda been here yesterday. Sgt. Fatty brought by two steelhead and a Coho salmon he caught, right where Pye Creek empties into the L.A. River. Big as your leg, all three of 'em. Took up the whole back of his wagon."

"I mean police business, Rube."

"Oh." The patrolman lifted his domed helmet and scratched. "Not that I know of."

"Well, anybody in the cells?"

"Uh, lessee . . ."

"I'll talk to the sergeant," said Teeheezal. "Make sure my horse stays in his stall."

"Sure thing, Captain." He led it around back.

The captain looked around at the quiet streets. In the small park across from the station, with its few benches and small artesian fountain, was the big sign *No Spooning by order of Wilcox P.D.* Up toward the northeast the sun was coming full up over the hills.

Sgt. Hank wasn't at his big high desk. Teeheezal heard him banging around in the squad room to the left. The captain spun the blotter book around.

There was one entry:

Sat. 11:20 P.M. Jimson H. Friendless, actor, of Los Angeles city, D&D. Slept off, cell 2. Released Sunday 3:00 P.M. Arr. off. Patrolmen Buster and Chester.

Sgt. Hank came in. "Oh, hello Chief."

"Where'd this offense take place?" He tapped the book.

"The Blondeau Tavern . . . uh, Station," said the sergeant.

"Oh." That was just inside his jurisdiction, but since the Wilcox village council had passed a local ordinance against the consumption and sale of alcohol, there had been few arrests.

"He probably got tanked somewhere in L.A. and got lost on the way home," said Sgt. Hank. "Say, you hear about them fish Sgt. Fatty brought in?"

"Yes, I did." He glared at Sgt. Hank.

"Oh. Okay. Oh, there's a postal card that came in the Saturday mail from Captain Angus for us all. I left it on your desk."

"Tell me if any big trouble happens," said Teeheezal. He went into the office and closed his door. Behind his desk was a big wicker rocking chair he'd had the village buy for him when he took the job early in the year. He sat down in it, took off his flat-billed cap, and put on his reading glasses.

Angus had been the captain before him for twenty-two years; he'd retired and left to see some of the world. (He'd been one of the two original constables when Colonel Wilcox laid out the planned residential village.) Teeheezal had never met the man.

He picked up the card—a view of Le Havre, France, from the docks. Teeheezal turned it over. It had a Canadian postmark, and one half had the address: *The Boys in Blue, Police HQ, Wilcox, Calif. U.S.A.* The message read:

Well, took a boat. You might have read about it. Had a snowball fight
on deck while waiting to get into the lifeboats. The flares sure were
pretty. We were much overloaded by the time we were picked up. (Last
time I take a boat named for some of the minor Greek godlings.) Will
write again soon.
            —*Angus*
PS: Pretty good dance band.

Teeheezal looked through the rest of the mail; wanted posters for guys
three thousand miles away, something from the attorney general of
California, a couple of flyers for political races that had nothing to do with
the village of Wilcox.

The captain put his feet up on his desk, made sure they were nowhere
near the kerosene lamp or the big red bellpull wired to the squad room,
placed his glasses in their cases, arranged his Farmer John tuft beard to one
side, clasped his fingers across his chest, and began to snore.

The murder happened at the house of one of the curators, across the
street from the museum.

Patrolman Buster woke the captain up at his home at 4:00 A.M. The
Los Angeles County coroner was already there when Teeheezal arrived on
his horse.

The door of the house had been broken down. The man had been
strangled and then thrown back behind the bed where he lay twisted with
one foot out the open windowsill.

"Found him just like that, the neighbors did," said Patrolman Buster.
"Heard the ruckus, but by the time they got dressed and got here, whoever
did it was gone."

Teeheezal glanced out the broken door. The front of the museum
across the way was lit with electric lighting.

"Hmmm," said the coroner, around the smoke from his El Cubano
cigar. "They's dust all over this guy's py-jamas." He looked around. "Part
of a print on the bedroom doorjamb, and a spot on the floor."

Patrolman Buster said, "Hey! One on the front door. Looks like somebody popped it with a dirty towel."

The captain went back out on the front porch. He knelt down on the
lawn, feeling with his hands.

He spoke to the crowd that had gathered out front. "Who's a neighbor here?" A man stepped out, waved. "He water his yard last night?"

"Yeah, just after he got off work."

Teeheezal went to the street and lay down.

"Buster, look here." The patrolman flopped down beside him. "There's some lighter dust on the gravel, see it?" Buster nodded his thin face. "Look over there, see?"

"Looks like mud, Chief." They crawled to the right to get another angle, jumped up, looking at the doorway of the museum.

"Let's get this place open," said the chief.

"I was just coming over; they called me about Fielding's death, when your ruffians came barging in," said the museum director, whose name was Carter Lord. "There was no need to rush me so." He had on suit pants but a pajama top and a dressing gown.

"Shake a leg, pops," said Patrolman Buster.

There was a sign on the wall near the entrance: *The Treasures of Pharaoh Rut-en-tut-en, April 20–June 13.*

The doors were steel; there were two locks Lord had to open. On the inside was a long push bar that operated them both.

"Don't touch anything, but tell me if something's out o' place," said Teeheezal.

Lord used a handkerchief to turn on the light switches.

He told them the layout of the place and the patrolmen took off in all directions.

There were display cases everywhere, and ostrich-looking fans, a bunch of gaudy boxes, things that looked like coffins. On the walls were paintings of people wearing diapers, standing sideways. At one end of the hall was a big upright wooden case. Patrolman Buster pointed out two dabs of mud just inside the door, a couple of feet apart. Then another a little further on, leading toward the back, then nothing.

Teeheezal looked around at all the shiny jewelry. "Rich guy?" he asked.

"Priceless," said Carter Lord. "Tomb goods, buried with him for the afterlife. The richest find yet in Egypt. We were very lucky to acquire it."

"How come you gettin' it?"

"We're a small, but a growing museum. It was our expedition—the best untampered tomb. Though there were skeletons in the outer corridors, and the outside seal had been broken, I'm told. Grave robbers had broken in but evidently got no further."

"How come?"

"Who knows?" asked Lord. "We're dealing with four thousand five hundred years."

Patrolman Buster whistled.

Teeheezal walked to the back. Inside the upright case was the gray swaddled shape of a man, twisted, his arms across his chest, one eye closed, a deep open hole where the other had been. Miles of gray curling bandages went round and round and round him, making him look like a cartoon patient in a lost hospital.

"This the guy?"

"Oh, heavens no," said Carter Lord. "The Pharaoh Rut-en-tut-en's mummy is on loan to the Field Museum in Chicago for study. This is probably some priest or minor noble who was buried for some reason with him. There were no markings on this case," he said, knocking on the plain wooden case. "The pharaoh was in that nested three-box sarcophagus over there."

Teeheezal leaned closer. He reached down and touched the left foot of the thing. "Please don't touch that," said Carter Lord.

The patrolmen returned from their search of the building. "Nobody here but us *gendarmerie*," said Patrolman Rube.

"C'mere, Rube," said Teeheezal. "Reach down and touch this foot."

Rube looked into the box, jerked back. "Cripes! What an ugly! Which foot?"

"Both."

He did. "So?"

"One of them feel wet?"

Rube scratched his head. "I'm not sure."

"I asked you to *please* not touch that," said Carter Lord. "You're dealing with very fragile, irreplaceable things here."

"He's conducting a murder investigation here, bub," said Patrolman Mack.

"I understand that. But nothing here has committed murder, at least not for the last four thousand five hundred years. I'll have to ask that you desist."

Teeheezal looked at the face of the thing again. It looked back at him with a deep open hole where one eye had been, the other closed. Just—

The hair on Teeheezal's neck stood up. "Go get the emergency gun from the wagon," said the chief, not taking his eyes off the thing in the case.

"I'll have to *insist* that you leave *now!*" said Carter Lord.

Teeheezal reached over and pulled up a settee with oxhorn arms on it and sat down, facing the thing. He continued to stare at it. Somebody put the big heavy revolver in his hand.

"All you, go outside, except Rube. Rube, keep the door open so you can see me. Nobody do anything until I say so."

"That's the last straw!" said Carter Lord. "Who do I call to get you to cease and desist?"

"Take him where he can call the mayor, Buster."

Teeheezal stared and stared. The dead empty socket looked back at him. Nothing moved in the museum, for a long, long time. The revolver grew heavier and heavier. The chief's eyes watered. The empty socket stared back, the arms lay motionless across the twisted chest. Teeheezal stared.

"Rube!" he said after a long time. He heard the patrolman jerk awake.

"Yeah, Chief?"

"What do you think?"

"Well, I think about now, Captain, that they've got the mayor all agitated, and a coupla aldermen, and five, maybe ten minutes ago somebody's gonna have figured out that though the murder happened in Wilcox, right now you're sitting in Los Angeles."

Without taking his eyes from the thing, Teeheezal asked, "Are you funnin' me?"

"I never fun about murder, Chief."

Three carloads of Los Angeles Police came around the corner on six wheels. They slammed to a stop, the noise of the hand-cranked sirens dying on the night. By now the crowd outside the place had grown to a couple of hundred.

What greeted the eyes of the Los Angeles Police was the Wilcox police wagon with its four horses in harness, most of the force, a crowd, and a small fire on the museum lawn across the street from the murder house.

Two legs were sticking sideways out of the fire. The wrappings flamed against the early morning light. Sparks rose up and swirled.

The chief of the Los Angeles Police Department walked up to where the captain poked at the fire with the butt end of a spear. Carter Lord and the Wilcox mayor and a Los Angeles city councilman trailed behind the L.A. chief.

"Hello, Bob," said Teeheezal.

With a pop and a flash of cinders, the legs fell the rest of the way into the fire, and the wrappings roared up to nothingness.

"Teeheezal! What the hell do you think you're doing!? Going out of your jurisdiction, no notification. It looks like you're burning up Los Angeles City property here! Why didn't you call us?"

"Didn't have time, Bob," said Teeheezal. "I was in hot pursuit."

They all stood watching until the fire was out; then all climbed into their cars and wagons and drove away. The crowd dispersed, leaving Carter

Lord in his dressing gown. With a sigh, he turned and went into the museum.

1913

If southern California had seasons, this would have been another late spring.

Teeheezal was at his desk, reading a letter from his niece Katje from back in Pennsylvania, where all his family but him had been for six generations.

There was a knock on his door. "What? What?" he yelled.

Patrolman Al stuck his head in. "Another card from Captain Angus. The sergeant said to give it to you."

He handed it to Teeheezal and left swiftly. Patrolman Al had once been a circus acrobat, and the circus folded in Los Angeles city two years ago. He was a short thin wiry man, one of Teeheezal's few smooth-shaven patrolmen.

The card was a view of the Eiffel Tower, had a Paris postmark, with the usual address on the back right side. On the left:

> *Well, went to the Ballet last night. You would of thought someone spit on the French flag. Russians jumpin' around like Kansas City fools, frogs punching each other out, women sticking umbrellas up guys' snouts. I been to a rodeo, a country fair, six picnics, and I have seen the Elephant, but this was pretty much the stupidest display of art appreciation I ever saw. Will write again soon.*
> *—Angus*
> *PS: Ooh-lah-lah!*

"Hmmph!" said Teeheezal. He got up and went out into the desk area. Sergeant Hank had a stack of picture frames on his desk corner. He was over at the wall under the pictures of the mayor and the village aldermen. He had a hammer and was marking five spots for nails on the plaster with the stub of a carpenter's pencil.

"What's all this, then?" asked the Captain.

"My pictures got in yesterday, Chief," said Sgt. Hank. "I was going to put 'em up on this wall I have to stare at all day."

"Well, I can see how looking at the mayor's no fun," said Teeheezal. He picked up the top picture. It was a landscape. There was a guy chasing a deer in one corner, and some trees and teepees, and a bay, and a funny-shaped rock on a mountain in the distance.

He looked at the second. The hill with the strange rock was in it, but people had on sheets, and there were guys drawing circles and squares in the dirt and talking in front of little temples and herding sheep. It looked to be by the same artist.

"It's not just paintings," said Sgt. Hank, coming over to him. "It's a series by Thomas Cole, the guy who started what's referred to as the Hudson River School of painting way back in New York State, about eighty years ago. It's called *The Course of Empire*. Them's the first two— *The Savage State* and *The Pastoral or Arcadian State*. This next one's called *The Consummation of Empire*—see, there's this guy riding in a triumphal parade on an elephant, and there are these armies, all in this city like Rome or Carthage, it's been built here, and they're bringing stuff back from all over the world, and things are dandy."

Hank was more worked up than the chief had ever seen him. "But look at this next one, see, the jig is up. It's called *The Destruction of Empire*. All them buildings are on fire, and there's a rainstorm, and people like Mongols are killing everybody in them big wide avenues, and busting up statues and looting the big temples, and bridges are falling down, and there's smoke everywhere."

Teeheezal saw the funny-shaped mountain was over in one corner of those two paintings.

"Then there's the last one, number five, *The Ruins of Empire*. Every-thing's quiet and still, all the buildings are broken, the woods are taking back everything, it's going back to the land. See, look there, there's pelicans nesting on top of that broken column, and the place is getting covered with ivy and briers and stuff. I ordered all these from a museum back in New York City," said Hank, proudly.

Teeheezal was still looking at the last one.

"And look," said Sgt. Hank, going back to the first one. "It's not just paintings, it's philosophical. See, here in the first one, it's just after dawn. Man's in his infancy. So's the day. Second one—pastoral, it's midmorning. Consummation—that's at noon. First three paintings all bright and clear. But destruction—that's in the afternoon, there's storms and lightning. Like nature's echoing what's going on with mankind, see? And the last one. Sun's almost set, but it's clear again, peaceful, like, you know, Nature takes its time . . ."

"Sgt. Hank," said Teeheezal, "When a guy gets arrested and comes in here drunk and disorderly, the last thing he wants to be bothered by is some philosophy."

"But, Chief," said Sgt. Hank, "it's about the rise and fall of civili-zations . . ."

"What the hell does running a police station have to do with civilization?" said Teeheezal. "You can hang one of 'em up. One at a time they look like nature views, and those don't bother anybody."

"All right, Chief," said Sgt. Hank.

That day, it was the first one. When Teeheezal arrived for work the next day, it was the second. And after that, the third, and on through the five pictures, one each day; then the sequence was repeated. Teeheezal never said a word. Neither did Hank.

1914

There had been murders three nights in a row in Los Angeles City when the day came for the Annual Wilcox Police vs. Firemen Baseball Picnic.

The patrolmen were all playing stripped down to their undershirts and uniform pants, while the firemen had on real flannel baseball outfits that said Hot Papas across the back. It was late in the afternoon, late in the game, the firemen ahead seventeen to twelve in the eighth.

They were playing in the park next to the observatory. The patrol wagon was unhitched from its horses; the fire wagon stood steaming with its horses still in harness. Everyone in Wilcox knew not to bother the police or fireman this one day of the year.

Patrolman Al came to bat on his unicycle. He rolled into the batter's box. Patrolman Mack was held on second, and Patrolman Billy was hugging third. The firemen started their chatter. The pitcher wound up, took a long stretch and fired his goof-ball from behind his back with his glove hand while his right arm went through a vicious fastball motion.

Al connected with a meaty *crack*; the outfielders fell all over themselves and then charged toward the Bronson place. Al wheeled down to first with blinding speed, swung wide ignoring the fake from the second baseman, turned between second and third, balancing himself in a stop while he watched the right fielder come up with the ball on the first bounce four hundred feet away.

He leaned almost to the ground, swung around, became a blur of pedals and pumping feet, passed third; the catcher got set, pounding his mitt, stretched out for the throw. The umpire leaned down, the ball bounced into the mitt, the catcher jerked around—

Al hung upside down, still seated on the unicycle, six feet in the air over the head of the catcher, motionless, sailing forward in a long somersault.

He came down on home plate with a thud and a bounce.

"Safe!" said the ump, sawing the air to each side.

The benches emptied as the catcher threw off his wire mask. Punches flew like they did after every close call.

Teeheezal and Sgt. Hank stayed on the bench eating a bag of peanuts. The people in the stands were yelling and laughing.

"Oh, almost forgot," said Sgt. Hank, digging in his pants pocket. "Here."

He handed Teeheezal a postcard. It had an illegible postmark in a language with too many Zs. The front was an engraving of the statue of a hero whose name had six *K*s in it.

> *Well, was at a café. Bunch of seedy-looking students sitting at the table next to mine grumbling in Slavvy talk. This car come by filled with plumed hats, made a wrong turn and started to back up. One of the students jumped on the running board and let some air into the guy in the back seat—'bout five shots I say. Would tell you more but I was already lighting out for the territory. Place filled up with more police than anywhere I ever seen but the B.P.O.P.C. convention in Chicago back in '09. This was big excitement last week but I'm sure it will blow over. Will write more soon.*
> *—Angus*
> *PS: Even here, we got the news the Big Ditch is finally open.*

It was the bottom of the eleventh and almost too dark to see when the bleeding man staggered onto left field and fell down.

The man in the cloak threw off all six patrolmen. Rube used the emergency pistol he'd gotten from the wagon just before the horses went crazy and broke the harness, scattering all the picnic stuff everywhere. He emptied the revolver into the tall dark man without effect. The beady-eyed man swept Rube aside with one hand and came toward Teeheezal.

The captain's foot slipped in all the stuff from the ball game.

The man in the dark cloak hissed and smiled crookedly, his eyes red like a rat's. Teeheezal reached down and picked up a Louisville Slugger. He grabbed it by the sweet spot, smashed the handle against the ground, and shoved the jagged end into the guy's chest.

"*Merde!*" said the man, and fell over.

Rube stood panting beside him. "I never missed, Chief," he said. "All six shots in the space of a half-dime."

"I saw," said Teeheezal, wondering at the lack of blood all over the place.

"*That* was my favorite piece of lumber," said Patrolman Mack.

"We'll get you a new one," said the captain.

They had the undertaker keep the body in his basement, waiting for somebody to claim it. After the investigation, they figured no one would, and they were right. But the law was the law.

Sgt. Hank scratched his head and turned to the chief, as they were looking at the man's effects.

"Why is it," he asked, "we're always having trouble with things in boxes?"

1915

Teeheezal got off the streetcar at the corner of what used to be Sunset and Ivar, but which the village council had now renamed, in honor of a motion picture studio out to the northwest, Sunset and Bison. Teeheezal figured some money had changed hands.

The P.E. Street Railway car bell jangled rapidly as it moved off toward Mount Lowe and the Cawston Ostrich Farms, and on down toward San Pedro.

In the park across from the station, Patrolmen Chester and Billy, almost indistinguishable behind their drooping walrus mustaches, were rousting out a couple, pointing to the *No Sparking* sign near the benches. He stood watching until the couple moved off down the street, while Billy and Chester, pleased with themselves, struck noble poses.

He went inside. The blotter on the desk was open:

Tues. 2:14 A.M. Two men, Alonzo Partain and D. Falcher Greaves, no known addresses, moving-picture acting extras, arrested D&D and on suspicion of criminal intent, in front of pawn shop at Gower and Sunset. Dressed in uniforms of the G.A.R. and the Confederate States and carrying muskets. Griffith studio notified. Released on bond to Jones, business manager, 4:30 A.M. Ptlmn. Mack. R.D.O.T.

The last phrase officially meant Released until Day Of Trial, but was station house for Rub-Down with Oak Towel, meaning Patrolman Mack, who was 6'11" and 350 pounds, had had to use considerable force dealing with them.

"Mack have trouble?" he asked Sgt. Hank.

"Not that Fatty said. In fact, he said when Mack carried them in, they were sleeping like babies."

"What's this Griffith thing?"

"Movie company out in Edendale, doing a War Between the States picture. Mack figured they were waiting till the hock shop opened to pawn their rifles and swords. This guy Jones was ready to blow his top, said they sneaked off the location late yesterday afternoon."

Teeheezal picked up the newspaper from the corner of the sergeant's desk. He scanned the headlines and decks. "What do you think of that?" he asked. "Guy building a whole new swanky residential area, naming it for his wife?"

"Ain't that something?" said Sgt. Hank. "Say, there's an ad for the new *Little Tramp* flicker, bigger than the film it's playing with. That man's a caution! He's the funniest guy I ever seen in my life. I hear he's a Limey. Got a mustache like an afterthought."

"I don't think anybody's been really funny since Flora Finch and John Bunny," said Teeheezal. "This Brit'll have to go some to beat *John Bunny Commits Suicide*."

"Well, you should give him a try," said Sgt. Hank. "Oh, forgot yesterday. Got another from Captain Angus. Here go." He handed it to Teeheezal.

It had a view of Lisbon, Portugal, as seen from some mackerel-slapper church tower, the usual address, and on the other half:

Well, I had another boat sink out from under me. This time it was a kraut torpedo, and we was on a neutral ship. Had trouble getting into the lifeboats because of all the crates of howitzer shells on deck. Was pulled down by the suck when she went under. Saw airplane bombs and such coming out the holes in the sides while I was under water. Last time I take a boat called after the Roman name for a third-rate country. Will write again soon.
—Angus
PS: How about the Willard-Johnson fight?

The windows suddenly rattled. Then came dull booms from far away. "What's that?"

"Probably the Griffith people. They're filming the battle of Chickamauga or something. Out in the country, way past the Ince Ranch, even."

"What they using, nitro?"

"Beats me. But there's nothing we can do about it. They got a county permit."

"Sometimes," said Teeheezal, "I think motion picture companies is running the town of Wilcox. And the whole U. S. of A. for that matter."

* * *

1916

Jesus Christ, smoking a cigar, drove by in a Model T.

Then the San Pedro trolleycar went by, full of Assyrians, with their spears and shields sticking out the windows. Teeheezal stood on the corner, hands on hips, watching them go by.

Over behind the corner of Prospect and Talmadge the walls of Babylon rose up, with statues of bird-headed guys and dancing elephants everywhere, and big moveable towers all around it. There were scaffolds and girders everywhere, people climbing up and down like ants. A huge banner stretched across the eight-block lot: *D.W. Griffith Production—The Mother and the Law.*

He walked back to the station house. Outside, the patrolmen were waxing the shining new black box-like truck with *Police Patrol* painted on the sides. It had brass hand-cranked sirens outside each front door, and brass handholds along each side above the running boards. They'd only had it for three days, and had yet to use it for a real emergency, though they'd joy-rode it a couple of times, sirens screaming, with the whole force hanging on or inside it, terrifying the fewer and fewer horses on the streets. Their own draught-horses had been put out to pasture at Sgt. Fatty's farm, and the stable out back converted into a garage.

The village fathers had also wired the station house for electricity, and installed a second phone in Teeheezal's office, along with an electric alarm bell for the squad room on his desk.

The town was growing. It was in the air. Even some moving pictures now said *Made in Wilcox, U.S.A.* at the end of them.

The blotter, after a busy weekend, was blank.

The postcard was on his desk. It had an English postmark, and was a view of the River Liffey.

Well, with the world the way it is, I thought the Old Sod would be a quiet place for the holiday. Had meant to write you boys a real letter, so went to the Main Post Office. Thought I'd have the place to myself. Boy, was I wrong about that. Last time I look for peace and quiet on Easter Sunday. Will write more later.

    —Angus

PS: This will play heck with Daylight Summer Time.

Teeheezal was asleep when the whole force burst into his office and Sgt. Hank started unlocking the rack with the riot guns and rifles.

"What the ding-dong?" yelled Teeheezal, getting up off the floor.

"They say Pancho Villa's coming!" yelled a patrolman. "He knocked over a coupla banks in New Mexico!"

Teeheezal held up his hand. They all stopped moving. He sat back down in his chair and put his feet back up on his desk.

"Call me when he gets to Long Beach," he said.

Sgt. Hank locked the rack back up; then they all tiptoed out of the office.

"Look out!" "Get 'im! Get him!" "Watch it!!"

The hair-covered man tore the cell bars away and was gone into the moonlit night.

"Read everything you can, Hank," said Teeheezal. "Nothing else has worked."

"You sure you know what to do?" asked the captain.

"I know exactly *what* to do," said Patrolman Al. "I just don't *like* it. Are you sure Sgt. Hank is right?"

"Well, no. But if you got a better idea, tell me."

Al swallowed hard. He was on his big unicycle, the one with the chain drive.

There was a woman's scream from across the park.

"Make sure he's after *you*," said Teeheezal. "See you at the place. And, Al . . ."

"Say 'break a leg,' Captain."

"Uh . . . break a leg, Al."

Al was gone. They jumped in the police patrol truck and roared off.

They saw them coming through the moonlight, something on a wheel and a loping shape.

Al was nearly horizontal as he passed, eyes wide, down the ramp at the undertaker's, and across the cellar room. Patrolman Buster closed his eyes and jerked the vault door open at the second before Al would have smashed into it. Al flew in, chain whizzing, and something with hot meat breath brushed Buster.

Patrolman Al went up the wall and did a flip. The thing crashed into the wall under him. As Al went out, he jerked the broken baseball bat out of the guy it had been in for two years.

There was a hiss and a snarl behind him as he went out the door that Buster, eyes still closed, slammed to and triple-locked; then Mack and Billy dropped the giant steel bar in place.

Al stopped, then he and the unicycle fainted.

There were crashes and thumps for two hours, then whimpering sounds and squeals for a while.

They went in and beat what was left with big bars of silver, and put the broken Louisville Slugger back in what was left of the hole.

As they were warming their hands at the dying embers of the double fire outside the undertaker's that night, it began to snow. Before it was over, it snowed five inches.

1917

The captain walked by the *No Smooching* sign in the park on his way to talk to a local store owner about the third break-in in a month. The first two times the man had complained about the lack of police concern, first to Teeheezal, then the mayor.

Last night it had happened again, while Patrolmen Al and Billy had been watching the place.

He was on his way to tell the store owner it was an inside job, and to stare the man down. If the break-ins stopped, it had been the owner himself.

He passed by a hashhouse with a sign outside that said "Bratwurst and Sauerkraut 15¢." As he watched, the cook, wearing his hat and a knee-length apron, pulled the sign from the easel and replaced it with one that said "Victory cabbage and sausage 15¢."

There was a noise from the alleyway ahead, a bunch of voices "get 'im, get 'im"; then out of the alley ran something Teeheezal at first thought was a rat or a rabbit. But it didn't move like either of them, though it was moving as fast as it could.

A group of men and women burst out onto the street with rocks and chunks of wood sailing in front of them, thirty feet behind it. It dodged, then more people came from the other side of the street, and the thing turned to run away downtown.

The crowd caught up with it. There was a single yelp, then the thudding sounds of bricks hitting something soft. Twenty people stood over it, their arms moving. Then they stopped and cleared off the street and into the alleyways on either side without a word from anyone.

Teeheezal walked up to the pile of wood and stones with the rivulet of blood coming out from under it.

The captain knew the people to whom the dachshund had belonged, so he put it in a borrowed toe sack, and took that and put it on their porch with a note. *Sorry. Cpt. T.*

When he got within sight of the station house, Patrolman Chester came running out. "Captain! Captain!" he yelled.

"I know," said Teeheezal. "We're at war with Germany."

A month later another postcard arrived. It had a view of the Flatiron Building in New York City, had a Newark New Jersey postmark, and the usual address. On the left back it said:

Well, went to the first Sunday baseball game at the Polo Grounds. New York's Finest would have made you proud. They stood at attention at the national anthem then waited for the first pitch before they arrested McGraw and Mathewson for the Blue Law violation. You can imagine what happened next. My credo is: When it comes to a choice between a religion and baseball, baseball wins every time. Last time I go to a ball game until they find some way to play it at night. Ha ha. Will write more later.
    —*Angus*
PS: Sorry about Buffalo Bill.

1918

If every rumor were true, the Huns would be in the White House by now. Teeheezal had just seen a government motion picture (before the regular one) about how to spot the Kaiser in case he was in the neighborhood spreading panic stories or putting cholera germs in your reservoir.

Now, last night, one had spread through the whole California coast about a U-boat landing. Everybody was sure it had happened at San Pedro, or Long Beach, or maybe it was in Santa Barbara, or along the Sun River, or somewhere. And somebody's cousin or uncle or friend had seen it happen, but when the Army got there there wasn't a trace.

The blotter had fourteen calls noted. One of them reminded the Wilcox police that the President himself was coming to Denver Colorado for a speech—coincidence, or what?

"I'm tired of war and the rumors of war," said Teeheezal.

"Well, people out here feel pretty helpless, watching what's going on ten thousand miles away. They got to contribute to the war effort *somehows*," said walrus-mustached Patrolman Billy.

Innocently enough, Patrolmen Mack and Rube decided to swing down by the railroad yards on their way in from patrol. It wasn't on their beat that night, but Sgt. Fatty had told them he'd seen some fat rabbits down there last week, and, tomorrow being their days off, they were going to check it over before buying new slingshots.

The patrol wagon careened by, men hanging on for dear life, picked up Teeheezal from his front yard, and roared off toward the railroad tracks.

The three German sailors went down in a typhoon of shotgun fire and hardly slowed them down at all.

What they did have trouble with was the giant lowland gorilla in the spiked *pickelhaube* helmet, and the eight-foot-high iron automaton with the letter *Q* stenciled across its chest.

The Federal men were all over the place; in the demolished railyard were two huge boxes marked for delivery to the Brown Palace in Denver.

"Good work, Captain Teeheezal," said the Secret Service man. "How'd you get the lowdown on this?"

"Ask the two patrolmen," he said.

At the same time, Mack and Rube said, "Dogged, unrelenting police procedures."

The postcard came later than usual that year, after the Armistice.

It was a plain card, one side for the address, the other for the message.

Well, here in Reykjavik things are really hopping. Today they became an independent nation, and the firewater's flowing like the geysers. It's going to be a three-day blind drunk for all I can figure. Tell Sgt. Fatty the fish are all as long as your leg here. Pretty neat country; not as cold as the name. Last time I come to a place where nobody's at work for a week. Will write more later.

—Angus

PS: Read they're giving women over thirty in Britain the vote—can we be far behind? Ha ha.

PPS: I seem to have a touch of the flu.

1919

Sgt. Hank didn't look up from the big thick book in his hand when Teeheezal came out of his office and walked over and poured himself a cup of steaming coffee. Say whatever else about the Peace mess in Europe, it was good to be off rationing again. Teeheezal's nephew had actually brought home some butter and steaks from a regular grocery store and butcher's last week.

"What's Wilson stepping in today?"

No answer.

"Hey!"

"Huh?! Oh, gosh, Chief. Was all wrapped up in this book. What'd you say?"

"Asking about the President. Seen the paper?"

"It's here somewhere," said Sgt. Hank. "Sorry, Chief, but this is about the greatest book I ever read."

"Damn thick square thing," said Teeheezal. He looked closely at a page. "Hey, that's a kraut book!"

"Austria. Well, yeah, it's by a German, but not like any German you ever thought of."

Teeheezal tried to read it, from what he remembered of when he went to school in Pennsylvania fifty years ago. It was full of two-dollar words, the sentences were a mile long, and the verb was way down at the bottom of the page.

"This don't make a goddamn bit of sense," he said. "This guy must be a college perfesser."

"It's got a cumulative effect," said Sgt. Hank. "It's about the rise of cultures and civilizations, and how Third Century B.C. China's just like France under Napoleon, and how all civilizations grow and get strong, and wither and die. Just like a plant or an animal, like they're alive themselves. And how when the civilization gets around to being an empire it's already too late, and they all end up with Caesars and Emperors and suchlike. Gosh, Chief, you can't imagine. I've read it twice already, and every time I get more and more out of it . . ."

"Where'd you get a book like that?"

"My cousin's a reporter at the Peace Commission conference—somebody told him about it, and he got one sent to me, thought it'd be something I like. I hear it's already out of print, and the guy's rewriting it."

"What else does this prof say?"

"Well, gee. A lot. Like I said, that all civilizations are more alike than not. That everything ends up in winter, like, after a spring and summer and fall." He pointed to the Cole picture on the wall—today it was *The Pastoral State.* "Like, like the pictures. Only a lot deeper. He says, for instance, that Europe's time is over—"

"It don't take a goddamned genius to know *that,*" said Teeheezal.

"No—you don't understand. He started writing this in 1911, it says.

He already knew it was heading for the big blooie. He says that Europe's turn's over, being top dog. Now it's the turn of America . . . and . . . and Russia."

Teeheezal stared at the sergeant.

"We just fought a fuckin' war to get rid of ideas like that," he said. "How much is a book like that worth, you think?"

"Why, it's priceless, Chief. There aren't any more of them. And it's full of great ideas!"

Teeheezal reached in his pocket and took out a twenty-dollar gold piece (six weeks of Sgt. Hank's pay) and put it on the sergeant's desk.

He picked up the big book by one corner of the cover, walked over, lifted the stove lid with the handle, and tossed the book in.

"We just settled Germany's hash," said Teeheezal. "It comes to it, we'll settle Russia's too."

He picked up the sports section and went into his office and closed the door.

Sgt. Hank sat with his mouth open. He looked back and forth from the gold piece to the stove to the picture to Teeheezal's door.

He was still doing that when Patrolmen Rube and Buster brought in someone on a charge of drunk and disorderly.

1920

Captain Teeheezal turned his Model T across the oncoming traffic at the corner of Conklin and Arbuckle. He ignored the horns and sound of brakes and pulled into his parking place in front of the station house.

A shadow swept across the hood of his car, then another. He looked up and out. Two condors flew against the pink southwest sky where the orange ball of the sun was ready to set.

Sgt. Fatty was just coming into view down the street, carrying his big supper basket, ready to take over the night shift.

Captain Teeheezal had been at a meeting with the new mayor about all the changes that were coming when Wilcox was incorporated as a city.

Sgt. Hank came running out, waving a telegram. "This just came for you."

Teeheezal tore open the Western Union envelope.

TO: ALL POLICE DEPARTMENTS, ALL CITIES,
UNITED STATES OF AMERICA
FROM: OFFICE OF THE ATTORNEY GENERAL

1. VOLSTEAD ACT (PROHIBITION) IS NOW LAW
   STOP ALL POLICE DEPARTMENTS EXPECTED
   TO ENFORCE COMPLIANCE STOP
2. ROUND UP ALL THE REDS STOP
   PALMER

Teeheezal and the sergeant raced to punch the big red button on the sergeant's desk near the three phones. Bells went off in the squad room in the tower atop the station. Sgt. Fatty's lunch basket was on the sidewalk out front when they got back outside. He reappeared from around back, driving the black box of a truck marked *Police Patrol*, driving with one hand. And cranking the hand siren with the other, until Sgt. Hank jumped in beside him and began working the siren on the passenger side.

Patrolmen came from everywhere, the squad room, the garage, running down the streets, their nightsticks in their hands—Al, Mack, Buster, Chester, Billy, and Rube—and jumped onto the back of the truck, some missing, grabbing the back fender and being dragged until they righted themselves and climbed up with their fellows.

Teeheezal stood on the running board, nearly falling off as they hit the curb at the park across the street, where the benches had a *No Petting* sign above them.

"Head for the dago part of town," said Teeheezal, taking his belt and holster through the window from Sgt. Hank. "Here," he said to the sergeant, knocking his hand away from the siren crank. "Lemme do that!"

The world was a high screaming whine, and a blur of speed and nightsticks in motion when there was a job to be done.

AFTERWORD

When I looked, at my story log for this, I couldn't believe my eyes.

I'd always remembered this out-of-chronology, as being written *after* lots of other stories, I worked on part of it in the summer of 1994, because I read part of it while teaching at the Clarion SF Writers' Workshop (then in East Lansing, MI). I finished the whole thing and read the long-hand copy at Armadillocon on October 9, 1994. I typed it up on October 10 and 11 and sent it off to Gardner Dozois at *Asimov's*, like some Columbus of the Imagination, on October 12.

Gardner sent back a Wandering Angus post card, taking it, on October 20, I got the contracts a few days later, then the money, and it was published in *Asimov's* in Feb. 1996.

It was included in my first e-book of all my movie- and radio- and tv-based stories *Dream-Factories and Radio-Pictures* by Electricstory.com (2001) and reprinted by Wheatland Press in 2005, both of which are still available.

This story came from two places.

I was reading about the Palmer (US Attorney-General) raids on suspected Bolsheviks, anarchists and foreigners of 1920. People got rounded up and deported on general principles. (One part of this became the celebrated Sacco and Vanzetti case which dragged on till 1927.) At some point I realized that if the raids had taken place in the Hollywood of our imaginations, it would have been the Keystone Kops of Mack Sennett who carried them out. The story began (after a mountain of research) to write itself.

The other impetus was that I'd just heard Connie Willis read her story "In The Late Cretaceous"—other people who heard her read it just *liked* it. When she'd finished, my jaw was hanging open a foot.

What she'd written was the first story I know of where the subtext is *right on the surface* (which means of course that the *real* subtext is somewhere else). What I mean is that there was a 1 to 1 correspondence between a small paleontology department at a cow college, and the last days of the dinosaurs.

Well, I'd show *her*! Connie Willis isn't the *only one* who can do that!

Like "Heart of Whitenesse" in vol. 1, this is one of the most jam-packed stories I ever wrote. I'd first read about Osvald Spengler in a piece called "Fafhrd and Me" by Fritz Leiber in an early *Amra* @ 1960. I tried, god knows I tried, to get through *The Decline of the West* (1922) all through

my high school and college years. One page and zzzzzzzzzzzzzzz—
Morpheus comes stealing in. Everything is just as I described it in the
story.

Plus I'd been looking at Thomas Cole's *The Course of Empire* series of
five paintings for years; the essence of Spengler in visual form, though it
predated him by 60 years.

It all came together—even the order of the monsters encountered has
a historical, chronological background (you could read up on it, but right
now, *trust me*). This one is soaked through and through with historical par-
allels, right on the surface.

Take that, Willis.

After I read this at that Armadillocon, many people came up to me
and congratulated me on writing a story that didn't *confuse* them, for a
change.

"Thanks, I think," I said.

MAJOR SPACER IN THE 21st CENTURY!

June 1950

"Look," said Bill, "I'll see if I can go down and do a deposition this Thursday or Friday. Get ahold of Zachary Glass, see if he can fill in as . . . what's his name . . . ?"

"Lt. Marrs," said Sam Shorts.

". . . Lt. Marrs. We'll move that part of the story up. I'll record my lines. We can put it up over the spacephone, and Marrs and Neptuna can have the dialogue during the pursuit near the Moon we were gonna do week after next . . ."

"Yeah, sure!" said Sam. "We can have you over the phone, and them talking back and forth while his ship's closing in on hers, and your voice—yeah, that'll work fine."

"But you'll have to rewrite the science part I was gonna do, and give it yourself, as Cadet Sam. Man, it's just too bad there's no way to record this stuff ahead of time."

"Phil said they're working on it at the Bing Crosby Labs, trying to get some kind of tape to take a visual image; they can do it but they gotta shoot eight feet of tape a second by the recording head. It takes a mile of tape to do a ten-minute show," said Sam.

"And we can't do it on film, kids hate that."

"Funny," said Sam Shorts. "They pay fifteen cents for Gene Autry on film every Saturday afternoon, but they won't sit still for it on television . . ."

Philip walked in. "Morgan wants to see you about the Congress thing."

"Of course," said Bill.

"Run-through in . . ." Phil looked at his watch, and the studio clock ". . . eleven minutes. Seen Elizabeth?"

"Of course not," said Bill, on the way down the hall in his spacesuit, with his helmet under his arm.

That night, in his apartment, Bill typed on a script.

MAJOR SPACER: LOOKS LIKE SOMEONE LEFT IN A HURRY.

Bill looked up. *Super Circus* was on. Two of the clowns, Nicky and Scampy, squirted seltzer in ringmaster Claude Kirchner's face.

He never got to watch *Big Top*, the other circus show. It was on opposite his show.

Next morning, a young guy with glasses slouched out of a drugstore.

"Well, hey Bill!" he said.

"Jimmy!" said Bill, stopping, shifting his cheap cardboard portfolio to his other arm. He shook hands.

"Hey, I talked to Zooey," said Jimmy. "You in trouble with the Feds?"

"Not that I know of. I think they're bringing in everybody in the city with a kid's TV show."

He and Jimmy had been in a flop play together early in the year, before Bill started the show.

"How's it going otherwise?" asked Jimmy.

"It's about to kill all of us. We'll see if we make twenty weeks, much less a year. We're only four to five days ahead on the script. You available?"

"I'll have to look," said Jimmy. "I got two *Lamps Unto My Feet* next month, three-day rehearsals each, I think. I'm reading a couple plays, but that'll take a month before anybody gets off their butt. Let me know'f you need someone quick some afternoon. If I can, I'll jump in."

"Sure thing. And on top of everything else, looks like we'll have to move for next week; network's coming in and taking our space; trade-out with CBS. I'll be real damn glad when this Station Freeze is over, and there's more than ten damn places in this city that can do a network feed."

"I hear that could take a couple more years," said Jimmy, in his quiet Indiana voice.

"Yeah, well . . . hey, don't be such a stranger. Come on with me, I gotta get these over to the mimeograph room; we can talk on the way."

"Nah, nah," said Jimmy. "I, you know, gotta meet some people. I'm late already. See ya 'round, Bill."

"Well, okay."

Jimmy turned around thirty feet away. "Don't let the Feds get your jock strap in a knot!" he said, waved, and walked away.

People stared at both of them.

Damn, thought Bill. I don't get to see anyone anymore; I don't have a life except for the show. This is killing me. I'm still young.

"And what the hell are we supposed to do in this grange hall?" asked Bill.

"It's only a week," said Morgan. "Sure, it's seen better days, the Ziegfeld Roof, but they got a camera ramp so Harry and Fred can actually move in and out on a shot; you can play up and back, not just sideways like a crab, like usual."

Bill looked at the long wooden platform built out into what used to be the center aisle when it was a theater.

"Phil says he can shoot here . . ."

"Phil can do a show in a bathtub, he's so good, and Harry and Fred can work in a teacup, they're so good. That doesn't mean they have to," said Bill.

A stagehand walked in and raised the curtain while they stood there.

"Who's that?" asked Bill.

"Well, this is a rehearsal hall," said Morgan. "We're lucky to get it on such short notice."

When the curtain was full up there were the usual chalk marks on the stage boards, and scene flats lined up and stacked in twenty cradles at the rear of the stage.

"We'll be using that corner there," said Morgan, pointing. "Bring our sets in, wheel 'em, roll 'em in and out—ship, command center, planet surface."

Some of the flats for the other show looked familiar.

"The other group rehearses 10:00–2:00. They all gotta be out by 2:15. We rehearse, do the run-through at 5:30, do the show at 6:30."

Another stagehand came in with the outline of the tail end of a gigantic cow and put it into the scene cradle.

"What the hell are they rehearsing?" asked Bill.

"Oh. It's a musical based on the paintings of Grant Wood, you know, the Iowa artist?"

"You mean the *Washington and the Cherry Tree*, the DAR guy?"

"Yeah, him."

"That'll be a hit," said Bill. "What's it called?"

"I think they're calling it *In Tall Corn*. Well, what do you think?"

"I think it's a terrible idea. I can see the closing notices now."

"No, no. I mean the place. For the show," said Morgan.

Bill looked around. "Do I have any choice in the matter?"

"Of course not," said Morgan. "Everything else in town that's wired up is taken. I just wanted you to see it before you were dumped in it."

"Dumped is right," said Bill. He was looking at the camera ramp. It was the only saving grace. Maybe something could be done with it. . . .

"Harry and Fred seen it?"

"No, Phil's word is good enough for them. And, like you said, they can shoot in a coffee cup . . ."

Bill sighed. "Okay. Let's call a Sunday rehearsal day, this Sunday, do two blockings and rehearsals, do the run-through of Monday's show, let everybody get used to the place. Then they can come back just for the show Monday. Me and Sam'll see if we can do something in the scripts. Phil got the specs?"

"You know he has," said Morgan.

"Well, I guess one barn's as good as another," said Bill.

And as he said it, three stagehands brought on a barn and a silo and a windmill.

Even with both window fans on, it was hot as hell in the apartment. Bill slammed the carriage over on the Remington Noiseless Portable and hit the margin set and typed:

MAJOR SPACER: CAREFUL. SOMETIMES THE SURFACE OF MARS CAN LOOK AS ORDINARY AS A DESERT IN ARIZONA.

He got up and went to the kitchen table, picked up the bottle of Old Harper, poured some in a coffee cup and knocked it back.

There. That was better.

On TV, Haystacks Calhoun and Duke Kehanamuka were both working over Gorgeous George, while Gorilla Monsoon argued with the referee, whose back was to the action. Every time one of them twisted George's arm or leg, the announcer, Dennis James, snapped a chicken bone next to the mike.

"Look at this," said Morgan, the next morning.

It was a handwritten note.

I know your show is full of commies. My brother-in-law told me you have commie actors. Thank God for people like Senator McCarthy who will run you rats out of this land of Liberty and Freedom.

Signed,

A Real American

"Put it in the circular file," said Bill.

"I'll keep it," said Morgan. "Who are they talking about?"

"You tell me. I'm not old enough to be a communist."

"Could it be true?" asked Morgan.

"Don't tell me you're listening to all that crap, too?"

"There's been a couple of newsletters coming around, with names of people on it. I know some of them; they give money to the NAACP and ACLU. Otherwise they live in big houses and drive big cars and order their servants around like Daddy Warbucks. But then, I don't know all the names on the lists."

"Is anybody we ever hired on any of the lists?"

"Not as such," said Morgan.

"Well, then?"

"Well, then," said Morgan, and picked up a production schedule. "Well, then, nothing, I guess, Bill."

"Good," said Bill. He picked up the letter from Morgan's desk, wadded it into a ball, and drop-kicked it into the wastebasket.

The hungover Montgomery Clift reeled by on his way to the Friday performance of the disaster of a play he was in. Bill waved, but Clift didn't notice; his eyes were fixed on some far distant promontory fifty miles up the Hudson, if they were working at all. Clift had been one intense, conflicted, messed-up individual when Bill had first met him. Then he had gone off to Hollywood and discovered sex and booze and drugs and brought them with him back to Broadway.

Ahead of Bill was the hotel where the congressmen and lawyers waited.

Counsel (Mr. Eclept): Now that you have taken the oath, give your full name and age for the record.

S: Major William Spacer. I'm twenty-one years old.

E: No, sir. Not your stage name.

S: Major William Spacer. That's my real name.

Congressman Beenz: You mean Major Spacer isn't just the show name?

S: Well, sir, it is and it isn't . . . Most people just think we gave me a promotion over Captain Video.

Congressman Rice: How was it you were named Major?

S: You would have had to have asked my parents that; unfortunately they're deceased. I have an aunt in Kansas who might be able to shed some light . . .

* * *

S: That's not the way it's done, Congressman.

B: You mean you just can't fly out to the Big Dipper, once you're in space?

S: Well, you can, but they're . . . they're light years apart. They . . . they appear to us as The Big Dipper because we're looking at them from Earth.

R: I'm not sure I understand, either.

S: It . . . it's like that place in . . . Vermont, New Hampshire, one of those. North of here, anyway. You come around that turn in Rt 9A or whatever, and there's Abraham Lincoln, the head, the hair, the beard. It's so real you stop. Then you drive down the road a couple hundred yards, and the beard's a plum thicket on a meadow, and the hair's pine trees on a hill, and the nose is on one mountain, but the rest of the face is on another. It only looks like Lincoln from that one spot in the road. That's why the Big Dipper looks that way from Earth.

B: I do not know how we got off on this . . .

S: I'm trying to answer your questions here, sir.

E: Perhaps we should get to the substantive matters here . . .

S: All I've noticed, counsel, is that all the people who turn up as witnesses and accusers at these things seem to have names out of old W.C. Fields' movies, names like R. Waldo Chubb and F. Clement Bozo.

E: I believe you're referring to Mr. Clubb and Mr. Bozell?

S: I'm busy, Mr. Eclept; I only get to glance at newspapers. I'm concerned with the future, not what's happening right this minute.

B: So are we, young man. That's why we're trying to root out any communist influence in the broadcast industry, so there won't be any in the future.

R: We can't stress that too forcefully.

S: Well, I can't think of a single communist space pirate we've ever portrayed on the show. It takes place in the 21st Century, Congressman. So I guess we share the same future. Besides, last time I looked, piracy was a capitalist invention. . . .

S: That's why we never have stories set further than Mars or Venus, Congressman. Most of the show takes place in near-space, or on the Moon. We try to keep the science accurate. That's why there's always a segment with me or Sam—that's Samuel J. Shorts, the other writer on the show—by the way, he's called "Uncle Sam" Spacer—telling kids about the future, and what it'll be like to grow up in the wonderful years of the 21st Century.

B: If we don't blow ourselves up first.

R: You mean if some foreign power doesn't try to blow us up first.

S: Well, we've talked about the peaceful uses of atomic energy. Food preservation. Atomic-powered airplanes and cars. Nuclear fusion as a source of energy too cheap to meter.

E: Is it true you broadcast a show about a world government?

S: Not in the science segment, that I recall.

E: No. I mean the story, the entertainment part.

S: We've been on the air three months, that's nearly sixty shows. Let me think . . .

E: A source has told us there's a world government on the show.

S: Oh. It's a worlds' government, counsel. It's the United States of Space. We assume there won't be just one state on Mars, or the Moon, or Venus, and that they'll have to come to the central government to settle their disputes. We have that on the Moon.

R: They have to go to the Moon to settle a dispute between Mars and the United States?

S: No, no. That would be like France suing Wisconsin. . . .

B: ". . . and other red channels." And that's a direct quote.

S: Congressman, I created the show; I act in it; I write either half the scripts, or one-half of each script, whichever way it works out that week. I do this five days a week, supposedly for fifty weeks a year—we'll see if I make it that long. I've given the day-to-day operations, all the merchandising negotiations to my partner, James B. Morgan. We have a small cast with only a few recurring characters, and except for the occasional Martian bad guy, or Lunar owl-hoot, they're all known to me. I never ask anybody about their politics or religion. All I want to know is whether they can memorize lines quick, and act in a tight set, under time pressure, live, with a camera stuck in their ear. The only thing red we have anything to do with is Mars. And it isn't channels; it's canals. . . .

S: . . . I have no knowledge of any. I'll tell you what, right now, Congressman, I'll bet my show on it. You come up with any on the cast and crew, I'll withdraw the show.

B: We'll hold you to that, young man.

R: I want to thank you for appearing for this deposition today, and for being so forthcoming with us, Mr. Spacer.

B: I agree.
R: You are excused.

There was one reporter waiting outside in the hallway, besides the government goon keeping everyone out.

The reporter was the old kind, press card stuck in his hat, right out of *The Front Page.*

"Got any statement, Mr. Spacer?"

"Well, as you know, I can't talk about what I said till the investigation's concluded. They asked me questions. I answered them as best as I could."

"What sort of questions?"

"I'm sure you can figure that out. You've seen the televised hearings?"

"What were they trying to find out?" asked the reporter.

"I'm not sure . . ." said Bill.

The government goon smiled. When he and the reporter parted ways in the lobby, Bill was surprised that it was already summer twilight. He must have been in there five or six hours. . . . He took off for the studio, to find out what kind of disaster the broadcast with Zach Glass had been.

Bill wiggled his toes in his socks, including the stump of the little one on the right foot, a souvenir from a Boy Scout hatchet-throwing contest gone wrong back when he was twelve.

He was typing while he watched *Blues By Bargy* on TV. Saturday night noise came from outside.

Then the transmission was interrupted with a PLEASE STAND BY notice. Douglas Edwards came on with a special bulletin, which he ripped out of the chundering teletype machine at his right elbow.

He said there were as yet unconfirmed reports that North Korean Armed Forces had crossed into South Korea. President Truman, who was on a weekend trip to his home in Independence, Missouri, had not been reached by CBS for a comment. Then he said they would be interrupting regularly scheduled programming if there were further developments.

Then they went back to *Blues by Bargy.*

"Look," said Phil. "James, you gotta get those rehearsing assholes outta here, I mean, out of here, earlier. When I came in Saturday to set up, I found they used all the drop-pipes for their show. I had to make them move a quarter of their stuff. They said they needed them all. I told 'em to put wheels on their stuff like we're having to do with most of ours, but we still need some pipes to drop in the exteriors, and to mask the sets off. And they're hanging around with their girlfriends and boyfriends, while I'm trying to set up marks."

It was Sunday, the start of their week at the Ziegfeld Roof. They were to block out Monday's and Tuesday's shows, rehearse them, and do the run-through and technical for Monday's broadcast.

"I'll talk to their stage manager," said Morgan. "Believe me, moving here gripes me as much as it does you. Where's Elizabeth?"

"Here," said Elizabeth Regine, coming out of the dressing room in her rehearsal Neptuna outfit. "I couldn't believe this place when I got here."

"Believe it, baby," said Phil. "We've got to make do." He looked at his watch. "Bill, I think the script may be a little long, just looking at it."

"Same as always. Twenty-four pages."

"Yeah, but you got suspense stuff in there. That's thirty seconds each. Be thinking about it while we're blocking it."

"You're the director, Phil."

"That's what you and James pay me for." He looked over at the stage crew. "No!" he said. "Right one, left one, right one," he moved his hands.

"That's what they are," said the foreman.

"No, you got left, right, left."

The guy, Harvey, joined him to look at the wheeled sets. "Left," he pointed to the rocket interior. "Right," the command room on the Moon. "Left," the foreground scenery and the rocket fin for the Mars scenes.

"And from whence does the rest of the Mars set drop in?" asked Phil.

"Right. Oh, merde!" said Harve.

"And they're the best crew on television," said Phil, as the stagehands ratcheted the scenery around. "They really are," he said, turning back to Bill and Morgan. "That way we stay on the rocket interior, and you leave, run behind the middle set, and step down onto Mars, while the space-phone chatters away. Also, you'll be out of breath, so it'll sound like you just climbed down fifty feet of ladder. . . ."

It was seven when they finished the blocking, two rehearsals, and the run-through of the first show of the week. Phil was right, the script was one minute and fifty-three seconds long.

Bill looked at the camera ramp. "I still want to do something with that," he said, "while we've got it."

"Wednesday," said Phil.

"Why Wednesday?"

"You got a blast-off scene. We do it from the front. We get the scenery guy to build a nose view of the ship. Red Mars background behind. Like the ship from above. You and Neptuna stand behind it, looking out the cockpit. You count down. Harvey hits the CO_2 extinguisher behind you for rocket smoke. I get Harry or Fred to run at you with the camera as fast as he can, from way back there. Just before he collides, we cut to the telecine chain for the commercial."

"Marry me," said Bill.

"Some other time," said Phil. "Everybody back at 4:00 P.M. tomorrow. Everything's set. Don't touch a goddamn thing before you leave."

Toast of the Town, hosted by Ed Sullivan, was on TV.

Señor Wences was having a three-way conversation with Johnny (which was his left hand rested on top of a doll body); Pedro, the head in the cigar box; and a stagehand who was down behind a crate, supposedly fixing a loose board with a hammer.

Halfway through the act, two stagehands came out, picked up the crate, showing it was empty, and walked off, leaving a bare stage.

"Look. Look!" said Johnny, turning his fist-head on the body that way. "There was not a man there."

"There was no man there?" asked Wences.

"No," said Johnny. "There was not a man there."

"What do you t'ink, Pedro?" asked Wences, opening the box with his right hand.

"S'awright," said Pedro. The box snapped shut.

"Come in here," said Morgan from the door of his makeshift office, as Bill came into the theater.

Sam was in a chair, crying.

Morgan's face was set, as Bill had never seen before. "Tell him what you just told me."

"I can't," Sam wailed. "What am I gonna do? I'm forty years old!"

"Maybe you should have thought of that back in 1931."

"What the hell is going on? Sam! Sam? Talk to me."

"Oh, Bill," he said. "I'm sorry."

"Somebody. One of you. Start making sense. Right now," said Bill.

"Mr. Sam Shorts, here, seems to have been a commie bagman during the Depression."

"Say it ain't so, Sam," said Bill.

Sam looked at him. Tears started down his face again.

"There's your answer," said Morgan, running his hands through his hair and looking for something to throw.

"I was young," said Sam. "I was so hungry. I swore I'd never be that hungry again. I was too proud for the bread line, a guy offered me a job, if you can call it that, moving some office stuff. Then as a sort of messenger. Between his office and other places. Delivering stuff. I thought it was some sort of bookie joint or numbers running, or money laundering, or the bootleg. Something illegal, sure . . . but . . . but . . . I didn't . . . didn't . . ."

"What? What!"

"I didn't think it was anything un-American!" said Sam, crying again.

"Morgan. Tell me what he told you."

"He was a bagman, a messenger between United Front stuff the Feds know about and some they probably don't. He did it for about three years."

"Four," said Sam, trying to control himself.

"Great," continued Morgan. "Four years, on and off. Then somebody pissed him off and he walked away."

"Just because they were reds," said Sam, "didn't make 'em good bosses."

Bill hated himself for asking; he thought of Parnell Thomas and McCarthy.

"Did you sign anything?"

"I may have. I signed a lot of stuff to get paid."

"Under your real name?"

"I guess so. Some, anyway."

"Guess what name they had him use sometime?" asked Morgan.

"I don't want to," said Bill.

"George Crosley."

"That was one of the names Whittaker Chambers used!" said Bill.

"They weren't the most inventive guys in the world," said Morgan.

"I knew. I knew the jig would be up when I watched the Hiss thing," said Sam. "When I heard that name. Then nothing happened. I guess I thought nothing would . . ."

"How could you do this to me?!!" yelled Bill.

"You? You were a one-year-old! I didn't know you! It wasn't personal, Bill. You either, Morgan."

"You know I put my show on the line in the deposition, don't you?"

"Not till Morgan told me." Sam began to cry again.

"What brought on this sudden cleansing, now, twenty years later?" asked Bill.

"There was another letter," said Morgan. "This time naming a name, not the right one, but it won't take anybody long to figure that one out. Also that they were calling the Feds. I was looking at it, and looking glum, when Sam comes in. He asks what's up; I asked him if he knew anybody by the name of the guy in the letter, and he went off like the Hindenburg. A wet Hindenburg."

Sam was crying again.

Bill's shoulders slumped.

"Okay, Morgan. Call everybody together. I'll talk to them. Sam, quit it. Quit it. You're still a great writer. Buck up. We'll get through this. Nothing's happened yet. . . ."

Live. The pressure's on, like always. Everybody's a pro here, even with this world falling apart. Harry and Fred on the cameras, Phil up in the booth, Morgan with him, Sam out there where the audience would be, going through the scripts for Thursday and Friday like nothing's happened.

He and Elizabeth, as Neptuna, are in the rocket interior set, putting on their spacesuits, giving their lines. Bill's suit wasn't going on right; he made a small motion with his hand; Fred moved his camera in tight on Bill's face; Philip would switch to it, or Harry's shot on Neptuna's face; the floor manager reached up while Bill was talking and pulled at the lining of the spacesuit, and it went on smoothly; the floor manager crawled out and Fred pulled his camera back again to a two-shot. Then he and Neptuna moved into the airlock; it cycled closed. Harry swung his camera around to the grille of the spacephone speaker; an urgent message came from it, warning Major Spacer that a big Martian dust storm was building up in their area.

While the voice was coming over the speaker in the tight shot, Bill and Elizabeth walked behind the Moon command center flats and hid behind the rocket fin while the stage crew dropped in the Martian exterior set and the boom man wheeled the microphone around and Fred dollied his camera in.

"Is Sam okay?" Elizabeth had asked, touching her helmet to Bill's before the soundman got there.

"I hope so," said Bill.

He looked out. The floor manager, who should have been counting down on his fingers five-four-three-two-one was standing stock still. Fred's camera wobbled—and he was usually the steadiest man in the business.

The floor manager pulled off his earphones, shrugged his shoulders, and swung his head helplessly toward the booth.

It's got to be time, thought Bill; touched Elizabeth on the arm, and gave his line, backing down off a box behind the fin out onto the set.

"Careful," he said. "Sometimes the surface of Mars can look as ordinary as a desert in Arizona."

Elizabeth, who was usually unflappable, stared, eyes wide past him at the exterior set. And dropped her Neptuna character, and instead of her line, said: "And sometimes it looks just like Iowa."

Bill turned.

Instead of a desert, and a couple of twisted Martian cacti and a backdrop of Monument Valley, there was the butt-end of a big cow and a barn and silo, some chickens, and a three-rail fence.

Bill sat in the dressing room, drinking Old Harper from the bottle.

Patti Page was on the radio, singing of better days.

There was a knock on the door.

It was the government goon. He was smiling. There was one subpoena for Bill, and one for Sam Shorts.

June 2000

Bill came out the front door of the apartments on his way to his job as a linotype operator at the *New York Times*.

There were, as usual, four or five kids on the stoop, and as usual, too, Rudy, a youngster of fifty years, was in the middle of his rant, holding up two twenty-dollar bills.

". . . that there was to trace the dope, man. They changed the money so they could find out where all them coke dollars were. That plastic thread shit in this one, that was the laser radar stuff. They could roll a special truck down your street, and tell what was a crack house by all the eyeball noise that lit up their screens. And the garage-sale people and the flea-market people. They could find that stuff— Hey, Bill—"

"Hey, Rudy."

"—before it All Quit they was goin' to be able to count the ones in your billfold from six blocks away, man."

"Why was that, Rudy?" asked a girl-kid.

"'Cause they wasn't enough money! They printed the stuff legit but it just kept going away. It was in the quote 'underground economy.' They said it was so people couldn't counterfeit it on a Savin 2300 or somebullshit, or the camel-jocks couldn't flood the PXs with fake stuff, but it was so they didn't have to wear out a lotta shoe leather and do lotsa *Hill Street Blues* wino-cop type stuff just to get to swear out a lot of warrants. See, that machine in that truck make noise, they take a printout of that to a judge, and pretty soon door hinges was flyin' all over town. Seen 'em take two blocks out at one time, man. Those was evil times, be glad they gone."

"So are we, Rudy; we're glad they can't do that even though we never heard of it."

"You just wait your young ass," said Rudy. "Some devious yahoo in Baltimore workin' on that right now; they had that knowledge once, it don't just go away, it just mutates, you know. They'll find a way to do that with vacuum tubes and such . . ."

Rudy's voice faded as Bill walked on down toward the corner. Rudy gave some version of that talk, somewhere in the neighborhood, every day. Taking the place of Rudy was the voice from the low-power radio station speakerbox on the corner.

". . . that the person was dressed in green pants, a yellow Joe Camel tyvek jacket, and a black T-shirt. The wallet grab occurred four minutes ago at the corner of Lincoln and Jackson, neighbors are asked to be on the lookout for this person, and to use the nearest call-box to report a sighting. Now back to music, from a V-disk transcription, Glenn Miller and His Orchestra with 'In the Mood.'"

Music filled the air. Coming down the street was a 1961 armored car, the Wells-Fargo logo spray-painted over, and a cardboard sign saying TAXI over the high windshield. On the front bumper was a sticker that said SCREW THE CITY TAXI COMMISSION.

Bill held up his hand. The car rumbled over to the curb.

"Where to, kindly old geezer?"

Bill said the Times Building, which was about thirty blocks away.

"What's it worth to you, Pops?"

"How about a buck?" said Bill.

"Real money?"

"Sure."

"Hop in, then. Gotta take somebody up here a couple blocks, and there'll be one stop on the way, so far."

Bill went around back, opened the door and got in, nodding to the other two passengers. He was at work in fifteen minutes.

It was a nice afternoon, so when Bill got off work he took the omnibus to the edge of the commercial district, got off there and started walking home. Since it was summer, there seemed to be a street fair every other block. He could tell when he passed from one neighborhood to another by the difference in the announcer voices on the low-power stations.

He passed Ned Ludd's Store #23, and the line, as usual, was backed out the door onto the sidewalk, and around the corner of the building. In the display window were stereo phonographs and records, transistor radios, batteries, toaster ovens, and none-cable-ready TVs, including an old Philco with the picture tube supported above the console like a dresser mirror.

Some kids were in line, talking, melancholy looks on their faces, about something. "It was called *Cargo Cult*," said one. "You were on an island, with a native culture, and then WWII came, and the people tried to get cargo, you know, trade goods, and other people were trying to get them to keep their native ways . . ."

"Plus," said the second kid, "you got to blow up a lotta Japanese soldiers and eat them!"

"Sounds neat," said the third, "but I never heard of it."

A guy came out of the tavern next door, a little unsteady, and stopped momentarily, like Bill, like everyone else who passed, to watch the pixie-vision soap opera playing in black and white.

The guy swayed a little, listening to the kids' conversation; then a determined smile came across his face.

"Hey, kids," he said.

They stopped talking and looked at him. One said "Yeah?"

The man leaned forward. "Triple picture-in-picture," he said.

Their faces fell.

He threw back his head and laughed, then put his hands in his pockets and weaved away.

On TV, there was a blank screen while they changed the pixievision tapes by hand, something they did every eight-and-a-half minutes.

Bill headed on home.

He neared his block, tired from the walk and his five-hour shift at the paper. He almost forgot Tuesday was mail day until he was in sight of the apartments, then walked back to the Postal Joint. For him there was a union meeting notice, in case he hadn't read the bulletin board at work, and that guy from Ohio was bothering him again with letters asking him questions for the biography of James Dean he'd been researching since 1989, most of which Bill had answered in 1989.

He was halfway back to the apartments, just past the low-power speaker, when six men dragged a guy, in ripped green pants and what was left of a Joe Camel jacket, out onto the corner, pushed the police button, and stood on the guy's hands and feet, their arms crossed, talking about a neighborhood fast-pitch softball game coming up that night.

Bill looked back as he crossed the street. A squad car pulled up and the guys all greeted the policemen.

* * *

"Today was mail day, right kids?" said Rudy. "Well in the old days the Feds set up Postal Joint-type places, you know, The Stamp Act, Box Me In, stuff like that, to scam the scammers that was scammin' you. That shoulda been fine, but they was readin' like everybody's mail, like Aunt Gracie's to you, and yours to her, and you know, your girlfriend's and boyfriend's to you, and lookin' at the Polaroids and stuff, which you some-times wouldn't get, you dig? See, when they's evil to be fought, you can't be doin' evil to get at it. Don't be lettin' nobody get your mail—there's a man to see you in the lobby, Bill—"

"Thanks, Rudy."

"—and don't be readin' none that ain't yours. It's a fool that gets scammed; you honest, you don't be fallin' for none o' that stuff like free boats and cars and beautiful diamond-studded watches, you know?"

"Sure, Rudy," said the kids.

The guy looked at something in his hand, then back at Bill, squinted and said: "Are you Major Spacer?"

"Nobody but a guy in Ohio's called me that for fifty years," said Bill.

"Arnold Fossman," said the guy, holding out his hand. Bill shook it.

"Who you researching? Monty Clift?"

"Huh? No," said Fossman. He seemed perplexed, then brightened. "I want to offer you a job, doesn't pay much."

"Son, I got a good-payin' job that'll last me way to the end of my time. Came out of what I laughingly call retirement to do it."

"Yeah, somebody told me about you being at the *Times*, with all the old people with the old skills they called back. I don't think this'll interfere with that."

"I'm old and I'm tired and I been setting a galley and a quarter an hour for five hours. Get to it."

"I want to offer you an acting job."

"I haven't acted in fifty years, either."

"They tell me it's just like riding a bicycle. You . . . you might think—wait. Hold on. Indulge me just a second." He reached up and took Bill's rimless Trotsky glasses from his face.

"Whup!" said Bill.

Fossman took off his own thick black-rimmed glasses and put them over Bill's ears. The world was skewed up and to the left and down to the right and Fossman was a tiny figure in the distance.

"I ain't doin' anything with these glasses on!" said Bill. "I'm afraid to move."

The dim fuzzy world came back, then the sharp normal one as Fossman put Bill's glasses back on him.

"I was getting a look at you with thick frames. You'll be great."

"I'm a nice guy," said Bill. "You don't get to the point, I'll do my feeble best to pound you into this floor here like a tent peg."

"Okay." Fossman held up his hand. "But hear me out completely. Don't say a word till I'm through. Here goes.

"I want to offer you a job in a play, a musical. Everybody says I'm crazy to do it; I've had the idea for years, and now's the time to do it, with everything like it is. I've got the place to do it in, and you know there's an audience for anything that moves. Then I found out a couple of weeks ago my idea ain't so original, that somebody tried to do it a long time ago; it closed out of town in Bristol, CT, big flop. But your name came up in connection with it; I thought maybe you had done the show originally, and then they told me why your name always came up in connection with it—the more I heard, and found out you were still around, the more I knew you had to be in it, as some sort of, well, call it what you want—homage, reparation, I don't know. I'm the producer-guy, not very good with words. Anyway. I'm doing a musical based on the paintings of Grant Wood. I want you to be in it. Will you?"

"Sure," said Bill.

It was a theater not far from work, a 500-seater.

"Thank God it's not the Ziegfeld Roof," said Bill. He and Fossman were sitting, legs draped into the orchestra pit, at the stage apron.

"Yeah, well, that's been gone a long time."

"They put it under the wrecking ball while I was a drunk, or so they told me," said Bill.

"And might I ask how long that was?" asked Fossman.

"Eight years, three months, and two days," said Bill. "God, I sound like a reformed alcoholic. Geez, they're boring."

"Most people don't have what it really takes to be an alcoholic," said Fossman. "I was the son of one, a great one, and I know how hard you've got to work at it."

"I had what it takes," said Bill. "I just got tired of it."

He heard on the neighborhood radio there had been a battery riot in the Battery.

Bill stretched himself, and did some slow exercises. Fifty years of moving any old which way didn't cure itself in a few days.

He went over to the mirror and looked at himself.

The good-looking fair-haired youth had been taken over by a balding old man.

"Hello," said Marion.

"Hello yourself," said Bill, as he passed her on his way to work. She was getting ready to leave for her job at the library, where every day she took down books, went through the information on the copyright page, and typed it up on two 4x6 cards, one of which was put in a big series of drawers in the entryway, where patrons could find what books were there without looking on all the shelves, and one of which was sent to the central library system.

She lived in one of the apartments downstairs from Bill. She once said the job would probably take herself, and three others, more than a year, just at her branch. She was a youngster in her forties.

Bill found rehearsals the same mixture of joy and boredom they had been a half-century before, with the same smells of paint and turpentine coming from the scene shop. The cast had convinced Arnold to direct the play, rather than hiring some schmuck, as he'd originally wanted to do. He'd conceived it; it was his vision.

During a break one night, Bill lay on the floor; Arnold slumped in a chair, and Shirlene, the lead dancer, lay face down on the sofa with a migraine. Bill chuckled, he thought, to himself.

"What's up?" asked Fossman.

"It was probably just like this in rehearsals when Plautus was sitting where you are."

"Guess so."

"Were there headaches then?" asked Shirlene.

"Well, there were in my day, and that wasn't too long after the Romans," said Bill. "One of our cameramen had them." He looked around. "Thanks, Arnold."

"For what?"

"For showing me how much I didn't remember I missed this stuff."

"Well, sure," said Fossman. "OK, folks, let's get back to the grind. Shirlene, lie there till you feel better."

She got to her feet. "I'll never feel better," she said.

"See—" said Rudy—"it was on January third, and everybody was con-gratulatin' themselves on beatin' that ol' Y2K monster, and was throwin' out them ham and lima bean MREs into the dumpsters. Joyful, you know—another Kohoutek, that was a comet that didn't amount to a bird fart back in them way old '70s. Anyway, it was exactly at 10:02 A.M. EST right here, when them three old surplus Russian-made diesel submarines that somebody—and nobody's still sure just who—bought up back in the 1990s surfaced in three places around the world—and fired off them surplus NASA booster rockets, nine or ten of 'em—"

"Why 'cause we know that, Rudy, if we don't know who did it?"

"Cause everybody had electric stuff back then could tell what kind of damn watch you was wearin' from two hundred miles out in space by how fast it was draggin' down that 1.5-volt battery in it. They knew the subs was old Russian surplus as soon as they surfaced, and knew they was NASA boosters as soon as the fuses was lit—'cause that's the kind of world your folks let happen for you to live in—that's why 'cause."

"Oh."

"As old Rudy was sayin', them nine or ten missiles, some went to the top of the atmosphere, and some went further out where all them ATT and HBO and them satellites that could read your watch was, and they all went off and meanwhile everybody everywhere was firin' off all they stuff to try to stop whatever was gonna happen—well, when all that kind of stuff went off, and it turns out them sub missiles was big pulse explosions, what they used to call EMP stuff, and all the other crap went off that was tryin' to stop the missiles, well then, kids, Time started over as far as ol' Rudy's concerned. Not just for the U S of A and Yooropeans, but for everybody everywhere, even down to them gentle Tasaday and every witchety grub-eatin' sonofagun down under."

"Time ain't started over, Rudy," said a kid. "This is Tuesday. It's June. This is the year 2000 A.D."

"Sure, sure. On the outside," said Rudy. "I'm talkin' 'bout the inside. We can do it all over again. Or not. Look, people took a week to find out what still worked, when what juice there was gonna be came back on. See, up till then they all thought them EMP pulses would just knock out every-thing, everywhere that was electronic, solid state stuff, transistors. That's without takin' into account all that other crap that was zoomin' around, and people tryin' to jam stuff, and all that false target shit they put up cause at first they thought it was a sneak attack on cities and stuff, and they just went, you know, apeshit for about ten minutes.

"So what was left was arbitrary. Like nobody could figure why Betamax players sometimes was okay and no Beta III VCR was. Your CDs are fine; you just can't play 'em. Then why none of them laserdiscs are okay, even if you had a machine that would play 'em? It don't make a fuckin' bit o' sense. Why icemaker refrigerators sometimes work and most others don't? You can't get no fancy embroidery on your fishing shirt: It all come out lookin' like Jackson Pollock. No kind of damn broadcast TV for a week, none of that satellite TV shit, for sure. Ain't no computers work but them damn Osbornes they been usin' to build artificial reefs in lakes for twenty years. Cars? You seen anything newer than a 1974 Subaru on the street, movin'? Them '49 Plymouths and '63 Fords still goin', cause they ain't got nothin' in them that don't move you can't fix with a pair o' Vise Grips . . .

"Look at the damn mail we was talking about! Ain't nobody in the Post Office actually had to read a damn address in ten years; you bet your ass they gotta read writin' now! Everybody was freaked out. No e-mail, no phone, no fax, ain't no more Click On This, kids. People all goin' crazy till they start gettin' them letters from Visa and Mastercard and such sayin' 'Hey, we hear you got an account with us? Why doncha tell us what you owe us, and we'll start sendin' you bills again?' Well, that was one thing they liked sure as shit. They still waitin' for their new cards with them raised-up letters you run through a big ol' machine, but you know what? They think about sixty to seventy percent o' them people told them what they owed them. Can you beat that? People's mostly honest, 'ceptin' the ones that ain't. . . .

"That's why you gettin' mail twice a week now, not at your house but on the block, see? You gonna have to have some smart people now; that's why I'm tellin' you all this."

"Thanks, Rudy," said a kid.

"Now that they ain't but four million people in this popsicle town, you got room to learn, room to move around some. All them scaredy cats took off for them wild places, like Montana, Utah, New Jersey. Now you got room to breathe, maybe one o' you gonna figure everything out someday, kid. That'll be thanks enough for old Rudy. But this time, don't mess up. Keep us fuckin' human— Morning, Bill—"

"Morning, Rudy."

"—and another thing. No damn cell phones. No damn baby joggers or double fuckin' wide baby strollers. No car alarms!"

Opening night

The dancers are finishing the Harvest Dinner dance, like *Oklahoma!* or "June Is Bustin' Out All Over" on speed. It ends with a blackout. The packed house goes crazy.

Spotlight comes up on center stage.

Bill stands beside Shirlene. He's dressed in bib overalls and a black jacket and holds a pitchfork. She's in a simple farm dress. Bill wears thick glasses. He looks just like the dentist B.H. McKeeby, who posed as the farmer, and Shirlene looks just like Nan Wood, Grant's sister, who posed as the farmer's spinster daughter, down to the pulled-back hair, and the cameo brooch on the dress.

Then the lights come up on stage, and Bill and Shirlene turn to face the carpenter-gothic farmhouse, with the big arched window over the porch.

Instead of it, the backdrop is a painting from one of the Mars Lander photos of a rocky surface.

Bill just stopped.

There was dead silence in the theater, then a buzz, then sort of a louder sound; then some applause started, and grew and grew, and people came to their feet, and the sound rose and rose.

Bill looked over. Shirlene was smiling, and tears ran down her cheeks. Then the house set dropped in, with a working windmill off to the side, and the dancers ran on from each wing, and they did, along with Bill, the Pitchfork Number.

The lights went down, Bill came off the stage, and the chorus ran on for the Birthplace of Herbert Hoover routine.

Bill put his arms around Fossman's shoulders.

"You . . . you . . . asshole," said Bill.

"If you would have known about it, you would have fucked it up," said Arnold.

"But . . . how . . . the audience . . . ?"

"We slipped a notice in the programs, just for the opening, which is why you didn't see one. Might I say your dancing was superb tonight?"

"No. No," said Bill, crying. "Kirk Alyn, the guy who played Superman in the serials in the Forties, now there was a dancer . . ."

On his way home that night, he saw that a kid had put up a new graffiti on the official site, and had run out of paint at the end, so the message read "What do we have left they could hate us" and then the faded letters, from the thinning and upside-down spray can, "f o r ?"

Right on, thought Bill. Fab. Gear. Groovy.

At work the next day, he found himself setting the galleys of the rave review of *Glorifying the American Gothic*, by the *Times'* drama critic.

And on a day two months later:

"And now!" said the off-pixievision-camera announcer, "Live! On Television! Major Spacer in the 21st Century!"

* * *

"... tune in tomorrow, when you'll hear Major Spacer say: WE'LL GET BACK TO THE MOON IF WE HAVE TO RETROFIT EVERY ICBM IN THE JUNKPILE WITH DUCT TAPE AND SUPERGLUE.

"Don't miss it. And now, for today's science segment, we go to the Space Postal Joint, with Cadet Rudy!" said the announcer.

Rudy: "Hey, kids. Listen to ol' Rudy. Your folks tried hard but they didn't know their asses from holes in the ground when it came to some things. They didn't mean to mess your world up; they just backed into one that could be brought down in thirty seconds 'cause it was the easiest thing to do. Remember the words of Artoo Deetoo Clarke: 'With increasin' technology, you headin' for a fall.' Now listen how it could be in this excitin' world of the future ..."

A few years later, after Bill and the show and Rudy were gone, some kid, who'd watched it every day, figured everything out.

And kept us human.

AFTERWORD

I'd always wanted to write a story with a fifty-year space-break in the middle of it, and now I have.

What I was trying to do here, among other things, was to show the changes in technology in that time; the ones we all now take for granted.

In 1950, long-playing records and 45 rpm singles had only been around a couple of years (1948). Everything *before* then had been Edison cylinders or shellac 78 rpms. TV had been started in the 1920s (see my "Hoover's Men" and "Mr. Goober's Show" in *Dream-Factories and Radio-Pictures*) but had only become a household actuality in 1946; the co-axial cable hadn't been laid coast-to-coast yet, so networks were in their infancy (and there was a freeze from 1948 to 1952 on issuing *new* television broadcast licenses by the FCC while they tried to work out a color television system: luckily RCA-NBC won out with an electronic color-compatible system, or else we'd now be watching stuff on a bastard half-mechanical, half-electronic non-compatible system backed by CBS). Even when the cable had been laid, shows were done twice (like on radio before it) because the broadcasts were *live*; so you did the show twice, like once at 8 P.M. Thursday for Eastern and Central, and again at 11 P.M. for the West Coast, and you gave the cowboys on Mountain Time kinescopes (film off a studio monitor) *next week*, in fuzzyvision. [To paraphrase *Sullivan's Travels*: "It won't play in Albuquerque." "What do they know in Albuquerque?" "They know what they *like*." "If they knew what they *liked*, they wouldn't be in Albuquerque."].

It was Desi Arnaz, of all people, who came up with the now-universal 5-cameras-before-a-live-studio-audience system (with his director of photography Karl Freund—director of *The Mummy* 1932 and *Mad Love* 1935—who came out of retirement to do so) and who realized you needed to *film* television series for broadcast *anytime anywhere*, and thereby caused the center of TV production to move to California (where the film production centers were) from New York City (where the actors for *live drama* were), when he did *I Love Lucy*.

Videotape was unknown as yet (though as I say, Bing Crosby was working on it. How come it was a Cuban conga-drum player and a crooner from Spokane who brought about what we watch on TV today?)

Remotes in those days were wired to a big mechanical motor that clamped to your channel knob; when you pushed the buttons on the big battery-pack in your hand, the motor *actually turned* the channel knob—

whirr-click. Otherwise you got up, walked to the TV and twisted the knob with your hand. (Remotes were to make cable and satellite TV possible.)

Cable was a gleam in someone's eye. (There were experiments with pay-TV, as it was called, as early as the late 1940s . . .) The movies, hit hard by television, had big signs up in theaters: "Stop Pay-TV"— because they *knew* that's what was going to *kill* them. The studios, except for a few small independents, would not release even their 1930s movies to TV. Warner Bros. with production way down, started leasing their stages to television producers; when they made a fortune without having spent *any* money, other studios jumped in. One maxim's always held true in Hollywood: *Money talks.*

Eventually Universal (where Karl Freund had worked) let loose its *Shock Theater* package to TV (another fortune) and Columbia put out all 160-something *Stooges* shorts (ditto). Eventually, all the studios broke down and went the route of Free Money and released all their backlog to television (at first with the proviso for new movies: it will be *at least* seven years before this shows up on television).

Most of this was way in the future as the story starts. And by 2000 A.D., *oh my*!

I got the idea for this too late (May 1999), because of all the talk about Y2K, when everything would supposedly quit working—computers, electronics etc.—because their programs had all originally been done in COBOL or other program languages in the 1970s—and there was no room on them for year digits starting with 2 rather than 1. . . and everything was supposed to quit at midnight, New Year's Eve, in what would become Year Zero.

I wrote the story hoping Kim Mohan, editor of *Amazing*, could take it and get it into print before Y2K (he was only working a few months ahead.) He wanted some revisions (he was *wrong*). So I wrote "London, Paris, Banana . . ." instead and sent it to him, which, when he printed it, killed *Amazing* the second, and so far final time; I'd killed it first in 1993, when he'd printed "Household Words, or: The Powers-That-Be"— both stories are in volume one of *Selected Fiction*. Anyway, I sent "Major Spacer . . ." off to editors *just leaving* for the Worldcon in Australia, who also when they got back a month later, also wanted revisions (they were *wrong*, too). It was Gordon van Gelder (then of *Fantasy & Science Fiction*) who suggested the present, much better title for the story (he was *right*.) Anyway, one thing led to another, we're *into* Y2K and NOTHING

HAPPENED—and the story had gone from being a piece of cutting-edge speculative fiction to being an alternate history, without me doing a damn thing. I published it as an original in *Dream-Factories and Radio-Pictures*. (I'd always put a new story in each of my original collections in case some deluded soul had already read all the stories in them— and I can't do that for a couple of books subtitled *Selected Fiction*, can I?)

You surely saw Monty Clift as he staggered on in the story. I hope you also noticed James Dean's walk-on (he bummed around early live TV in New York City before going west and becoming the most famous 24-year old dead man in history) and Zachary, or Zooey, Glass who was also an early-TV actor, when not helping his sister over nervous breakdowns and spiritual crises. They were put in to give the story verisimilitude. And the production methods (and political tenor of the times) are pretty much as I describe them.

I read this just after finishing it, on May 27, 1999 in Kane Hall (a swell auditorium) at the University of Washington, with a *Tom Corbett, Space Cadet* lunchbox beside me, a Senor Wences cigar-box Pedro, and in a paper-bag space helmet (in appropriate spots) to rousing applause, as we say.

Vonda McIntyre stood up in the audience as soon as I finished and said "I'm going home and firing up my Osborne!"

Score another one for retro-science.

THE OTHER REAL WORLD

SUNDAY. "Stranger on the Shore"

Bobby sat in the small beachside park watching the waves come in from Japan.

It was a park put up by the WPA twenty-five years before, probably nice once, that had been allowed to run down. There were a few picnic tables, some missing slats from the tops, three firepits and a poured concrete bench overlooking the ocean.

An old lady there once told him that it had once been quite popular with families just after the war. Then bodybuilders had started using it, and the kinds of crowds they attracted, she'd said, arching her eyebrows, and then the Colored had moved into the area, and now look at it.

Now, looking at it, he saw a couple of surfer guys paddling around out there, and their girlfriends lying on towels on the beach, even though it was October, and a guy walking a dog back and forth, eyeballing the girls' butts.

Bobby came here because he usually wasn't bothered. There were two orders of french fries from the In-and-Out Burger a mile away beside him.

He heard a car pull into the parking lot, a door slam, and the sound of a tinny transistor radio playing "Fly Me to the Moon (Bossa Nova)" getting closer.

"You gonna eat all those fries?"

"No, I was hoping some dork grad-school physicist would come along and want some."

"Hello, Bobby. Swell mood."

"Hello, Stewart. Plenty to make me this way. Sorry. What's up?"

197

"Went by the place, you weren't there, you weren't at the pool hall, figured you were here."

"Turn that thing down."

Stewart fiddled with his shirt pocket, turned off the brown and silver radio, took his Chesterfields out of the other pocket and lit one up.

Bobby moved away from him on the bench, coughing. "What's up?"

"Saw Gadge at your apartments," he said. "Pomphret's busting his chops again at j.c. Making him think and stuff. The bastard."

"He was making everybody think when we were there; why should he quit now?"

"Yeah, but you know how Gadge is. He says when he first saw the prof, six or seven years ago, he was a science reporter named Johnson; now he's at the junior college teaching English and his name is Pomphret."

"Maybe he's got a half-twin brother or something? Anyway, what's on Gadge's mind?"

"You know, since he discovered girls, he wants to be called Brian?"

"Yeah, yeah."

"Well, he said he talked to Dobie, and Dobie's worried about his dad again."

"From what I hear," said Bobby, "His dad ain't been the same since he had to go up into the hills and identify his brother Joe's body in the swimming pool at that crazy old bat's house. That was before my time, though."

"Well, there's that. There's also trouble with Dobie's uncles. His dad's a triplet, you know; Joe was a younger brother. Anyway, there's him, Herbert T., then there's his brother Norbert E. who used to be the taxi service in some podunk town, and then there's Elbert P., who everybody used to call Pinky and worked in a male psycho ward in New York."

"Okay. Triplets. What's the deal?"

"Well, Pinky—that's Elbert P.—got to looking through some state records and ran across their birth certificates. Pinky was always told he was born last. But the records say that was Norbert E. He can't be Pinky—he's Herbert T. or he's Norbert E. but he can't be Elbert P. So Norbert's Pinky, or Dobie's father is—"

"What does this have to do with anything?"

"Well, now Herbert T. thinks he may be Pinky. And Norbert doesn't know who he is."

"I think Dobie's runnin' his dad crazy, hanging around with beatniks, chasing after girls who only want rich guys when he ain't got two nickels to rub together—"

They were interrupted by singing from below the rise at the edge of the park: "Medea—I just met a girl named—Medea—" off key, very off key.

Stewart walked to the edge of the park and looked down. "Go somewhere else, squirts!" he yelled. He walked back.

"It's just that Opie and young Theodore," he said. "Go on."

"I said, Dobie's running his father as crazy as his dad's worrying about which triplet he is. How did we get off on this?"

"You asked me what Gadge said. I'm telling you the truth, Ruth. He's worried about Dobie's—"

"Sorry I asked in the first place. God, I wish life was as simple as wondering whether I'm me!"

"Gal trouble?"

"I don't want to talk about it."

"Suit yourself."

They watched the ocean in silence. Stewart finished his fries. "Well," he said. "I better get back and check on Roger. Want to shoot some pool later?"

Roger was Stewart's little brother, who hadn't spoken in six years.

"Naw. I'd rather brood."

"OK." said Stewart. "You might want to check the news when you get back—you may not have heard out here on Despondence Slough Point, but some big-ass deal's up in Washington, cars coming and going all day, Kennedy flew back from campaign-stumping for senators in the midwest. Not that I give a rat's ass." He paused. "And I wouldn't go selling Dobie's friend too short. Regiomontanus was a Krebs." He got in his Merc and left.

Bobby brooded for an hour or two, then that lost its charm. He went back to the parking lot.

As usual, there were notes stuck under his windshield wipers, two under the left and one under the right. He pulled that one out. It said: "Don't listen to those guys!! I'll top any of their offers by $75. Call Spud," then a phone number.

Bobby's car was a 1946 Ford Super Deluxe wagon: pale green hood and fenders, black top, with light blond wood doors, sides and back, and rear door. It had a green Continental kit and whitewall tires.

Every gremmie and would-be ho-dad on the coast was always trying to buy it from him, so they could use it to haul their surfing-boards and beach-bunnies around in it and look cool. He tore up the notes and threw them in the park garbage can.

He got in, made sure the greasy rag was handy on the floorboard, the one that he used when the gears hung between first and second, when he would have to jump out in the street, open the hood, yank the shift-levers even, and start all over again. It was happening more frequently lately.

No matter. He put it in reverse, swung out, shifted and headed for home.

Trouble or not, his rod was not for sale.

MONDAY. "I Remember You"

Bobby came in from work, took a quick shower, and lay down on his bed, which was three steps from either the door or the shower.

He looked around at his place. What a dump. He had to make some more money, or something, and get out of here.

He looked up at the wall where there was a license-plate holder. Above, it said "DC Cab" and below "Call Lawrence 6 1212." The license plate itself was number H0012. He'd gotten it when he was eleven. He remembered the day he'd gone to the cab company to get it, the day they changed all the license plates for the next year. It hadn't cost him anything: by then everybody seemed to have forgotten everything that had happened.

He'd had it with him ever since, in DC at the boarding house; when he and his mom had moved to California for her new job in '54, when his mom died in '58 and he'd been out on his own.

He also remembered, back in '51, that the first thing he'd done that summer night was to beat the shit out of Sammy, the neighbor kid, for putting the finger on Mr. Carpenter. "They was Army guys!" said Sammy that night as Bobby pounded some more on his snotty nose, "What could I do? Don't hit me!" But Sammy knew he had it coming.

He turned on the radio. "—will make an address in about six more minutes. Meanwhile, here's 'Sea of Heartbreak' by Don Gibson, from way way back last year in 1961—" The music came up.

There was a knock on the door, then Stewart came in. "Hey, turn on the box. Kennedy's gonna blow off his bazoo in a few minutes."

Bobby switched on the TV, fiddled with the rabbit ears and the tinfoil till Channel 9 came in as well as it ever did. Some afternoon game show was wrapping up.

Stewart fired up a Chesterfield with the flame-thrower Zippo he used.

"God, those things stink!" said Bobby.

"You don't like smoking, move to another country." said Stewart. He rebreathed his own smoke three or four times.

"That kind of smoking went out in the Stone Age." said Bobby.

"The hell," said Stewart. They heard a motor-scooter buzz up outside.

Gadge, who lived in the same apartments, came in the door with his books under his arms.

"Kennedy talking yet?" he asked, dumping his books all over the floor. "Pomphret's busting our asses again."

"That right? Well—"

The TV had gone to the network logo, and a "Please Stand By—Special Bulletin" card. The announcer said: "We take you now to the White House where the President of the United States will address the nation."

Bobby looked at the clock. Four P.M. PDT. That would be 7 o'clock on the East Coast.

* * *

"—within the past week, unmistakable evidence has established the fact that a series of offensive missile sites is now in preparation on that imprisoned island. The purpose of these bases can be none other than to provide a nuclear strike capability against the Western Hemisphere.

"This government, as promised, has maintained the closest surveil-lance of the Soviet military buildup on the island of Cuba—"

* * *

It was weird listening to this. It was coming out of the TV. It was com-ing out of the radio that Bobby had forgot to turn down. The President was saying it. Nukes in Cuba, a few minutes flight away from DC. Bobby knew all the DEW radars were in Canada, Alaska, Greenland, pointed north, over the Pole, toward Russia. They fired those things off from Cuba, you'd be dead where you sat.

* * *

When it was over, and the quarantine—Kennedy's word for blockade —was announced, Gadge said "Gee whiz!"

Stewart was quiet.

"Where's the admiral?" asked Bobby.

"He had to get back to the Pentagon last Friday. Some big-cheese reunion of the old code-breakers or something . . . Hey, wait! I bet it had something to do with this!"

Howard Waldrop

Gadge started to laugh.

"What's so funny?"

"Boy!" he said. "I just got a picture of Krushchev and Kennedy waving their dongs at each other, their hair all standing up straight . . ."

"Krushchev doesn't have any hair," said Stewart.

"He does on his back." said Bobby.

"Yeah, well, it's just a big-dick contest!" said Gadge.

"It's a big-dick contest with H-bombs," said Stewart.

"Hey," said Bobby, looking at him, "you're the one who's usually a card. Why so glum?"

"I better get home," said Stewart. "No telling how Roger's taking this. See you guys later."

"Lemme put this in perspective," said Bobby, stopping him at the door while turning off the TV, and turning the radio back up, which was playing Bert Kaempfert's "Wonderland by Night" from 1960. "Kennedy thinks he's got problems, what with Russians and missiles and Castro in Cuba. Me, I gotta find a shifter gate collar for a '46 Ford."

* * *

After they had gone, Bobby put on the First Family album on his Silvertone record player. He listened and laughed. He liked the way Vaughn Meader, as Kennedy, said "Cuber."

TUESDAY. "Wheels"

The junkyard was as crummy-looking as most, but it was bigger.

There was a parking strip, and a tiny office you had to go through, attached to a barn-size building with a couple of garage doors through which you could see the entire history of the internal-combustion engine and the transmission stacked up to the ceilings. Beyond that was about two miles of 10-foot-high fence topped with four strands of barbed wire with a sign every fifty feet saying "Patrolled by Vicious Dogs." There was a big wrecker with the junkyard name on it, and a smaller one made out of a pickup, dark blue with a dribble of pink paint on the left fender, that was unmarked. On one side of the garage-part, hoods of cars and trucks were stacked up like rental boats at a lake in the off-season. There were four or five cars out front when Bobby pulled up. He took out some wrenches and screwdrivers and went inside the office.

A fat guy was on the phone. His hands looked like he'd cleaned them last during the third Roosevelt administration. He held up one of them. He finished talking and hung up.

"First thing you do, kid, you go to that stack of pads there and you write your name and address and you sign and date it."

"I thought I was at a junkyard," said Bobby.

"Hoho. So you are, kid. This is for my insurance company. Something happens to you out there, and you've signed the form, I don't care. You don't sign it, you don't get in on your quest for the perfect hot rod."

Bobby stepped over to the pad of mimeographed forms, read it—the standard "own risk" crap, wrote out his name and address, signed and dated it.

"Letting lawyers doing your thinking for you, aren't you?"

The guy sighed. "You got cars, glass and junk, you get insects and worms. You get insects, including bees and wasps, and worms, you get birds and rats. You get birds and rats, you get snakes, many beneficent, but including the coast rattler, the copperhead and the mocassin. You reach for the headlight assembly on an El Dorado and grab a handful of coast rattler, you die.

"I really don't have time for a nature lecture, kid. I just don't want anybody asking me in county court why I let idiots in such a dangerous place. That is the short answer. You through?"

"Yes."

"Happy hunting."

* * *

The junkyard rose slowly toward the back of the place, up toward the hills maybe a mile away. Bobby assumed any Ford Super Deluxes they had had been stripped long ago; he'd have to look at any Ford made between '46 and '49, including pickups. He had a tracing of the shifter gate collar, top and side view he'd made after Kennedy's speech yesterday; he figured while the thing was working at all, he'd better take it off, trace and measure it, and put it back on before he went to the junkyard. He'd had to hand-jerk the gears eight times today, including two blocks before he got to the junkyard. His hands weren't much cleaner than the guy's who ran this place.

* * *

An hour later and no luck. Every early postwar Ford he'd seen was stripped back to the firewalls, most missing the steering columns, even the wheel hubs. He'd found lots of wasp nests, and once thought he heard a snake under a car when he climbed up on the bumper—maybe it was just a lizard or frog or rat.

* * *

He was near the back of the place. Off to one side was a long pen full of the snarliest dogs he'd ever seen, ten or twelve of them. They were barking and bounding off the double-reinforced cattle fence that looked like it had been through a waffle-maker. The dogs' feet never seemed to touch the ground. Geez.

There was a slow rise at the back of the place, mowed grass on it, a mound. In the middle of the mound was what looked like a bank-vault door. Above the door and to one side was a dark indented slit in the mound.

Bobby jumped down inside the front of a '54 wagon, made, he knew, too late after they changed everything, but he looked anyway.

* * *

Some minutes later a truck pulled up through one of the narrow twisting lanes between the junkers and drove around to the back of the mound. The truck was from the Pure Water people; a guy got out, hooked up some hoses, and let Newton do the work, as Stewart was always saying when gravity was involved.

Bobby walked closer. He saw that the inset slit above the door contained the business end of a submarine periscope.

He knew then that he was looking at a pretty serious fallout shelter. So the junkyard guy was going to bunker-up during WWIII, instead of taking his chances outside with all the radioactive mu-tants. To each his own.

* * *

He found what he was looking for on a 1951 Chrysler. They weren't supposed to have parts that would fit Fords. He checked the drawing twice and measured three times. Same adjustable screw sleeves and everything.

He tossed it up in the air and caught it a few times. He walked to the edge of the mowed grass around the fallout shelter. The water truck was long gone. The dogs were going crazy. The sun was heading down in the drink, and they were getting restless. Maybe they lived for each night, hoping just once somebody would be out in the place when they were turned loose. He saw there was a big lift-gate at the front of the pen, and a walkway above it so the gate could be pulled up and the dogs couldn't get to whoever opened it. This was some operation.

* * *

He went back to the office just as the big back overhead garage doors of the engine and transmission graveyard opened, and a kid with sun-streaked-blond hair jumped back in another wrecker, towing a car that looked like a photograph of a wave on the hook. The car was all blue; all the glass had been spiderwebbed, and it was hilled and vallied in six places. It must have spun on the top, or gone under a moving van. Bobby didn't see any blood as it went by him.

"Out in the 34 area," the fat guy was saying to the kid. The kid nodded, looked at Bobby, bounced away.

"You look happy. What you got, kid?"

"Shifter gate collar."

"Shifter gate collar? Well, normally that would be 50¢. But being how the world's gonna end this week, that'll be a quarter. You'll need it to get up in the hills to the people who'll steal and rob and kill you."

"Thanks," said Bobby, handing him two dimes and a nickel. "I see you're ready."

"That I am. But don't come around when it happens thinking I'll let the whole world and his uncle in. All my family's ready too, 'ceptin' that boy you saw there; he says he'll take his chances."

"Well, he may be right," said Bobby. "Maybe people are more or less good. Maybe they'll help each other if that happens."

"Kid," said the fat guy. "Prepare yourself for one big disappointment."

* * *

There were two more names and phone numbers stuck under his windshield wipers. He crumpled them up, threw them on the seat. He jerked up the hood, undid the top screw from the old shifter gate collar, crawled under, backed the bottom screw out, pulled off the old collar, slipped the new collar over the column till it snapped into place, put in the bottom screw, climbed out from under, pulled the gear rods down, put in the top screw. He wiped his hands on the rag, got in, ran through the gears letting the clutch in and out. Smooth as silk. All that aggravation fixed for a quarter. He turned on the radio. The DJ was saying, "and now, here's the Republican campaign song for 1964," and Ray Charles came on singing "Hit the Road, Jack."

Then Bobby noticed the fat guy and his sun-blond kid standing on the office porch looking at him.

"Hey, kid." said the guy. "My son wants to know if you want to sell your car?"

Bobby cranked up and put it in reverse.

"Not for all the farms in Cuber," he said, and drove away.

WEDNESDAY. "West of the Wall"

Roger, who was thirteen, was putting together an Aurora model of the Frankenstein monster. He had it standing up on its tombstone base, its left arm outstretched and in its shoulder socket, and the two halves of the right arm together and held with rubber bands while the reeking airplane cement dried.

"You okay, kid?" asked Stewart, coming in and putting his papers on the chair nearest his bed in the room they had shared for six years.

Roger shook his head yes.

"School okay?"

Roger shrugged.

"Yeah, I know what you mean. Neat Frankenstein."

Roger pushed the box, with all the parts already broken off the sprues, over toward him. He pointed to the sides, with its pictures of Dracula and the Wolfman, and the slug-line "Collect 'Em All!"

"I'll bet you can hardly wait for your next allowance, huh?"

Roger smiled, then went back to gluing.

* * *

The hall phone rang and Miz Jones the housekeeper answered it. She talked a few minutes, then called Sarah, the admiral's sister to the phone.

Sarah was upset when she came into the boys' room. "It's the admiral," she said. "He wants to talk to Roger a minute, then you," she said to Stewart.

Roger ran out into the hall. After a couple of minutes he came back in, pointing over his shoulder with his thumb.

Stewart picked up the receiver.

"You okay, Admiral?" he asked.

"Yeah, yeah, Stewart, I'm fine as could be. Eating good old Navy chow again, working with some of the old gang. Look, Stewart—" he said, then stopped. "I—"

"We'll be fine, Admiral. It's you we're worried about."

"Yeah, well, I was fine for about forty years before you was born, kid. I want you to know how—uh—"

"Hey! I want you to know how much I—me and Roger—appreciate all you and Sarah and Miz Jones did for us. Especially for Roger, Admiral. We couldn't have been an easy thing—"

"Aw, hell. All I said was give me those kids; they need something like a parent right now, and I don't have time to argue with you."

"Wasn't like ordering around swabbies on a boat, though, was it?" asked Stewart.

"Well, no," said the admiral. "But I got you, didn't I?"

Then he cleared his throat. "Look, Stewart. This thing might get a little hairy. Keep on top of stuff. Get Roger and Miz Jones and Sarah somewhere safe, if it comes to it. You're the man of the house right now."

"Of course I will, Admiral," said Stewart.

"Well, gotta get off the blower here—they're only giving everybody one call. I oughtta know, I signed the order myself. And I'm strict." He laughed.

"Admiral, we—"

"Get back to your books, Stewart. Tell Sarah and Miz Jones I'll be back the minute this little flap is over."

"Sure thing," said Stewart. There was a transcontinental click on the other end of the line.

* * *

Stewart remembered the first few days after the lab explosion that took his mom, dad and that fugitive Nazi scientist whose body was found in the debris with them. Roger of course had never spoken afterwards. Stewart had been in a daze—he'd been doing his math homework one minute; the next the lab across the driveway and half the house were gone. It was two days before his hearing had come back.

The admiral, who'd been working with his parents the week before, and who was on his way back from Washington when it happened (the week after the collapse, then sudden reemergence of the Soviet Union, when it looked like the messages his dad had been getting from Mars were faked by the Nazi from South America) got there in the first few hours while the ruins were filled with firemen, police, FBI, and the military.

Aunt Jessica and Uncle Hume had wanted to adopt them, but of course the State of California said, "They're actors. New York actors, mostly, and they have kids of their own."

So the admiral said "Give them to me. Those boys need me." The State reminded him he wasn't married. "You're right," he said. "I figured if I needed a wife, the Navy would have issued me one. But I've lived in the same house when not on blue-water duty for twenty-four years, my sister lives with me, and we've had the same housekeeper for twenty of those years, and we don't intend to change now. And I don't want either boy to go into the Navy—assuming the little one starts talking again—they got too many brains for that, I've seen their IQ scores. They'll have to get real jobs when they grow up, like everybody else. I'll give them a good solid home and I'll take care of them till they're ready to leave. Now tell an admiral in the US Navy he hasn't got the onions to be a fit parent."

A week later they'd moved into the admiral's house, and their lives had been swell ever since.

* * *

Stewart watched Roger finish the Frankenstein monster while he fiddled with what was turning out to be some Fibonacci curves. He plugged in some unknowns.

Roger climbed into bed, staring at the monster, which he'd put on the top of the bookcase that was the footboard to his bed. He'd put it there, striding toward him off its graveyard base, arms outstretched for him.

He reached down under his bed, from the ragged pile there, and took out *Famous Monsters of Filmland* #12, which seemed to be his favorite. He went to sleep with his bedlamp on, the magazine across his chest.

Stewart got up, put the magazine back in the pile, pulled the covers up around Roger, and turned off his light.

Then he went downstairs to raid the refrigerator.

THURSDAY. "Because They're Young"

"Ready to go?" asked Stewart.

"I don't know," said Gadge.

"What do you mean? All this stuff getting you down? I'm the one who's worried the hell about Roger, and the admiral. I'm here. I'm ready. I want to see some flicks."

"Look," he went on. "I been zombieing around for three days. I haven't had the fun of fighting over groceries and lugging five gallon cans of gasoline home, or stocking a fallout shelter, or buying shotgun shells. I been moping around and worried about my little brother, who hasn't said a word in six years anyway."

"How is Roger?"

"Who knows! No different than always. Watches the news. Don't change the subject. Are you coming with me to the drive-in or not?"

"Look, Stewart. Everything's pretty spooky right now. I mean, what if there's World War Three while we're there . . .?"

"Listen at you. All the Russian ships slowed down but the one that's fifty miles out ahead of the others. It won't reach the blockade till Saturday. Nothing's gonna happen till then. Besides, what would you do? I mean, supposing you only had an hour to live?"

"That's easy," said Gadge. "Send both Veronica and Angela Cartwright to my room. Have Hayley Mills wait outside in case they don't kill me . . ."

"Right! There you go! And where is it you can ever ever hope to see girls like that?"

"At . . . at the movies," said Gadge. He sighed. "Let's go."

* * *

There were only a dozen other cars waiting to get into the Luau Drive-In, with its neon Hawaiian party going on on the backside of the screen facing the road. There were red neon flames where the pig cooked; a guy's neon hands plucked on his neon ukelele strings; two hula girls' hips moved back and forth in their neon green grass skirts.

"Look, guys," said the owner who was taking tickets, and who lived in the house that was the screen, with its upper story porthole windows. "Not enough people show up, there won't be movies tonight. We'll announce it and give your money back as you exit."

"Whatta ya mean, no show?"

"Kid, the world might end any time."

"Yeah, well," said Stewart, "if it doesn't you'll regret being out our six bits."

* * *

The sound piped in over the speakers before the show started was the local radio station. The DJ was saying "and that was Charley Drake with 'My Boomerang Won't Come Back.' And now here's one from way back in 1959 to take us up to the news . . ." "Quiet Village" with its rainfall and bird noises and tinkling piano came on.

"I'll go get some crap to eat." said Gadge. He got out and headed back toward the concession stand as the floodlights around the screen came on with the dark.

* * *

He got back in with the big cardboard carrier. There were two big bags of popcorn, two big Cokes, two Clark bars, a big box of Dots and a roll of Necco wafers.

"How much I owe you?" asked Stewart.

"Man, this place is expensive," said Gadge. "It came to a dollar-ten in all. If you don't want any of the Dots, give me 50¢."

* * *

There were previews, then a cartoon (an old Looney Tunes) a newsreel and some more previews, and then the first of the triple feature started to roll.

"I really don't know why I'm here," said Gadge. "Hayley Mills isn't in any of these movies—I'm sure she's not in *Bride of the Gorilla*—when it was made she would have been about two years old."

"Where's your spirit of adventure?" asked Stewart. "Maybe you'll see another girl of your dreams in this. Or *Poor White Trash*. Or *High School Confidential?*"

"Yeah, right. If they were my age when these things were made they'd be about forty by now . . ."

"Come on. Where's your appreciation of cinema history?"

Raymond Burr, the guy who played Perry Mason on TV, was having trouble in the jungle.

"Seriously," said Gadge, biting into the Clark bar. "How is Roger?"

"He seems okay," said Stewart. "Well, no different anyway. He just watches TV more. He's been in study-hall for two days. They sent some of the special ed kids home Tuesday—some of them got too upset. He still answers any yes or no question you ask him, shakes his head, like he always has. I talked to his shrink last week before all this happened."

"What'd he say?"

"Same stuff as you and me heard growing up. Post-wonder effect. It wears off or it doesn't. Not enough of us around to figure out if everybody comes out of it or not. I mean, it's what, a decade or less . . . Bobby was one of the first and that was only eleven years ago."

"It was sure as hell less time for me than since this movie was made." said Gadge.

* * *

Stewart awoke with a start. Gadge was snoring away in the passenger seat. Stewart looked at the screen. It was another movie—a guy in a black hat was doing something bad.

He looked at the clock on the dash. Only 9:30—this must be *Poor White Trash*. Yeah, there was Peter Graves.

"Hey," said Stewart. "Wake up."

"Huh, what? Huh?"

"You know the idea I had about going to the movies to forget our troubles?"

"Yeah?"

"Bad idea."

"Bad idea," Gadge repeated. He looked up at the screen. "What happened to the gorilla?"

"Wrong movie," said Stewart. He cranked the motor, put the speaker back out on its hook on the post, and drove toward the exit with his parking lights on.

There were still two cars way out in the back row, their windows steamed up. The lights in the snack bar were already out.

"Wake me up when we get to my place," said Gadge.

Then he was snoring again.

Stewart was thinking about "My Boomerang Won't Come Back." When the song first came out, there was a line in it about practicing till you were black in the face. Now the song said blue in the face. Go figure. The Aborigines must have a tough union.

FRIDAY. "Gazachstahagen"

Bobby said, "A Raymond Burr gorilla movie?"

"If I'm lyin', I'm dyin'," said Stewart.

They were sitting in Stewart's '53 submarine Merc at the Hi-Spot, eating burgers. Stewart had swung by to pick up Bobby just as he'd swung in from work with his paycheck in his pocket. They went by Bobby's bank, where he cashed his check and put $8.00 in his savings account, and then they'd driven here.

"That guy was always having trouble with gorillas, wasn't he?"

They had the same radio station on in the car as the one piped in over the drive-in's speakers. The song ended and the DJ said ". . . and that was Larry Verne with 'Please Mr. Custer' and then Ben Colder's 'Don't Go Near the Eskimos' and a happy oog-sook-mook-ee-ay to you, too . . ."

Then the news came on and it was grim. The blockade waited for the Russian ships: the one out ahead of the others, the *Grozny*, was still coming on strong, the others slow behind it. The President and cabinet were meeting in the War Room. Absenteeism in schools and jobs was running 35%, 50% at defense plants on the East Coast and the Midwest. Stores all over the US were out of toilet paper, bulk foods and batteries. There was price-gouging all over; some stations were selling gas for as much as 50¢ a gallon. The weather forecast came on, then the DJ played Jack Scott's "What in the World's Come Over You?"

"And Gadge thought this was a big bluff thing," said Bobby.

"Yeah, well . . ." Stewart chewed on his fries. "Look. Don't you sometimes wish . . . I don't know . . ."

"What?"

"I mean, look at us. You, me, Gadge, especially Roger. All that stuff we went through. It didn't change a goddam thing."

"Well, how do we know it didn't change anything?"

"Okay, Mr. Philosophical. Everybody knows there's guys from outer space. Well, one, and his big robot enforcer. They went away. We never heard from them again. Then everybody thought my and Roger's dad was talking to Mars; things went crazy. The Russian Orthodox Church overthrew the Commies, for god's sakes . . ."

"For about a day—" said Bobby.

"For about a day. Then Krushchev and Beria came down on them like a ton of bricks. It was like, you know, a little holiday, and then business back to Commie usual.

"And Gadge—his gramps makes a robot. Then all kinds of spy stuff—where Pomphret comes in; Commie spies. Then it's over. Gramps sends up the robot in a souped-up V-2. It's never seen or heard of again. 'Cranky Old Man Shoots Robot Into Space.' The end. Two years later—Ooops! Sputnik!"

"Your point being?"

"Nothing changed. Not one thing. We're right back to Us vs. Them, like The World is all there is, like we're all that matters . . ."

"Well," said Bobby. "Most people can't handle the idea we're not alone; that strange and marvellous stuff happens all the time, that—that—"

"But it did happen. We saw it; they saw it; they went crazy, too. But to them, it wasn't personal. It was just The News; then something else took its place. It was just this year's tortilla Jesus."

"We got on with our lives. Well, except for Roger," said Bobby. "Why shouldn't people who weren't even there?"

"Yeah, but Truman? Eisenhower? Kennedy? Krushchev too. They saw what happened. You don't see any of that influencing foreign policy, or scientific research, or anything. Just business as usual. Now look where it's got us!"

"You expecting somebody to drop down from Pluto and straighten this out?"

"No. That would be the easy way out of this mess our world leaders have gotten us into."

"Well, what do you want?"

Stewart looked over the steering wheel out into the big plate glass window of the Hi-Spot where the carhops whizzed by on roller skates.

"I want a world better than this one," he said. "I want a world with shadows, and wet streets, and neon lights flashing 'Hotel' 'Hotel' outside my windows. Everything here seems to be taking place in a grey flat light. I want to be able to smoke like Robert Mitchum, and drink all day and night like Barton Maclane, and never, ever blow my beets. I want—I want to break someone's heart, or have mine broken, in the rain . . ."

"Why, why," said Bobby, ". . . you . . . you're a romantic! Take me back to my place before I become so filled with cheap sentiment that I can't move."

"Asshole," said Stewart, and flashed his lights for the carhop to come and take the tray.

* * *

They pulled up in front of the apartments. Things looked different.

There were two times in his life when Bobby had gone somewhere to do something, and when he got back found the world completely changed.

One had been in 1951. He'd gone off of play baseball in the neighborhood park, and when he got back, he found that his mom and

Carpenter had gone off in the cab, and the rooming house was full of cops, FBI men and MPs.

The other was tonight, when he stepped out of Stewart's car and realized his 1946 Ford Super Deluxe wagon was gone.

* * *

He awoke from a dream of Hayley Mills, in a t-shirt and a pair of shorts, climbing over a high fence.

Gadge got up and took a pee, then got back in bed.

What a week. Teachers on his case. Russians with missiles all over, bad gorilla movies, and now Bobby gets his woodie stolen.

He turned on his radio; the DJ was babbling, it was 2:30 in the morning. Good thing he only had a language lab on Saturdays at noon.

Ral Donner's "The Girl of My Best Friend" came on, a Golden Oldie from way back last year.

He thought of Gramps; he could see him and the robot like it was yesterday. Gramps had been dead four years now; the robot had been gone five. After all that stuff with the Commie spies, Gramps had shot the robot off in the V-2 the Army had given him, a year before Sputnik. They'd lost contact with the robot and the rocket a few minutes after takeoff, and that was that. While he was still little, ten, eleven years old—he held out hope that the robot was still up there. He'd watch the night sky for hours at a time for some blink of light, some flashing thing passing overhead. Nothing.

When they made that crummy movie based on Gramps, they hoked it all up. There wasn't any telepathy-thing with him and the robot. It was a fairly simple big machine and could perform some simple functions. That didn't mean Gadge hadn't loved it, and Gramps.

And there wasn't a love-interest for his mom, either. They made all that stuff up. His mom had died three years ago. He had enough money left over from Gramps to go to junior college, and live in these swell apartments, and eat and put gas in the Vespa, and that was about it. There was more money coming when he turned twenty-one.

As if the Russkies would ever let that happen, now.

What he mostly remembered about the night he and Gramps went to the planetarium for the supposed lecture (a cheap Commie trick to kidnap them) was that there had been a bunch of teenagers in a circle out in the parking lot; in the middle two of them were having a knife-fight. He'd watched from the back seat, between the two big Commie refrigerators with bad haircuts, as they pulled away. One of the juvies was throwing down his knife.

Then the Russkies had put the sack over his head and thrown him down on the floorboards, and one kept his feet on him the whole trip out to the Last Chance Garage.

Orphans. We're all orphans in one way or another, Gadge thought. His dad was killed in Korea; his mom, Gramps and the robot in the last five years. Bobby's dad had bought it at Anzio, and his mom got cancer five years ago; Stewart and Roger's mom and dad were blown up in a lab fifty feet from them, five years ago.

The Cold War was sure rough on kids.

Now the radio was playing Neil Sedaka's "Happy Birthday, Sweet Sixteen." Yeah right, thought Gadge. Welcome to the future, kid. Fifty megatons, right up your butt. Like the posters people printed, of the toothless old man in the jet helmet—"Sleep Tight Tonight. Your Air National Guard Is On The Job!"

He turned off the radio and went back to sleep.

At some point in the night, Hayley Mills climbed down the other side of the fence, real slow.

SATURDAY. "Midnight in Moscow"

Things began to happen pretty fast that morning.

Bobby was staring at the empty space where his car had been in front of the apartments.

The guy in the house across the street, who had talked to the cops the night before—he told them the wrecker had been "black or blue" and that "it had a big hook on it"—walked over to him.

"I just remembered something. You know, in the excitement and all. I had been watching TV when I saw the cops over here, after I'd seen the tow truck pull your car off. The TV was showing pictures of little Caroline Kennedy playing with her pony Macaroni at the White House. They were near that tree house JFK had built for her, out in the back yard. You could—"

"What was it you remembered," asked Bobby. It would probably be something like "The tow truck had wheels on it."

"—oh yeah. That wrecker had some pink or lavender paint on the front fender. You think that's enough we should call the cops back? You think it'll help get your car back?"

"Thanks." said Bobby. "I don't think we should call the cops about it. But I think it'll help get my car back."

The guy looked at him funny, then scratched his head. "Well, okay." he said.

* * *

From the field up on the side of the hill—a failed subdivision, a few houses further up, roads paved, then gravel, then dirt, then nothing, going nowhere—Bobby could look down over most of the junkyard. Up here, at the back, closest to him was the fence, the bunker, and the dog pens, then nothing but acres of cars; far away the office and the garage.

All three tow trucks were outside. He looked through Gadge's 80 x 300 binoculars he'd borrowed before Gadge had to go off to his language lab.

The back garage doors, facing him, were open. His wagon wasn't there. And for a Saturday, the junkyard was pretty empty.

He was listening to his transistor radio. The news was that all the Russian ships had stopped except the *Grozny*, which came on toward the American quarantine line.

It was hailed.

It didn't stop.

A Navy destroyer escort fired a shot across its bow.

The Grozny steamed on toward Cuba.

The Navy shot off its rudder.

The news got out about twenty-seven minutes after it happened.

* * *

Things really started happening down at the junkyard then.

People moved around at the office. A few minutes later a couple of cars pulled in, and women and kids got out of the cars that drove into the garage and came out back. They carried boxes and blankets and dolls, and after awhile they came out of the mazes between the cars and went into the bunker.

The fat guy closed the place up and came back toward the fallout shelter in a '59 Ford pickup. The back end was full of shotguns, rifles and ammo boxes. He and some other guys carried the stuff inside.

Then nothing happened in the junkyard for two hours.

* * *

Not much happened anyplace. The teletype between Washington and Moscow must have been red-hot. The radio said the *Grozny* was boarded, and it was full of wheat, tractors and medical supplies. This left the Americans with red faces, and a ship they'd disabled dead in international waters.

Some Cuban tugs were sent out.

Meanwhile the rest of the Russian freighters got up good heads of steam and plowed toward that imprisoned isle.

* * *

Bobby's back was killing him. Nothing moved in the junkyard. A couple of cars pulled up out front, saw the place was closed, drove away. The dogs in their big pen figure-eighted back and forth: they knew something was up.

Then the bleach-blond kid and the fat guy came out of the bunker. They talked. The fat guy handed his son some money. The kid walked out through the junkyard, through the office, got in the big wrecker and left.

Then for a while nothing happened but the radio. One of the songs it played was "Asia Minor" by Kokomo, and Bobby Darin's "Beyond the Sea," a song Bobby had always liked.

* * *

A half-hour later the big wrecker came back, pulling Bobby's wagon. The kid opened the doors and pulled it into the big garage, closed and locked the front garage doors, and walked back out to the bunker. The fat guy met him. The kid handed him a pink slip and some money back. Nice touch.

The junkyard owner went back inside the fallout shelter. The kid went up on the catwalk—the dogs were banging themselves against the side of the pens and gate. The kid opened the lift-gate like a sluice. Dogs squirted out like water from Grand Coulee Dam.

The kid jumped down on the outside of the fence—dogs slamming against it and barking and growling all along it. They seemed a little confused being out in the daytime, and the kid walked along the fence to the front of the place and got in one of the cars and drove away.

The radio said a disc jockey in Cleveland had just been fired on-air for dedicating a record to Nikita Krushchev, and then playing the Cuff-links' "Guided Missile (Aimed At My Heart)."

* * *

Bobby was on the pay phone three blocks over to Stewart.

"Yeah, well. Get on over here—we gotta work fast."

"Everybody here's upset," said Stewart. "Sarah's fluttering around like ZaSu Pitts. It looks like it's even getting to Roger."

"What if I sent Gadge over?"

"I thought he had class?"

"They cancelled it. He was already home when I called him by mistake trying to call you. They're all shook up out at the college, too."

"You think this is a good idea? I mean, this is looking like it."

"And if the world doesn't end, I've lost my wagon for good. Soon it'll be purple and pink and the wood'll be dark teak. And legal-like, too."

"Hang tight, then. I'll be over as soon as Gadge gets here."

Bobby called Gadge back. Gadge didn't want to go, with everything looking serious and all.

"Look," said Bobby. "What if WWIII happens? Can you see yourself riding away from the Apocalypse on a Vespa? Come on, Gadge—"

"Call me Brian. I told you that a thousand times."

"Ga—Brian. There's three or four cars at Stewart's place. Something happens, you all jump in two or three and take off."

"I wanna go with you guys, if I'm going anywhere. I know something's up."

"Look, G—Brian. I do not know how long this is gonna take. Stewart's worried about everybody there. Roger likes you; you'll calm him down; he'll calm Sarah and Miz Jones down; everybody will be calm, including you."

"Roger gives me the creeps sometimes."

"Yeah, well, remember what he went through and what you went through. I'm pretty sure everything gives Roger the creeps. Look. Just do it. I'll give you—I don't know—money."

"Never mind that," said Gadge. "I'll do it. What you said about A-bombs and motor-scooters made sense."

"You're a pal," said Bobby.

"Yeah, right."

* * *

Stewart showed up with food and blankets. He looked the place over. He was formulating a plan. But first he said:

"You should call the cops. There's your wagon. There they are."

"Nah. The kid's gone. There's dogs all over the place. The cops'll get their asses eaten getting in there, or they'll have to shoot all the dogs. What if, say, it's not mine? I know it is, you know it is. They gotta get a judge to sign a warrant. And the fat guy didn't do it. It's the kid."

"Call the cops," said Stewart. "No matter how much trouble it is, no matter how many fallout shelters they gotta look in to get a judge."

"No," said Bobby.

"Why not?"

"Because now it's personal."

"I knew you were going to say that," said Stewart.

* * *

"Look at the setup," said Stewart. "How do you think they get the dogs back in the pens in the mornings?"

"Uh . . ."

"You climb up on that catwalk there, from outside the fence. You throw food in the pens. You open the gate. They come in. You close the gate. That'll be my job."

"What's mine?"

"While I'm doing that, you open the front garage door and you drive your wagon out. You pick me up, two blocks over that way. Or, things still being quiet, I walk back to my car up on the hill and drive myself home. We go to the nearest cops and you tell them you found your car. Someday, when no one's looking, you back-shoot the kid."

"There's things that can go wrong with your plan, as I see it . . ." said Bobby.

"Yeah. I can fall in the pens and get eaten up. Or the people in the bunker see what they think is someone stealing a car they think is legally theirs, and they shoot you full of big holes. Other than that, what's there to worry about?"

Stewart got up.

"Where you going?"

"You think food for the dogs is gonna walk down here? And how are the front garage doors locked?"

"Slaymakers as big as toolboxes," said Bobby. "Oh."

"Oh is right. Stick tight."

"What if the kid comes back and starts doing stuff to the car?"

"The kid ain't coming back today or tonight unless bombs start dropping; if they do, he ain't gonna be thinkin' about chopping and channeling your rod. If he were coming back, he wouldn't have let the dogs out, because then he's gotta put 'em back in again. He'll be back tomorrow when they usually put the dogs back in. Ever read any Pavlov? I thought not."

"Well—"

"Worst comes to worst, Bob," said Stewart, "you can always call the cops."

He left. While he was gone, Bobby doodled in the sand with his finger the symbols: ♀ ☿ ☀ † ∞

* * *

It was dark. They lay wrapped in their blankets. The lump of ten pounds of raw meat—$2.00 worth—lay over to one side, double wrapped in three yards of cellophane. Hopefully the dogs couldn't smell it up here. Occasionally a shape moved in the junkyard; one of the dogs looking for something to kill. Sometimes there was a dogfight.

"Guy in the store said raw meat was the one thing that wasn't selling. Nobody wants to take fresh meat down in a fallout shelter. Gave me a big-guy discount."

The bolt-cutters lay between them, the size of a small lawnmower. Stewart got them from a tool rental place a mile away.

"See," said Stewart. "We could be home. We could be playing Scrabble®. We could set our alarm clocks and get out here tomorrow at dawn. But no. You gotta play like Tom and Huck rescuing Jim, when Jim's just fine."

"Shut up," said Bobby. "I'm just as cold as you are."

"Ah, yes," said Stewart, "but the difference is, you want to be cold, not me."

* * *

At some point in the night Bobby woke up. Stewart was mumbling in his sleep.

Bobby turned on his radio. It was 4 A.M., Pacific time. Some minutes before, daylight already out over the Atlantic, over central Cuba, either the Russians or the Cubans had shot down an American U-2 spyplane.

"Wake up!" said Bobby.

"Huh?" asked Stewart, sitting up.

"We're in deep kim-chee. The timetable's been moved up."

SUNDAY. "Monster Mash"

Just dawn.

* * *

They'd put the blankets and stuff in Stewart's car up on the hill. Then Bobby'd taken the long way around, and stepped out of the weeds and watched till Stewart climbed out on the catwalk. He heard and watched as the dogs made a beeline for the pens.

He cut the bolt of the lock on the right-hand door. It popped apart like cheap swing-chain. These things must have about six million tons of torque, he thought, admiring the boltcutters. He lifted the garage door— what a racket—then closed it in case anyone was driving by.

His car was still up on the wrecker hooks. He threw the boltcutters inside.

He went to the wrecker, cranked it up, tried to figure out which gears and levers did what. He pulled one. Nothing happened. Then another. His car moved an inch.

He thought he heard yelling. He killed the motor. He heard yelling.

A blur of a dog shot through the back garage doors and bounced off the wrecker.

About that time, the front garage door opened. There stood the bleached-blond kid with a pistol in his hand; beyond him a car with its lights on idled.

The dog went over the kid's head and lit out for San Pedro.

The kid fell on his back and started emptying the pistol into the ceiling.

Bobby cranked up, gunned the wrecker motor and roared out of the garage, missing the kid by a foot with the fishtailing Ford wagon.

* * *

"Geez!" said Stewart, when Bobby roared to a stop for him two blocks away. "Now we're the thieves! Head for my place. We'll call the cops from there!"

"What happened?" asked Bobby, grinding the gears.

"The dogs didn't all come in. Then they must have seen me from the bunker, 'cause I saw guys with guns. About then I saw the kid pull up out front. I yelled as much as I could running as fast as I could. I think they shot at me—I heard shots anyway. I don't think I got the gate all the way down, either. The place is probably full of mutts. Geez!"

They swung out on the road. They didn't hear any sirens; no one was chasing them yet.

"Hey!" said Bobby. "This thing doesn't have a radio!" Stewart turned on his pocket transistor. He had to hold it up against the door handle to get better reception.

Groovy Ray Poovey was running down the Top Ten of the week: "That was #5, Frank Ifeild's 'I Remember You,' now here's #4!" and the Crystals' "He's Not A Rebel" came on.

"Great driving music." said Stewart.

* * *

They turned a corner a couple of miles from Stewart's house. "That was #3 this week," said the DJ, "The Contours' 'Do You Love Me?' Here's the #2 record for the week of October 28, 1962, the Four Seasons with 'Sherry.'"

Bobby and Stewart wailed along with the falsetto Frankie Valli, nodding their heads back and forth. Stewart looked out the back, over the Ford. No one chasing them still.

Bobby downshifted, ground the gears. The wrecker rolled to a stop.

"Damn!" He found first again.

"Now," said Groovy Ray Poovey, before we find out what that #1 song is, we'll play a—" his voice went into echo-chamber bass "—Old One From-m-m-m the-th-th Vault-ault-ault-ault." And out came the piano notes of Floyd Cramer's "Last Date" from 1960.

* * *

"Swing over on Lattner," said Stewart. "It's downhill. Geez, you were doing fine for awhile. What happened?"

"I must have been running on adrenaline. Hey—what's this?" He was down in some kind of compound grandma gear. He started over. The rig started moving more than half a mile an hour again.

"And now," said the DJ "the number one tune of the week, and you know what it is—"

There was the sound of a creaking door, bubbles, a dragging chain . . .

And the mellifluous voice of Bobby "Boris" Pickett doing "Monster Mash."

It stopped. There was dead air. Then a weird high warbling tone came over the radio as they got in sight of Stewart's house.

"*Video portum*," said Stewart, his face ashen.

* * *

The Conelrad warning came on the radio. Sirens started up all over the city.

Bobby slammed the wrecker to a stop. He fiddled with the levers. His Ford dropped to the ground.

Gadge, Miz Jones, Sarah and Roger ran out of the house carrying blankets and food. Bobby undid the hooks, fished around for his keys, cranked the wagon.

Gadge and Miz Jones jumped in the car with him. Stewart and Sarah got in the admiral's sedan. All over the neighborhood people were running around like crazy.

"Get in, Roger!" yelled Stewart.

Roger stood facing north, looking far up into the sky.

He turned back and looked over his shoulder at the two waiting cars.

He did a little clumsy dance.

"Oh boy, oh boy!" he said. "Now you're really gonna see something!"

* * *

Over the Conelrad warble, over the sirens and crashes and car horns, over the Pole, the missiles came down, passing some going the other way.

For Bill Warren, Joe Dante, David J. Skal, and William Schallert:
keep watching the skies, guys.
And for Aunt Ethel Simpson, 1914-2000.

Glossary

1) "Stranger On The Shore"—by Mr. Acker Bilk. The first pre-Beatle British record to make #1 in America, the week of May 26, 1962. It was used in the film *The Flamingo Kid*, which was set in 1962. If you're an alto sax or B-flat clarinet player, and can play this, you'll have all the girls (or boys) you want hanging around the bandstand. . . .

2) In-and-Out Burger: for real and true.

3) "Fly Me to the Moon (Bossa Nova)": just making its way onto the charts.

4) Bobby (Benson): see *The Day the Earth Stood Still* (1951). Hereafter *DTESS*.

5) Stewart (Cronyn): see *Red Planet Mars* (1952). Hereafter *RPM*.

6) Gadge: Brian "Gadge" Roberts. See *Tobor The Great* (1954). Hereafter *TTG*.

7) Pomphret (Also spelled Pomfrett, Pomfritt): English teacher, at first, in high school, then Peter Piper Junior College (j.c.). See the television series *The Many Loves of Dobie Gillis* (1959-1963). Played by William Schallert, one of the dedicatees of this story.

8) Johnson: see *TTG*. Played by Schallert, too. See also some of the many books around on the CIA's use of journalists, teachers, etc. as "covers" during the 50s through the 70s.

9) Dobie: Dobie Gillis, of the novel by Max Schulman and the TV series. Played by Dwayne Hickman. Blonde the first season, brunette afterwards.

10) Dad: Herbert T. Gillis. Played by Frank Faylen.

11) Brother Joe's body: see *Sunset Boulevard* (1950).

12) Norbert E.: taxi driver from Bedford Falls. See *It's A Wonderful Life* (1946). Bert and Ernie are the taxi driver and cop there. Since neither I nor anyone else remembers which is which, I made up the name Norbert E. so it could stand for either Bert or Ernie. (You have to watch me every minute.) Played of course by Frank Faylen. (Yes, Bert and Ernie on *Sesame Street* are named for the pair.)

13) Elbert P., "Pinky": see *Lost Weekend* (1945). Played of course by Frank Faylen.

14) "Medea": a standard kids' goof-off version of "Maria" from *West Side Story*.

15) Opie and young Theodore: either it's Opie Taylor (played by Ron Howard) of *The Andy Griffith Show* and Theodore Cleaver (played by Jerry Mathers) of *Leave It To Beaver*, or Stewart is just using his Eddy-Haskell-type (Ken Osmond) sarcastic voice (as *LITB* would have it "to give some squirt the business") about a couple of nondescripts.

16) Running his father crazy: the Frank Faylen catchline on TMLODG was "I gotta kill that boy! I just gotta!"

17) Roger was Stewart's: see *RPM*. The six years started where RPM ends.

18) Krebs, Maynard G.: The first beatnik on television. Played by Bob Denver, later Gilligan (no first or middle name) on *Gilligan's Island*.

19) Bobby's car: it's a woodie, a wood-panelled station wagon, as described. Surfing was just starting big. Woodies were status symbols, and utilitarian, for carrying (as then called) surfing-boards to and from the beach.

20) Gremmie: short for gremlin. Ho-dad wannabees. They had everything they needed for surfing except a board and a car ...

21) Ho-dad.: hotshot surfers who knew how to hang ten, shoot the pier, run a pipe, etc.

22) "I Remember You" by Frank Ifeild: the second British song to bust the top 5, at #3 in the fall of 1962.

23) Lawrence 6-1212: the number Helen Benson and Mr. Carpenter must have called to get a cab. See *DTESS*.

24) H0012: the license plate of the cab Helen and Carpenter took. See *DTESS*.

25) When he was eleven: okay—we've got to do this sooner or later. The chronology: *DTESS* is the only one of the three movies that takes place the year it was made, i.e. 1951. *TTG*, made in 1954, is set in 1957 or 1958, as Gadge's dad was "killed in Korea seven years ago." Unless he was killed in a peacetime accident in 1947, he died sometime after June 25, 1950, which puts the movie in 1957, at the earliest. *RPM* was made in 1952, but takes place "at the next closest opposition of Mars," which would have been in 1956. This is why everybody is the ages they are in the story ...

26) Sammy: Sammy blabbed about the cab to the Army and FBI men at the boarding house. Most people forget Bobby is never seen in the movie again after the scene where his tennis shoes are wet from the dew at the Mall.

27) "Sea of Heartbreak": as it says (#21, 1961).

28) Rabbit ears and the tinfoil: remember broadcast television?

29) The admiral: Admiral William "Bill" Carey. Played by Walter Sande, an actor you instantly believed in any role. See *RPM*.

30) "Wonderland By Night" as it says (#1, 1960).

31) The First Family: Album of the Year Grammy. Comedy record by Kennedy imitator Vaughn Meader. Events made this album sound very strange in later years.

32) "Wheels": instrumental by the String-A-Longs (#3, 1961).

33) Date it: once you could go to any junkyard in America and pry off anything you wanted and pay something for it and take it home. As in so many

things, California led the nation in fear-of-lawsuit.

34) Time for the nature lecture: He just gave one. This junkyard owner in 1962 understood ecology better than most people still do.

35) Mu-tants: as it was pronounced in so many 1950s sf films, including *The Day The World Ended* (1955).

36) Steal and kill and rob you: see *Panic in Year Zero* (1963).

37) "Hit the Road, Jack" (#1, 1961): I heard this, from a DJ, in 1961, over the air.

38) "West of the Wall": Miss Toni Fisher (#37, 1962). About lovers separated by the Berlin Wall, which went up in 1961. August, to be precise.

39) Model of the Frankenstein monster: hot off the mold in 1962.

40) Miz Jones, Sarah: I made them up. This is fiction, and you have to do some of that, you know?

41) After the lab explosion: for this paragraph, see *RPM*.

42) Aunt Jessica and Uncle Hume: Jessica Tandy, Hume Cronyn.

43) I figured if I needed a wife . . . : old Navy/Marine saying.

44) *Famous Monsters of Filmland* #12: there are three movies (now four, but *13 Days* doesn't count and I don't include *Missiles of October,* which was made for TV) set during the Cuban Missile Crisis: *The Steagle* (1971), Joe Dante's (another dedicatee) *Matinee* (1992), both set in the US; and *The Butcher Boy* (1995), set in Ireland, Kennedy's spiritual homeland. It was David J. Skal (another dedicatee) who pointed out that 1962 was the height of monster-worship, in his book *The Monster Show* (1993).

45) "Because They're Young": Duane Eddy instrumental (#4, 1960). Theme music to the movie of the same name, starring Dick Clark.

46) Fighting over groceries: this is in *Matinee.* This is also for real, too. People stayed home from work, got in their fallout shelters, etc. Leigh Kennedy wrote about it in her novel, *Saint Hiroshima.*

47) All the Russian ships: the news stuff I give for the bulk of the story is accurate. Up to a point . . .

48) Veronica and Angela Cartwright: hubba-hubba 12- and 13-year-old sister actresses (*Make Room for Daddy, The Birds*) in 1962 and hubba-hubba actress sisters now, too.

49) Hayley Mills: daughter of Sir John, sister of Juliet. Hubba-hubba at 12 in 1962, even more so now. Started with Disney. Tore a hole in the screen.

50) Six bits: that's 75¢ to you young whippersnappers. That was on a regular night. On "carload nights," usually Monday and Tuesday, as many people as you could cram in or on a car got in for 50¢ for the whole load.

51) "My Boomerang Won't Come Back": as it says (#21, 1962).

52) "Quiet Village": instrumental by Martin Denny (#4, 1959).

53) Give me 50¢: about what half this stuff would cost in 1962, without the box of Dots.

54) *Bride of the Gorilla* (1951), *Poor White Trash* (1957), *High School Confidential* (1958): this is a pretty spavined lineup even for a 1962 triple feature at a drive-in.

55) Guy in a black hat: this is from *The Big Chill* (1983).

56) Peter Graves: Graves played Chris Cronyn, Stewart's dad, in *RPM*. (You have to watch me every minute.)

57) "*Gazachstahagen*": instrumental by the Wild-Cats (#57, 1959).

58) Always having trouble with gorillas: *Bride of the Gorilla* (1951); *Gorilla At Large* (3-D, 1953).

59) Larry Verne, "Please Mr. Custer (I Don't Wanna Go)" (#1, 1960).

60) Ben Colder, "Don't Go Near the Eskimoes" (#62, 1962). Ben Colder was Sheb Wooley, who had a hit in 1958 with "Purple People Eater" (#1). He was supposed to record "Don't Go Near The Indians," which became a hit for Rex Allen (#17). This song was a parody of the one he should have recorded. Sheb Wooley's the second person you see in *High Noon* (1952) after Jack Elam. He's Frank Miller's brother, Ben.

61) Oog-sook-mook: phonetic equivalent of the Eskimo chorus in this song.

62) 50¢ a gallon: gasoline was @ 22.9¢ a gallon in 1962.

63) "What in the World's Come Over You?": as it says (#5, 1960).

64) Okay, Mr. Philosophical: see *DTESS, RPM, TTG* for details.

65) Roller skates: it was true. Also in *American Graffitti* (1973).

66) "The Girl of My Best Friend": Ral Donner (#19, 1961).

67) He thought of Gramps: see *TTG*.

68) A bunch of teenagers in a circle: that would be Jim and Buzz with the knives. See *Rebel Without A Cause* (1955). The Griffith Planetarium is used again at the climax of that movie; in *TTG* (1954), *Phantom From Space* (1953), *Invaders From Mars* (3-D, 1953); *War of the Colossal Beast* (1958), and is the nightclub in *Earth Girls Are Easy* (1989).

69) "Happy Birthday Sweet Sixteen": as it says (#6, 1961).

70) "Midnight in Moscow": instrumental, Kenny Ball and his Jazzmen (#2, 1962). An even better version was by the Village Stompers in 1965.

71) Macaroni: I'm not making this up. Millions of people were worried about what would happen to this horsie if WWIII started.

72) "Asia Minor" by Kokomo (#8, 1961): rock version of Grieg's Piano Concerto in A (get it?) Minor.

73) "Beyond the Sea" by Bobby Darin (#6, 1960): this is Darin's version of Charles Trenet's "La Mer" in 1945.

74) "Guided Missile (Aimed At My Heart): 1961.

75) ♀ ☿ ✳ † ∞: The symbols drawn on the blackboard at the opening of every episode of *Ben Casey*. "Man. Woman. Birth. Death. Infinity." would intone Dr. Zorba, head of neurosurgery. Dr. Zorba was played by Sam Jaffe. Jaffe also played Professor Barnhardt in *DTESS*. (You have to watch me every minute.)

76) Kim-chee: only Koreans, or people in California, would know what kim-chee was in 1962.

77) "Monster Mash": Bobby "Boris" Pickett, #1 the week of the Cuban Missile Crisis. See Skal's *The Monster Show*.

78) "I Remember You": as it says.

79) "He's Not A Rebel": as it says. We're doing the top 5 of the Cuban Missile Crisis Week 1962. Also next two songs.

80) "Last Date": instrumental, Floyd Cramer (#2, 1960).

81) *Video portum*: "I see the port/home."

* * *

Helpful in the writing of this story: *That Old Time Rock and Roll: the chronicle of an era 1954-1963* by Richard Aquilla (1989); *The Billboard Book of #1 Hits* by Fred Bronson (1985 ed.); *The Golden Age of Novelty Songs* by Steve Otfinoski (1999). And of course dedicatee Bill Warren's *Keep Watching the Skies: American Science Fiction Movies of the 1950s: Vol. one: 1950-1957* (1982) *and Vol. two: 1958-1962* (1986).

AFTERWORD

I was sitting on a rock above the Highway 530 bridge on the Sauk River in Washington state, changing flies. Dave Myers (*not* the Dave Myers the disc-jockey who's married to SF writer Sydney van Scyoc, *nor* the Dave Myers who writes for the *Post-Intelligencer*, but my friend David E. Myers) was out in the middle of the Sauk, tied into some monster salmon. (Dave has a theory about winter steelhead flies: dark day, Brad's Brat. Bright day, Brad's Brat. Today he couldn't keep those *pesky* 20 lb. coho salmon off it.)

Anyway, I'd been thinking about a story.

"Who's your favorite kid's part in 1950s SF movies?" I asked him, real loud.

"The kid from *Day the Earth Stood Still*," he yelled back.

"Mine too," I yelled. "But he's *already* in there. I need a couple of others."

Dave got the coho in finally, released it (the Sauk is *never* open for salmon) and then tied into either another coho or a giant Dolly Varden, I forget which—those days are all a blur—you remember the good days; the ones you forget are the 18º F. ones with a 15 mile an hour wind when you have to hold your rod under water between casts to melt the ice off your line guides, are out the *only* seven hours of daylight and catch *nothing*.

Anyway, once we got back to the cabin attached to the Oso Store, and I'd cooked some supper, and Dave had taken back off to Seattle, I sat down and *really* started working on this story.

I wanted to write about what the lives of SF movie kids of the 1950s would have been like later.

The story had a different direction at first, based on something told by Bill Warren in his two-volume definitive work of SF movies of the 1950s *Keep Watching The Skies*; having to do with the theft by someone in the 60s of the original robot from *Tobor the Great* (1954). The original concept was to be trying to get the junked Tobor for "Gadge."

The story wasn't working right, telling me this *wasn't* the story it wanted me to write about 50s SF kids. It began to change, getting fuller and deeper.

I'd known from the first it would be set (like Joe Dante's movie *Matinee*) during the Cuban Missile Crisis, which for those of you not born at the time, was pretty much just like I describe it (except for the last few pages) here.

I hoped I was doing something swell.

When I finished typing the final draft on December 9, 2000 out in

Oso, WA, I sent it to Eileen Gunn, who at the time was running the webzine InfiniteMatrix.net and complaining that Ellen Datlow was getting *all* my good stuff. She kept it as long as she decently could (without sending me a contract or money) but sent it back on Feb. 28, 2001, explaining that her backers were getting antsy about the site ("That's why they're called backers, Eileen," I said, "because they *back out*.") I sent it to Ellen Datlow anyway at Sci-Fiction.com; she wrote back taking it but wanting the glossary at the end of the story so whippersnappers wouldn't get lost. I sent that off, got contracts and money later, and it went up July 18, 2001.

This got some strange reviews (including one by a guy who admitted from the outset that the *only* 2 SF films he'd seen, made before *Star Wars*, were *2001* and *Metropolis* . . .) and was pretty much ignored worldwide.

A footnote: When I was writing this, no one knew about it but Dave.

Just after I finished it, I wrote to Steven Utley and told him I'd just finished a story called "The Other Real World."

"Strange," Steven wrote back. "I just finished a story called 'The Real World,'" (one of his many Silurian Tales, forthcoming from PS Publishing in two volumes). Coincidence, or *what?*

A BETTER WORLD'S IN BIRTH!

"The Past ain't dead. It ain't even past."
–William Faulkner, *Requiem for a Nun*

1
Arise, Ye Prisoners of Starvation!

The whole thing began, I am told, with the sound of falling books in the Peoples' Department of Culture.

In my initial inquiry, I pieced together the following:

Comrade Dichter, the chief clerk, was at her desk when she heard the books fall—one, two, three—inside the office of the Peoples' Minister of Culture. There was the sound of a chair scraping on the floor and a muted cry.

Comrade Dichter rose from her desk, knocked once, and opened the door to the inner office. The Minister of Culture was an old man nearing retirement (he had fought on the barricades of the Revolution as a man of thirty-five) and had not been in the best of health for a few years, though still a tireless worker. Dichter feared to see him slumped over his desk or lying on the floor, victim of a stroke or seizure.

She was more surprised to see him standing, backed to the leftward wall of his office, staring toward his private bookcase on the right wall, an excited look in his eyes.

His chair was overturned near his desk where he had risen quickly. Several books and the right-hand bookend, which had held them on the corner of his iron desk, lay on the floor.

He breathed heavily, and put out one hand toward the wall, as if reaching for a curtain or to close a window.

"Comrade Minister," asked Dichter. "What is?"

He turned his head toward her. His eyes shone with fear, or something more.

"Karl . . ." he said. "Karl Marx was standing there, wearing his last suit and trailing the rope they hanged him with!"

Only then did the Peoples' Minister of Culture lie down, like a man lowering himself into his usual bed at home, stretch himself out full-length on the floor of his office, and die with a small sigh.

Since this involved the head of the Department of Culture, and one of the original Revolutionaries, the Peoples' Department for Security was called in.

In this case, me.

I went back to Department headquarters to make my initial report to my boss.

I boarded Peoples' Traction Company Tram #4 at the corner of Tannhäuser Boulevard and Street of the Peoples, on which all the government departments were located. I looked over my notes of interviews with six Culture workers, and the doctor who had treated the Peoples' Minister for the last twelve years.

Workers on bicycles, a few pedicabs, and one vehicle based on the eastern rickshaw, pulled by two sturdy proles in tandem, passed the steam tram. It was true what people said; Dresden was a more beautiful, quieter, and hygienic city since horses had been banned three years ago, freeing half the street cleaners for more important jobs. (Rome, 2000 years ago, had taken a halfway measure, forbidding the city to equine traffic between sunup and sundown, which meant only that it was noisier, and you stepped in road-apples in the darkness.) Here and there one of the new self-propelled vehicles sputtered by, giving off whale-oil fumes.

It was late in the year with a hint of snow in the air under the gray sky. Not the picture people have of Dresden. It was warm in the tram, however, the few blocks I rode, thanks to the new electrical heating coils over the seats.

I stepped out; the Peoples' tram moved away, and I went in and reported to my Section chief.

2
The Union We of All Who Work

Dirkmann had his booted feet up on his large desk. It had once belonged to some minor functionary in the Old Regime.

"So?" he asked, cocking his head to one side so his good eye was on top.

"The Minister of Culture died of a coronary, or a cerebral hemorrhage. He had been in poor health. Evidently it was triggered when Karl Marx, whom he had known, or rather the *figure* of Karl Marx, stepped out of his bookcase."

Dirkmann raised his eyebrow, the one over the bad eye. He took down his feet and sat upright slowly in his chair.

"He saw Karl Marx." It wasn't a question.

"According to the chief clerk."

Dirkmann reached into his desk files and came up with four blue *pneumatique* letters.

"That makes one Marx, one Engels, and now three Wagners in the last week."

"So . . ." I said. "A—"

"—Spectre is Haunting Europe," finished Dirkmann. "Or, spectres. And Dresden, if not the whole of the continent." He looked over the blue forms. "All to current or former officials who knew them. Your case is the only one involving death—the woman who saw Engels has been put to sick-bed by her doctor, though. I've sent copies upward—yours will join them. At least the Leader will not have just statistics to read, if the copies get that far. Right now I need a three-paragraph summary. Then go home. Tomorrow," he said, "don't come here. Go directly to the Peoples' Archives. Start learning everything you can about Wagner."

"But," I said, "surely the Department has some expert, someone it can call on?"

"It does," said Dirkmann. "*He* saw Wagner Tuesday." He pointed to one of the blue letters. "He's been quite drunk since."

"I'm not the least bit musical," I said. "I can't carry a tune, or whistle. Others who can would be better."

"There's irony for you, Comrade," said Dirkmann. "Someone named Rienzi who can't whistle! I said, research everything. The music was only about one-tenth the man. Work your way through *that* on momentum. I want you to know as much about the man as anyone who wasn't there. Talk to whomever you must. Find out why this is happening after twenty-three years."

"Surely *you* can't believe . . ."

"Ah, yes!" said Comrade Dirkmann. "The Peoples' Federated States of Europe does not believe in ghosts or goblins! It believes in the innate perfectibility of Man! *There's* your Hegelian dialectic in a nutshell. We no longer have the Church's Heaven and Hell; we have the Worker's Heaven on Earth!"

"Very well. Why would *you* be interested in this, then?"

Dirkmann looked at me with his bad eye.

"It's personal," he said. "These ghosts are messing with *my* town."

Every school, gymnasium, and university student thinks they know Wagner's story. I thought I did, too, until I was handed this case.

The usual précis goes something like this: Born, 1813, Leipzig, his stepfather perhaps his true father; brothers and sisters; bad academia and gambling; desire to write poems and plays, then opera: *Die Feen; Das Liebesverbot; Rienzi; Der fliegende Holländer; Tannhäuser; Lohengrin;* the start of one on Jesus and one on Buddha; some notes about the Norse. While writing and composing these, a series of itinerant jobs as choral and orchestral leaders in Prague, Riga, and elsewhere. Marriage to the actress Minna Planer; poverty in Paris; escape from creditors in the night, to end up as kappelmeister to the Court of Saxony, 1846; eventual conversion to the revolutionary party, the *Vaterlandsverein,* 1847; hero of the Dresden Revolution, May, 1849; First Leader of the Peoples' Federated Revolutionary State, 1849–1853 (during, and just after which, all Germany became a Peoples' Republic); adoption of a son, 1852; execution by the Prussian forces of the Counter-Revolution, 1853; disinterment and entombment in the Wall of Martyrs, Dresden, 1854, following the collapse of Prussia. In other words, idol and fount from which all European (with the exception of Britain) revolutions and Peoples' Republics sprang.

The night before going to the Archives, I reread Hannebolt's *Richard Wagner: Peoples' Martyr* (we'd all had to read it at University), made some notes, and took them with me the following morning.

The chief archivist seemed surprised when I presented my credentials and told him what I was here for.

"Except for a few foreign scholars, sent by their governments to look for specific things Wagner might have said about *their* countries, hardly anyone comes here looking for anything. Most of it, you know, has been printed somewhere—the State Publishing House did forty-nine volumes —copies of those are here, too—and it has been twenty-three years since his martyrdom. For what specifically are you looking? The papers of the Provisional Government? His writings on music theory?"

"I suppose I want to look at it *all,*" I said.

The archivist laughed. "Excuse me, Comrade." He gestured for me to follow him. We walked down a short hall and turned. He unlocked the door, revealing four rooms, one after the other, extending into the darkness. There were floor-to-ceiling shelves in the first room, with four reading desks near the door, and in the far corner boxes and map files, all labeled.

"Where would you like to start?" he asked.

I looked at my notes. "His letters to friends, 1849–1850. The official papers by him on the Erfurt Crisis of 1851. Records of the Prussian Counter-Revolution in Dresden of 1853. *Some* of the music."

The archivist pushed a button. Three clerks appeared. He rolled off a series of numbers; they scurried away. He seated me at one of the desks and turned on its new Ruhmkorff lamps, bathing the reading table with a soft blue glow.

"You may leave anything here when you're done for the day," he said. He handed me a dozen red ribbons. "Place these on anything you wish kept out for tomorrow. The others I shall return to the stacks myself. If you wish more, or anything, press the button. The *taza de alivio* is the first door on the left. Enjoy your research," he said, and departed.

In a few minutes the clerks had put a dozen boxes, ledgers, and notebooks on the desk, then they too departed.

I was alone with Wagner and history.

3
Fruits of the Peoples' Works Are Buried

In the writings of one of the lesser-known of the original Revolutionaries, I ran across the following:

Of course, revolutions are fun! You can drop a piano from a fourth-floor window onto some poor conscript—caught between shooting at you, and being shot for not shooting at you—and watch him pop like a tomato. There is a sense of great personal satisfaction—I did *my* part in the collapse of some nodding Charles or Louis or Roderigo, even if it were just to kill some poor fool who'd rather be up here throwing furniture down on me. *He* is dead—Long Live the Revolution! It was not his fault he was the tool of backwardness and repression; it is not my fault I am the agency through which the Forces of Destiny work themselves out. Might as well execute Bösendorfer for making the piano in the first place! I work for a world where people will never have to make a choice between shooting me and being shot for *not* killing me on sight.

August Roeckel, 1850

The third day of the Revolution, everyone knows, Wagner borrowed a cart and took his wife, his dog Peps (a monster that could have pulled a cart), and a parrot to his sister's house in Chemnitz, forty kilometers away. He was on his way back next morning when he started meeting refugees from Dresden, telling him to turn around, the Revolution has failed. Then he met the owner of the cart, who was in another with his household goods and two grown sons. Wagner returned his cart and weary horse to the man, and continued on foot back toward the city. He met more and more people, including members of the Revolutionary Council, who told him the Prussians were coming.

What most don't know is that he continued on for another kilometer before his will faltered; that he had in fact retraced his path for two kilometers back toward Chemnitz when he spied, coming in from a side road from the direction of Poland, a large group of armed men, singing and yelling.

They had come from Bohemia to aid the Revolution and had heard no news yet. More than half were drunk—they had come upon an abandoned wagonload of wine two villages back.

Heartened, Wagner told them he was a member of the Revolutionary Council, out scouting for the reinforcements—and here they were! He put himself at their head, and marched them back into the now-burning city, singing "La Marseillaise." What remained of the Revolutionary Council – that being Bakunin and Roeckel—came out to meet them.

And less than an hour after taking their places on the barricades, word came that their king, the King of Saxony (safely twenty kilometers away), had accepted the crown of the constitutional monarchy offered by the Frankfurt Assembly, in the name of the Peoples' Federated Revolutionary States.

The fighting went on for another two days—the Poles at the forefront —then a miracle. The Prussians were recalled to put down a minor revolution of their own, leaving only the battered army of the Old Regime to withdraw to the nearest border to await developments.

Wagner threw a last grenade at the hindmost of the Saxon army stragglers, from his nest in the bell tower of the Kreuzkirche, and yelled, "Good riddance, running dogs of the bourgeois lickspittles!"

Up in the tower with Wagner was a new arrival—he'd entered

Dresden while Wagner had been turning around for Chemnitz before meeting the Poles. His name was Emil Gaspard, later known to history as Eisenmann.

The first thing Wagner did the next day was send for Engels, who was in Frankfort, and Marx, who was of all places in Prussia. They came, *toots sweet*.

From Wagner's personal notebook:

Last night, troubled by bad news from *just everywhere,* I fell asleep on my campaign bed while reading dispatches. I had a strange dream, uplifting and nightmarish at the same time.

I was in a strange city filled with water—it must be Venice though I have never been there—and I was an old man. When I moved, my joints ached and my heart was as heavy as lead.

But the strangest aspect was that the woman I was with— Minna was nowhere about—who must be my wife, was Liszt's daughter, whom I met when she was eleven years old five years ago, in 1848; now a grown plain but stylish woman.

I was at a desk in a sumptuous apartment in some villa. And I was writing not party essays or speeches, but music once again, music such as I nor the world had ever heard before! I knew it was my masterpiece. I wrote the last note of the last bar. And at that moment my heart ruptured and I died. Liszt's daughter saw and rushed toward me; her hands grabbed me as all faded to black—

I awoke with a start to find my glasses broken where I had rolled onto them in my sleep, and myself crying—and then Bakunin barging in, singing, already smoking the vilest cigar to be had, and behind him Marx, Engels, and Roeckel, all full of plans for the relief of Erfurt . . .

One day nineteen years before Wagner's revolution, Emil Gaspard (now known as Eisenmann, the Leader of the VDDR) turned a corner in Paris and witnessed a soldier shoot Emil's neighbor, Monsieur J-P Fleury, right between the eyes.

Emil had been heading for his father's *boulangerie* when he heard a great tumult in the street ahead. He'd run and leaned around the corner just in time to see the act.

The fact that M. Fleury had been raising his walking stick at the soldier did not change the violence of the act that ensued.

Immediately several other civilians beat the crap out of the soldier. Then they stepped back to a handy pile of paving stones three meters away and stoned him with enough bricks to make the foundation of a small shop. Someone took his rifle, cartridges, and bayonet, and ran away.

There were sounds of firing up the street; smashing furniture, the screams of women and men, the neighing of horses cut short by musketry. Emil ran toward his father's place of business in time to see soldiers roll a cannon around a farther intersection, then fire it into a mob that crossed from a side street, tearing away limbs and heads, covering the walls with blood and offal.

A second cannonade tore into people beside the bakeshop. Flames spewed from its shattered facade. Emil ran to the shop, slipping on a boot and foot. The back door to the place stood open; his father and the baker-boys must have gotten away.

Soldiers marched down the street then, serried out in a wedge, cannon foremost, trundling it before them. Heat and flames grew around Emil.

An officer walked slowly by. Emil grabbed a dough-paddle bigger than himself and stepped out behind the man. Emil brought the paddle down with such force that he was lifted from the ground. The officer sank to his knees.

Emil grabbed the two pistols and holsters with their cartridge box from the wounded officer. When he tried to pull the man's saber from its scabbard, it proved too heavy and unwieldy.

"What do you think you're doing there, boy?" asked a sergeant, standing over him, a rifle in his hand.

Emil shot him right between the eyes and grabbed his rifle before it fell to the ground. He ran off toward the end of the street where a barricade was going up.

It had been a hot July day in Paris in 1830, and Emil was ten years old. As he ran down the street, he caught a glimpse of three men watching him from a balcony.

After Charles X had slunk out of the city, and the July Revolution ended, a servant showed up in the Gaspard home with a visiting-card from a famous painter.

So it was that Emil found himself posing beside a half-naked lady, and a student in the green top hat and red velvet coat of the National Guard, while M. Delacroix painted his famous picture "Liberty Leading the People, 28 July 1830," a few days before the painter left on a long-planned trip to Algiers.

Emil was quite bored, standing there in this fashion fifteen minutes at a time, holding up the two pistols, trailing the cartridge box, with that ridiculous beret on his head. But at the end of three days he was paid what amounted to his father's income for a month, and that was the only income the family had seen since the shop had burned down.

As he said goodbye, he realized M. Delacroix was one of the three men who had watched him from the balcony.

From Wagner's personal notebook:

Bakunin said one night: "This revolution's over. I've got other cities to be burning, other soldiers to be depressing. My work here is done; it has been for at least a year, but I've stayed on from good comradeship and a vast sense of accomplishment.

"A toast, comrades" he said. We stood.

"To further revolutions in the minds of men . . ." We all lifted our glasses to each other, and placed our hands over our hearts.

It was the saddest, and at the same time, most encouraging leave-taking I have ever had.

4
For Justice Thunders Condemnation

They marched Wagner out to the wall behind the Municipal Building the day after they hanged Marx and Engels.

In the tumult of the last few days there had not been time, nor had it been safe enough, for a large crowd to gather, but there was now a respectable and respectful one; some of the men with their hats off; some people holding up children so, as they said according to political leanings, they could see and remember either the death of a peoples' hero, or the just desserts of a rabble-rousing villain.

The firing squad was a handpicked group of Saxons, though the officer was a Prussian.

"Are there any last words, Herr Wagner?" asked the interim bailiff, after reading the death warrant.

Wagner, it is said, had difficulty clearing his throat. His voice was weakened from shouting orders this last week of fighting, and of arguing in court the day before. It barely carried past the firing squad, but then, the first part of the speech was addressed only to them.

"Remember . . ." he said with great trouble, "Remember me, when you, yourself, stand here." And then his voice rose to take in the crowd. "Lady Liberty!" he said. "Show us your tits!"

And then they shot him.

In the crowd stood Eisenmann, with a newly shaved head and a fake beard, and from that moment on his resolve was set.

It took a year of large struggles, small defeats, and then the Consolidation, before the geopolitics of revolution were settled, and the Peoples' Federated German Republic was a reality, with Eisenmann at the head of the Peoples' Council, and later the Republic's Leader.

It took a further three years before his first order as head of state came to fruition.

One by one the soldiers who executed Wagner were sought out and arrested, if still in Germany, and brought to the Old Jail, which had miraculously stood through all the strife since 1849. Two men were extradited from Switzerland; one from the new Polish state to the east. One was kidnapped from Paris, when legal means failed, from under the nose of the Sûreté, put on a barge as cargo, and pulled up rivers and down, back to Dresden.

The coffin containing one who was dead was dug up from the burying ground of a small riverside hamlet thirty kilometers away.

At last there were·eleven of them, in jail with the coffin, and they were taken out to the wall behind the Municipal Building.

Eisenmann himself read out the death warrants.

One of them yelled, "But what did I do? I was only following orders!"

Then Eisenmann read Roeckel's account of Wagner's last day, ending:

"It is said, with difficulty his last words came. His voice, weakened with shouting the last week, and from speaking in court, barely carried past the firing squad, but the first of his speech was addressed to them only.

"'Remember...' he said, 'Remember me, when you, yourself, stand here.'"

Then they *understood* history.

Then the firing squad shot them, and the coffin.

5
Behold Them Seated in Their Glory

The lettering on the office door stated:

PEOPLES' DEPARTMENT ON THE FORMER MONARCHY
HOURS MON-WED, FRI 0900-1500
THURS 1000-1400

I knocked.

"Come," said a voice.

I went in. It was a one-person office, no clerk; just a desk, some shelves full of documents, a State-issue wastebasket that needed emptying, and a stein full of nibbed steel pens beside an inkwell.

"Comrade Rienzi, from the Peoples' Department for Security." I was wearing my uniform today. "To interview you about Wagner."

"Ah! Yes. I have your letter ... somewhere here ... I'm afraid I knew him only as a small boy, as you are no doubt aware, being able to do the math."

"No matter, Comrade King," I said. "Perhaps some small memory will be of help to us."

"Perhaps," he said. He wore his hair in the old fashion. "The poor Minister of Culture and suchlike."

I gave him a look.

"Oh, we have our sources," said Comrade King. "You'd be surprised how much there still is to do, twenty-seven years on. There are still lawsuits and bills of requisition from my grandfather's time. They had a very relaxed view of justice and economics in those days, before the Revolution. We still hear things, of the here and now."

He settled himself in his chair. "I shall miss the Minister of Culture; he was, as they say, a cultured man. He was of great service to the State. I worked closely with him cataloging the palace contents several years ago."

"But you did know Comrade Wagner?"

"Yes. What I mostly remember was his height. He had none. Yet he was the *only* adult who never bent over, or kneeled down, to talk to my sister and me—of course he didn't have far to go, but he treated us as adults, worthy of a conversation. More so than with my father, who you know was something of a scatterbrain. The one kingly thing he did was accept the Constitution of the Frankfort Assembly. And he knew it. He and Wagner worked closely for the three years remaining to Wagner's Provisional Government. My father's the one you really should have talked with, the poor man."

"Wagner was originally kappelmeister to your father's court?"

"Wagner was first and foremost *for* Wagner. I read quite a bit about him as I grew up–but after himself he loved music. I've read his proposal for reorganizing the Court Musicians and Theaters—sometime around 1847 or so—quite a thorough piece of work; rejected though by my father's advisors of those times. I'm sure what he really wanted was a good orchestra so *his* operas could be performed—both the ones he'd already written, and those great whapping things he was always threatening to do."

"A perfectly logical conclusion," I said.

"What I remember most was that he loved Beethoven, especially the *Ninth*. He performed it every Palm Sunday from 1846 until two weeks before the Counter-Revolution. Every time he did it he came alive, conducting, not like his usual State concerts. Of course, during the original Revolution the Opera House (and so much more) burned down; the next year it was performed in some barn of a place. It was still wonderful. And the Peoples' Federated Revolutionary State was still new. I believe that was when the nation came together, that Palm Sunday of 1850. It's the first time I felt that this thing might really work. All the leaders took some part, including Roeckel–the father of the present State Conductor—who was a musician. I forget what Marx did—but they all sang on 'Ode to Joy,' we all did, in the audience too. It was quite wonderful. I wish every citizen, now, could have been there then, like I was."

"Do you remember Wagner, or Engels, or anyone mentioning the occult?"

"Well, Wagner's early stuff was full of fairies, and magic swans and such. I heard he always wanted to do one about the Norse gods, and was always reading Wolfram von Eschenbach. But the real supernatural? I don't think so. He was more of a mystic than anything. As I said, what he believed in was Wagner."

I rose. "Thank you for your time, Comrade King."

"Glad to do it, Comrade Rienzi," he said, walking me to the door. "It was nice to get my head out of these musty legal papers this little while."

We shook hands, and I left.

There was a message from Dirkmann at my apartment:
The wind is from the west.

This meant I had to go see him, as the office of the Leader, Eisenmann, had asked him a question, which he had to ask me.

6
"No Rights," she says, "Without Their Duties."

To celebrate this, their Centennial Year of 1876, the United States of America had driven out its witches, warlocks, and demons, in other words, atheists and spiritualists. Which meant that Europe, and especially the Peoples' Federated States of Europe, was full of them.

Obviously they were all being watched.

I nodded to the police informant on duty at the corner of Engels and

Bakunin. He discreetly ignored me. I felt the pressure of his gaze on the back of my neck as I went down the walkway on Bakunin and turned up the path to the second house.

The door had one of the new electric bells. A plate, still new, in the middle of the door, read: MRS V.C. WOODHULL—SITTINGS AND ADVICE. Below this was an engraving of an ancient Greek—Demosthenes, or I miss my guess.

A foreign domestic received me. I presented my card–an assumed name and address, one of the standards issued by the Department. On it I had written, *My soul is troubled. May I have a sitting?* The domestic receded farther into the house like a cuckoo returning to its clock.

I looked around the spacious parlor. There were many photographs, including one of Commodore Vanderbilt and the current American President James G. Blaine (who had evidently been of no help to Mrs. W. in the matter of deportation). Perhaps exile makes the heart grow fonder. On the bookshelves were numerous editions of Demosthenes, both in the original and many foreign translations.

The domestic reappeared and presented me with a folded note on an American Flag tray. *Please join our circle at 2000 hours tonight,* it said, and was signed, *Mrs. Vict. C. Woodhull.*

I went back to the Peoples' Department for Security, and went through a few files.

Perhaps it was another police spy on the corner that night, playing a hurdy-gurdy and with a baboon on a chain. Perhaps not.

The baboon walked up to passersby, nudged them in the sides, and held out its hand. When it received a coin, it tipped its cap, and took the coin to the bucket next to the player. Were the man a spy, it was understood he got to keep all the money the ape collected.

* * *

The séance room was on the second floor, in a heavily curtained and tapestried open landing at the top of the stairs.

Seven people were there, three of whom I recognized; two couples I did not. The domestic brought us small cakes and bitter Russian tea. Two of the men waiting, I discerned, had fortified themselves beforehand.

And then Mrs. Woodhull appeared from farther down the landing.

"Welcome," she said, "for any troubled in heart, for those longing for advice from those who have crossed over."

She was a stunning woman for whom, in a bourgeois society, middle-age would hold no terrors. Her clothes were somber gray and black; she wore a demure necklace from which hung a simple medallion of hammered bronze. Her hair was swept up and back in the new fashion, but it did not give her a severe appearance, as it did most women.

She looked at each of us in turn.

"Many years ago," she said, "while I was in Cleveland, in the United States of America, I was very troubled like yourselves. As I sat at my desk, a man dressed in a toga appeared to me and told me to go to 17 Great Jones Street in the city of New York. I asked him who he was, and he told me Demosthenes, and then he dematerialized.

"I immediately took my family by train to New York; we arrived at the house with all our baggage, and with no idea of what the future held.

"We knocked, and a woman answered the door, and asked 'Did you come about the house?'

"We entered. The house was furnished but had been emptied of all personal effects of the previous owner. In the entry hall were many bookcases, all empty except one, which had a single book lying open upon one shelf.

"I went to it. It was *The Orations of Demosthenes*.

"From that moment my future changed, always for the better, and now I find myself many thousands of kilometers away, helping those who are troubled as I was before the spirit of Demosthenes appeared to me, and pointed the way."

(Conveniently, I thought, leaving out the ten years of scandal, and exile from her native country.)

"Come," she said, pointing. "Let us go to the Table of Confidence, where we may ask for surcease from worldly torments and doubts."

We went to that Table; beneath its fringed cloth covering, I noticed it was made of oak, and its legs were quite hollow.

7
What Have You Read in All Their Story?

I returned to my room to find Dirkmann sitting in my desk chair, his feet up, reading one of my volumes of Hegel and smoking a Turkish cigarette. He didn't have a key to my place.

He brought his feet down, brushed ash off the blotter.

"Remarkable man, that," he said, closing the book and putting it back in its place on the shelf. "He should have lived to see the Revolutions. Or

stayed around and talked to Marx, after Marx got out of knee-pants. I'm
sure he had no idea of the fires he lighted in the minds of men."

"To what do I owe this honor?"

"You remember our little talk yesterday, no?"

"Yes?"

"I'm to take you somewhere."

"What if I hadn't come home?"

"I knew where you were. Learn anything of use?"

"That maybe the Americans had the right idea. I've rarely seen a better
cold reading, and a perfect one for the name I used, which implies seven
hours of research on someone's part. Also, of everyone else there, I believe
there was no more than one stooge out of the eight. The usual noisy accou-
terments and dim manifestations. Very impressive, with the intellectual
content of a good fart."

"So I've heard," said Dirkmann. "No disturbances in the ether? No
impending catastrophes? No Day of Judgement coming down on us like a
lowering pot lid?"

"Not as far as Frau Woodhull has seen."

He stood up. "Follow me."

It was near 0300 when we stood before an unmarked door. We'd gone
through a series of basement corridors, from our Department, to the
Department of Justice, to somewhere across the street, and down a couple
of blocks, until I assumed we were in or near the Peoples' Department of
Agriculture.

Dirkmann knocked once, then twice more. We went in.

Other than a guard in the corner, *he* was alone.

There was a pitcher of water on the desk, one glass, and a bowl of
grapes (grown no doubt in the chemical nurseries somewhere upstairs–
they say there's a fine experimental wine about to be put on the mar-
kets).

We came to attention and Dirkmann saluted for us both.

He waved his hand.

"Your report?" Dirkmann asked me.

"Comrade Leader," I said, for it was he before me. "I've found no
reason to believe Peoples' Martyrs Wagner, Engels, or Marx had interest
in the occult or expressed any desire to return to this Earth. Of course they
all met violent, quasi-legal ends, as you yourself witnessed. Former Leader
Wagner was somewhat mystical—but it seems a backward-looking view at
the past glories of the German peoples, before becoming leader of the

forward-looking Revolution. You may or may not know he wanted to write an opera about it."

He nodded.

I didn't know whether to go on or not.

"Your report on the spiritualists?" prompted Dirkmann.

"As far as the séances I attended, Comrade Leader, business seems to be as usual. I have visited two spiritualists in two nights, the last of whom has a huge foreign reputation as the best and most skilled. There seems to be no disturbance among them—the usual ploys to gain confidence or financial advantage."

His eyes moved to Dirkmann again.

"We have no explanation for the visitations," said Dirkmann. "Other than the medical and the mental."

Comrade Leader sat back, spread his arms and shrugged his shoulders.

"The only conclusion we could come to," said Dirkmann.

Comrade Leader opened his hand toward the door.

We turned smartly and left.

Comrade Leader Eisenmann had looked exactly like his posters. He had been portrayed since his thirties as being somewhere in his early forties, so he now looked only a few years older than the official portraits; gray at the temples, hair thinning some at the top (he was not wearing his usual Peoples' Guards hat tonight). His eyes were still the same as those in the Delacroix painting. The rest of his face was hardened by time, but still recognizable as the French baker's son.

We were halfway back through the Knossos-like maze of corridors and hallways when I asked Dirkmann, "Does he ever speak?"

Dirkmann lifted his shoulders and sawed his levelled hand back and forth in a sometimes—yes sometimes—no motion.

The next morning the arrests began.

8
No Claims on Equals Without Cause

There have been many arrests before, hundreds of them. That's why there is a Peoples' Department for Security.

News of the arrests was on the street when I awakened. Bullermann, Erkheit, and Sensucht. All members of the Peoples' Committee; all in the original Revolution alongside Wagner, Marx, and Engels. Erkheit and

Bullermann were in the *Vaterlandsverein* before Wagner, even. Intellectuals all.

The rumor had it that there would be a trial on very grave charges.

Meanwhile, they were being held in our cells, not over at the Department of Justice.

The smart ones always end up in our jail.

I entered the headquarters and nodded to the senior officer on duty in the lobby. My gaze went up to the large official State-issue painting on the mezzanine above. It and one other painting ("Night Watch in the Kreuzkirche Tower") were in every government building, and had been reproduced countless times in lithographs and engravings for homes.

This painting was of Wagner's exhortation before the *Vaterlandsverein* two months before the outbreak of the original Revolution, in March of 1849. He stands at the rostrum in the old Assembly Hall, one hand upraised, eyes lifted, giving the famous speech about the need for freedom for the artist and the common man that led directly to the creation of the Citizens' Militia. It is as iconic a moment as you could hope for in the history of the Revolution.

There are many upturned faces in the painting, some recognizable, some not. Roeckel, of course, and, turned slightly away, like Judas in the old religious paintings of "The Last Supper," the three men who had first led the Revolutionary Council but then slunk away to Chemnitz as soon as they got the first whiff of grapeshot. One person near the front raises his copy of *The Communist Manifesto,* hot off the press, so Marx and Engels make in-absentia appearances. Very stirring, very representational of the ideas in the air at the time.

As I said, the painting is so omnipresent it has become like wallpaper in our lives. We have all passed by it a thousand times without looking at it.

Today I stopped and took it in.

I know now he has been there all the time, just a small detail. Over at the edge of the stage, among other excited young men, is Eisenmann—then still Emil Gaspard. You can tell it's him by the floppy red beret he was always depicted in when young (here and in "Night Watch") and the small tricolor pin on his lapel, showing he had still not become a citizen of the adopted land to which he would someday become Comrade Leader. He would at the time have been twenty-nine years old.

I have seen the painting or reproductions of it most of my life (I believe the original was painted in 1854, just after the end of the Prussian Counter-Revolution).

It is only just now, after my time in the Archives, that I know the meeting of the *Vaterlandsverein* took place while Eisenmann was six weeks away from starting toward Dresden. I believe he was still teaching at the Workingman's College and organizing petition drives in Paris, his nose to the wind, sniffing for the next hot spot in Europe, which he and everyone else thought would be Prague.

Perhaps this was artistic license on the painter's part? But then someone who put Marx and Engels present only in spirit would have found a way to put Eisenmann there *inabsentia*, too.

I walked from one end of the mezzanine to the other, taking in the whole monumental painting, noting faces and figures, the play of light and shadow (there are torches in the audience, besides the early candle-and-gaslight from chandeliers over the stage), the small touches in the painting.

It is, through familiarity, mostly background to office work. As far as such things go, it is a decent piece of Socialist-Realist art—there are far worse examples around. And this is probably the copy of a copy of a copy by a sixth-hand copy of the original from the State Art Studio.

I looked at the Eisenmann figure once more—if you don't know the iconography, he's just one more excitable boy-man, thrilled by Wagner's words, at the edge of the painting.

The eyes are the same as the ones in the Delacroix painting; the same ones I looked into a few hours earlier this morning.

Those eyes saw two full Revolutions, a Counter-Revolution, and the final, successful Second Revolution, which flamed throughout Europe (except Britain). I looked into those eyes in the painting.

They looked back.

I felt nothing.

9
No Room Here for the Shirk

I returned to the Peoples' Archives, and as I walked into the lobby, I saw the Chief Archivist rise from his desk and hurry toward me.

"Comrade Rienzi," he said, "we wondered when you were coming back to your book."

I misunderstood him for a moment. "I originally had no plan to come back," I said, "though the pull of this place is overwhelming."

"We left your book out, as per instructions," he said.

"My instructions?"

"The one with the marker," he said.

I distinctly remember closing all the books and placing the dozen ribbons in a stack on the left of the table.

"Thank you," I said. "Is there anyone else here?"

"Comrade Roeckel, the younger, looking at Wagner's music. He came in this morning."

"Very good," I said, and went down the hallway into the reading room.

A man in his twenties had three weighty tomes open before him; I could see the staff lines on the pages all the way from the doorway. He was at the third table down. He looked up at me, nodded, and went back to copying with a pencil on one of the stack of loose sheets of paper beside him.

At the desk I had used two days ago lay a notebook with a ribbon marking a place in it. I knew it to be Wagner's last notebook, just before the Prussian Counter-Revolution of 1853—a time of scarcity, this last notebook had not been uniform with his regular notebooks, but purchased from some local source. It was larger and slimmer than the others I had looked at. I had glanced through it on my previous visit—but from what I had seen the contents were mostly hurried jottings—days of battle and unrest everywhere—and weeks would be skipped in some places. The official correspondence from the period was more informative, so I had lain this one aside.

I placed other books atop it later in the day. But I had put all twelve ribbons aside. All the books should have been cleared away that evening.

I sat down in the chair and opened the book to where the ribbon was.

I read the page to the bottom. It was Wagner's thoughts on the reorganization of the government—much like his paper in the pre-Revolutionary days on the orchestra—and the last paragraph began: "But I must warn others here now, or whoever follows me in this office, never to put too much faith or pow—"

I turned the page and read: "As respects the Peoples' Department of Goods and Services, the need will be seen for coordinating railway and shipping schedules so that essential. . . ."

I turned the page back, thinking I had turned two together and missed one. The page with the ribbon in it was number 89. The next page was number 91. I looked closer. I took a magnifying glass from its holder at one of the empty tables and examined the two pages.

Page number 90 had been very professionally razored out of the notebook.

I opened the notebook back to the first unnumbered front flyleaf and worked my way through it. Pages number 23 and number 39 were missing, but they had no pendant sentences.

I went back to the Chief Archivist.

"You have a list of yesterday's visitors?"

"There were no visitors yesterday," he said.

"No one?"

"Not a mouse."

"And Comrade Roeckel is the only one in this morning?"

"True."

"And you trust your clerks?"

"Explicitly," he said. "Is something wrong?"

"They have no curiosity of their own? I mean, surrounded by the Peoples' Archives?"

"They are products of the State Librarians School. Curiosity has been bred right out of them."

He looked at me. "I sense something is wrong," he said.

"If it is, it's my memory, Comrade Archivist. Thank you."

I went back to the reading room. Might as well kill two birds with one stone.

"Comrade Roeckel," I said, showing my badge. His eyes grew wide, then calm again. He stood.

"I see you're busy. Please sit. This is in the line of another inquiry. You knew Peoples' Martyr Wagner?"

He laughed. "When I was four, he was martyred. Good thing I was only four at the time, or we wouldn't be having this conversation." He knew that I knew the Prussian Counter-Revolution had put to death the children of all Revolutionary leaders over the age of ten, figuring children under that age had not been indoctrinated in Revolutionary concepts more so than any other schoolchild.

"I only have one memory of meeting him—people tell me it was just after the last Palm Sunday concert he ever conducted—it was just a bunch of people and music to me at the time. He turned my cap backwards and patted me on the shoulder. Not much to remember of a great leader and composer, but that's all I have."

"And your father was one of the few to get away during the Prussian Counter-Revolution, was he not?"

"Happily for the Second Revolution," he said, "but it was a miserable time for me. I was six when he and Comrade Leader Eisenmann came back at the head of the Peoples' Army. That was the happiest day of my life."

"If I may ask, what brings you to this place of dead facts?"

"I'm reinstating Comrade Wagner's works into the State Concerts—

there was a great vogue for them in the first few years of the Second Revolution, but he's fallen out of fashion, except with small town orchestras. I want people in the capital to appreciate him again as a composer, not as just the leader of the people he was.

"Right now I'm copying some of his unpublished works for the concert after next. I hope eventually, next spring, to have again a full performance of Beethoven's *Ninth Symphony*—only not, as in the old days, on Palm Sunday, but for the Peoples' Day, May 8, when the first Revolution succeeded at Dresden, as Wagner and Comrade Leader Eisenmann climbed down from the tower and declared the Peoples' State."

I knew him to be State Conductor for the Peoples' Symphony and Opera, following in the footsteps of his late father. I also knew he had served with distinction as a sailor six years ago on the *Battleship Kropotkin* in the sea war against the Turkomen.

"The present concerts are warm-ups for the next season," he said. "We hope to do them monthly till then. The first is this Saturday—we've been rehearsing it for a month."

"I should very much like to attend," I said. "The Palm Sunday concerts seemed to have quite an effect on everyone who attended them."

"Except me, at the time," he said. "I remember all I wanted to do was play with a rubber spider activated by an air-bulb I had just gotten; instead I had to sit and listen to a bunch of grown-up noise. It was only later, when I learned to read music, that I realized what I had missed. Beethoven, like Wagner, is quite out of fashion, too. There's of course the rage now for symphonies and concerti celebrating battles and treaties. I'll see there are tickets for you, Comrade . . . Rienzi. Saturday evening."

"One more question. Was *that* book there on that table when you arrived?"

He looked toward the table. "I don't know if it's that *exact* one," he said, "but there was a book there when I came in."

"And no one else has been here?"

"Only the Chief Archivist, bringing me these things," he said, pointing with his pencil to the monster books. "No one else."

"Thank you very much. I look forward to the music."

I was halfway back to the office when I realized I had never looked for what I had gone to the Archives for.

On the mezzanine of the Peoples' Department for Security, workmen were moving things around. I went up.

There was a lighter rectangle on the wall where the official painting had been. I saw it over at the left; workmen wrestled it onto a long wheeled dolly.

"What is, Comrades?" I asked.

The workman with the order-book said, "Standard maintenance, Comrade. Your official painting goes in for cleaning. We hang another that's been cleaned, from somewhere else, here. Eventually, yours goes to some other department; any department, in fact, that takes Subject-Size II-B, and so on ad infinitum. We do this every day of the year except State holidays; throughout all the Peoples' Republics there are teams like us doing the same work. You might say we have about the best job security in the Peoples' Federated States of Europe."

"Thank you," I said. "Quite more than I wanted to know."

"We aim to be thorough, Comrade," he said.

I came out of my office later and passed the painting.

It was brighter and cleaner; it seemed to glow as if it were new.

Wagner still orated; Eisenmann was still over there where he shouldn't have been; Marx and Engels's names were still on the book.

Only, in the middle of the audience, where no one ever looks anyway, Erkheit, Sensucht, and Bullermann were gone, their faces replaced by those of nondescript rabble-roused hotheads.

10
No More Tradition's Chains Shall Bind Us

I sent August Roeckel Jr. a *pneumatique* to confirm my ticket.

He sent me an invitation to meet him for lunch at the Café München.

I arrived at one door just as he appeared at the opposite entrance. We sat at a table in the middle of the café.

"Most pleasant," I said, as we ate bowls of spicy potato soup. "I had merely wanted to confirm my ticket."

"I remembered another thing I wanted to tell you about," said Roeckel. "Although it was not about Former Leader Wagner, at least, not directly. I had heard rumors about recent . . . let us say, visitations, and enquiries. I hope I may be of help."

"These . . . visitations seem to be the worst-kept secret in the history of the Revolution," I said.

"The memory that came to me—I had quite forgotten it—was while my father was away, while the Prussians were here. We children of the Revolutionary leaders were kept at an orphanage—most of us were by that time true orphans, or separated from our mothers while the Junkers decided what to do with them.

"We were getting the usual Prussian-style kindergarten instruction in saluting and close-order drill, along with the rest of the children. At the end of the period, the other children were marched off to watch an instructional Punch and Judy show. We however were double-timed to more instruction, this time from a dead ringer for the later Bismarck.

"We were stood at attention while he explained to us that, as sons and daughters of the original Revolutionaries, we would be denied certain privileges until such time as we proved ourselves worthy as the other children.

"We could hear the laughter and high voices from the other end of the school, and it was more than one of us—I don't remember which of the forty or fifty of us it was—could take anymore.

"'But Herr Professor,' she asked, 'What have *we* done? Why *us?*'

"The professor grabbed her wrist, jerking her toward him, then opened her palm and smacked it three times with his rod, his face turning crimson and purple.

"'*Here,*' he yelled at her, 'there is no *Why!* There only *Is!*'

"I had forgotten that till an hour ago. The memory is connected with Comrade Wagner. The contrast of being taught under the Revolution, and what we would have had under the Prussians, had there not been the Second Revolution under my father and Eisenmann. Good thing, too, their own people rose up and tossed them out and joined us, and got rid of those soldier-bastards."

Then he looked at me. "Sorry to go on and on. I guess you had to have been there to understand."

"My parents moved here from Italy," I said, "the third year of the Second Revolution, to support the workers' dream. Then they went back to Italy, when the Revolutions spread there, and gave their lives in the assault on the Vatican. I was just too young to have been part, raised here by an uncle and by this State."

We talked more, and he told me the last concert rehearsal had gone swimmingly.

"It will not be the usual thing," he told me. Then he explained.

There was no organ grinder on the corner, nor street-clogger, nor other police spy, that I could tell. I walked directly to the second house, up the walkway, and jerked the bell-pull.

Mrs. Woodhull herself opened the door.

"I was expecting you," she said.

"And why is that?"

"Because you were the only one present under false pretenses. And the only skeptic."

"I needed to determine if you could or could not help me."

"And?"

I shrugged my shoulders. "I hope so," I said.

"You are still a skeptic. You know the spirits can sense that? They usually do not respond to doubt."

"Perhaps I am less skeptical today."

"Something has happened since the night before last," she said. It wasn't a question. She reached out slowly and touched my forehead. "You have been given some sign?"

"Please spare me the professional tricks. I know you would normally give me the answer I want. You will find that very hard, for I can formulate neither the question I need to ask, nor the answer I want."

She looked up at me and widened her eyes: naturally, that is what she would do to convince me my case was different from the many thousands before.

"I see you are very troubled," she said. "I will try to help, though your doubts may hold the truth back."

"I will, of course, pay your usual fee for a private sitting," I said.

"There is no need in this case, Mr. Rienzi," she said.

We sat at the Table of Confidence, next to each other, our hands touching.

"Do you feel the charge of the Spirits?" she asked.

"No. Of course not."

"Do you see the pendant ectoplasm trying to form over our heads?"

"No."

"Do you have a sense of expectation, of breakthrough and release from your dreads?"

"No."

She stood up, pulling me with her, clasping both my hands.

"Come with me," she said.

We had sexual relations in her bedroom, while things that might have been ectoplasmic snakes wriggled and crackled up the walls and across the ceiling, and fell down among the bedclothes, writhing, and changing from blue to green and back again.

11
To Free the Spirit from Its Cell

I went into his office.

Dirkmann sat behind his desk; he was not, as usual, slouched somewhere over it or along it.

He looked at me, then began taking off his shoulder holster, something I had never seen him without in all the years of working with him.

"Did you hear the news?" I asked. "They are going to try The Three on charges of being spies for *both* England and Japan?"

"I have heard the news," he said.

"But England and Japan have been at war for two years! These charges are absurd!"

Dirkmann reached in his pocket and took out his badge and placed it on his desk atop the pistol.

"*What* are you doing?"

"I am making sure I don't do anything rash," he said.

Then he reached up and began pulling at his bad eye. He jerked out a long stringy thing. I started to look away. He moved his hand back and forth, and something resembling colloidon came out with a snap.

Both the eyes that looked back at me were perfectly good.

Only then did he lean back in his chair and put his boots up on his desk, throwing the rubbery stuff into the State-issue wastebasket.

"What is happening?" I asked.

"In just a moment, you should leave," he said. "This will not be a popular place to be seen in. You're a good secret cop. Keep your nose clean, and you'll end up with some cushy job in a tourist town on the Baltic, keeping an eye on rich visitors, who are, of course, never *the* trouble.

"Be prepared to be reassigned—everyone still standing will be given other jobs. You'll probably see Dresden again within five years—don't get antsy or discouraged. There are much worse things than a working exile."

"I want to keep working with you," I said.

"Ha!" he laughed. "No you don't."

"You're the best man who ever held this job."

"Ah, Antonio. Sometimes being the best person for a job *is* the problem."

"But . . ."

"Time to go. It's near the close of business on a Friday. Worry only on late Fridays, and weekend nights," he said.

I came to attention to salute him.

"Cut the crap," he said. As I turned to go, he said, "Some things you don't need to be a psychic to know."

On my way past the painting on the mezzanine, a colonel and six men armed with carbines passed me, going the other way.

I walked through what was usually the beautiful city of Dresden on a gray day much like the one on which I'd gone to make my initial investigation at the Peoples' Ministry of Culture. It seemed weeks ago, and yet was only a few days.

I watched the gas and new electrical lights come on in the State shops and cafés, and in the homes and private establishments. In the government offices, lights showed where people worked late, going about the government's business.

Time to visit a restaurant, and have a hot chocolate, and contemplate this city where Comrade Wagner premiered *Rienzi* thirty-four years ago in those last days of monarchs and aristocrats—that lost world of privilege and class, and indifference to the common man, of which my family had been an example.

I sat bolt-upright in my bed, reaching for my pistol.

I had been almost asleep when the thought came to me, filling me with dread. I had a *frisson* and a horripilation and broke out in a cold sweat.

My automatic pistol was shaking in my hand. I put it down with a clatter beside my holster on the somnoe.

What if there had been no sightings of Wagner, of the other early leaders of the Revolution? What if it were part of some plot, some machination so vast I could not imagine it, by someone, some hand I could not fathom? It would have to be so immense no one person could see it whole. Its reason unknown, involving dozens, hundreds, perhaps thousands. Why? Are enemies of the Revolution at work?

Was it easier to believe in ghosts and spirits, or some gigantic plot?

And then: Am I unknowingly part of it?

Then I remember the words of Dirkmann, and of Mrs. Woodhull.

It would seem to be—to believe in ghosts. Of a kind.

12
Earth Shall Rise on New Foundations

I have left a note on my night stand which explains nothing.

It will be 1800 hours. I will make my way slowly through this beautiful Revolutionary city in the light snowfall, to the Peoples' Concert Hall, where the People are.

I shall take my seat in the great Hall, and we the audience shall settle down. Then Comrade Leader Eisenmann and his entourage will enter his State box, and we shall rise and applaud, and he will join in the applause, as what we are all expressing is not our enthusiasm for him, but what he represents, twenty-seven years of the Peoples' Revolution.

Then after his entourage is seated, the lights will come down and the darkened orchestra will tune up, and then the lights will come up and dim again and Roeckel will come out to applause, and he will raise his baton.

And the curtain will open on four musicians and their instruments:

The twenty-five-year-old Franziska Marx will have her concertina.

Jean-Jacques Engels, child of Engels and either Mary Burns or her sister Lydia—opinions vary—will be on musical saw.

Friegedanke Wagner, adopted son of Minna Planer and Former Leader Wagner, also twenty-five, will be at the glass harmonica.

And August Roeckel III, six-year-old son of Roeckel the conductor, will be on ocarina.

And they will begin to play the "Ode to Joy" from Beethoven's *Ninth Symphony.*

The music will be ethereal.

Only when they finish will the audience rise to its feet and shout. By then I will be elsewhere in the Hall.

Underneath my civilian overcoat I will have on my dress uniform; I will have made my way to the leftward of the hallways leading to the State boxes, and checked my coat with the attendant there, as if I were late.

Everyone knows Comrade Leader Eisenmann attends every performance in the Peoples' Hall; what they don't know is that he always leaves after the first interval of whatever program is being presented.

I will wait in the corridor while the applause for the "Ode to Joy" dies down and the lights dim again, and the orchestra strikes up the "Wedding March" music from *Lohengrin,* and the ushers and soldiers in the hallway come to attention, and Eisenmann and his people leave the State box and come down the corridor toward me.

Perhaps his eyes will meet mine again as they had two days before; he will take me in and categorize me from long experience: security policeman, dress uniform, seen before, some report or other; or maybe more than that.

He will be near me, surrounded by people who would step in front of the Kolm Express if he told them to do so.

The music will swell as a door is opened somewhere.

My machine pistol is a comforting weight in my hat, which is under my arm.

His bodyguards will be fast.

I will be faster.

E. G. EISENMANN
1820–1876

COMRADE LEADER,
PEOPLES' FEDERATED STATES
OF EUROPE   1854–1876

"Death to the Enemies of the
Peoples' Revolution!"

AFTERWORD

I wrote this, as I told someone, so next school board election you'll go down and vote the straight Trotsky ticket, and put Creation Science back in the superstitious garbage can where it belongs.

I'd wanted to write this for, oh, thirty years or so, since I'd first read about Wagner's involvement in the Dresden Revolution of 1849 (like *most* things, the Germans were about a year behind the rest of Europe, which had exploded in 1848). I'd known from real life that Bakunin would be there—the quoted opinion of him in the story was said *many* times by *many* people during his peripatetic incendiary career.

I also knew it was going to be a damnably long story, and would take place later on in the world Wagner had created; essentially revolution contemplated in—well, *not* tranquility, but retrospect. And I didn't have time to stop and do it, except for 50 years of notes.

Then along comes Golden Gryphon with the idea of a series of limited edition chapbooks, of novellas, in the early 00s. (I may be wrong, but I think *only* mine and one by Alastair Reynolds were published.)

I'd moved from Oso, Washington, back to Texas (Ft. Worth) in 2002, with this as my next project. I worked and worked for three months all fall, and I mailed this off after finding the last copy shop open on Christmas Eve afternoon—the rest had closed early—of 2002, and taking it across the strip mall and priority-mailing it to Golden Gryphon a few minutes *before* the post office closed.

They paid me a much-needed chunk of change for the edition rights on January 23, 2003, by which time I'd moved *back* to Austin, which I'd left 8 years before. It was published soon after. (There may *still* be a few copies left at Golden Gryphon.)

Writing these is one thing; you have a great sense of accomplishment. Then you do the donkey-work, proofing, ancillary matters which seem to *never end.* Then the work comes out and you get a new sense of self-worth.

This one was especially swell: not only had I finally done it after 50 years but they'd gotten Nicholas Jainschigg to do the front *and* back covers (more on Jainschigg see the afterword to "*Fin de Cyclé*"). I'd sent him drawings and photos for research while I was *still* writing the story. On the front cover was the appropriate 1849 Wagner in a Lenin pose in front of a hammer-and-sickle flag; on the back cover a painting inspired by Delacroix' *Liberty Leading The People* (from the 1830 Paris revolution) only instead of Liberty, there was an opera Valkyrie with a spear.

Just perfect.

* * *

The epigraph to the novella is a sign some anonymous one hung around the neck of the statue of Lenin that's in Fremont Peoples' Park in Seattle: "Workers of the World—Sorry."

Other Books by Howard Waldrop

The Texas-Israeli War: 1999 (with Jake Saunders, 1974)
Them Bones (1984)
Howard Who? (1986)
All About Strange Monsters of the Recent Past (1987)
A Dozen Tough Jobs (1989)
Night of the Cooters (1990)
Going Home Again (1997)
Dream Factories and Radio Pictures (2003)
Custer's Last Jump and Other Collaborations (2003)
Heart of Whitenesse (2005)
Things Will Never Be The Same: Selected Fiction Volume One (2007)

Chapbooks

You Could Go Home Again (Cheap Street, 1993)
Custer's Last Jump (with Steven Utley) (Ticonderoga Press, 1998)
Flying Saucer Rock and Roll (Cheap Street, 2001)
A Better World's in Birth! (Golden Gryphon, 2003)
The Horse of a Different Color (You Rode In On)/The King of Where-I-Go
(WSFA Press, 2006)

OTHER WORLDS, BETTER LIVES
A HOWARD WALDROP READER

First Edition

September, 2008

Other Worlds, Better Lives by Howard Waldrop was published by Old Earth Books, Post Office Box 19951, Baltimore, Maryland, 21211. 2000 copies with 1700 as trade paperbacks and 300 as hardcovers have been printed by Maple-Vail Book Manufacturing, York, Pennsylvania. The typeset is Adobe Caslon and Futura Condensed, printed on 55lb Glatfelter Offset Cream. Design and typesetting by Robert T. Garcia, Garcia Publishing Services, Woodstock, Illinois.

LOCUS Award Finalist for Best Collection (2007)

THINGS WILL NEVER BE THE SAME
A Howard Waldrop Reader: Collected Short Fiction 1980-2005

Things Will Never Be The Same is Old Earth Book's first retrospective of Howard Waldrop's works. It contains sixteen short stories accompanied by afterwords by the author. Many of these are award nominees and winners. All expand your world-view with a unique delight and wit, that can only be described as "Waldropian."

Contents: "The Ugly Chickens," "Flying Saucer Rock and Roll," "Heirs of the Perisphere," "The Lions Are Asleep This Night," "Night of the Cooters," "Do Ya, Do Ya, Wanna Dance?," "Wild, Wild Horses," "French Scenes," "Household Names," "The Sawing Boys," "Heart of Whitenesse," "Mr. Goober's Show," "US," "The Dynasters," "Calling My Name," and "King of Where I Go."

On *Things Will Never Be The Same*

"[*Things Will Never Be The Same* is] all the best Waldrop, or as near as makes no never mind, slammed between two covers and set out as a dare to the reading public: a greatest hits collection that includes all of the stories that passers-by are likely to have heard of. It's a feast of unrestrained, relentless fictional excellence, one great story after another."　　　　　*—Green Man Review*

"There's no better writer alive than Howard Waldrop, and here are all his best stories, with funny and fascinating afterwords—you need this book."
　　　　　—Tim Powers

"It always feels like Christmas when a new Howard Waldrop collection arrives, and this one is as crammed with wonderful presents as Santa's sack. This is even better than getting a BB gun!"　　　　　*—Connie Willis*

"Old Earth Books has put together a wonderful collection of short stories by one of science fiction's great masters, Howard Waldrop. Waldrop writes the funniest, most bent short sf you've ever read . . ."　　　　　*—Cory Doctorow, BoingBoing.com*

TRADE PAPERBACK • ISBN 978-1-882968-36-7 • $15.00
(1-882968-36-0)
HARDCOVER • ISBN 978-1-882968-35-0 • $45.00
(1-882968-35-2)

Order from www.oldearthbooks.com or

Old Earth Books • Post Office Box 19951
Baltimore, Maryland • 21211-0951